Standing alone in the doorway was the king. The ruler, anointed by priests and priestesses, of all the lands of Attolia, the official father of the people, the lord of the barons who'd one by one sworn him their oaths of obedience, the undisputed, uncontested, and absolute sovereign of the land. The swollen discoloration by his mouth closely matched the elaborate purple embroidery on his collar.

"Most people in your circumstances would kneel," said the king, and Costis, who had been staring transfixed, belatedly dropped to his knees.

MEGAN WHALEN TURNER

THE KING OF ATTOLIA

A Greenwillow Book

An Imprint of HarperCollins*Publishers*

The King of Attolia
Copyright © 2006 by Megan Whalen Turner

EOS is an imprint of HarperCollins Publishers.

www.harperteen.com

The text of this book is set in Adobe Caslon.
Book design by Chad W. Beckerman.

The Library of Congress has cataloged the hardcover edition
as follows:
Turner, Megan Whalen.
The king of attolia / by Megan Whalen Turner.
p. cm.
"Greenwillow Books."
Summary: Eugenides, still known as the Thief of Eddis, faces palace intrigue and assassins as he strives to prove himself both to the people of Attolia and to his new bride, their queen.
ISBN 978-0-06-083577-4 (trade bdg.)
ISBN 978-0-06-083578-1 (lib. bdg.)
ISBN 978-0-06-083579-8 (pbk.)
[1. Kings, queens, rulers, etc.—Fiction. 2. Soldiers—Fiction. 3. Loyalty—Fiction. 4. Robbers and outlaws—Fiction. 5. Adventure and adventurers—Fiction] I. Title.
PZ7.T85565Ki 2006 [Fic]—dc22 2005040303
10 11 12 13 LP/CW 10 9 8 7 6 5 4

First paperback edition, 2007

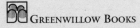
GREENWILLOW BOOKS

THIS BOOK IS DEDICATED WITH GRATITUDE TO
ELIZABETH CRETTI. WITHOUT HER TIRELESS EFFORT,
IT COULD NOT HAVE BEEN WRITTEN.

THE KING OF ATTOLIA

The queen waited. Sitting at the window, she watched the lights of the town glow in the last of the long twilight. The sun had been down for hours and it was still not fully dark. True dark wouldn't come, except in the odd unlit corners. The lanterns would burn all night as the people moved from celebration to celebration until they greeted the sun's return and the new day and staggered home at last. They celebrated, with wine and music and dancing, a day they had thought would never come. The queen's wedding day. She sat at the window, watching the lights, listening for the music, waiting for her husband.

In Attolia, a woman came to her husband on the wedding night. In Eddis, a man came to his bride. They had chosen to keep the custom of Eddis. The Eddisians could see this as the queen bowing to the Eddisian customs of her new husband, but the Attolians would see the queen still flouting the traditional duties of an Attolian woman. It was a careful dance of shadows and unsubstance, but under it all, there was a marriage of two people. Today she had yielded the sovereignty of her country to Eugenides, who had given up everything he had ever hoped for, to be her king.

In the palace's great open court, filled with tables and the glowing lanterns in colored paper shades, Ornon, the Ambassador from Eddis, smothered a yawn and the smile that followed it as he considered the future of the former Thief of Eddis. He and Eugenides were old adversaries, and the happy vision of the Thief fettered by the responsibilities of sovereignty warmed his heart. It was far more satisfying than any petty revenge Ornon might have planned. The Queen of Eddis knew his thoughts from across the room and gave him a look that made him sit straighter, take another sip of wine, and turn his smile toward his dinner companion.

On the palace wall, a young guard on duty looked out over the town with much the same view as the Attolian queen had from her window. He was missing the celebrations, but he didn't much care for drinking and brawling, and he didn't mind. He liked being stationed high above the palace. The solitude, and the time away from the noise of the barracks and his companions, gave him space to think. These stints on the upper reaches of the palace walls were his favorite. There was no danger he needed to watch for: no ships of Sounis's could reach their harbor, no armies would be dropping from the hills across the valley. Attolia's most dangerous enemy was already within the palace and an enemy no more, he supposed. Costis could have been asleep for all his duty mattered, this night. Still, he straightened to attention and tried to look alert as his captain came up beside him.

"Costis," said the captain, "you are missing the feasting."

"So are you, sir."

"I don't mind." No emotion colored the captain's voice.

Deeper into the night, when the official banquets in the palace had ended, far from the still-noisy celebrations in the streets of the city, the Secretary of the Archives idly shifted the papers on his desk. More than anyone, he had cause to fear the new king. He had approached the queen privately and suggested they discuss means of limiting the king's power. Eugenides was young; he was untrained, impetuous, and naive. He would be easy to control once the power of his Eddisian advisors waned, as it necessarily must. The queen had responded with a look that was all the warning Relius needed to know that he had overstepped his authority. He withdrew with apologies. He would leave the fate of the king to the queen, but would not pretend to himself that he was not afraid.

COSTIS sat in his room. On the table in front of him was a piece of paper meant to hold a report on the squad of men he directed. He'd scratched out the first few lines of the report and written underneath the beginnings of a letter to his father. It began, "Sir, I must explain my actions," and then stopped. Costis couldn't explain his actions. He rubbed his face with his hands and tried again to compose his anguished thoughts into cold words and orderly sentences.

He looked over the mess in his quarters. His small trunk of clothes was tipped out onto the floor. The tray that had sat in the top of it to hold his sleeve links and buttons and pins was thrown down by the bed. The links, the spare buttons, and the small image of his god were scattered everywhere. His books were gone. He'd had three. So, he assumed, was his wallet with what money he kept in his room. That was a pity. He would have given the money to his friend Aristogiton. His sword was gone from its rack on the wall. He would have given that to Aris as well.

The two soldiers who'd brought him back from the training ground, almost dragging him along by their grip at his elbows, had taken every sharp thing out of the room. They were veterans, who'd served in the Guard for most of their lives. They'd searched his small trunk and dragged the thin mattress, as well as the blanket, off the narrow bed frame. One had pulled down Costis's sword and swept up his knife from the windowsill while the other had collected his papers, crumpling them together in his fist. Without looking at him again, they'd gone. Costis had turned the stool upright on its three legs. They had left his cloak pins, his plain everyday one and his fancy one with the amber bead. He had been a little surprised. His good pin was fibula-shaped with a shaft four inches long and as thick as a cornstalk. It would be as effective as a sword, if Costis chose to use it. Even the smaller pin would do; two inches in the right place was all it took.

As Costis had considered, without any real motivation, the possibilities of the cloak pins, the curtain across his doorway had swept back and one of the soldiers had returned to kick his feet briskly through the detritus on the floor, quickly locating the cloak pins. After scooping them up, he had checked the floor again to see if there were more. He had seen the sandal straps and taken those. He'd looked Costis over once and shaken his head in contempt as he left.

Costis looked back at the letter in front of him. It was almost the only paper they'd left him. He shouldn't waste it, but he didn't know how he could explain his actions to his father when he couldn't explain them to himself. He'd broken a sacred oath, had destroyed his career, his life, and perhaps his family in one moment. It was unnatural to look back at events and be unable to believe that what you remembered could actually have happened.

It was afternoon. He'd made no progress on his letter since morning, when the sun had been slanting into the narrow window and filling the small room with light. The sun had climbed over the roof of the barracks and the room was grown dim, lit only indirectly by the sunlight falling into the narrow courtyard between barracks. Costis was waiting for the queen. She had left the palace for the first time since her marriage and had gone hunting. She was to eat at midday at one of the lodges and return sometime in the afternoon.

Costis got up from his stool and paced for the hundredth, the thousandth time across the room. He would be sentenced when she returned, almost certainly to death. Even worse than death would come if she thought that he had acted as part of a conspiracy or that even one member of his family had known of his actions in advance. If that happened, his family would have to leave the farm outside Pomea in the Gede Valley. Every single one of them, not just his father and his sister, but uncles, aunts, and cousins. Their property would be forfeit to the crown and they would be no longer members of the landowning class, but would be okloi—merchants if they were lucky, beggars if they were not.

Of course, even he had had no foreknowledge of what was going to happen. He would never have guessed that he could so compound calamity with disaster, but the truth hardly mattered now. Costis thought of the papers they had taken away and tried to remember exactly what was in them that could be mistaken for plans of treason. The Secretary of the Archives could see treason in a single word. One hint of a plan and Costis would be put to torture instead of hanging in the morning. He knew that when torture began, Truth, which had mattered very little to begin with, soon mattered not at all.

He stepped to the window and looked out at the shadows falling on the barracks across from him. The midafternoon trumpets would be sounding soon and the watches would be changing. He was supposed to be on the palace walls. Behind him he heard the curtain rings sliding on the rod across his doorway. He turned to face the men who would take him to the palace.

There were no guards. Standing alone in the doorway was the king. The ruler, anointed by priests and priestesses, of all the lands of Attolia, the official father of the people, the lord of the barons who'd one by one sworn him their oaths of obedience, the undisputed, uncontested, and absolute sovereign of the land. The swollen discoloration by his mouth closely matched the elaborate purple embroidery on his collar.

"Most people in your circumstances would kneel," said the king, and Costis, who had been staring transfixed, belatedly dropped to his knees. He should have bowed his head, but he couldn't take his eyes from the king's face. Only the king's returning stare broke his rigor, and he finally lowered his head.

The king stepped to the table, and out of the corner of his eye Costis could see the jug held in his hand, a finger looped through the handle and two cups pinched in his fingers. The king lifted them onto the table, putting the jug down first. With a flick of his hand he sent one of the cups spinning into the air, and carefully set the other on the wood. Catching the one in the air as it began to fall, he set it delicately beside its partner. He moved casually, as if this little bit of juggling was second nature. Yet it was necessity made into grace because the king had only one hand.

Costis closed his eyes in shame. All the events of the day, which had been so nightmarish and unreal, were terribly, terribly true, the mark beside the king's mouth unmistakable and incontrovertible, every knuckle of Costis's fist indelibly represented there.

Eugenides said, "You did swear less than two months ago to defend my self and my throne with your life—didn't you?"

He'd gone down like a rag doll.

"Yes."

"Is this some Attolian ritual that I am unaware of? Was I supposed to defend myself?" He had one hand; he couldn't have defended himself against a man both taller and heavier, a whole man.

"I beg your pardon."

The words were those of a gentleman. They sounded odd, even to Costis, under the circumstances, and the king laughed briefly, without humor. "My pardon is not a matter of civil pleasantry, Costis. My pardon is a very real thing these days. A royal pardon would spare your life."

A royal pardon was impossible. "I just meant that I am sorry," Costis said, helpless to explain the inexplicable. "I have never, I would never. I—I . . ."

"Don't usually attack cripples?"

Costis's shame closed his throat. He heard the wine being poured into a cup.

"Put the mattress back on your cot, sit down, and drink this."

Moving stiffly, Costis did as he was told. By the

time he took the cup and sat gingerly in the presence of the king, the king himself was seated on the stool, leaning back against the wall behind him with his legs out and crossed at the ankle. Costis couldn't help thinking he looked like a printer's apprentice after a bar fight and not at all like a king. He took a drink from his cup and stared into it in surprise. The wine was chilled. Sweet and clear, it was like liquid sunlight and better than anything Costis had ever had in his life.

The king's smile spread slowly. "A royal prerogative, that wine. Be careful of it, it isn't watered. Have you eaten today?"

"No, Your Majesty."

The king turned his head and shouted at the curtain, and after a moment there were footsteps in the corridor and the curtain was drawn aside. Laecdomon, one of the men of Aristogiton's squad, stood in the doorway. Aris was a friend of Costis's. It couldn't be pleasant for him to be standing guard outside with his squad.

The king asked for food to be brought from the mess hall. Looking contemptuous, Laecdomon bowed and went away.

"That's a loyal servant I could do without," the king said quietly as he turned back to Costis. "No doubt he thinks the food is for me, and he will bring a hard loaf and olives sealed in a jar."

Costis couldn't blame him for his opinion of

Laecdomon. He'd never liked the guard. Laecdomon was a little surly, a little aloof, and Costis had been glad not to have him in his own squad. Aris didn't much like him either, but complained more often of another one of his squad, Legarus, whom he called Legarus the Awesomely Beautiful. In addition to a pretty face, Legarus was born to a landowning family, as Aristogiton was not. Legarus would never rise to squad leader no matter how elevated his family, and this occasionally caused tension in Aristogiton's squad.

The king interrupted Costis's distracted thoughts.

"Tell me, Costis, why do people persist in offering me food I can't eat and then looking like wounded innocents when I point out that I can't cut it myself? Or open a jar? Or apply soft cheese with a trowel, much less a butter knife?"

Because you're a jumped-up barbarian goatfoot who abducted the Queen of Attolia and forced her to accept you as a husband and you have no right to be king, was Costis's thought. Aloud, he said, "I don't know, Your Majesty."

Guessing at the thoughts, Eugenides must have found them amusing. He laughed. Costis hid his flush in another swallow of the wine. It was cool in his mouth, and it eased the sick tight ball of despair in his belly.

"Where are you from, Costis?"

"Ortia, Your Majesty. The Gede Valley above Pomea."

"How big is the farm?"

"Not big, but we've held it for a long time."

"The house of Ormentiedes, isn't it?"

"Yes."

"You're a younger son?"

"My father is."

"You would have been hoping for land for service?"

Costis couldn't speak. He nodded.

"Costis."

Costis looked up.

"If it wasn't premeditated treason, she won't take the farm."

Costis waved his hand, unable to put into words his knowledge that the truth of his crime was less important than the seeming.

"I am king," Eugenides pointed out mildly.

Costis nodded and drank again. If Eugenides was the sovereign ruler of Attolia, why were they both sitting, waiting for the queen to return? If the king guessed again at Costis's thought, he made no sign this time. He swung his legs back and stood up to refill Costis's glass. Costis shivered, wondering if he should allow the king to serve him. Should he stand when he had been told to sit, should he help himself to the king's wine? Before he could decide what was best, Eugenides had replaced the jug on the table and dropped gracefully back to the stool.

"Tell me about the farm," said the king.

Haltingly, unsure of himself in this interview that was as unreal as the rest of the day, Costis took refuge in the training of hierarchy and did as he was told. He talked about the olive groves and the corn crops, the house he shared with his father and his younger sister. In between his words, he sipped his wine and the king refilled his cup. The gesture was less startling the second time. As he thought of the farm, Costis's words came more easily. His father had quarreled with his cousin who was the head of the family, and they had moved out of the main house when Costis was young.

"Your father lost the argument?"

Costis shrugged. "He said the only thing worse than being wrong in a family argument was being right. He said a particular dam wouldn't hold through the spring. When it didn't, we moved out of the house."

"Not very fair."

Costis shrugged again. It had suited him. The house was small, meant for one of the farm's managers, but it was private. Costis had been happy to be away from his cousins.

The king nodded in understanding. "I didn't get along with my cousins either. They held me face down in a rain cache once and wouldn't let me up until I repeated several filthy insults about my family. Not that I would admit that to anyone but you." He sipped his wine. "We've gotten along better recently, my cousins and I. Perhaps something similar will happen as you get older."

Costis finished the wine in his cup and wondered

what sort of creature you would have to be to forgive your cousins a history like that. He shrugged. The king sounded like an old man giving advice to a child. The official father of the people was younger, Costis thought, than he was himself, and Costis was very young to be a squad leader. Anyway, Costis's relationships with his cousins would have little opportunity to mature if he was going to be dead by morning. No doubt that was why the king felt safe in his embarrassing revelation.

The king refilled Costis's cup.

When he sat again, he said, "Don't give up so soon, Costis. Tell me why you hit me."

Costis swallowed the wine in his mouth.

"Or should we review? You and your friend came through the entryway while you were repeating all the insults you no doubt heard from my dear attendant Sejanus. I understand he was off drinking with his old friends from the Guard last night. Aristogiton must have missed the fun. Was he on duty?"

"He's okloi. His family has no land. Sejanus wouldn't drink with him."

"But your family are patronoi? And you and Aris are friends?"

"Yes."

"How unfortunate that the arched entryway amplified your words so well. I thought I was being magnanimous when I pretended not to have heard."

"Yes, Your Majesty."

"I was talking to Teleus then, wasn't I? He called you over to join us. I think we were trying to gloss over the unpleasantness. Do you remember? We were discussing whether or not I would train with the Guard."

"Yes, Your Majesty."

"And you . . . ," he prompted.

"Hit you, Your Majesty." Costis sighed.

He'd pulled the king around and swung his fist into the king's startled face, knocking him to the dusty ground of the training yard, where he rolled, howling and cursing and dirtying the fine white cloth of his blouse.

"Why?"

"I don't know."

"How can you not know why you hit someone?"

Costis shook his head.

"It must have been something I said. Was that it?"

"I don't know." He knew. The king had commiserated with Teleus on having men so inept that they allowed their own queen to be abducted.

"You must admit, Costis, that I did whisk her right out from under your noses."

"It was nothing you said. Y-Your Majesty was, of course, entirely correct," Costis said, hating him.

"Then why?" the king badgered plaintively. "Tell me, Costis, why?"

Costis didn't know why he said what he said next,

except perhaps that he was going to die and he didn't want to do it with a lie on his lips.

"Because you didn't look like a king," he said.

The king stared in mild astonishment.

Costis went on, growing angrier with every word. "Sejanus says you're an idiot, and he's right. You have no idea even how to look like a king, much less be one. You don't walk like a king, you don't stand like a king, you sit on the throne like . . . like a printer's apprentice in a wineshop."

"So?"

"So—"

"You mistook me for one of your cousins?"

Costis surged on. "So, everything Teleus said was right. You have no business wanting to practice with the Guard. You can practice with the rest of the useless aristocrats in the court, you can call up a garrison of Eddisians to train with if you want."

"There aren't any Eddisian soldiers in the palace," the king interrupted to point out.

"They are half an hour away in Thegmis port. They are scattered all over the country like boils. You can send for them. We are the Queen's Guard, and you can leave us alone. Teleus was *right*. You had no business—"

Shocked at his own words, Costis lifted his hand for another swallow from his cup and paused, looking into it. It was empty. He rolled it in his fingertips and tried to think. How many times had the king filled it? *Have you eaten?* the king had asked before he sent for food that still hadn't come, that he had known wouldn't come soon. How many cups of unwatered wine had there been? Enough that his joints felt watery and his head was light. Enough that his tongue was loose in his head. He looked up to meet a mild, inquiring look from the king.

He wasn't an idiot, whatever Sejanus said. He was a conniving bastard.

"Who put you up to it?" the king asked quietly.

"No one," snapped Costis.

"Teleus?" the king prompted softly. "Tell me it was Teleus and I'll see you pardoned."

"No!" Costis shouted. He jumped to his feet, and his hands balled into fists. The cup in his hand fell unheeded to the floor and smashed. He could feel the heat of the rage and the wine in his face. The curtain in the doorway was swept aside.

The queen had arrived.

Costis gaped, as breathless as if the air had been driven out of him by a blow. He hadn't heard the sounds of her arrival. He looked at Eugenides, still sitting on the stool. The king hadn't been distracted by the noise Costis was making. He must have heard the footsteps in the hall. He'd spoken softly so that those approaching wouldn't hear him. But they had certainly heard Costis. They had heard him shouting at the king. Smashing wine cups. Now they could see him standing over the king like a threat.

Costis took a ragged breath. He wanted to kill the king. He wanted to cry. He dropped to his knees before his queen and lowered his head almost to the floor, covering his face with his hands, still balled into fists, tightening knots of rage and bitter, bitter shame.

· CHAPTER TWO ·

COSTIS heard the queen's voice over his head. "Do tell me why I should come to the barracks to speak to my guard?"

And Eugenides answered, as calmly, "You could have summoned him."

"You would have come, too? Following like the tail behind the dog?"

"Am I insufficiently kinglike? Costis has been telling me so."

"Unkingly, in so many ways, My King. Not the least of which is listening to your guard tell you so."

Eugenides accepted the rebuke without a word.

"You haven't ordered a hanging," said the queen.

Costis fought with the desire to throw himself onto his stomach and crawl toward the queen. He'd never been so helpless. Like a fly in a web, the more he struggled, the sooner he would be lost.

"No," said the king. Costis hoped silently. "I don't

want to hang him." Costis's hopes fell and shattered. He cursed himself for believing even in the smallest corner of his heart that the king might try to prevent the loss of his family's farm.

"You will *not* meddle with the machinery of justice," the queen warned.

"Very well, then," said the king casually. "Hang them both."

"Him and which other of my most loyal servants, My King?" Her voice never rose, every word was cool and precise, and her anger made Costis, still on his knees, shake.

"Teleus," said the king with a shrug, and the queen was silenced.

"It was premeditated, then," she said at last.

Gods defend them both, it wasn't premeditated. Costis pushed himself up from the floor.

"My Queen." He spoke as calmly as he could and looked up at her face as she turned to look down at him. He would rather have done anything than draw her attention.

"You have something to say?" She spoke as if her dog had suddenly sat up and begged to be heard.

He shouldn't have addressed her as His Queen. He should have said Your Majesty. She was always "Your Majesty" no matter who addressed her, but if he was a traitor, she was no longer His Queen. The thought brought a twisting pain in his chest. He'd served her with the unrelenting loyalty of every member of her Guard, from the day he was recruited. Teleus himself had selected him, younger than most trainees, for service, and after a year of training had selected him again for the Queen's Guard. He didn't look away from her gaze as he spoke.

"Your Majesty, please, it was stupidity, not treason. Let me prove it, if I can. Please don't hang my Captain for something that was only my fault." He was too afraid even to speak of the farm.

"Do you know what you offer?" asked the queen.

"No, Your Majesty," Costis admitted in a whisper. He didn't know the details and didn't think he should try to guess at them now. He was scared white already. "But I will do anything."

"Oh, very well," said the king petulantly, as if he were losing a game of chess. "Don't hang Teleus. But I don't see how you can hang Costis if you won't hang his superior officer."

The queen turned back to face him. "I could hang *you*," she said.

Eugenides looked up at her. "You missed your chance for that," he said.

The queen lifted a hand to briefly cover her eyes. "It is remarkable how you cloud my otherwise clear vision," she said. "What is it you propose?"

"I propose that you let me trade him to Teleus. His life in return for Teleus's good behavior."

"Go on," prompted the queen.

"Teleus thinks well of him. He performed well at the Battle of Thegmis, and his name was mentioned to you when he was promoted to squad leader."

Costis winced, having dreamed that he might someday hear that his name had been mentioned to the queen. Not like this.

"I am willing to offer Teleus Costis's life if Teleus is willing to guarantee my continued well-being."

"He is the Captain of your Guard. Your well-being is the object of his employment," said the queen.

"Your Guard," said the king.

"Your Guard," insisted the queen.

"Then how do you explain the sand in my food? The snakes in my bed? The persistent little shoves between my shoulder blades whenever I am at the top of a long flight of stairs?"

"A snake," repeated the queen.

"A black one. A friendly one."

Costis had never heard anything like the silence that followed. It went on and on, as if he had suddenly been struck deaf, like the ritual silence of a temple, only much, much worse.

"Teleus." When the queen finally spoke, it was only in a whisper, hissing the final sibilant.

Costis heard the curtain rings slide on the rod. Teleus would have been standing just outside in the passage. Costis could have looked up to see the captain's face, but

Costis's head had moments before sunk slowly back toward the floor into his hands.

Sejanus had related stories of the pranks played on the king by his attendants. They had seemed riotously funny when retold around the table in the mess hall. They seemed less funny now. If someone could put sand in the king's food, who could not put poison there as well? If someone put a black snake in his bed, why not a viper? If they succeeded in pushing him downstairs . . . There were Eddisian soldiers, just a few, here and there, all over Attolia. No one doubted the damage they could do if the war with Eddis recommenced. And begin again it would if the king died suspiciously in the first few months of his reign.

"My favorite," said the king, "was the hunting dogs released in the courtyard as I passed through it."

The whole palace knew about the hunting dogs. The guards had laughed and laughed when Sejanus offered his firsthand account. Sejanus had said the king had been so scared he'd turned green, standing on the stairs outside the palace doors until the dogs were collared and dragged away. He'd warned their keeper he would have all the dogs slaughtered like goats if it happened again.

"Teleus?" prompted the queen.

"I didn't know, Your Majesty." It wasn't an excuse. It was an admission of failure.

"Why didn't you say something sooner?" Attolia demanded of the king.

The king answered, speaking slowly. "Because I had not yet been knocked down by a member of my own Guard."

Sejanus had said the king wouldn't tell the queen about the pranks because he didn't want to admit that he was too weak to deal with his own attendants. He just pretended not to notice, to his attendants' ever-increasing amusement. Being attacked by his own Guard was not something the queen could fail to overlook.

"So, a bargain," suggested the king. "Teleus, I give you Costis's life and you start doing your job."

Costis knew the answer before Teleus spoke. It was no secret that the captain despised the new king. He wouldn't have accepted a drink of water in a fiery hell from Eugenides, much less the life of Costis. Costis, according to the strict rules that ordered Teleus's life, deserved his fate, and Costis, even in the privacy of his own skull, couldn't disagree. He had time to think again of the gibbet that would be built on the parade ground, of what it would be like to hang, of his father's shame.

"Take the bargain, Teleus," commanded the queen abruptly.

"My Queen?" Teleus didn't believe his ears either.

"Take it."

"As you wish, My Queen," said the captain, sounding as stunned as Costis felt.

"You wanted a sparring partner this morning?" the queen said, turning back to Eugenides.

"I did."

"Costis will serve you well," she said, and swept out of the room. The rings slid again across the rod. The leather curtain dropped, and the only sound was that of the many receding footsteps in the hall.

Costis was still hunched over, blinking his amazement into the darkness of his hands cupped over his eyes. When the crowd of footsteps had reached the stair at the end of the hall, he finally lowered his hands to the floor on either side of his knees. He rested them gingerly on the wood boards, as if there had been an earthquake and he wasn't sure it was over. He sat up slowly. The earthquake wasn't over. The king still sat on the stool, his legs still stretched in front of him, still crossed at the ankle.

The king rubbed his face with his hand, pausing to finger gently the bruise beside his mouth.

He said at last, "That was terrifying, but I suppose you are used to excitement?"

Costis stared at him blankly.

"She wouldn't hang Teleus. She doesn't have anyone to replace him."

As if the king had risked Teleus's life in an effort to save Costis, instead of failing in an attempt to eliminate one of the queen's most powerful supporters. Costis knew what he had seen.

"I told you she wouldn't take the farm." Eugenides smiled, entirely without royal dignity, and left.

◆ ◆ ◆

"Do you still wish you'd hanged me?"

She hadn't heard him come in, but he had moved an inkpot on her desk, sliding it across the wood so that she would know he was there before he spoke. He was considerate in every detail. She didn't turn.

"Men's necks have been broken by a single blow," she said.

He tossed a cushion to the floor and stepped around her to settle on it, sitting cross-legged near her feet. "I can't keep on apologizing," he said.

"Why not?" she asked, over his head.

"Well," he said pensively, "I think you would be bored."

It was vain to hope that he might cease to have things to apologize for. "What happened?" she asked coldly, and Eugenides hunched his shoulders and minded the fringe on the pillow under his ankle, laying each thread out straight.

"I was angry at Teleus. Costis came to his rescue." He scattered the fringe back into a tangle. "I thought you were going to hang poor Costis."

"I would have if you hadn't chained him so neatly to Teleus."

"Like an anchor to drag him down," the king agreed.

"I thought that we had an agreement about Teleus."

"We did. We do," the king assured her.

"So you risk him to save the life of a treacherous, worthless guard?"

"You called Costis your loyal servant earlier."

"He was a loyal servant earlier. He is no longer. You will not rehabilitate him with me."

"Of course not," he said humbly.

She released a sigh of frustration and asked reluctantly for the truth. "Were you lying?"

"I never lie," he said piously. "About what?"

"The sand, the snake."

For a young man who never lied, he seemed surprisingly unoffended by the question. "You should ask Relius. Your Secretary of the Archives has suspected something for weeks and has all but turned himself inside out trying to find out more."

"Then why didn't you speak?"

"I don't want the kitchens purged, or the guards."

"You want to save people from punishment they deserve?"

"Oh, no," said the king, "I only want to be sure that those that deserve it the most are the ones punished."

"Say the word, then, and they will be."

He only shook his head and she gave up for the moment.

· CHAPTER THREE ·

Costis woke earlier than usual the next morning, when one of the barracks boys knocked on the frame of his door.

"Captain's orders," he called. "Everyone not on duty is to be on the parade ground in full uniform at the dawn trumpets." Costis could hear the same orders repeated down the hall by another boy.

"I'm supposed to spar with the king," he said groggily.

"Captain said to tell you not today, that he has asked the king to begin training tomorrow."

"All right, thank you," Costis said, and the boy moved to the next door. Costis pushed aside his blanket and got to his feet. Aris had helped him set his room in order the night before, and everything was back in its place. The bits of broken wine cup were swept into a pile. The king's empty wine amphora still sat on the table with the remaining wine cup. When he had time, Costis would have to carry them back to the palace kitchens or send them back with a boy.

Costis got dressed. He pulled on his undershirt and a leather tunic, a leather kilt under the chain skirt that hung from his waist. He had guards for his shins and shoulders and a breast and back plate that hung from his shoulders and buckled together under his arms. Aris had brought back his kit the night before. He'd agreed with Costis that the king would exact his revenge in their sparring session this morning, but evidently the king would have to wait.

Costis belted on his sword after he had pulled it from its scabbard to check its edge. The chain at the collar of his cloak hooked to his shoulder guards, so that the cloak hung down his back without tangling his arms. He had no gun, because he wouldn't be on duty. Each soldier owned his own sword, but the guns belonged to the queen and were locked in the armory. Only guards on duty with the queen carried them, and they collected them before going on watch and returned them when their duties were completed.

When he was dressed, Costis went downstairs and out to the court that lay between the barracks. There were other guards there, but no one spoke to Costis. They looked away and stepped back as he walked up to the fountain. He splashed a little water on his face and used the dipper to get a drink, careful to keep his face turned away from the other guards, as if there were something fascinating on the far side of the narrow court. He went back into the barracks to find his squad and make sure they would be ready at the parade ground by the appointed hour. Diurnes in particular was sometimes slow to move in the morning.

This morning, however, his men were up and ready, waiting for him and looking him over in speculation. He had only to nod a greeting and then lead them toward the parade ground. Costis's squad was in the Eighth Century. When the dawn trumpets sounded from the walls, he was in line, beside his squad, one of more than a thousand men standing in orderly blocks across the parade ground, waiting for their captain.

Teleus didn't keep them waiting long. He signaled, and the centurions one by one called their ranks to order. When they were finished, the only sounds to be heard across the wide parade ground were the distant calling of birds and the muffled noises of the city waking on the far side of the palace walls. On the parade ground, no one moved or spoke until Teleus raised his voice to shout, "Costis Ormentiedes."

Costis felt the twitch that ran through the men around him. No one dared move to look at him except Diurnes, who turned his head just slightly, in order to watch the squad leader from the corner of his eye. Costis didn't know what he should do and was relieved to see his centurion arrive at the end of his rank. The centurion jerked with his head, and Costis stepped from the line and paced to the center of the field.

He and the centurion turned smartly on their heels and moved together to stand below the podium, looking up at their captain.

With a few words, the captain stripped Costis of his rank of squad leader.

"By the will of the king, you may be relieved of your oath to serve him. You may take your things and leave the palace this morning. Do you choose to go?"

Costis hadn't anticipated such a question. He'd assumed Teleus meant to dismiss him from the Guard entirely in order to thwart the king. Suddenly he was offered a choice to go or stay. His tongue felt wooden and he had to force the words out of his mouth. "I'll stay, sir." When Teleus continued to look down at him, Costis realized that he had spoken too quietly. "I'll stay, sir!" he shouted.

Teleus lifted his head to shout over the parade ground. "By the will of the king, any one of you today may be released from your oath to serve him. Any man who chooses may leave his rank, collect his belongings, and leave the palace without penalty." Across the parade ground, not a man moved.

"You will be given time to consider your decision," said Teleus. He nodded again at Costis, who returned to his rank but not to his squad. He followed the centurion to the end of the rank and took his place with the unassigned men there. The Guard remained at attention. Several minutes passed, and then several more. There was a very quiet murmur as a few daring men whispered a comment to their mates. There was the barest scuffling of boots. A centurion cried out to his men to dress their ranks, and the scuffling ceased.

While they stood, the sun rose higher in the sky until its rays struck the ground at the western edge of the parade ground. Those still standing in predawn chill envied their comrades their place in the sun, until the chill disappeared and the sun rose higher and the Palace Guard still stood at attention. At the change of watch, the centurions called out the men for duty, but the rest remained. Those men who had been on watch arrived in twos and threes and quietly filled in the empty places. Teleus, who had remained standing in front of his men, offered again to release any man who chose to leave the king's service, but no one moved. It was afternoon and the day wore on. The watches changed, offering a respite to those who had duty. For a few, the heat and the dehydration were overwhelming. They keeled over like trees. The centurions ordered them carried off the field, but when they revived, they came back to their places.

It was summer and the day was long. The sun finally began to drop toward the horizon, and the shade crept out from the western wall of the parade ground. The sweat cooled. An evening breeze blew an unwelcome chill down the backs of the soldiers, and they shivered in place, but they didn't shift. The sun dropped further.

The trumpets had blown for the end of bird watch and the beginning of bat, and every man of the palace Guard had had hours to consider his oath when finally Teleus shouted, "Long live the king!"

"Long live the king!" the Guard answered, and was dismissed.

In silence, they moved heavily back toward their barracks. As they reached their courtyards, a few groaned, swinging their arms to loosen stiffened muscles. Costis turned for the barracks door, intent on retreating to his room until the storm Teleus's discipline had provoked lessened a little in its fury. He knew he would have to face the Guard, just not yet.

Four or five men stood talking just inside the door, and he couldn't get through. As Costis tried to slip behind them, he heard one say, "We know who is to thank," and he flinched.

A hand reached out of the crowd for him, forcing Costis to stop. "Oh, I don't know, Seprus, I don't think we can blame everything on poor Costis." The hand and the voice belonged to Sejanus. Until his appointment as one of the king's attendants, he had been a lieutenant in the Queen's Guard. He was the second son of the Baron Erondites and had, no doubt, been selected as an attendant because of his father's power and not because Erondites was any friend of the queen's.

Gods alone knew how Sejanus came to be in the barracks, though of course the whole palace must know of Costis's disgrace and Teleus's discipline. The Guard had been standing in view of the palace all day. It was impossible that anyone would not know the full story, and there was nothing to stop Sejanus's coming to the barracks if he chose and if he wasn't called at the moment to serve the king.

"No, I don't think you can blame the last straw on the donkey's back, gentlemen." He ruffled Costis's hair as if he were a boy. "If the king has finally lost his temper, I think you'd better look to the sand in his bed as the cause. Sand in your sheets is such an aggravation, especially when that's all that's in your bed." The men around him laughed. Sejanus pushed Costis toward the stair, and gratefully he went while the guards were distracted by their former lieutenant's comments about the king, the sand, and his sleeping habits.

"There were a few other aggravations, weren't there?" one of the guards asked Sejanus.

"I'm sure I don't know," Sejanus answered with one of his cool smiles.

"Relius will," said the guard. "Relius will know by morning." There was more laughter. The Secretary of the Archives had his own army of spies to ferret out any information he desired.

Once on the stairs, Costis was shielded from the view of the room, and he reached back to pluck the sleeve of Aristogiton, who was standing nearby, a fringe member of Sejanus's group of seasoned, but not yet veteran, soldiers. Aris twitched his arm free, but Costis grabbed him at the elbow and conveyed with a sharp tug his intention to pull Aris up the steps backward if necessary, and Aris gave in.

Even so, Costis nearly dragged his friend through the dark to the top of the narrow stairs. He stopped just below the landing. There was a lamp there that cast its light on Aris's upturned face. Costis, on a higher step, bent over his friend.

"Tell me," he said in a fierce whisper, "that you don't know anything about the pranks Sejanus has been playing on the king."

"Why would I?"

"Don't lie to me, Aris. I saw your face!"

"I—"

"What have you done?"

Aris rubbed his head. "I think I delivered the message that said that the king wanted to review the hounds in the lion court."

"What do you mean, you think?"

"It was written on a folded sheet. How was I supposed to know what it said?"

"But you knew something was wrong? Why would you be sent with a message from the king? Who gave it to you to deliver?"

"Costis . . ."

"Who? And why did you deliver it, you fool?"

"What was I supposed to do? Say no?"

"The thought might have crossed your mind!"

"Well, of course, it would have crossed yours, Costis, because you're not an okloi. You want to know who asked me to deliver the message? The second son of the man my father pays his taxes to. What was I supposed to do? What would you have done?" Aris threw up his hands. "I know what you would have done. You would have said no, and damn the consequences, because you have a sense of honor as wide as a river. I am sorry, Costis, I guess I don't."

"Well, maybe I don't either," Costis snapped. "Or I wouldn't have taken a sacred oath to protect a man and then knocked him flat on his back."

Aris snorted.

Costis paused to collect his temper. He had never felt so irrationally hot-blooded. He didn't like the feeling, though he knew other soldiers often did. "What are you going to do?" Costis asked, and Aris could only shrug.

"Relius will know who delivered the message, if he doesn't already. Tell the captain before Relius does."

"What happens to my family, then?" asked Aris.

"What happens to you if you don't tell the captain?" Aris thought it over. "Maybe I should."

It was Costis's turn to shrug. He didn't want to sound like a hypocrite. "I think it's the right thing to do."

"So, so, so," said Aris, "at least my honor will be intact."

"And that's very important," said Eugenides.

Aris and Costis both jumped at the sound of the king's voice. He stood on the landing above them like an apparition. His dark hair melted into the darkness behind him, while the light of the lantern fell on the white linen of his shirt and the gold threads embroidered in his coat seemed to glow. After a brief moment of horrified paralysis, Aris leapt to attention. Costis had known the voice as soon as he heard it. He didn't look at the king, but rather behind him, searching for the attendants that he thought must be there. He was a second later pulling himself to attention.

It was impossible that Sejanus would be downstairs talking about the king's sleeping arrangements if he knew his lord was standing on the landing upstairs, but just as impossible that the king could be there without his attendants and without Sejanus's knowing it.

Eugenides leaned forward and whispered into Aristogiton's ear. "Speak to Teleus in the morning," he said just loud enough for Costis to hear as well. Then he stepped behind the wall of the stairwell into the corridor that ran alongside it. There was no sound of footsteps. When Costis bent to look around the wall, the king was gone.

Costis woke the next morning before the dawn trumpets and dressed with a sense of dread, oddly familiar. It was the same feeling he'd had whenever he'd gone off to meet his tutor, having spent his day playing in the woods instead of preparing his lessons. Whatever happened this morning, the bruises, like the marks left by his tutor's willow switch, would fade, and Costis was certainly no stranger to bruises. He tried to encourage himself with the thought that he could have been facing a hanging, not a beating. But it had never been the fear of bruises that sickened him when he faced his tutor, and he felt distinctly uncheerful as he walked toward the training ground.

He arrived early. No one spoke to him. The Guard ostracized those in disgrace. The captain did come to stand beside him, but did no more than nod a greeting. When the king came, he was accompanied by four of his attendants as well as his guards. He left them all at the entrance of the training ground and walked across the open space alone. He arrived at Costis and Teleus and nodded a greeting at them both. He had his practice sword with him and tucked it under his right arm in order to wave a hand in invitation. Costis winced. The captain would have thoroughly humiliated any of his own Guard who treated a practice sword so thoughtlessly.

"Shall we begin with the first exercise?"

Costis obediently assumed the stance for the simple practice of thrust and parry in prime. He knew that the king was not a soldier, but he was surprised that Eugenides had not at least mastered the basics with a sword. Perhaps he had lost his skill along with his right hand, but Costis thought the king should have adapted to fighting with his left. There had been time to learn since the queen had caught him traipsing through her palace and cut off his hand. Back when he was the Thief of Eddis, before he'd stolen the throne of Attolia as well as its queen.

Teleus dropped back and pretended not to watch. The rest of the Guard did the same. The flesh crawled between Costis's shoulder blades.

"Your guard is low," Eugenides said calmly, and Costis took his attention off the guards around him and looked at the king. Eugenides put one eyebrow up. Costis had to pull his chin down to stop his head from shaking in disgust. He wasn't a very talented swordsman, and he didn't have the experience of the veterans around him, but he was a damned long way further down the road than first exercises in prime.

Eugenides read his mind and smiled wickedly. Costis clenched his teeth, adjusted his sword, and fixed his gaze on the embroidered front of the king's tunic.

The king didn't move. Costis stood with his sword extended while the king stood with his own sword still tucked into his armpit. Costis's arm and shoulder began to burn. The wooden practice sword was weighted to feel as much like a real sword as possible, and it was no joke to hold it extended as the moment stretched on, especially as his muscles were still stiff from hours of immobility the day before.

Finally the king stepped into position. He knocked Costis's sword aside and completed the thrust, stopping just a bit before Costis's breastbone.

"Again?" he said.

Costis returned to position. And so it went. The king may not have had the skill to engage in a pretend battle and give Costis the beating everyone in the Guard assumed he had coming, but the king could and did commence exercise after exercise only to leave Costis immobile in the middle of it, straining his muscles to keep his body motionless and to conceal the effort immobility demanded. He was determined not to let the effort show. He concentrated on the point of the sword held out in front of him and willed it to be still, as the least waver at its point would reveal his strain.

The king, after his first mocking smile, addressed himself to the practice as if it held his whole attention. His concentration was worse than the mockery had been. If he had laughed, Costis could have been angry and his anger would have given him strength, but Eugenides was almost preternatural in his calmness as he moved his sword for a thrust, back to a ready position, to the block, marked by the quiet *tack* as the swords hit, to the thrust, and to ready again. *Tack*, thrust, ready, *tack*, thrust, ready.

Costis wanted to throw back his head and howl. This was the king the gods had given Attolia?

At last, the men around them began to break off their exercise and move away. Costis expected every repetition to be the last, but the king seemed oblivious and only remarked, "Again?" after each.

The other soldiers had left. The only people on the open ground between the palace walls and the barracks were Costis, the king, Teleus, and the king's attendants lounging near the entryway. One of the king's attendants approached. He was taller than the king, about as tall as Costis, expensively dressed and heavily built.

"Your Majesty?" he said, in cool, arrogant tones.

Eugenides lowered his sword and stepped back from Costis to look around at the empty field. He looked up at the position of the sun.

"I see the day is passing," he said mildly. "Thank you, Costis." He nodded dismissal. Costis stepped back and almost stumbled. The king saw the hesitation and raised an eyebrow. Costis had no doubt that his concern concealed malicious delight. He bowed and strode away. Behind him he heard the king speaking to Teleus, but he didn't listen.

He went from the training ground to the mess hall, hesitating for a moment in the doorway. No one greeted him. No one even looked at him. He looked, but didn't see Aristogiton. Costis hoped that it was because he was on duty, but suspected Aris had avoided a situation where he must either throw in his lot with Costis or publicly ignore him. Costis headed toward the kitchen, and the line of men gathered there melted out of his way. He collected a bowl of ground cereal and a dish of yogurt and a handful of dried fruit. He sat at a long table at the side of the room.

He looked at the food and couldn't bring himself to eat.

He was too proud to get up and leave.

A bowl dropped, not lightly, onto the table beside him. The wooden bowl hitting the wooden table announced like a knock on the temple door that someone had come to sit beside him.

"Aris, don't be a fool."

"Too late to change now," said Aris as he stepped over the bench and sat beside Costis. He looked around the room, daring anyone to object. Instead, after a moment, one of the other squad captains, senior to both of them, stood up from his table and crossed the room to join them.

"It isn't," he said as he dropped onto the bench, "as if we weren't, every one of us, happy to see him knocked flat on his back."

One by one, the other squad leaders joined the group, and Costis passed from one kind of embarrassment to another, less painful but no less acute, as they teased him about his practice session with the king.

Costis put his elbows on the table and rested his chin in his hands, pointedly ignoring the rest of the table, but knowing privately that the weak feeling in his knees was relief. He no longer had a squad, but he was still a member of the Guard, not a disgraced outcast.

The other squad leaders ate and moved on. Aris stayed a little longer. "You should eat," he pointed out to Costis.

"I will," Costis promised. He'd been too sick and then too embarrassed to get on with his breakfast. "Why do you think they did it?" he asked, grateful but puzzled to have been brought back from exile.

"They like you," said Aris. "They respect you."

"Why?" asked Costis, unaware that he might be admirable in any way.

Aris put his head in his hands, an image of despair at such naiveté. "That, Costis, is the difference between you and, say, someone like Lieutenant Enkelis. You didn't think you deserved to be promoted after Thegmis; you said you were just doing your duty. Enkelis never lets a good job go by without taking credit for it. He wants to be captain someday, so he makes sure he is better than anyone else. You just want to be better, and that's why everyone thought you'd make centurion and lieutenant and maybe captain, someday. They wanted you to be captain. They'll never want Enkelis." Aris drained his cup and stood. "I'm on duty soon. You should eat."

Costis didn't take his advice immediately. He was thinking. Too soon he felt a hand on his shoulder.

"Wash and dress," Teleus said. "The king wants to see you."

Costis looked at him in bewilderment.

"Hurry," Teleus prompted.

After one regretful look at his breakfast, for which he had finally acquired an appetite, Costis went. With Teleus standing there, he couldn't even snatch a fig. He hurried to his room to collect his gear and carried it in his arms down the stairs and across the courtyard to the baths.

The Guard's baths were in a building as big as one of the barracks. It had a domed top as elegant as anything designed for the patriarchs of the court, though its insides were fairly utilitarian. There was no time for the steam room and the strigil afterward. Costis dumped his clothes onto a bench and hurried to the tepidarium to scoop a bucket of hot water out and dumped it over his head. There was a hard lump of soap sitting in a stone dish that he used to scrub himself. There was no lather. Aris said that the lumps provided in the bath-house weren't soap at all, but stone, and that they cleaned by abrading the dirt from the skin, not soaping it away. He scooped more water out to rinse himself, and stepped back across the slate floors, careful that he didn't slip.

A valet appeared with a scrap of cloth to dry him and

helped Costis into the clothes. Once the breastplate was buckled in place, the valet stepped back, and Costis shrugged his hands helplessly. "I haven't got a coin. I'm sorry." All of his money had disappeared. There would be no more until the next payday.

The valet waved a hand in forgiveness and Costis hurried away.

Teleus led the way up to the palace. Following his captain, Costis worried and wondered what the next stage of his fate might be. The captain had said only that the king wanted to see him and expected him at breakfast. Nervously, he followed Teleus through the many hallways and rooms of the palace, at first familiar then increasingly less so. As a member of the Eighth Century, Costis had never been in the inner palace. Some of the doorways were guarded, and at each, the guards saluted Teleus and he nodded as they passed. Finally they crossed a narrow courtyard and went through an arched tunnel that led to a terrace overlooking the queen's garden. Waiting there were the queen's attendants, a table laid with dishes and breakfast, and, sitting alone at the table, the queen.

She glanced up at Teleus, but didn't speak. Teleus took a position near the entrance to the archway and waited. Costis did the same.

The king arrived, preceded by his own squad of soldiers and his attendants. His hair was damp and unoiled. His skin looked freshly scrubbed. He noted Costis as he passed him and turned his head to give him a brief smile as if acknowledging a point that Costis had scored in arriving first.

"You're late," said Attolia to her husband.

"My apologies," said the king. One of his attendants pulled out a chair for him and he sat at the table. The attendants bowed and withdrew, leaving the king and queen alone except for their guards.

"That waistband doesn't go with that coat," said the queen.

"As you have already noted, I was late." Eugenides bent his head to look at his waist. His coat was yellow, and so was the waistband, but the shades were not the same. "My attendants have triumphed this morning in their quest to make me look foolish."

"You are unhappy with your attendants," the queen said. The flesh between Costis's shoulders crawled at the implied fate of any man or woman who failed the queen's expectations.

"Oh, no," said the king. "There's no need to boil them in oil. No doubt in time their taste will improve."

"Perhaps if you did not order your clothes in colors that would suit a canary?"

The king tilted his head to one side and eyed her for a moment as if weighing his response. "You're right," he agreed placidly. "I should stick to an Eddisian tunic in black with black embroidery and shiny black boots. I can powder my hair with gray like a Continental, and you can pretend you married my father."

The queen waved at the guard around them, and the soldiers withdrew, out of hearing distance, but not before they heard the queen tell her king that his father at least had a sense of dignity.

"And he's never late for breakfast," observed the king, taking a bite of a pastry.

When breakfast was over, the king stepped around the table and bent to kiss his wife's cheek. This assertion of ownership, the queen endured like stone. Costis was transfixed. He struggled to imagine her own mother kissing the queen and balked, seeing instead an adult Attolia somehow shrunk to the size of a child. Distracted by the image, he was late to realize that everyone on the terrace was looking at him. The king had motioned him to approach and waited with one eyebrow raised.

When Costis stepped forward, the king looked him carefully up and down. He leaned closer to peer at the buckles on Costis's breastplate, while Costis counted back in his head the number of days it had been since he'd polished them. The king's subsequent look of dissatisfaction left Costis certain that somewhere there was a buckle undone or an unburnished spot on his breastplate.

"I understand you are now an unassigned guard?"

"Yes, Your Majesty."

The king addressed his captain. "Is he going to dangle like a loose thread from your tidy schedule?"

"I am sure I can find a use for him, Your Majesty."

"I have a place ready made," said the king. "He can serve me."

"The units that serve the king are fully made up, Your Majesty, but we could enlarge one unit if you like."

"No, not in someone else's squad."

"You want him detached from the Guard?" Teleus was puzzled.

"I thought as . . . lieutenant."

Teleus was stunned.

"Yes." The king nodded his head with sudden decision. "I want him promoted to lieutenant-at-large, and I want him assigned to me. Every day from now until I dismiss him. Morning and afternoon. I will inform him if I want him with me in the evenings. He can begin now."

"Costis has not been trained as a lieutenant," Teleus protested politely. "He does not know the protocols for serving within the inner palace."

"He can learn as he goes." The king lifted the gun out of Costis's hand. A lieutenant didn't carry one. He passed it to Teleus to dispose of, and waved in dismissal.

When Teleus still stood, the king waved again, shooing him off like a trespassing pigeon. The captain bowed, cast a look at Costis full of dire warning, and retired.

"I believe he was instructing you not to disgrace yourself," said the king, and then turned to his attendants. "Where are we going this morning?" he asked.

The day that followed took on the same nightmarish impossibility of the day before. Bewildered, Costis followed the king and his attendants and guards as they led the way through the convoluted passages of a palace pieced together by at least seven known architects over a span of uncounted years. He observed the king's tutorial on olive production and taxation. When it was over, the king asked Costis whether he thought it was better to levy a tax per tree or try to estimate olive production year to year.

"I don't know, Your Majesty," Costis answered.

"Hmm," said the king. "I thought you grew up on a farm?"

The tutorial on olive production was followed by a lesson in Mede. As the king wandered around the room, obviously bored and unreluctant to show it, Costis tried to stay alert. The king seemed to know by divine inspiration when his attention wandered.

"Costis. The word for *death* in Mede, I can't remember it."

Costis racked his brain, searching that part of the mind that remembered the last few words it had heard without actually understanding them. "*Shuut*," he said at last. Clearly annoyed, the king asked him another question and another until Costis couldn't produce an answer, and then a few more questions after that. The conjugation of *to hit*, the word for *traitor*, the word for *idiot*.

"Forgive me, Your Majesty. I didn't hear that part of the lesson," said Costis. None of those things had been mentioned by His Majesty's tutors.

"You might pay attention to what's going on around you, instead of daydreaming. My life does depend on it, you know."

Costis thought perhaps he'd died and somehow crossed the river into hell without noticing the trip.

At last, one of the attendants stepped forward to say that it was time for the king to return to his apartment to eat. The king's instructors thanked the king with every appearance of sincerity.

In the hallway, the king dropped back to walk behind his attendants and beside Costis.

"So, Costis," he said, "have you learned all you need to know of Mede?"

"No, sir," said Costis, judging that to be the safest answer.

The king yawned, covering his mouth with his hand. "Me neither," he said.

They had reached a corner. The attendants who had been in front of them had politely slowed until the king was once more even with his retinue. Sejanus murmured a direction.

The king looked around. "I thought it was that way." He pointed.

"No, Your Majesty," the attendants patiently chorused.

The entrance to the king's apartments, like the queen's, was always guarded. The king nodded at the guards and passed through the door from the corridor. Costis hesitated, unsure if he should wait in the hall or pass through himself. A hand between his shoulder blades impelled him forward. Through the door, he found a guardroom, elegantly paneled in wood, lit by deep windows in the far wall. It was the entrance room to the king's private chambers, and it held more soldiers and one of Teleus's lieutenants. Costis himself, he remembered with a shock, was also one of the captain's lieutenants.

The guards standing around the room at attention must moments before have been occupying the benches that lined the walls. The king waved, a gesture of simultaneous recognition and dismissal, and the guards settled from the rigor of attention to a slightly more relaxed but respectful posture. A guard opened a door to the king's right, and he passed through, followed by his attendants. Costis knew from palace rumor and from Sejanus that the room beyond must be the king's bedroom. There was no other anteroom.

These were not the royal apartments with layers and layers of social defense, anterooms, audience rooms, and more anterooms, between the guardroom and the queen's most private space. The queen had not vacated the king's apartments, and Eugenides had evidently declined to move into what were traditionally the queen's rooms. If he had, his rooms would have connected through interior doors to the king's suite and nighttime traffic between the rooms would have been a matter for speculation and not public record. As it was, the king could not visit the queen without an embarrassing trek through a roomful of his guards and attendants, down a corridor, and along the same public path past the queen's guards and her attendants. It was well known that this had never happened. The king rarely visited the queen's apartments and only during the day. The queen had never been in these apartments.

"You may go if you like, Costis," the king called from the inner room. "But don't be late getting back for the afternoon court."

The door closed and Costis was left standing. He looked helplessly at the lieutenant, who stared back with an appraising look. He looked over Costis's shoulders at the veterans in the squad behind him. The hair on Costis's neck crawled as the veterans offered their silent report. It may have been positive; the lieutenant smiled and told Costis that he was off duty.

"Then I just leave?"

"That is so. Be sure to get back in time to escort him from here to the afternoon court. I'll make sure one of the men on duty in the afternoon tells you where to stand in the Audience Hall."

Only as Costis stepped into the passage outside the king's apartment did he realize he had no idea how to get out of the palace. He looked over his shoulder at the guards outside the king's door. They looked blandly back, and Costis wasn't fool enough to ask directions. Taking a deep breath, he decided to retrace his steps to the main part of the palace. Once there he would be on familiar ground.

He found that he had memorized most of the route. It twisted and turned so often that at last, curious at its convolutions, he stopped to explore a little in the passages around him. By happy chance, he found a wide corridor that led directly to the center of the palace. Relieved, he headed for the barracks to look for Teleus.

He spent most of his precious time off duty searching for the Captain of the Guard without finding him. Giving up at last, he snatched some bread out of the mess hall and headed back to the king's apartments, only to be stopped at the entrance he had chosen to the inner palace. No one had questioned him on the way out, but to readmit him, they demanded authorization. When he explained, they looked at him doubtfully, but sent word to the lieutenant assigned to the captain's office. Teleus must have left instructions because the messenger came back with authority for Costis to pass, and the guards sent him on his way.

By the time Costis finally reached the king's apartments, he was late. There was no time to get instructions about where to stand. Costis had no sooner stepped into the guardroom than the king swept out and Costis had to follow.

The afternoon court was held in the Audience Hall in the center of the palace. Costis had seen Attolia's throne room before, but not often enough for it to have lost its effect on him. Eugenides didn't seem to notice the mosaics or the towering columns several stories tall that supported the roof.

The titular King of Attolia dropped onto the throne beside the queen's and smiled at her. "It's not my fault I am late," he said with childish delight. "Costis didn't come back after he ate. I waited and waited."

Attolia declined to respond. Costis, obeying the hissed instructions of a chamberlain and the helpful wave of one of the other guards, found a place to stand against the wall and watched the business of the state. The queen directed everything. No one addressed the king, and he never spoke. Costis's interest waned, and he grew bored but was careful to keep the expression on his face attentive. The king didn't bother. In fact, during one baron's particularly drawn-out accountings of his tax payment, the king leaned his head back and closed his eyes, to all appearances asleep.

Finally the court session drew to a close. Those who hadn't been heard would have to come the next day. The king and queen rose. They were surrounded by their attendants and guards and escorted away. In the corridor, they paced along, side by side.

"You can speak during a court session," the queen pointed out, in a dry voice.

"I can," agreed the king. "I thought about telling Artadorus he needed a haircut."

"That would have been impressive, not only speaking, but speaking in your sleep."

"I was listening," the king said, aggrieved. "I closed my eyes to listen better."

"What did you hear?"

"I'm not sure," he said. "That's why I was listening so closely. I may have to ask the baron to repeat some parts of his report on his grain tax."

"I am sure you can arrange an appointment."

"I am sure I can, too."

Dismissed at last, Costis returned to the barracks. As exhausted as if he'd spent the entire day in a battle, he staggered upstairs and along the narrow hall to his tiny but private quarters. The leather curtain that served as a door was pulled back. The room was empty, stripped of every single possession; even the thin mattress on the bed was bare, his blankets missing. Feeling utterly defeated, Costis sank down on the three-legged stool the king had occupied the day before and wondered what he was supposed to do next.

He hadn't sat there long when a barracks boy arrived.

"Captain's orders are that you are to attend him immediately."

Costis thanked him and turned his steps wearily back down the stairs and across the grounds to the collection of rooms that included Teleus's office and his quarters. A narrow staircase climbed an outside wall to a small landing and a door. Costis knocked.

Teleus was at his desk writing. There was a tray near his elbow holding bread and cheese as well as an amphora and a wine cup. Relius, the Secretary of the Archives, sat on a stool nearby with another wine cup in his hand. He nodded to Costis. Costis suppressed the shudder that went with a chill down the back of his neck. Teleus continued to write. Costis waited.

"He'll try again, you know," Relius said to the Captain of the Guard, continuing the conversation Costis had interrupted. "When he is more sure of himself, he will move against us both."

"If we are valuable servants of the queen, she will preserve us, as she has so far," said Teleus, checking a schedule and re-inking the nib of his pen.

"And if we are not valuable?" Relius asked.

"If we are not valuable, why should she defend us?" Teleus asked.

Relius sighed. "No one could doubt our value," he said, "but no man is indispensable. I taught her that myself. Many years ago." He sipped his wine. "You could leave," he suggested to Teleus.

The captain looked up from his work. "So could you," he responded. "But you won't, and neither will I." He went back to his writing.

Relius stood and placed his wine cup on the tray. He arranged his clothes, easing the creases from the expensive material. He took a moment to smooth his already perfect hair. Then he patted Teleus's shoulder, smiled at Costis without speaking, and left. Costis waited.

At last Teleus put down his quill. "You were a year younger than the age limit when I accepted you. I made an exception for you, do you know why?"

"No, sir."

"Another year on your uncle's farm might have ruined you, and I didn't want your skills to be wasted. They have been, though, haven't they? You threw them away."

"I am very sorry, sir."

"I'd like to think a desire for justice temporarily evicted common sense, but it's hard to justify attacking someone so incapable of defending himself, however contemptible he may be and," he added, "however much your comrades might congratulate you for it."

Costis opened his mouth, but found no words to speak, and anyway, Teleus held up a hand.

"Your gear has been shifted to one of the lieutenant's quarters. The boy will show you which one."

"Sir, I don't understand."

"What don't you understand, Lieutenant?"

"How can I be a lieutenant, sir?"

"Because you have been promoted by the king's whim, far beyond your merits. If the king succeeds in eliminating me, you might be the next Captain of the Guard. It's a joke, Costis. You are a joke. If you don't want the king's joke to be a success, then do your duty, and do it well. No doubt there are other men he will attempt to destroy. We don't have to make it easy for him. Here is your schedule." He pushed a paper across the desk. "You will have all the regular duty of a lieutenant as well as dancing attendance on the king. I am damned if I am going to have a lieutenant that doesn't actually serve as one. Dismissed."

Out on the steps, Costis stopped to look at the schedule. He stared at the sheet in consternation. The king hadn't needed to hang him; he would be dead of exhaustion within the month. He almost turned back to Teleus, but there was no point. His feet carried him slowly down the stairs to the barracks boy who was waiting to show him to his new quarters.

· Chapter Four ·

In the morning, Costis got a better idea of what the captain had meant when he had said that the king's sense of humor was playing itself out. Costis thought it was not humor so much as sheer vindictiveness.

The training session with the swords was as tedious as the day before. With long, painful pauses, they practiced the early exercises over and over. Afterward, Costis hurried to clean himself in the baths and then went to present himself in the king's guardroom. He had the day's passwords and arrived without delay.

The king had bathed but was not yet dressed.

The door between the bedchamber and the guardroom was open, and Costis could hear every part of the process of dressing the king, and see most of it. From the conversation, he attached the names he already knew to some of the men waiting on the king. Hilarion, the heavyset attendant, was the second son of a coastal baron. He brought the king the wrong trousers and was sent back to the wardrobe. Dionis, who was the nephew of another baron, brought him the wrong shirt. He was also sent back to the wardrobe, somewhere through a doorway on the opposite side of the guardroom from the king's bedchamber. Nothing seemed to suit the king, and the attendants passed back and forth across the guardroom with rejected items. At first Costis blamed the king's vanity, but slowly he realized that this was all a dance enacted by the attendants and directed by Sejanus. The guards on duty watched in amusement. Sejanus winked as he passed Costis with an ink-stained sash.

The king had chosen a Mede style of dress with a long, open coat over his shirt and tunic. The longer belled sleeves of the coat should have concealed the cuff and hook he had in place of his missing hand, but the coat the attendants brought had been miscut by the tailor. The sleeves were too short. Not only the hook but the entire cuff stuck gracelessly out of the sleeve. The king sent it back.

Sejanus, smoothly conciliatory to the king's face, pushed his arms backward into the sleeves of the coat as he was leaving and stared in silent consternation at his arms, sticking out of the shortened sleeves all the way to the elbow. He waggled the fingers on his left hand and then turned in horror to his right hand, where his fingers were bent in the shape of a hook. Snatching at the sleeve with his left hand, he pulled his right hand in until it was hidden, then tucked it under his left arm, hiding it further, and looked around in mock chagrin. Someone in the guardroom, staring in over Costis's shoulder, choked on a laugh, and the three attendants standing in front of the king, in his view, were suffused and rigid.

There seemed to be little that the king could do to control his attendants. He might dismiss them from his service, but Costis guessed that dismissing them would only reveal his inability to control them. So Eugenides sat, with his jaws locked, and ignored Sejanus.

Presently, when he'd been given clothes and been obsequiously helped to dress, the king called Costis. He looked him over closely, as he had the day before.

"Are you a typical example of the Guard, Costis? I am a little surprised. After all, you aren't really soldiers, and given that you serve a mostly decorative function, I would have expected you to be more . . . decorative."

Most of the attendants had the kindness to look uncomfortable, knowing that Costis was paying for their transgressions. Hilarion glared at the king, safely out of his line of sight. Sejanus only looked amused. He raised his eyebrows and smiled as if he expected Costis to share the joke.

In this way, Costis fully realized his new function. He had been elevated from obscurity so that there would be some victim in the pecking order lower than the king.

If the king hoped to make Costis, and through him the Guard, look foolish, he had chosen the wrong target. That day, and every day, the soldiers of the Guard treated him as a lieutenant, and not as a joke. With the king, he served as the butt of the king's humor, but the men of the Guard, some veterans twice his age, saluted Costis with pointed rigor and deferentially called him sir. Even Teleus made no distinction between how he treated Costis and how he dealt with his other lieutenants. The attention made Costis uncomfortable at first. He felt like a fraud, but the show of respect was no sham. The Guard wanted him to be a lieutenant, not an imitation of one, and their confidence in him supplied the strength he needed to suffer the king's company with dignity.

He had support from another source as well, an anonymous one. He thought it was Sejanus, but had no proof that it was the king's most successful tormentor that sent a package from time to time with notes on the king's lessons. The first one arrived the second day of Costis's new duty. Costis sat in his lieutenant quarters and examined what he'd found waiting for him on the bed. It was a flat package in a cloth wrapper tied with string. A folded note had been slipped under the string.

"To assist in your lessons," it said, "from one who wishes you well in your contest." That, Costis thought, defined his role in no uncertain terms. Whether he wished it or not, he was an opponent of the king.

Costis opened the cloth wrapping and found a collection of vellum sheets, neatly folded, covered in writing. He carried the paper to the window and read over someone's detailed notes on the structure of the Mede language. The handwriting was square but uneven, as if the hand that held the quill had been shaking. If it was Sejanus, he had probably been laughing as he wrote. Several pages were covered back and front with vocabulary lists. Costis glanced through the lists, looking for the words the king had quizzed him with the day before. The infinitive of *hit* and the words for *traitor* and *idiot* had been added to the bottom of the list.

Costis looked back at the note. It was unsigned. The package might have come from one of the king's instructors, but it was more likely to be one of the king's attendants. Sejanus was clearly the leader even though the attendant Hilarion was oldest and Philologos, the youngest attendant, an heir to a baron, was the highest in rank. Costis looked over the sheets again. He wished he'd gotten a written explanation of the issues involved in olive production. He thought he would need one.

"Thank you, Costis," said the king, dismissing him.

"Thank you, Your Majesty," said Costis, dismissed.

The king crossed through the middle of the training ground and met his attendants on the far side. In a crowd, they passed through an arch and out of sight. As they disappeared, Costis turned for the archway behind him, the king's exit releasing him from his polite position. The soldiers cleared a path for him, and he hurried. His clothes and gear were waiting for him at the baths. He had just enough time to duck into the cavernous building through a side door, skirt the cold-water plunge, and cut through the steam room to the dressing room beyond. The steam room was usually empty so early in the morning, and the few occupants knew who he was and why he was hurrying. They shouted encouragement instead of curses as he passed through in a draft of cold air.

Between the steam room and the dressing rooms, a valet waited with a bucket of warm water to dump over him. Costis soaped hastily and was doused again. The valet handed him a cloth, and he dried himself as he headed toward his clothes. With the valet's help he got dressed as quickly as possible, had his greaves buckled on and his breastplate buckled over his shoulders and under his arms. He bent his head so the man could run a comb through his hair, while he fumbled for a coin, which he couldn't afford to give away. It was a ritual gesture. The valet waved it away with a smile.

Sheepishly, Costis dropped it back into the purse hanging from his belt.

"You are making me famous," said the man, patting him on the back as he turned him toward the door. "Valet to the King's Own Guard."

Passing between the barracks, Costis ran, holding his sword stable with one hand so that it didn't bang against his leg, and using the other hand to hold the breastplate so that it would not ride up and chafe under his arms. Once he reached the end of the barracks, he had to drop to a walk, the fastest walk he could manage while maintaining the dignity of Her Majesty's Guard.

He climbed up the steps to the upper palace and made his way through the twisting corridors and across atriums under light wells until he reached the last open court before the archway to the terrace. The guard there shook his head. The king had not yet come down to breakfast. Costis turned back to a nearby stairway and waited at the bottom, listening.

The king timed his morning training precisely. It was still the same dull repetition of basic exercises, and when it had finally dragged to its end, Costis had just enough time to get himself clean, but not enough time to rest in the steam room or even soak himself in the hot baths. The king never cut his time so short that he might be excused if he skipped the wash and came to his post less than perfectly tidy, so Costis rushed. If he was lucky, then Costis got to the king's chambers before the king had finished his own, rather more elaborate bath and robing. If Costis was late, he could join the king on the breakfast terrace, taking his place unobtrusively by the archway. The king said nothing, though he never failed to notice Costis's arrival, nor did the queen, who eyed him inscrutably for a moment across the breakfast table whenever he appeared. The very worst mistake Costis could make was to meet the king on the way down. It gave the king a clear, drawn-out opportunity to comment on Costis's lateness, his dereliction of duty, his inability to meet even the basic requirements of a member of the Royal Guard, and his appearance. If the king did miss an opportunity to complain about his hair, the polish on his buckles, the state of the leather straps—all things that Costis spent hours late into night trying to perfect—Sejanus would draw the king's attention to the fault. It seemed unlikely behavior from an ally who sent notes on the Mede language and Attolian political history, but Sejanus seemed far more interested in the entertainment of the contest between the king and the guard than in who won it. Sejanus liked his jokes. Costis was growing tired of them.

After breakfast, the king kissed the queen, a practice Costis still resented, and condescended to be swept off to his daily tutorial in which various counselors and ministers tried desperately to educate him in his responsibilities in spite of his obvious lack of interest.

The meeting on wheat production seemed to be a recitation of the yield of every wheat field in the country in the last year. Costis tried unsuccessfully to pay attention. They were a half hour into the list when the king asked, "What's the difference in the wheat?"

"Excuse me, Your Majesty?"

"The different kinds of wheat you keep mentioning. What's the difference?"

The two men looked at each other. The king waited, leaning back in his chair with one booted ankle crossed over his knee.

"Pilades would be most helpful. If Your Majesty would excuse us?"

The king waved one hand, and the two men hurried away and returned with Pilades, a bent older man with wisping white hair and an expression of delight on his wrinkled face.

"If Your Majesty would like to see, I have samples here." He reached into a variety of small bags that he was carrying and dumped handful after handful of grain onto the table. Dust rose in a cloud, and the king winced, waving his hand in front of his face. Pilades didn't notice. He called the king's attention to the formation of the seeds, to the number of the seeds, to their shape. He dumped more piles onto the table and explained the advantages of each, which one yielded the largest crop, which survived the most inclement weather, which could be planted summer or fall. Many facts Costis knew, having been raised on a farm. Some were new, and the lecture, once begun, was clearly unstoppable.

The king, who normally wandered away to a window

during meetings like this, sat immobilized. He had little choice. If he so much as shifted in his seat, Pilades moved in closer, hovering over him with zeal. No doubt he rarely got a chance to expound to this extent and was reluctant to lose the king's attention. The king made a few abortive attempts to escape but was ultimately forced to sit and listen.

Over the king's head, the counselors and the attendants exchanged glances of awed delight. When Pilades finally wound down, the king, his face blank, thanked him. He thanked the two men he'd begun the meeting with and suggested that perhaps they could finish their business at another meeting, or better— they could just give him a written summary and he would look over it sometime himself. They nodded; the king rose and escaped into the hall. Once there, with the door closed, he put his face in his hand.

"Thank gods I didn't ask about fertilizer," he said.

Costis almost laughed out loud. A glance told him that the others in the entourage were also amused, but they were smirking at the idea of the king sitting through another lecture. Only Costis shared the king's vision of the dedicated Pilades dropping handful after handful of various animal wastes onto the tabletop and discussing their individual merits.

The king met Costis's eye and smiled. Costis looked away. When he looked back, the king's smile was gone as well.

"Gentlemen, I think I've suffered enough for the morning. Pelles, why don't you tell my next appointment I'm not coming?"

"Your Majesty is supposed to meet with Baron Meinedes before lunch," said Sejanus.

"Well, I am not going to," said the king. "I'm going back to my room."

Pelles bowed and excused himself. The rest started down the hall. At the first intersection of passages the king spoke again. "Directly back to my room, please, gentlemen."

Sejanus bowed, offering the king the lead. Eugenides stepped forward. He led the way without hesitation, and Costis wondered how long the king had known that his attendants and his guards led him on a dance of unnecessary twists and turns every time they crossed the palace.

Certainly the king stepped out confidently ahead of his entourage. When he reached the main passage, he crossed it and then turned down a narrower passage that led to an even narrower staircase. The attendants, who might have been worried that their game had been discovered, began to be amused instead. The king climbed three flights without speaking and stepped into a passage lit by small windows near the roof. There were tiny offices on either side. Startled faces looked out from the doorways, and men walking with scrolls and tablets in their hands froze and then bowed as the king passed. Costis had no idea where they were. He didn't think the attendants knew either. They all followed the king into an office, then through it and out onto a balcony beyond, and stopped.

They were at a dead end, looking out over what had once been an interior courtyard that was now a hall, partially roofed over, with a light well in the center. The roof above their head was supported on rafters that butted into the balcony at their feet.

The royal quarters were somewhere on the far side of the atrium, and there was no way across except to sprout wings and fly.

The attendants smiled.

The king stared angrily at the railing in front of him.

"Perhaps not the most direct route," he said. The attendants continued to smile as he led them back to the hallways and back past the men still standing with their scrolls and tablets. They bowed again as the king passed. He went down the stairs again, just one flight, turned left and left again to circumnavigate the atrium, and then turned right to reach a passage on the far side. They were again in familiar territory, and even Costis knew which way to turn to reach the king's rooms.

Even after the detour, they were early and unexpected. The guards in the hall pulled themselves to attention, and the one knocked on the doorway to alert those within of the king's arrival. The king walked through the doorway and turned on his heel to face his attendants.

"Out," he said.

"Your Majesty?"

"Out," said the king. "All of you." He waved the guards toward the door as well.

"Your Majesty cannot mean—"

"His Majesty does mean . . . and His Majesty has had enough for now, and you may go. Have a holiday. Get a cup of coffee. Chat with your sweethearts. Out."

"We could never leave you unattended," Sejanus said in a voice smooth and provoking.

"Your Majesty, it wouldn't be right," protested the squad leader, the only one genuinely concerned. He knew his duty, and it did not involve deliberately leaving the king unguarded. Teleus would have his head.

"You can guard me from the hall. The door is the only one into the apartment. You can attend me," he said to his attendants, "from the hall."

"Your Majesty, that is unacceptable," Sejanus said. "We simply cannot leave you all alone."

The king looked as if he was going to throw the words back in Sejanus's face. Then his vindictive eye fell on Costis.

"Costis can stay," he said.

"I think not, Your Majesty." Sejanus smiled the words, all condescension, but the king stopped him.

"Am I king," he said flatly, "or shall I call my wife for corroboration?"

He would never admit to the queen that he couldn't

control his own attendants, but none of them, not even Sejanus, could risk calling his bluff.

"Bit in his teeth," someone muttered as they filtered through the door to the hallway. Lamion was the last one out. He looked back and at the king's glare hastily pulled the door closed behind him.

Eugenides turned to Costis. "No one walks through that door, Costis. No one comes through any of the doors into this guardroom, is that clear?"

"Yes, Your Majesty."

"Good. Come in here first."

He walked into the bedroom, and Costis followed to the door.

"Move that chair, please. I want it in front of the window." It was an armchair, awkward but not heavy. Costis hesitantly lifted it and moved it as the king desired.

"Facing the window or away, Your Majesty?"

"Facing."

The king sat. Costis stood. The king held out his hand, without looking at Costis, and said, "Take that off for me." He meant the ring on his finger. It was a heavy seal ring, of solid gold with the seal carved into the face of a ruby.

Costis carefully pulled on the ring, but it was a close fit. He had to hold the wrist with one hand and work the ring off the finger by pulling hard.

"I'm sorry, Your Majesty," he said as he tugged.

"Don't apologize," said the king. "I can't imagine that removing seal rings is in your professional training. Unless they give the Guard special training in looting corpses?"

Costis didn't think it funny. "They do not, Your Majesty." He pulled hard and the ring came off.

"Leave it on the desk," said the king, and looked away.

Costis remembered that Teleus worried what damage this young man would do as he started to feel his power. Angry, he stalked to the desk and dropped the ring on its leather top with a thump. The king ignored him. Costis continued out of the room. The king hadn't said to close the door, so he didn't. Let him ask, he thought, but the king didn't. Costis picked a spot where he could stand without a view of the king sitting in front of the window. He stood stiffly at attention, and he waited.

So far as Costis could tell by listening for sounds of shifting weight in the chair, the king didn't move. Minutes ticked past. There was no sound from the bedroom. The king had probably decided to take a nap.

"Costis," he said at last. "Come move the chair back. Then I suppose you had better let the lapdogs back in."

In spite of himself, Costis was amused at the image of the king's elegant courtier attendants as a pack of poorly trained house dogs.

Later, in his own quarters, as he was getting ready for bed, Costis wondered who put the king's seal ring back on and if the attendants wondered how he got it off. He looked at his own left hand, where he wore a small copper ring with a seal on it of Miras, the soldier's patron god of light and arrows. As a trainee, Costis had joined the Miras cult with his friends. They each wore the copper ring, though it turned their fingers green.

Tentatively he pushed at the ring with his thumb, trying to remove it without using his right hand. He hooked it on the edge of the tabletop to no effect. Finally he put his finger in his mouth and worked it off with his teeth. He spat the ring into his palm and dropped it onto the table, where it sat reflecting the candlelight. Costis shuddered as if someone had walked over his grave. He put the ring back on his finger and went to bed, trying to think of other things.

❖ CHAPTER FIVE ❖

I N a small audience room, Relius delivered his report
to the queen. In the past, they had been alone for
these meetings. Now, the new king attended as well.
While Relius talked, Eugenides sat with one booted
ankle over his knee and watched a gold coin flip across
the backs of his fingers.

It was a distraction, but the queen did not take her
attention off Relius. He was being as elliptical as possible, trying to inform her, without alerting the king, of
the intrigues within her court. Eugenides's failure to
exercise his authority meant that others were maneu-
vering to exercise it for him. Several different parties
hoped to woo the king to their side, to make him speak
for their interests.

Briefly, the queen looked at Eugenides and back at
the Secretary of the Archives. It had not escaped her
notice that both these men, exquisitely tailored, had
chosen clothes for this occasion that complemented

her own. This was not as prescient as it seemed. Her wardrobe was fairly uniform, in spite of her new husband's suggestions that she expand it. It amused her that their sartorial choices clashed so completely with each other. Eugenides's loosely cut coat in the Mede style, more like a robe, was red silk shading to orange. Relius dressed in the Continental style, his tunic, a deep wine color, tailored close to his body and matching the short velvet cloak he affected even in summer.

His clothes were an expression of his power. He alone of the queen's advisors had been with her the length of her reign. He had been the illegitimate son of a steward in a baron's villa, and she had seen, the first time they met, that he could teach her what she needed most, the manipulation of men and power. He had been her teacher, and she had rewarded him with wealth and influence.

Eugenides had grown bored with moving the coin across his fingers. He began tossing it into the air and catching it. He was distracting Relius, an accident, or more likely a calculated effort to unsettle the secretary. As the coin rose higher and higher into the air, Attolia drew her foot back slightly and kicked the king in the ankle. He jumped and turned to her in outrage. The coin dropped behind him, and he plucked it out of the air without looking.

He glanced at Relius and back at her. He'd missed

nothing, she was certain. Eugenides held out the coin; it was a gold stater with her head on one side and the lilies of Attolia on the other.

"Lilies, I rule, heads, you do," he said, and threw the coin into the air.

"Lilies, you rule, heads, you throw again," said Attolia.

The coin dropped. Eugenides looked at it and then showed it to her. "No need," he said. The coin sat in his palm, obverse, showing the lilies of Attolia. He flipped it again and again and again. Each time it landed showing the lilies. He threw the coin and this time caught it in his closed fist. Without looking at it, he slapped it onto the embroidered sleeve of his coat and took his hand away. It was lilies again.

"I think we are finished here," Attolia said. "Was there anything more, Relius?"

"No, Your Majesty."

With affected disinterest, the king shrugged his shoulders and palmed the coin from his sleeve. "Thank you, Relius, for your report. As always, I am grateful for your thorough presentation of the information." He inclined his head, and Relius bowed himself out.

The king rarely missed an opportunity to insult the Captain of the Guard, but to the Secretary of the Archives he was unfailingly polite. It made Relius feel ill. For now the king was a puppet of the Eddisians, but that would change. Within the year, some power in

Attolia would pull his strings, and Relius was determined that the power would be the queen's. Like Teleus, he would stay with his queen no matter the cost.

He wanted to dismiss the coin toss as sleight of hand. Any circus performer could control the drop of a coin, but he'd been puzzled. The queen had been undismayed; she had seemed almost vindicated in her manner. It had been the king who had been more disturbed with each toss of the coin. He'd looked almost sick, Relius thought, by the time he put the coin away.

Relius loitered in the arcade outside the audience room until the king left with his attendants. Walking away along the arcade that lay perpendicular to the one where Relius lurked, the king pulled the coin from his pocket. He looked at the gold stater in sudden disgust and pitched it hard between the columns of the arcade into the shrubbery that filled the courtyard garden. Perplexed, Relius returned to his work.

When the palace was quiet, and it seemed only the royal guards could still be awake: "Baron Artadorus."

It was a whisper on a breath of air so shallow it wouldn't have stirred a cobweb, but it combined with the touch of a blade on his neck and woke the baron instantly.

The night-light was out. He could make out nothing but a dark shape leaning over him, close enough to put lips near his ear to whisper into it. Whoever it was wasn't standing by the bed, but sitting on it. This intruder was in the royal palace, in the baron's private apartments, in his bedchamber, sitting on his bed, and had arrived there waking no one, not even the other person in the bed.

The blade was sharp, never mind how a man without a hand could hold a knife.

"Your Majesty?" the baron whispered.

"I have had a most interesting discussion with a man named Pilades. Do you know him?"

"No, Your Majesty." The steel was warming to the temperature of his skin. He could feel the edge biting.

"He works in the Ministry of Agriculture."

"I'm sorry, I—"

"He's been telling me all about the grain that grows in different parts of the country."

"Ah," the baron said weakly.

"Ah, indeed. How long, Baron?" the king whispered, still leaning close enough that the baron could have taken him in his arms, had he been a lover instead of a murderer. "How long have you been misreporting the kind of grain that you grow? How much have you avoided paying in taxes?"

The baron closed his eyes. "This was the first time, Your Majesty."

"Are you sure?" The knife-edge bit deeper.

"I swear it."

"I remind you that there are records that can be checked."

"I swear it, Your Majesty, this was the first time." His eyeballs strained to the corners of his eyes, striving to see the king's face. "You will tell Her Majesty?"

The king's laugh was silent, no more than a puff of warm air against the baron's cheek.

"I am here in the night, holding a knife-edge at your throat, and you worry that the queen will learn about your error? Worry about me, Artadorus."

It was blackmail then, thought the baron. "What do you want, Your Majesty?"

The king laughed again, without a sound. "For you to pay your taxes, for a start," he breathed.

He lifted the knife-edge away and rose noiselessly from the bed. He crossed the room as silently, but when he'd gone through the door, he closed it behind him with a snap. In the bed beside the baron there was a sleepy murmur, not his wife, thank the gods, his wife would have been awakened by the whispered conversation.

His bedfellow stirred beside the baron and sat up. "Did you hear something?"

"You dreamed it," said the baron. "Go back to sleep."

For a long time, he lay in his bed thinking. Clearly he had been a fool. A fool not to realize that the king might be inept and inexperienced and still be dangerous. A greater fool to take Baron Erondites's suggestion that the queen might be distracted by her new marriage. Erondites, never a friend of the queen's, had seen that prudence had kept Artadorus loyal all these years, and greed might lead him astray. It was he who had set this trap by suggesting a means of avoiding the queen's taxes, and sprung it by informing the king of the tax scheme the baron was attempting. The baron dismissed the reference to Pilades and the Ministry of Agriculture. This king would never have discovered the business on his own. It was Erondites who had betrayed him, building his influence with the king and preparing to blackmail this baron into working with the king and against the queen. There was only one thing to do. The night was warm, but the baron lay under his bedcovers, chilled through.

At breakfast the queen spoke to the king.

"Baron Artadorus sent me a message asking to see me before breakfast. He has asked to be excused from court."

"Has he?" The king feigned lack of interest.

"He said he had business to oversee at his home."

"Oh?"

"Something to do with his accounts."

"Hmm."

She warned him with a look.

"Did he fall on his sword?" the king asked.

"Not physically."

"Ah," said the king.

She crossed her arms and refused to speak to him again.

"The baron met with the queen this morning. He has been excused from court." Sejanus, meeting his father briefly in an out-of-the-way courtyard, relayed the news.

"Has he?" said his father, mildly surprised but not distressed. "No doubt he is heading home to edit his accounts. It doesn't matter. The error has been recorded, and correcting it won't erase the crime."

"And if he confessed to the queen already?"

"If he had confessed to the queen, we would all know. Surely you remember what happened to the last person who attempted to defraud the royal treasury?"

There were no more snakes in the king's bed and no more sand in his food. The Captain of the Guard and the Secretary of the Archives had taken steps to insure that. Palace misbehavior became more subtle. The food that arrived for the king's lunch, which he ate alone, except for the oppressive company of his attendants, was always unsuited for consumption by a one-handed man. As the king made every effort to conceal his handicap, the attendants made every effort to emphasize it. If the king wanted his bread sliced, he had to ask. If he stubbornly declined to ask, then Sejanus, or Hilarion, would make a show of distress that they had forgotten to slice it for him. Twice more the king locked himself in his rooms. Both times he allowed Costis and only Costis to stay with him.

The attendants, as careless as they appeared, spent their time exiled in the outer corridor, sweating at the thought that the queen might pass by. She surely knew that the king ousted his attendants from his presence, but she seemed willing to turn a blind eye, so long as she was not faced with the pack of them kicking their heels in the passage.

"Her Majesty must appear to support the king," Sejanus reminded his peers. "Otherwise, I am sure she wouldn't care how much we irritated the king."

On a rare evening when Costis was neither on duty nor asleep, he talked with Aris in his quarters.

"Until I die, I think," Costis said. Aris had asked how long Costis thought he would serve as lieutenant. "Probably of boredom." Lying in a pose of intense apathy, with his feet on his pillow and his head hanging a little over the edge of the short cot, he stared at the ceiling. His expression of distaste was the one he had to be careful to keep off his face when on duty.

"So you think the promotion is permanent?"

Costis reconsidered. "No. He can't really mean to leave me as a lieutenant. It's all pretend and mockery, not a real promotion. I suppose he will get tired of this eventually and I will be demoted back to squad leader. Or line soldier."

"Or dismissed from the Guard."

Costis rolled his eyes to look at his friend. Aris had said aloud what Costis had been trying not to think.

Costis shrugged, not an easy thing to do when partly upside down. "If he's going to do that, I wish he'd do it and get it over with instead of leaving me halfway to nothing, waiting and waiting for the fatal blow. Maybe he's waiting until boredom kills me . . . or I kill ex-Lieutenant Sejanus."

"What? Kill our brave and clever and beautiful Sejanus?"

"With my bare hands," said Costis. "If he points out one more tarnished buckle or loose thread on my uniform to the king, I am going to pop his eyeballs out with my thumbs, and I don't care how beautiful he is or how clever."

Aris chuckled. "Careful . . . remember, he's an idol to us all." Sejanus was wealthy and influential, and generous with his spending money. As lieutenant, he had had the admiration and envy of most of the Guard.

Costis lifted his head to drink the last of the wine out of the cup he'd been dangling over the edge of the bed, the rim pinched in his fingers. When the wine was gone, he lowered his arm to set the cup on the floor. "He's funny," Costis admitted. "He can make you laugh so hard it hurts." He yawned suddenly and rubbed his face with the heels of his hands, pushing his fingers into his hair and pulling on the curls until his scalp protested. Gods, he was tired. "But underneath the jokes and the gibes and the playacting, there's nothing there but . . . spite. There isn't anything he won't laugh at."

He looked at Aris. "Did you know that already?" he asked.

"I admire him," said Aris. "I haven't ever liked him." Aris shrugged. "That might be sour grapes. I am sure he doesn't like me."

"Sour grapes for me, too, then," said Costis. "You, me, and the king."

Aris made a face at the company he was in.

Costis smiled. "You do have to admire him. Sejanus, I mean. Not the king, of course. He tells Hilarion, who supports the queen, that any attack on the king, even so much as a mismatched stocking, is a blow for the queen. The next day, he might tell Dionis, whose family has never supported the queen, that to ridicule the king will shame the queen as well, and somehow he is perfectly convincing."

"They don't notice that he has no loyalty to either side?"

"They don't care." Costis stopped to think. "Or they are afraid of the wrong side of his tongue. He can make anyone who crosses him sorry. Philologos doesn't like all these pranks. He's his father's heir, not some wild younger son, but Sejanus pulls everyone's strings like a puppet master."

"Does he pull the king's strings?"

"The king?" Costis yawned again. "Well, he fights more than the others. He is always trying to balk Sejanus, but I swear half the time he doesn't realize he's doing exactly what Sejanus wants. And when he does spike him, it is by accident. Sejanus spent all night setting up some prank in the music room, and the king chose that day to walk in the garden."

"How angry was Sejanus?"

"Oh, he laughed. He always laughs, even when the joke is on him."

"What does the king do, when the joke is on him?"

Costis put one hand over his eyes. "First he pretends not to notice, but you can tell how angry he is because his face gives away everything. Then he summons the poor stupid guard Costis Ormentiedes and makes him wish he'd never been born."

"Poor Costis," said Aris.

"Poor Costis indeed. Do you know what is most difficult?"

"Tell me," said Aris.

Costis smiled at his friend's dry tone. "Remembering that he is the king and that I can't wring his neck."

"Maybe he'll go after Sejanus's brother and leave you alone."

"I wish he would," said Costis fervently.

Sejanus's brother was Erondites the Younger, called Dite. He was their father's heir. Where their father was one of the queen's oldest enemies, Dite was one of her most fervent supporters.

Dite was a poet and musician and widely assumed to be the author of a rude song circulating through the palace and the Guard. Costis had learned it in the mess hall earlier in the evening. The sort of tune that stuck in a man's head, with a chorus that repeated over and over, it was a humiliating portrayal of the king on his wedding night, set in flawless classic pentameter, and Costis was going to have to be very careful not to hum it by accident in the king's presence.

"Or anyway, I would wish Dite the worst," Costis said, "if I didn't know how happy it would make Sejanus to see his older brother drawn and quartered."

Sejanus played a careful game, serving the queen but never disavowed by his father. The baron scorned Dite, and spoke of him only in terms of withering contempt, but Dite was still his heir.

Eugenides evidently shared the baron's contempt for his older son. He made no secret of his dislike for Dite. Nor did Dite bother to conceal his contempt for the king. The king insulted Dite with barbaric directness. Dite's responses were more subtle, in the Attolian fashion, and no less cutting. The song was only the most recent example.

"I have heard that the king taunts him almost as much as he baits you."

"He must think it's safe. The Baron Erondites isn't going to complain on Dite's behalf."

The next morning, the king was almost crisp in his practice moves, but clearly many miles away in his thoughts. Costis wondered if he was thinking of Dite. Someone had been whistling the tune to "The King's Wedding Night" in the training yard that morning. The delicate unmistakable notes had trickled into silence as the king arrived. He must have heard them, but he'd made no sign. Costis sighed in contempt, and the king's wooden sword skipped over the top of Costis's guard and knocked him hard in the temple.

Costis backpedaled automatically in a defensive crouch in case of further attack, but the king had lowered his sword and was standing still, looking exasperated.

"Ice!" he shouted in the direction of the boys watching from along the wall, and one of them scampered away.

Costis's head was ringing and one half of the world looked oddly bright and dark at the same time. He had a hand cupping the pain, but still held the practice sword in the other. The king gently tugged it away. Costis put both hands over his face. It hurt.

"I'm sorry," said the king.

"My fault," Costis gasped politely.

There was a crowd forming around them. "Let me see it."

Costis lowered his hand and the king reached up to turn his head. "Can you see out of that eye?"

"Yes, Your Majesty."

"You're sure? Cover the other eye."

Costis did as he was told. The world still looked odd. The figures around him were limned with darkness, but clear.

"It was the flat." Teleus spoke from somewhere out of Costis's line of sight.

The king sighed. "It was the edge," he said. "Gods' love, Costis, served by a swing in prime. How embarrassing for both of us."

It was embarrassing. Hitting your opponent in the face while sparring wasn't supposed to happen. Hitting him with the edge of the wooden sword instead of the flat was even worse. But being hit by a swinging stroke in prime by an inept one-handed opponent was the depths of humiliation. Costis sighed.

"My fault, Your Majesty."

"Yes, it was," the king agreed affably. Costis looked up sharply and found the king smiling pleasantly for a change. "My fault, too," he said apologetically. "I lost my temper."

When the boy came back with ice from the kitchens

wrapped in a cloth, Costis put it against his face.

"Go lie down," said the king. "Teleus can take you off the duty schedule today."

"I'll be fine, Your Majesty."

"Of course you will. Enjoy your day off."

Costis would have protested again, but his face hurt, and the idea of a day off was a temptation.

"That's better," said the king. "Keep up that obedient attitude, Lieutenant, and you could be Captain of the Guard someday. It's true, the queen would never have you, but we could both be assassinated, and you could be captain to my heir. Don't give up hope just because chances are slim."

"For the assassination or the heir, Your Majesty?" asked Costis.

There was silence.

Costis looked up, hearing too late what he'd said and realizing to whom he had said it.

The king was openmouthed with surprise. So were a number of people nearby.

Costis lifted his other hand to his eyes, and didn't realize that the laughter he heard was coming from the king.

"Costis, you're picking up bad habits from my attendants. You aren't even half cocked on unwatered wine as an excuse. Shall we blame it on the pain in your head?"

"Please, Your Majesty. I am sorry if—"

"Not at all," said the king, "not at all." He lifted the

ice away from Costis's face to check the bruising one more time. "But why would I worry at all about assassination when I have such a stout Guard to defend me?"

He patted Costis gently on the shoulder and left.

In spite of its poor beginning, Costis did enjoy his day off. Teleus made him lie down in his room for most of the morning, until they were both sure the blow hadn't affected his eyesight. By that time, Costis was starving and looking forward to a leisurely midday meal. He hadn't put his bottom on a bench to eat at midday since he had begun serving with the king.

He thought he would eat alone, but there was a crowd still in the mess, and they waved him to join them. He swung a leg over the bench and sat down to find himself surrounded by amused faces.

"A swing in prime?" someone said.

He tried to brazen it out. "I had to let him hit me sometime."

In silence they weighed this. Then they laughed in his face.

That evening, as usual since the wedding, the king and queen dined with their court. Ornon, the Ambassador from Eddis, was there as a matter of diplomatic etiquette. He was not a happy man. After dinner, the tables would be cleared away and there would be dancing. The queen and king would dance first, then the queen would retire to her throne, and the king would politely circulate through the room, returning to sit with her from time to time. Without fail, Ornon could predict that the king would dance with the wrong people, the wallflowers, the younger daughters of weak barons, nieces and unmarried older women of no importance. He would pass over the older daughters presented to him and the women of the powerful families with whom he was supposed to be forming alliances. It wasn't through ignorance that he erred. Ornon had told him often which women to dance with, but the king claimed he couldn't remember. Ornon thought it more likely that the king had reached his limit and refused to force himself through one more politically motivated performance.

Not looking forward to the rest of his evening, Ornon picked at his dinner and wondered why he had ever thought it would be amusing to watch the Thief of Eddis suffer. That he was suffering was indisputable. In the beginning the young king had answered the subtle and not-so-subtle Attolian insults and condescensions with private jokes of his own. Because the Attolians considered only themselves capable of subtlety, they missed his ripostes entirely or took his more cutting comments as accidents. Ornon had bitten his tongue on more than one occasion. He was willing to admit, if only to himself, that glaring at the king on these occasions had been a mistake. Not only did it further incite

Eugenides, but it had convinced the Attolians that the Ambassador for Eddis at the court of Attolia had little respect for the king, which only contributed to their contempt.

The Attolians were mistaken. Ornon had the greatest respect for the Thief of Eddis, much the way he respected the business edge of a sword. He wondered how the Attolians thought Eugenides had managed to become king if he was the idiot they assumed him to be. Perhaps because they had never seen him as the Thief, with his head thrown back and a glint in his eye that made the hair on the back of a man's neck rise up. The Attolians had only seen this new and uncomfortable king. Ornon himself wondered what had become of the Thief. Ornon had seen no sign of that character in Eugenides since the wedding.

That, too, might have been his fault. He had warned Eugenides that he would have to keep his temper under control and his tongue between his teeth. He knew how much Eugenides would hate playing this role, and he'd looked forward to seeing Eugenides's cockiness stifled and his sharp tongue checked.

Ornon hadn't meant for the king to be seen swallowing one insult after another as if he had no spine at all. As a ten-year-old boy, the Thief of Eddis could stop a grown man in his tracks with a single look. Where had that look gone? It worried Ornon that Eugenides's role as Thief might have been an essential aspect of his confidence and strength of character. Perhaps both were gone, now that he had left Eddis for good. If so, it boded poorly for the country of Attolia.

The Attolians only thought that they wanted a weak king. A weak king meant uncertainty. If the king didn't wield the power in the country, all kinds of other people would fight to wield it for him. They would fight to gain power and fight to keep it. Some of the fighting would be public, with rebellions and civil wars; more of the fighting would be secret, with poisonings and political murders. Unless the queen continued to hold power, it would be an ugly future for her nation.

Ornon looked at the queen. Perhaps she would continue to rule as sovereign. No one would have anticipated her power when she had first taken the throne. She might still hold the throne alone, but Ornon thought she had reached the end of her resources. She had held her fractious barons and forced them to bow to her authority, but the Mede Empire wanted this little country and the countries of Eddis and Sounis as well. Attolia couldn't keep her barons in check and fight off the Mede Empire at the same time. She had driven the Mede off once, embarrassing their ambassador. That embarrassment would weaken the ambassador, Nahuseresh, but it was only a matter of time before he and his brother, the next emperor, returned to attack this coast of the Middle Sea. No one who had any foresight doubted that the Mede would eventually return.

When they did, the state of Attolia would have to be united in opposing them. The queen could command her barons, but not unite them. There was too much bloody history between her and too many of her barons. For the same reason, no one of the barons could have become king. They needed a neutral person to take the throne. Eugenides.

Ornon shook his head. Not all plans work out. This one may have been a failure. Eugenides had stopped trying to respond to the Attolian insults. He allowed himself to be heckled and badgered from place to place. He hated being in the public eye, and Ornon knew it. He'd expected a great deal of pleasure in watching Eugenides, with whom he shared a long and complicated history. What Ornon hadn't expected was this feeling of floating downstream with no one at the tiller in a boat headed for a waterfall.

He looked at the king. Eugenides was wearing the same coat to dinner as he had the night before. More worrisome, he'd smacked a guard in the head during sparring that morning. The Attolians assumed it was an accident, but Ornon knew better. Something had made Eugenides lose his temper, and that was the greatest danger of a weak king. Weak kings who lost their tempers were notoriously destructive. Eugenides had matured lately, but he'd been a hothead for many more years before that.

There was a lull in conversation, and in the quiet, someone from a side table addressed the king. "Your Majesty," he asked innocently, "is it true that your cousins once held you down in a water cache?"

Ornon, in the act of putting down his wine cup, paused.

"Is it also true that they wouldn't let you out until you agreed to repeat insults about your own family?"

The man speaking was across the hall from Ornon, but his voice carried. He was one of the younger men, with his hair long and curled, his clothes fashionable. He was one of Dite's set, Ornon thought. Dite and his younger brother Sejanus both seemed to be particular banes of the king's existence. Eugenides bridled any time Dite was near. Given that the two Erondites brothers hated each other, one would think that the king would get along with at least one of them, but he didn't.

Eugenides, who had been pushing his food around on his plate, finally raised his eyes and Ornon's wine cup hit the table with a crack and a splash.

Hastily righting the cup, Ornon cursed himself for even thinking about Eugenides's past, as if his thoughts had stirred Eugenides's more malevolent aspect to the surface. In this mood Eugenides was unlikely to yield to any hints or warnings delivered the length of the table by Ornon. He wouldn't even look at Ornon. Short of throwing a dinner roll at him, there was no way to get his attention.

The dandified Attolian who had spoken, a patron, but not a baron by any means, glanced at the queen to see if she approved, but she was looking the other way. The king shrugged his shoulders slightly and said, "I could send you to ask them."

The man laughed. His laughter was edged with contempt. "It would be a long trip, Your Majesty. I would so much rather hear the answer from you."

"Oh, the trip would be quicker than you think," said the king, pleasantly. "Most of my male cousins are dead."

The silence that had begun at the head table had spread to the edges of the hall. The Attolian's smile grew uncertain.

The king didn't smile back. Those who understood shifted uncomfortably in their seats.

The late war between Eddis and Attolia had cost Eddis dearly. She had suffered and lost on a greater scale than the larger, richer nation of Attolia, but at the end of the war, the Thief of Eddis had become the king of Attolia. And whether Eugenides of Eddis could send an Attolian courtier to his death to carry a question to his cousins in hell was a question that courtier was suddenly not interested in exploring. He wished, with intensity that surprised him, that he hadn't listened when Dite had suggested this little joke. The young man looked again to his queen, this time for rescue; she was still looking the other way.

"Forgive me, Your Majesty, if I offended," he murmured to the tablecloth.

The king said nothing. He met Ornon's worried look from across the tables and returned it with a widening smile that Ornon knew well. Eugenides was angry and pleased to be so. Leisurely, he reached for his wineglass and drained the little wine that was in it.

Unable to think where else to look, Ornon looked to the queen. His entreaty must have been plain because she smiled with a hint of amusement, and turned to Eugenides. As he contemplated his empty cup, she lifted hers.

"Take mine," she said.

People sitting nearby recoiled. Eugenides choked on the wine still in his mouth. There was no one in the room unaware that Attolia had used poison hidden in her own wineglass to rid herself of the first husband she had been forced to marry.

Eugenides continued to cough, his shoulders shaking. He threw his head back, gasping, and finally seized the breath he needed to laugh outright. Helplessly holding his sides, he looked at the queen. She only looked back without expression, and he laughed harder. The Attolians, one and all, watched with increasing dislike.

"No fear of that, my dear one," he said, his voice slightly strained, "and look, no need." He gestured toward his wine cup, which the wine boy had refilled, lunging forward with the amphora so hastily that the wine had splashed onto the cloth below. "I see my cup is full as well."

Conversations slowly resumed. The court lost its troubled expressions. The strange moment had passed. Once again, the Attolians had seen that the king was nothing more than a clown. Ornon was staring at his plate, relieved and angry at the same time, wishing that the Attolians could know how close they had come to disaster, and grateful that they didn't. He looked across the tables at the young man whose insult had roused the danger. That one, he thought, looking at the courtier's white face, had looked Eugenides in the eye. He knew how near disaster he had been. Ornon turned to look at the queen only to find her looking back at him, the hint of a satisfied smile still on her face. She'd proved her strength, and Ornon bowed his head in respect.

Later, the tables were cleared away for dancing. Under cover of the noise of shifting chairs, the queen spoke. "I'm sorry."

"For what?" asked her husband.

"For that young man. I would have seen you send him after your cousins gladly except that he is an undersecretary for provisions to the navy."

He shook the apology away and smiled, but his smile was distant. She followed his gaze, looking out over the court. She was seeing her dead. He, no doubt, was seeing his. She knew that he had both hated and loved those cousins who were now beyond both love and hate.

"A dance," the king said, "will mend everyone's spirits." He stood and offered her his hand. Together they took the first step down from the dais as the music started, and stopped before they took the second. The drum, which had started with a slow rhythm, playing alone, was joined by the shrill voice of a mountain pipe.

It was a traditional Eddisian tune that might have been a compliment to the new king, except that none of the Eddisian traditional dances could be danced with only one hand. Attolia thought of her music master, directing the music from a low balcony to one side of the room, blithely hounding the king with the notes, reminding him of all that he had lost. "Him, I will have flayed," she said, meaning it.

The intolerable tension she felt in Eugenides's grip eased. Her statement had been less calculated than her offer of wine, but it had had the same effect, easing the strain she knew he felt.

"I wouldn't," he said. "I have no doubt it is the careful hand of Sejanus making the music here and not the music master at fault. Dance with me," Eugenides said, turning toward her suddenly, bubbling with energy and mischief. Her heart sank. He had been pushed beyond his limits once already, and she had pulled him back, but she did not manage him like a dog on a chain. His wildness sometimes frightened her.

"No," she said repressively, and was unprepared when he pulled her down the steps in spite of her refusal. She staggered, and struggled for her balance, but he didn't let go of her hand. The court hissed in barely concealed rage to see their queen treated so. Even those who opposed the queen liked the Eddisian less.

"The court is watching," she pointed out.

"I thought you wanted me more exposed to the public eye?" he teased.

"I reverse myself," she said coldly, "and argue for a little circumspection." She tugged at his hand, but he didn't release her. She gave up, unwilling to be seen trying to pull away.

"You don't think I can do it."

She didn't think he could.

"I don't care what they think."

She knew that. It worried her.

"No," said the queen, but she wavered.

He sensed it and smiled. "Am I king?" he asked, irrepressibly.

It was the one argument she was in no position to deny. She wanted him to be king, and he was resisting it with all his will.

"Of course." She acquiesced, but she was angry now. The pink in her cheeks showed it. The music had stopped, and the court was silent. No one could have overheard their quiet words, but anyone who could see the king's face knew what he had said and what the queen had answered.

Radiating delight in the face of people who hated him, Eugenides led the queen to the middle of the empty space in front of the musicians. He looked at the floor, as if choosing his spot carefully, and brushed the stone with his shoe before looking up.

"You know the steps?"

"Of course," the queen answered again, tight-lipped.

"Of course," the king echoed. "Well, your part will be the same, just reach as if you were expecting me to take you with my right and I will use only my left."

"Simple," said the queen, putting out her hand.

"Very," said the king, taking it.

He shook away the stiffness of her arm. "Don't be afraid. Before I stole Hamiathes's Gift out from under your nose, these were the only dances I knew."

"I am not afraid," she said coldly.

"Good," said the king. "Neither am I."

He nodded to the musicians, and first the drum and then the pipes began. The king and queen faced each other and began the steps, their feet mirroring each other, their left hands clasped. Attolia's right hand, which should have been holding the king's left, hung down at her side.

"Why were these the only dances you knew?"

"Because no one would dance with me. Thieves are never popular."

I know why, thought Attolia, but aloud she asked, "Why are you familiar with the square dances?"

The music quickened.

"My mother taught me. We danced them on the rooftops of the Megaron. According to legend, the Thief and any partner the Thief chooses will be safe."

"You are king now," she pointed out.

"Ah, but they say that if the king dances, the entire court can safely dance with him."

"Spare me," said Attolia, "and my court, from dancing on the roof."

"It probably only works in Eddis."

They were called square dances because the entire dance took place in one small square, the dancers' feet never moving outside it. The line dances, in the same way, were danced up and down an imagined line. Both dances began slowly, but as the music continued, the dancers had to move faster and faster, their feet repeating the same pattern over and over. At the end of each cycle, Attolia spun away from the king and then back to face him. They clasped hands and spun together and then began again. The music soon increased to a pace that left no breath for talking.

As Attolia spun, she felt a tug at her hair and, turning back, felt another. Then she felt her carefully arranged hair slipping down on her neck. Eugenides, minding the pattern with his feet and spinning the queen with one hand, had been pulling out her hairpins one by one when her back was turned. The rest of the pins loosened, and her hair dropped free. It swung out as she spun and the last of the pins bounced and slid across the marble floor.

The queen was several inches taller than Eugenides, and he leaned back to counter her spin. To those watching, it didn't seem possible that he could succeed, but with one hand, and no visible effort, he defied the laws of the natural world. Phresine, the queen's senior attendant, watched them from behind the throne as her queen danced like a flame in the wind, and the mercurial king like the weight at the center of the earth. Faster and faster they moved, never faltering, until the music shrilled at an impossible tempo and the pattern gave way to a long spin, each dancer reaching in with one hand and out with the other, holding tight lest they fall away from each other, until the music stopped abruptly and the dance ended.

The queen's hair and her skirts swung and then settled. Coolly she pulled the hair away from her face and used one strand of it to wrap the rest into place behind her.

The king's brow furrowed. Spinning slowly, he looked down at the floor around him.

"Aha," he said, and walked away, bending to pick something up. As he walked back, he tucked his hand into his sash and pulled it out again full of hairpins.

He offered them to her.

"If you will excuse me, my lord, I will retire to replace them."

"Of course," said the king, echoing sweetly her earlier short-tempered answers. He bowed.

The queen inclined her head and turned. She walked back up the steps, past the thrones, and through the doorway there, collecting her attendants as she went.

Gen had returned to the throne and settled onto it looking smug. Phresine, leaving with the queen, heard Elia murmur under her breath, "Well, that was revealing."

"Only to those with eyes to see," murmured Phresine back.

Ornon, standing nearby, silently agreed.

Costis spent the evening happily unaware of the events in the throne room, writing long-overdue letters to his father and sister. He'd written only briefly since his disgrace and received more letters than he had sent. His sister's letters were filled with the inconsequential details of the farm. The birth of a new cousin and a new calf were announced in the same sentence. Thalia was more interested in the cow and knew Costis would be, too. He took comfort in her pretense that she was untouched by the disaster he had made of his life.

He knew she wasn't. Thalia and his father would have Costis's disgrace flung in their faces every day by the rest of the family, but his father also didn't mention it. He only assured his son of his support. Costis was glad of the letters and read them over and over, but they were hard to answer.

He prepared for bed early and in a glum mood.

The glum mood didn't leave him in the night.

"Is the eye bothering you, Costis?" asked the king the next morning.

"No, Your Majesty."

"Perk up, then, won't you? You're making me feel guilty."

After breakfast, the king declined to meet his tutors. "We have an appointment in the garden," he said to the queen as he excused himself. It was news to Costis, but apparently not to the attendants. After kissing the queen, the king went down the steps from the terrace. The attendants started across the terrace to join him, but he paused on the steps long enough to wave them back. Only the guard accompanied him.

Below the terrace was the queen's garden. Costis had assumed that the "queen" in its description was his own queen, but had learned from one of the other lieutenants that the garden had been for many years the private retreat of Queens of Attolia. It stretched from the edge of the terrace out to a wall that encircled it on three sides, separating it from the rest of the palace grounds. On the remaining side, a low stone railing edged the garden. No more was needed to protect the queen's privacy. On the far side of the railing, the ground dropped in a sheer face to an open court below.

The garden was laid out with hedges that divided the garden beds. In many places, the hedges grew high enough to form leafy tunnels and the green walls of outdoor rooms. In the center of the garden, a series of these rooms, interconnected by green corridors, gave the appearance of a maze when viewed from the terrace. It wasn't a true maze, and no one could be lost in it, but it provided privacy and at the same time security. The hedges were too thick for even a persistent assailant to break through quickly. The queen could walk there alone, leaving her guards at the arched entrances.

The king followed the path that ran along the balustrade. A summer wind twisted dust into spirals that blew against the stone wall below the garden and disintegrated as the wind was deflected upward. Some of the dust rose as high as the garden and made Costis's eyes burn. The king turned away from the wind toward the maze. Waiting there, in the space before an arched entryway, were a squad of guardsmen, the Guard Captain, and, surrounded by the guards, Erondites the Younger.

Costis knew him on sight. Dite's path had crossed the king's before, and Costis had seen him often. He was much like his brother, Sejanus, though he wore his dark hair long and curled in the fashion of the elite young men of the queen's court. He was elegantly dressed in an ornamented open coat, but he had his hands in his pockets, and looked simultaneously contemptuous and afraid.

"Hello, Dite," said the king. Costis was behind him, and could only hear the smile in Eugenides's voice, not see it in his face. Costis winced. The king had found someone else lower in the pecking order than Costis himself. He had needed only to ask Relius, the Secretary of the Archives and the queen's master of spies, who wrote "The King's Wedding Night." Relius would have known who was responsible for publicly insulting the king.

"I thought we should talk," said Eugenides.

Costis exchanged glances with the guard beside him, then looked away.

"About what, Your Majesty?" Dite was going to try to brazen it out. Costis wished he wouldn't. It was only going to make a scene that promised to be very, very ugly take even longer. Dite was a fool. He might have been immune, as the heir to a powerful baron, but everyone knew he wouldn't get any protection from his father. And if his own father wouldn't bring a complaint to the throne about the treatment of his son, no one else could.

"Why, about that very amusing song you wrote." Before Dite could deny it, the king turned to Teleus. "You have guards at the rest of the entrances. You've cleared it?"

Teleus nodded, and the king turned back.

"We can have a private talk, Dite."

"I still don't know what about, Your Majesty."

"Well. The errors in your representation, for a beginning. There were a few, you know. I'm sure you'll want to present a factual account once you hear the details." The king paused, to be sure he had Dite's full attention. He did. He had the undivided attention of every man around him. "She cried."

Dite recoiled. "Your Majesty, I don't—"

"Want to hear this? Why not, Dite? Don't you want to put it into your song? The queen wept on her wedding night. Surely you can find rhymes for that? Walk with me, and I can tell you more."

"Your Majesty, please," Dite said, shaking. "I'd rather not hear more. If you would excuse me." The whole court knew he was in love with the queen. The whole country knew it. He took a step backward, but Teleus stood directly behind him and blocked any escape.

The king slid an arm that ended in a shiny silver hook to the middle of Dite's back and gently but firmly forced him through the archway. "Walk with me, Dite," he insisted.

Costis was left with the rest of the guardsmen, breathing unevenly through teeth that were clenched so hard they hurt.

"Bastard," someone behind him hissed.

"He should worry about being assassinated," said another man.

"Steady," said Teleus.

"Captain . . . ," the guard protested.

"Shut up," Teleus snarled.

No one spoke after that.

Dite and the king walked for half an hour in the garden. When they returned, Dite looked subdued, but surprisingly calm.

Once through the archway, he turned and dropped to his knees in front of Eugenides, who said amiably, "Get up, Dite."

"Thank you, Your Majesty."

"Have lunch with me tomorrow?"

Dite looked up from a surreptitious check of the dirt smudges on the knees of his fine trousers, and smiled. "Thank you, Your Majesty. I'd be honored."

The king smiled. Dite smiled. They parted. Dite went off alone and the king, followed by his stunned guardsmen, walked back to the terrace where the breakfast dishes had been cleared away. The queen was gone. The wind blew across the empty stone pavement.

By the day's end, the entire palace knew of Dite's defection to the king's support. Costis reviewed the evidence of his own eyes over and over in his head and still couldn't believe it. He was thinking of it as he prepared for bed. He was about to blow out the light on his desk when he heard footsteps approaching. He looked up from the flame to see Aris leaning on his door frame.

"Have you heard the latest?" Aris asked.

"I was there," said Costis. "I saw Dite myself."

Aris corrected himself. "Not the latest, I suppose. The almost latest. Have you heard what went on last night at dinner?"

Costis shook his head. Aris related his information, picked up at the mess. "If being high-handed is your idea of how a king behaves, I think he has worked it out. You might not think he can act like a king, but he thinks he can."

It didn't get exactly the response that Aris had expected.

"He told *me* that story, Aris. The night I thought they were going to hang me. He said his cousins were worse than mine, that they used to hold him face down in the water until he was willing to insult his own family. He said"—Costis paused to think through what he was saying—"he said he wouldn't mention such a thing to anyone but me. I suppose he thought I was going to be dead the next day."

"You didn't tell me."

"No, of course not," said Costis. "He only told me because he thought I wouldn't live long enough to tell anyone else. I couldn't repeat it."

Aris was looking amused. "You think I am ridiculous, don't you?" Costis asked.

"I do," Aris admitted. "But, as a low-minded and practical sort of fellow, I'm glad someone has ideals and sticks to them."

"If the king didn't tell that story to anyone but me, he'll think I have been passing it around. Why didn't he say something about it this morning when we sparred?"

"Would he?" Aris asked.

"I don't know," Costis admitted. "But he's not going to go on believing that I'm some kind of loose-mouthed gossiper."

"Loose-mouthed gossip seller," suggested Aris, and at Costis's puzzled expression, he looked amused again and rolled his eyes.

"Do you know how much that humiliating tidbit about the king was worth?" Aris asked. "However it *did* get to Dite's friend, you can be sure someone was very well paid on the way."

Costis was horrified.

"Does he think that I sold that story to someone?"

Aris shrugged.

Costis swore, cursing the king in every particular.

He was still angry the next morning. He was determined to say something to the king at the first opportunity, and that was to be during their morning training together. The king didn't look as if he were holding a dire insult against Costis. But then, Costis thought, the king never looked the way he was supposed to. He just stood there, patiently waiting for Costis to put up his sword for the same pathetic basic exercises. Costis didn't move. He stood very proudly, with his shoulders square, and rushed into what he had to say.

"Your Majesty, if you believe I sold that story about your cousins—"

The king interrupted before he was finished. "I would never accuse you of such a thing."

"—well, you are mistaken, I assure you," Costis insisted. Only after he'd spoken did the king's words sink in.

The king laughed. Costis held on tight to his temper. The men around him were turning to stare.

Stiffly Costis said, "You may think poorly of me, and I think poorly of myself, but I did not spread that story."

"Too slow to find a buyer? Better luck next time."

Costis lifted his chin a little higher. "I would never stoop to revealing information I knew was private."

"Not even if you don't like the person whose privacy you are protecting?"

"Especially not then," said Costis, and hoped his disdain showed.

"I see." The king only looked more amused. "First position, this morning? I'll try not to hit you in the face again. It will be harder if you keep sticking your chin out like that."

Costis left the training ground defiantly satisfied. He may have sounded like an ass, in fact, he knew he had, but he'd shown the king he had some pride left. He was very pleased with himself, at least until he was summoned by the queen.

Costis was hurrying, as usual, from the king's apartments at midday. He had to move sharply to get something to eat in the Guards' mess and then be back in time for his duty in the afternoon. It would have been easier to carry bread and cheese in his belt, but that was a uniform violation. He could have skipped the meal, but his stomach had shown an embarrassing tendency to rumble in the quiet of the afternoon court sessions.

One of the queen's attendants, Imenia, approached him in the passage, and he stepped aside to allow her to pass, but she stopped.

"The queen wishes to speak to you, Lieutenant," she said.

Costis gaped. "Me?"

The attendant responded with a stare.

Costis stammered an apology. "Forgive me, where shall I go?"

Imenia condescended to nod and turned away, expecting him to follow, which he did. He knew the names of the attendants, and had been slowly putting those names to the faces he saw at the afternoon courts and at the dinners. Imenia was not the first of the queen's attendants, but she was among the most senior.

Feeling light-headed, only partly because he'd had no food at all that day, he followed to the door of the queen's apartments. Imenia nodded at the guards in the hallway there. They neither challenged nor even looked at Costis. They seemed somehow more impressive than the men who guarded the king. Beyond the doorway, the guardroom of the queen glowed with light from the windows near the ceiling. The room was far larger than the king's guardroom, paneled entirely in wood inlaid with mosaic pictures. Costis stared.

He'd thought the king's apartments were the height of opulence, until he saw this room, not even an audience chamber, merely the guardroom. The noise of his boots, crossing the carpetless floor, reminded him that he hadn't come to admire the walls. He handed his sword to the guard waiting to take it and made haste after Imenia, who hadn't slowed.

She passed through one of the open doors on the far side of the guardroom and down a passage, then turned into a narrower passage that was lit indirectly by light from the windows in the rooms opening off it. She stopped at a doorway and waved Costis in. The queen waited for him in the small audience room. Her chair was the only furniture.

The queen looked him over impassively and spoke to the point. "What is the king doing when he retires to his room without his attendants?"

Costis wished the queen had asked him her question the day before, when he hadn't just told the king he wouldn't stoop to distribute gossip. He could almost hear what Aris called his ideals crashing to the ground like a pile of sticks. This wasn't gossiping; this was his queen asking him a direct question, or alternatively, asking him to betray the privacy of the king, who was his sovereign, or alternatively, a goat-footed throne-stealing interloper. Costis thanked the gods he could keep his conscience clear and answer, "I don't know, Your Majesty."

"Don't know, Lieutenant, or won't tell?"

"I don't know, Your Majesty. I am sorry."

The queen looked thoughtful. "Nothing?"

Costis swallowed.

"Do you mean to say that as far as you are aware, he spends the entire time sitting and looking out the window and nothing else?"

"That's correct, Your Majesty," Costis said, relieved that it was the truth.

"You may go."

Costis stepped backward through the door and retraced his steps to the guardroom. The attendant who had brought him was nowhere to be seen. Costis held up his head but he couldn't shake the sensation of creeping away from the majesty of the queen. That, he told himself, was what a sovereign should be.

One morning in the Guards' bath, the valet was buckling on Costis's greaves when he spoke. "I have a friend," he said quietly, "who heard something the other day."

Costis, warned by the tone of his voice, kept his own low. "What did he hear?"

"Two men talking. You know how it is in the plunges, people think they are going on too quietly to be heard, but suddenly every word they say seems to be going directly into your ear."

"Yes," said Costis. Everyone knew that the curved roofs of the baths sometimes caused strange echoes to carry unexpected distances. "I've had that happen to me. But usually it's a vet talking about the girls he's left behind."

"These two weren't talking about girls."

"Go on," said Costis.

"Well, I will," said the valet, "because it's been worrying me and I'd like to pass it on and then forget it. The one asked the other if things were going well, and the other said yes, just as planned, he thought he would be successful in a few more weeks. He said he thought the first man would be very pleased with the results. Those were his words, 'very pleased with the results.' "

"So?" said Costis. "They could be talking about anything, managing a farm, training a horse."

"I don't think so," said the valet. He finished with the greaves and stood, face to face with Costis. "It was the Baron Erondites and Sejanus."

Of course, it would be Sejanus, Costis thought. "I suppose," he said slowly, "that Baron Erondites served in the Guard under the old king, and as Sejanus was still a guard until he became the king's attendant, they both have privileges to use the Guards' baths . . . if they didn't want anyone else in the court to see them talking."

"Exactly," said the valet. "And now I am going to forget I ever heard anything." He stepped back. Thinking hard, Costis left for the palace.

Dite had been cut off in every way from his family, though the baron had stopped short of disinheriting him. People thought he still held out hope that Dite might come to his senses. In contrast, the baron was publicly fond of Sejanus, providing him with an allowance and keeping his town house open for Sejanus's use. It was Sejanus who made it clear that he was a loyal member of the Guard, and kept his distance from his father. People might have thought that his loyalty was more to the Guard itself, and to his career in it, than personally to the queen, but having your greatest loyalty be to your own career wasn't a crime, really, or there would be more people in the queen's prisons. Sejanus certainly shared his father's opinion of his brother, Dite, and Dite returned the favor. They made it abundantly clear whenever they chanced to meet. Sejanus called Dite a fop and a coward. Dite sneered at Sejanus and referred to him as a sweaty uncultured pig, but he had been forced to watch in helpless rage one evening as Sejanus cruelly cut through his lyre strings one by one, while their friends looked on in amusement or discomfort, depending on where their sympathies lay. Because Sejanus would be heir if Dite were disinherited, his animosity was not surprising and didn't suggest any disloyalty to Attolia.

But a murmured conversation in an out-of-the-way corner did. It sounded like a conspiracy, and no conspiracy that had Baron Erondites as a member could be good for the queen.

The question was what to do with the information. It had obviously worried the valet, so he had passed it on to Costis, which made some sort of sense, though he wished the valet had chosen someone else. Now that Costis was the possessor of the information, what was he going to do with it?

Tell Relius. Costis's lip curled in distaste at the idea, but telling the queen's master of spies was the obvious course of action. Relius knew everything about every palace intrigue. Perhaps he already knew about this one and it was old news. At any rate, this was not gossip, and no gentlemanly rules applied. Loyalty to the throne was all that was needed to guide Costis's actions, that and a sense of self-preservation. Like the valet, Costis would pass on the information and then try to forget as quickly as he could that he had ever known it.

He watched Sejanus more closely that day. Suspecting his motives, Costis found everything about Sejanus even less amusing. He resolved to speak to Relius as soon as he was dismissed by the king.

In the afternoon, the king and queen sat to hear the business of their kingdom. At least, the queen sat to hear the business; Costis was still not sure what the king was doing. Costis paid more attention than Eugenides seemed to. He found many things surprisingly interesting, some things distasteful, and some horrifying.

The king, on the other hand, seemed to find everything boring. He slumped back on the throne and stared at his feet or at the ceiling. He never appeared to be listening and at times appeared to be asleep, though Costis suspected him of feigning the sleep just to be provoking. If so, the queen remained unprovoked. She coolly administered the court as if the king were not there.

Only once had the king seemed alert, when one of Relius's men reported the first rumors that the barons of Sounis had risen in revolt against him and that his heir, Sophos, had disappeared, probably having been abducted by the rebels. Even then the king had had no comment to make. He had spoken in court only once, and that was only because he had been blatantly nudged by the Eddisian advisors.

That day a discussion had been going on for some time about where to garrison Eddisian troops. The barons who hosted the troops paid for their upkeep, and several had complained of the unfair distribution of the burden. One of the assistants to the Ambassador from Eddis had turned to the king and asked point-blank, "What does Your Majesty think?"

"What?" Eugenides had to shake himself out of a daydream. He glowered at the Eddisians, angry at being disturbed.

Ornon cleared his throat. "Baron Anacritus would like to be relieved of the burden of supporting our garrison. We are discussing where else they might be stationed."

"Baron Cletus is next door. Put them there."

"Ah," said Ornon diplomatically. "Our engineers have observed that there is a gorge which makes that posting tactically . . . compromised." It made the posting tactically useless, as it separated Baron Cletus's land from every major travel route. Costis had been listening while all this had been explained in detail. He had caught back a sigh, not looking forward to hearing it all again, but he was spared by the king's whim.

Eugenides waved his hand and said airily, "Build a bridge."

There was much surreptitious eye rolling, but the king had been asked for his decision, he'd made it, and it had to be taken seriously. The discussion turned to the logistics of bridge building. Afterward, as they traveled together toward the royal apartments, Eugenides had prided himself on his performance. "Very clever," the queen had said dryly. Costis noticed that he never saw the assistant to the Ambassador from Eddis after that. No one addressed the king anymore, and he went back to woolgathering.

He was certainly not paying attention to a report on the organization of an upcoming trip that the royal retinue would take at harvesttime when the door behind the throne opened and Relius slipped between the guards posted there. He came in at the back of the room so that he could step up to the thrones from behind and lean down to whisper into the queen's ear. Like the Captain of the Guard, he continued to address himself only to Attolia unless forced to speak to Eugenides.

In response to Relius's message, Attolia dismissed most of the court. The few people scattered through the large room waited in near silence, the only sound the light footsteps of the Secretary of the Archives as he crossed the open marble floor to the door of an anteroom. The heels on his elegant leather shoes tapped. The short cape that hung from his shoulders billowed against a coat even more expansively embroidered than the king's. The guards at the door opened it on his signal, and he stepped inside, reappearing as an escort to a slow-moving party. One man was carried in a chair, and another, with his eyes bandaged, was led by the hand. The third man walked on his own but with a shuffling gait that suggested an injury.

They came before the queen, and slowly the people left in the throne room drew around them. Costis's drowsiness fled.

"They were arrested simultaneously, or very nearly," said Relius.

"In the same place?"

"No, Your Majesty. One in Ismet, one in Zabrisa, one in the capital."

Zabrisa and Ismet were the names of Mede towns. Zabrisa, Costis knew, was on the coast. There was a map of the Mede Empire in the room where the king met with his Mede tutor, but Costis couldn't recall seeing Ismet on it.

"Then the first arrested did not betray the others?" said the queen.

"No, Your Majesty. None of them even knew of the others."

"Then you have a larger tear in your net."

"I believe so. Immeasurably so, Your Majesty. There

are sources who should have warned me by now of these events . . . had they been able."

"I see," said the queen. Attolia's spies in the Mede Empire were strangely silent. Frightened into hiding, Costis guessed, or dead.

"Who betrays us, Relius?" asked Attolia.

"My Queen, I will know by this time tomorrow, I swear it."

Attolia turned to the men before her. "How is it that you have returned if you were arrested by the Mede Emperor?"

"We are messengers, Your Majesty, from the emperor's heir."

"And your message?"

"He is preparing an army against you, Your Majesty. We were read the provisions for the forces, the levies of men, weapons, and food."

"Fetch them chairs," ordered the queen. When the two standing men had been gently cared for, seated in chairs and supported with pillows, she said, "Go on."

"The armies he is gathering are vast, Your Majesty. The entire empire is directed against us."

"The Continent has armies as well. They will not let us be so easily overrun."

But the spy shook his head. "The Heir Apparent says to tell you that the Continent will not act on hearsay, nor act in time. His forces are spread across his empire, and he will keep them so until the navy is ready.

He will deny that he intends to invade until he brings his army together at the harbor. Once they have swept over the Peninsula, the Greater Powers will have no easy means to evict them. The Heir says they won't even try. They have their own battles to fight among themselves."

"The next Emperor of the Mede is sure of himself, indeed, if he sends you back to me with messages of his intent. In my experience, patronoi, my opponent's self-confidence is usually my best asset."

"My family are okloi, Your Majesty. We have no land of our own," the man said humbly.

The queen disagreed. "You have all three served Attolia well. There will be land for you. The secretary will see to it." Relius escorted the men away.

When they were gone, the queen made no move to resume business. She stared into space. The king spoke at last.

"The Mede are returning sooner than you expected."

"Not necessarily," said the queen. "The old emperor still lives. The Heir cannot move until he takes the throne. He is consolidating his power more quickly than I had hoped, however."

"Is it Nahuseresh pushing him?"

Attolia shook her head. "I am afraid it is his own desire motivating him. Relius says that Nahuseresh remains out of favor."

"Yes. Relius." The king paused. "Your master of spies is a liar, and this time he is lying," the king said slowly, "to you."

Attolia frowned, then almost imperceptibly shook her head.

"Have him arrested," said the king. After another pause he added unequivocally, "Now."

If he succeeds in having me killed, you could be the next Captain of the Guard. What, then, if the king destroyed Relius? Who would replace him?

Costis hardly breathed. The king hadn't ordered the arrest himself, though he could have, but he had directed the queen to do so, in public. Now they would see if the queen could protect her own or not.

"Fetch Teleus," she said, and a messenger hurried from the room.

You might not think he can act like a king, but he thinks he can.

They waited like a wax tableau. Costis wondered if others' thoughts were racing silently in circles, as his were. The queen gave no indication what she was thinking. Not even her gaze shifted until Teleus was standing in front of her. Her husband was sovereign of Attolia, and her country was riddled with Eddis's soldiers. She ordered the arrest of her secretary.

"There will be no mistakes made, Teleus," warned the queen. "It will be done immediately."

Once the captain had gone, they returned to the

tableau. Time slid slowly past, and no one spoke, no one moved. They waited. The doors opened, but it was the Eddisian Ambassador. He bowed to the throne and moved quietly to a space along the wall. The doors opened again, and this time it was Teleus. He had his guards and, surrounded by them, the Secretary of the Archives. Stunned, the court turned back to the king. The truth was on Teleus's face and on Relius's. The Secretary of the Archives was guilty.

"He was writing this," said the Captain of the Guard, shaking a collection of papers in his hand. "He tried to take poison when he saw us in the doorway, Your Majesty."

"Is the paper a confession?"

"Yes."

They walked Relius across the room, and he dropped to his knees before the throne. He stared forward like a man who sees nothing clearly except his own death, for whom the sounds of the world are nothing but a muffled din.

Blank of expression, he raised his eyes to the queen. "May I explain?"

The queen looked down at him and said nothing. His lips moved as if he was speaking, but there were no words. He closed his eyes briefly, and he struggled for a breath to begin. "When I told you that I did not know who betrayed us . . . I lied," he admitted. "I had already realized that it can only be my fault. I visited a woman in the town. You know of her, you knew when she left me. I thought she was tired of me, but I should have understood when she disappeared that I let her see too much, that she was a spy for the Mede." He held his head in his hands. "My Queen—"

Teleus hit him in the back of the head, so hard that he sprawled forward onto the marble steps of the thrones' dais.

"She is Your Majesty, to you!" the Captain of the Guard snarled.

"Teleus." The queen reined him in with a word, but his face, unlike the queen's, showed all his rage and his sense of betrayal.

"The poison?" she asked Relius. He had pulled himself back to his knees.

"I was afraid," he said.

"Understandably so," said Attolia. "But does an innocent man keep poison at hand?"

"My—Your Majesty," Relius corrected himself. "I failed you," he said. "I failed you, but I swear I never meant to betray you. I was writing all this, so that you would know. I did not mean to hide it from you. You must believe me," he insisted.

"Must I, Relius?"

If all he had taught her was true, there was only one answer to her question.

His lips formed the word, but he couldn't force it out. He shook his head.

"No," agreed the queen, speaking softly. "Take him away."

When he was gone, no one in the court moved, afraid to be the first to draw her eye.

"You will observe?" the king said.

"I must," said the queen.

"I can't," the king admitted.

"Of course not," said Attolia. She turned to the chamberlain, whose role it was to issue people in and out of the royal presence, and said, "We are through here." It signaled the end of the court session for the day. Any further business would be postponed. The chamberlain bowed and began to clear the room. When the king stood, all stopped where they were and bowed respectfully as his guard gathered and escorted him away. Costis glanced back once to see the queen still sitting alone on her throne as the room emptied.

No, Costis thought. The king would not observe Relius's interrogation. It would mean a return to the rooms underground where Eugenides had been imprisoned, where he had lost his right hand. If he looked sick—and he was so pale he was almost green—Costis thought it was not at the idea of Relius's suffering, but rather at memories of his own.

They returned to the king's rooms. He stopped in the guardroom.

"What is the time?" he asked, rubbing his face with his hand like a man distracted. He didn't even look pleased with his success in eliminating Relius.

"Just coming to the half hour, Your Majesty."

"Very well." As he walked into his room, he reached for the door, blocking his attendants with his arm. "Knock in an hour," he said. "Don't bother me before then."

He closed the door in their faces.

"Well," said Sejanus, "I suppose not even you are necessary, then, Costis, when the king retires to gloat. I wonder why he doesn't do this when he wants to crawl into his hole and lick his wounds. It would save us standing in the hallway."

Costis thought it was probably because the king didn't want to move the chair for himself, and he probably wanted to be sure the attendants wouldn't wander into the room in spite of his orders to leave him alone.

He jumped when he heard the bolt shoot in the door. He hadn't been aware that there was a bolt. Sejanus laughed at his surprise.

"He does that every night," he said. "I think our little king doesn't trust us. We have to knock like okloi at the temple in the morning and wait until he opens it for us."

Attolia returned to her apartment and sent her attendants away. She sat at the window. There was a deliberate click of a door closing, but no other sound.

She thought of Relius. In the first year of her reign, when she was a young queen with nothing to guide her but her wits and civil war on her hands, her guards had found Relius spying on her and dragged him out from under a wagon. Who was his master? they had asked, and he'd answered, No one. Entirely for himself, he had wanted a glimpse of the queen. Standing in his muddy clothes, the illegitimate son of a household steward, Relius had offered to serve her. He offered her everything she needed to know of her enemies. He had taught her the craft of manipulation and intrigue, teaching her to use men as tools, and as weapons, and to survive in a world where trust had no place. Never trust anyone, had been his first and most important lesson.

"Not even you?" she had laughed, back then when she had still laughed sometimes.

"Not even me," he had answered her seriously.

Only through pain can you be sure of the truth, he had taught her, and she must have truth at any cost. Her nation depended on it.

She had to know the truth.

The silence around her was a gift, and she took refuge in it. For this brief time she did not need to move or speak, did not need to tease apart the truth from the lies of Relius's betrayal, did not need to justify her action or her inaction. Her king found no such refuge in stillness. He preferred to pace. She had seen it often enough already, back and forth as silent as a cat in a cage. But he could be still as well, as skillful in stifling movement as in moving, as silent as sunlight on stone. He knew that the stillness was as near as she could come to peace, and he offered it to her.

When Phresine knocked to say that it was time to dress for dinner, she waited for the click of the latch and then she called her attendants in.

When the hour was up, it was time for the king to dress for a state dinner, and Costis was dismissed. He marched back through the palace with the squad of guards also relieved from their duty. They had left the palace proper and were on the terrace, moving toward the stairs that led down toward the Guard's compound, when they crossed the path of Baron Susa.

Costis knew him by sight, as he was baron over the land where Costis's family farm was. He nodded at the baron politely and was surprised when the baron called him by name. Costis stopped. So did the squad.

"Perhaps you could send your men on," suggested Susa. "I only want a moment of your time to chat with a fellow countryman."

Reluctantly, Costis sent the men back to the barracks.

"So, Costis Ormentiedes," said the baron, "you have become quite the confidant of our king, have you not?"

Costis wished he could call the men back. He was rattled by the fall of Relius. Their presence would have deflected anything Susa wanted to say, but it was too late. Susa was waiting for an answer.

"No, sir. I wouldn't say so, sir," Costis said carefully. Just as Aris had been hesitant to cross Sejanus, Costis would be very careful not to offend Susa. As landowners, Costis's family was not as vulnerable as Aris's. Susa couldn't raise the taxes on the land, or seize any of it, and an Attolian landowner, no matter how small his holding, held the rule of law on his own land, but Susa could still make things uncomfortable for the Ormentiedes.

"I understand that he has requested you for special service, even allowing you to attend him privately?"

"The king is—" Costis paused to look down at the ground, hoping that he radiated embarrassment. "The king is exercising his sense of humor, sir."

"Ah?" prompted Susa.

"I've been doing nothing but basic exercises on the training ground since I . . . came to his attention." Costis was afraid he might be overdoing the shame-faced act, so he lifted his head and pulled himself to something like attention, in the process managing to look even more harassed. "I am on the walls at night regularly, sir, and at the court in the afternoon. The extra watches are . . ."

"Capricious?" asked Susa.

Costis's expression hardened. "I would never say so, sir." To call the king capricious was a step too far even for Susa.

"And the private audience for a dishonored squad leader?"

"His Majesty chose to dismiss his attendants, and when they protested leaving him entirely alone, he selected me as a replacement. I don't believe, sir, that that was a compliment to myself but rather a reflection of the king's relative pleasure with his attendants, sir, which was at the time low." Were there too many "sirs" in that answer? he wondered.

"I see," said Susa. "Nonetheless, you have absorbed a certain amount of information you would be glad to relay, I am sure, Lieutenant."

Costis hoped his expression didn't give away his horror at the proposition. However the Undersecretary of Naval Provisions had gotten his information, more than just the king assumed it came from Costis, probably because of the scene he had made on the training ground. He wanted to turn on his heel and walk away, but he couldn't. Neither, he knew, could he offer Susa what he wanted.

"Not much, really, sir," said Costis. He remembered his audience with the queen. "Nothing beyond that he spends the time alone looking out the window." He shrugged an apology for the insignificance of his information.

Susa's eyebrows went up. He didn't think it was insignificant. It was apparent Costis had revealed something very important indeed. "Thank you, Squad

Leader." He offered a coin, which Costis took after a moment's hesitation, not knowing how to refuse it, and then Susa went away.

Costis walked on through the palace and down to the Guard's barracks, knowing himself entirely guilty of what the king had not condescended to accuse him of.

· CHAPTER SIX ·

THE stool hit the wall with a satisfying crash.

"I was going to sit on that," Aris pointed out mildly. He was lying on the bed, where he had been waiting for Costis. "Anyway, I planned to sit there once you showed up. What has happened now?"

"Only that I have done something stupid. STUPID."

"You told the king you aren't a gossipmonger?"

"No," said Costis. "I mean, yes, I told the king. That's not the stupid thing I did."

"You're sure?"

Another time Costis might have laughed. "I told the king I would not sink so low that I would reveal private information about him."

"And?"

"The queen summoned me at noon to ask what the king did when he was alone in his rooms."

"Ah. "

"How could I not tell the queen anything she asked?"

"You are still here—and breathing—so I assume you did tell her?"

"She wanted to know if he did anything besides looking out the window the whole time. I said not that I knew of. I thought I wasn't telling her anything new and I wasn't refusing to answer her because I don't know anything anyway." He held up his hands, begging Aris to tell him this answer had not been unreasonable.

"So?" Aris was reserving his judgment. He knew that there was more coming.

"So Susa just asked me the same thing."

"Ah."

"Stop saying that!"

"Did you tell him?"

"I thought it was meaningless, only now I think it wasn't. It was important. I just didn't know it."

"But you said the queen already knew."

"No," said Costis, "the queen *guessed* it. Then she asked me in a way that I would confirm it if it was true." He rubbed his face with his hands. "I am so sick of people who all seem to be smarter than I am and know more than I do. I want to go back to the farm. These people make my family look easy to get along with."

"Well, at least no one knows, this time," said Aris. "Why are you looking at me like that?"

"Well, because I have to tell him, don't I?"

❖ ❖ ❖

Aristogiton didn't agree. He and Costis argued back and forth as he tried to convince his friend not to expose himself to further difficulties. What difference, after all, could it make if the king spent time looking out the window? What of interest could he possibly be looking at?

Costis didn't know and couldn't guess. "But it is important, Aris. You have to see that. And if it's important to the queen and to Susa, it means that it will be something used against him."

"Then tell him that you told the queen. You can't be blamed for that, and if Susa throws it in his face, the king will think it came from the queen. He'll never learn otherwise."

Costis shook his head. "If Susa is going to attack him, he should know."

"Why?" demanded Aris. "You don't care if he gets poisoned tomorrow."

"I don't care if he gets poisoned as long as it doesn't have anything to do with me."

Aris looked at him in speculation. "You do care if he gets poisoned," he said.

Costis admitted the point with a sigh. "If he choked on a bone and died, I wouldn't care. But I can't . . . I sound like a sanctimonious old philosopher, but I can't stand by and watch people get murdered, Aris. I never meant to have anything to do with people like this. I wanted to be a soldier."

"You wanted to be Captain of the Guard someday," observed Aris.

"That was before I realized what it meant."

"So what do you want now?"

"I want to retrieve some grain of self-respect. That's about the total of my ambition at this point. I'll tell him about Susa and I'll tell him about Sejanus while I'm at it, and maybe if I'm blessed by the gods, he'll have me exiled to a nice penal colony in Thracia."

Having decided to speak to the king, Costis had to wait for an opportunity. He didn't dare speak out at sword practice in the morning. There were too many people nearby to overhear him. He meant to wait until the king next dismissed his attendants. He began to be afraid that the king had retreated to his rooms alone for the last time, especially as he had demonstrated his willingness to lock his attendants out of his room when he wanted his privacy. Moreover, in the process of winning over Erondites the Younger he seemed to have found a new means of arranging a little peace for himself. Between appointments, he sometimes walked in the garden. On days when the king might have the time free in his schedule, the gardens were emptied. The king could order the guards into position at various points and walk between them alone.

Every day Costis debated with himself whether he should speak to the king at their morning training, but in an agony of indecision he held off. As he told Aris, it was no place for a private exchange. He could suggest to the king that he needed to speak to him alone, but he already knew, from his last attempt to address him during training, that the king wouldn't cooperate. It was more likely he would turn the moment into a scene from a farce and draw the attention of everyone within hearing, perhaps alerting Sejanus in the process. Costis waited.

Ornon also waited, and worried. Relius had fallen. The Office of the Archives was in disarray. The king hardly spoke to his barons. He spent more and more time distancing himself from the court. He rarely addressed the queen in public, though Ornon was told Eugenides still claimed a proprietary kiss at breakfast.

"Your Majesty." Sejanus had to repeat himself before the king finally called his thoughts back to the matter at hand.

"What?"

"I'm very sorry, Your Majesty, but the blue sash appears to have ink stains on it as well."

"Never mind," said the king. "Just bring me—"

Bring him what? Costis thought. If the king broke down and said, "Bring a sash, any sash," the attendants would bring him one that didn't match the style or color of his coat. If he came up with a particular sash, they would claim again that it was stained with ink, or that it had been sent to be cleaned. This could continue all morning, and the king was late, with all his attendants standing around in poses of mock subservience, and Sejanus visibly smug.

"Bring me all the sashes that aren't stained, dirty, or otherwise abused," said the king wearily. "And I will pick one."

It was a solution. The king seemed tired, not triumphant. The attendants excused themselves, calculating how much more time could be wasted fetching and delivering the sashes from the wardrobe, the least likely first, until almost every single sash the king owned was draped across the bed and hanging from the furniture around the room.

Finally the king was dressed and ready to leave. He and his entourage were on their way to the temple of Hephestia. There had been no morning training and would be no breakfast with the queen. This was a signal occasion when the king visited the new temple, still under construction on the acropolis above the palace. By all accounts, the last time Eugenides had addressed the Great Goddess, she'd answered by smashing windows all over the palace. The storm that day had probably been a coincidence, Costis thought, but it made a man think twice, and he hoped today's visit provoked no such response.

They left the palace through the gate near the

stables and the kennels and proceeded up the Sacred Way on foot. The new temple to Hephestia was being constructed on what remained of the foundations of the old Megaron. The king and queen had been married here at a temporary altar. Since then, new courses had been laid to make the walls of a naos, provisionally roofed in canes. The rest of the foundation was open, as all that remained of the earlier building were the basal stones, in some places still covered by mosiacs in tessellated patterns. Resting on these were haphazard piles of stonework that would be used to enlarge the foundation before the pillars, lying in pieces nearby, were stepped. The king wove his way between the stonework piles, heading toward the door to the naos and a priestess who waited for him there.

"This is the end of your journey, Your Majesty."

"I am seeking an answer from the Great Goddess and have come to speak with her Oracle."

"She knows your question, and your answer."

"I have not yet delivered it." The king held up a folded paper in his hand.

"She knows it," the priestess repeated.

The king tried to push past. "Then she can tell me the answer."

The priestess held out an arm that stopped him in his tracks. "She will not."

"Then I will ask the Great Goddess myself."

"You may not."

"You think to come between *me* and the Great Goddess?"

"No one of us can be separated from the Goddess," said the priestess, but she still held up her arm. Costis wondered if the two would come to blows, and if they did, what was he supposed to do? Help the king violate a temple? Watch while the king was chucked off the temple foundation by the priestesses?

Luckily for him, a commanding voice came from the interior of the naos. The Oracle herself stepped from the darkness into the doorway. Hugely fat, she was wrapped in a peplos of livid green that seemed to glow with its own light against the dark interior behind her. Her meaty fingers twitched the paper out of the king's hand. She opened it, and without reading it, without even looking at it, she tore it in half. Still cold, she handed one half back to the king.

Eugenides looked down at the paper in his hand. The men behind him craned to see it. There was nothing left but the signature of the king, written left-handed in square letters, ATTOLIS, at the bottom of the page.

"Your answer," said the priestess.

The king crumpled the paper in his fist and threw it on the ground. Without a word, he stalked from the doorway, across the open foundation of the temple, and leapt across a construction ditch to firm ground without looking back. His guard and his attendants hastily followed. Exchanging looks, rolling their eyes, and with shrugs, they had to break into a trot to catch up. It was clear that the Oracle could upset the king more in one morning than even Sejanus could in several months' time. Eugenides never slowed and he never looked back all the way down the Sacred Way to the palace and from the gates of the palace to his apartment, where he arrived in such a fury that the guards stationed there actually jumped to attention.

In his guardroom, he turned at last to face his attendants and snarled at them, "Get out."

Still surprised and puzzled by the scene at the temple, the attendants withdrew without argument. The king pointed at Costis and at the door to the passageway, then walked into the bedroom. Costis quietly closed the door to the passage, and followed the king to move the chair near the window. The king threw himself into the chair, and Costis backed out of the room.

In the guardroom, he stood by the door to the outside passage and waffled. It would take more nerve than he anticipated to take the step forward into the doorway and draw the king's attention. The door was open. Costis had left it open the first time and the king hadn't objected, so he assumed it should remain open. It would take three steps to reach it and clear his conscience.

He didn't move. He reviewed his argument with Aristogiton, but still arrived at the same conclusion. If he wanted to redeem himself, he needed to admit to the king what he had done. Then he reviewed just how much he wanted his self-respect. Too much, he finally decided, and stepped toward the doorway.

The king sat with his feet on the chair and his knees drawn up to his chest, looking over them and out the window. So motionless was he, and so silent the progress of his tears, that it was the space of a breath before Costis realized the king was crying. When he did, he stepped hastily back out of sight.

"What is it, Costis?" The king's voice was quiet. He must have caught the movement from the corner of his eye.

Reluctantly, Costis stepped forward. "I'm sorry, Your Majesty."

"All will be well, I am sure. Is there something you wanted to say?"

Costis looked up from the floor. All traces of the king's tears were gone, so perfectly erased that Costis almost doubted that he had seen them at all.

"Uh—"

"You interrupted me so that you could say uh?"

Costis blurted out the words. "I told the queen that you sat here and looked out the window."

The king continued to watch whatever held his attention outside. "She is your queen. You could hardly decline to answer her questions."

"I also told the Baron Susa."

The king turned away from the view. He was expressionless. Costis stammered an apology and an explanation. Helplessly he fumbled for the coin he had carried everywhere since that day and held it out to the king. "I don't want it," he said. "I didn't do it for money, I didn't mean to do it at all."

The king turned back to the window.

Costis stood, his hand still out, the silver coin lying in his palm, waiting for the penal colony.

Finally the king spoke, very quietly. "I apologize, Costis. I've put you in an impossible situation. Why don't you let my entourage back in, and you may go."

"Go, Your Majesty? The guard doesn't change until the end of the hour."

Eugenides shook his head. "You may go now," he said.

"What should I do with the coin?"

"Dedicate it. I am sure some god or priest will appreciate its value."

Costis backed out of the door again. Numb, he admitted the king's attendants and the guards.

"I've been dismissed," he said to the squad leader. The squad leader nodded, and Costis stepped into the passage.

"What, Lieutenant? Are you going?" the guard there asked cheerfully.

"I've been dismissed."

"An early day. Congratulations," the guard said. Costis headed down the dim passage.

It wasn't just an early day. The king was done with him. His stay in limbo was over. He told himself he should be happy, and he wondered why he didn't feel more relieved. Maybe he was shaken by the king's tears, but he didn't want to think about those. He had cleared his conscience and hadn't been sent to a penal colony; the future should look brighter. He wondered what the king found so interesting to look at out the window.

Descending a narrow staircase on his way back to his barracks, he was presented with the answer. As Costis turned on a landing and began to descend the next flight, he was directly across from a window in the outside wall of the palace. The window opened in the same direction as the king's, and there, summer-bright and framed by the darkness of the stairwell, was the same view. Costis passed it, and then went back up the stairs to look again. There were only the roofs of the lower part of the palace and the town and the city walls. Beyond those were the hills on the far side of the Tustis Valley and the faded blue sky above them. It wasn't what the king saw that was important, it was what he couldn't see when he sat at the window with his face turned toward Eddis.

Costis's heart twisted sympathetically. He sternly reprimanded that weak and traitorous organ, but he couldn't help remembering that his own homesickness had sucked the life out of every day when he had first left the farm. His initial summer in the barracks had been the worst. He'd never been more than a few miles from home in his life, and as much as he despised his cousins, he would have given a month's pay to see one of their familiar faces. The sick feeling had gradually faded as he had made a place for himself in the Guard, but Costis remembered it too well not to recognize it in the king's face when he had seen him looking so hopelessly out the window. What must it be like to know that you couldn't ever go home? To leave behind the mountains, where Costis had heard it never got really hot even in the summer, to live on the coast, where the snow rarely came? Small wonder if the king had passed up other, more gracious apartments to have one that had a bed-chamber with a window facing toward Eddis.

So what? Costis started down the stairs again. Why should he care, really, if the king was homesick? Eugenides had brought it on himself. He should have stayed in Eddis. No one wanted him in Attolia, not the queen, certainly, not the Guard, not his attendants ...

"Dammit!" Costis stopped again. He'd forgotten to tell the king about Sejanus.

There was no point in going back. Cursing more quietly, he continued down the stairs.

· CHAPTER SEVEN ·

W HEN Costis got back to his room, he found
Aristogiton wearing a smile as wide as his face.

"I've been dismissed," Costis said bluntly, not in the
mood for humor, just as Aristogiton announced, "I've
been promoted."

Both said, "What?"

"I've been dismissed," Costis said again.

"You told him about Susa, then, not just the queen?"

"Yes."

"And he threw you out in a rage."

"No. He apologized to me and said very politely that
I could go."

"Apologized?"

"Nicely."

"The bastard."

Costis nodded his head in agreement. "I hate him."

"You didn't manage it, then, the grain of self-respect?"

"No," said Costis. "Not a remnant the size of a grain

of wheat, not the size of a grain of sand. If he had been enraged, if he'd sent me to some hell in Thracia . . ."

"You'd feel like you deserved it and you'd take it like a man. You do know, don't you, that if you'd sold out to Susa on purpose, you could be a completely honorless but happy villain gloating over your silver?"

"I left it on the Miras altar on the way here."

Aris groaned.

"I'm sorry. I am spoiling your good news. You've been promoted?"

"I and my entire squad," said Aristogiton, "have been elevated to the Third. I begin my new duties tomorrow."

"The Third? You'll be in the palace?"

"I'm assigned to the king." Aris smiled at Costis's disbelief. "I was looking forward to watching him humiliate you."

"But that's impossible. You can't be eligible for that kind of promotion."

"Thank you so much for your judgment of my reputation."

Costis smiled. "I apologize unreservedly. I am a swine. Obviously you belong in the Third, should be a centurion of the Third, a lieutenant no less."

"Well," Aris admitted, "I am pretty sure we all owe it to Legarus the Awesomely Beautiful."

"Ah," said Costis, enlightened. "Promoted for his pretty face?"

"And he's wellborn, and he's too stupid to be promoted on his own, but if I'm promoted, and with me goes my squad . . ."

"Then Legarus serves honorably in the Third, and has a ready access to the palace—and probably someone in the palace."

Aris said, "Yes, I think that's it, but I have no sticky notions of honor, and you won't hear me complaining because I have undeservedly been made squad leader in the Third. On the contrary, I intend to celebrate." He lifted the amphora he held in his hand. "While I am celebrating, you can drown your sorrows," he told Costis.

"I would be delighted," said his friend.

Much later, he asked Aris a question that had been preying on his mind. "Do you think the Thief wanted to be king?"

"Of course," said Aris.

Costis, taking this as a straight answer, was unprepared when Aris added, "Who wouldn't want to be married to the woman who cut off his right hand?"

Costis looked up, startled.

"Everyone talks as if it's a brilliant revenge," said Aris, "but I'd rather cut my own throat than marry her, and she hasn't chopped any pieces off me."

"I thought—"

"I was her loyal guard? I am. I would march into the

mouth of hell for her. I will never forget that I would be bending over a tannin vat now and for the rest of my life if not for her. I might have been a soldier under her father and have marched myself into the ground and died choking on my own blood in the dirt and never have been even a squad leader—not me, not the son of a leather merchant. Look at me now, with a squad in the Third. Miras guide us, I worship her. But I am not blind, Costis. I feel about her the same way every member of the Guard feels. She is ruthless."

He leaned forward, pointing a finger in Costis's face. "And it is a good thing she is, because she wouldn't be queen if she weren't. She is brilliant and beautiful and terrifying. It's a fine way to feel about your queen, not your wife," he added.

Costis blinked.

"There isn't one womanly bone in her body, and you cannot believe any man in his right mind would want to marry her. If the Thief had wanted to be her husband, he would have forced the issue of heirs. He hasn't, has he? If you ask me," Aris continued, "it was Eddis's plan all along. I hear men dismiss her as just a woman, and I think we of all people should know better. If she weren't every bit as brilliant and as ruthless as Attolia, there would be a king in Eddis. I will bet any price you name that the Thief was as loyal to his queen as we are to ours." Aris shrugged. "So Eddis sent him to be King of Attolia. Poor bastard. I'll stick to marching into the mouth of hell, myself." He looked at Costis and shrugged again. "Just my opinion. I'll go back to my wine."

Costis, looking down into his own wine cup, shook away thoughts of the king.

"Not your business anymore," said Aris.

"Not my business," Costis agreed.

The queen was agitated, but no sign of it showed as she stood at the table sorting the papers that lay on it. "There was no need to ask Teleus who was in command in the border forts in the northeast. You already know."

"I do?"

"You were provoking him."

"Why would I do that?"

"And you asked me to recall Prokep from his fort ten days ago so that you could meet him."

"Did I?"

The queen shook her head. It had been an awkward meeting between herself and the king and Teleus, with Teleus as stiff as a poker and Eugenides draped in his chair like a cat. The king had asked Teleus who was in charge of the forts on the border with Magyar and when the general in charge of the region would next be in the capital to deliver a report on his charge. Teleus had answered every question with barely veiled contempt, but had agreed to keep Costis on light duties until the king had made up his mind about a suitable transfer.

The queen began packing papers into a diplomatic pouch. "I wish you and Teleus got along better."

"I wish Teleus weren't an idiot."

If the queen heard him, she gave no sign, only finishing with the pouch and then setting it aside.

✦ ✦ ✦

In the mountain country of Eddis, the days were shorter than in coastal Attolia. The lamps in the palace had been lit and the late summer evening was almost over when the Queen of Eddis summoned Sounis's magus, who was officially her prisoner. The magus had just returned the day before from an unsupervised exploration of the hinterland, where he had been collecting differing versions of various folktales from people in isolated communities. Queen and magus shared a fondness and a respect for Eugenides, the former Thief of Eddis. Once the magus was seated and had a cup of wine near to hand, the queen handed him the most private report from her ambassador to Attolia, Ornon, and waited patiently while he read through it.

"I see," said the magus. "I did wonder why your ambassador's assistant was returned so precipitously. I assumed it was Gen who gave him that black eye. It must have been beautiful when it was fresh."

"No, that was Ornon," Eddis informed him dryly. "As you see, the assistant took it upon himself to try to force Gen's hand."

"I can see that he failed," said the magus, turning the

✦ 151 ✦

paper to read the sentences that crossed the page. "But I am not sure I understand the significance of the bridge."

"Cletus and Anacritus are both allies of the queen's. They pay ruinous fees to a third baron, Minos, for use of the only bridge across that gorge for miles. Anacritus needs it to get to his pasturage, Cletus's people must use the bridge if they are going to get any of their produce to market. Neither can afford the labor to build a bridge himself. Attolia has wanted to build one for years, but hasn't been able to do so without showing blatant favoritism that would enrage Minos, technically also a supporter of hers."

"Now you are building a bridge for her?"

"Ornon had no choice," Eddis said with a hint of irony, "but to graciously offer the labor of the Eddisian garrison."

The magus nodded. "So the Baron Minos has no grounds for complaint and the Barons Anacritus and Cletus, who found the garrison of Eddisians a burden—"

"—are now deliriously happy," Eddis agreed.

"Gen still looks inept," observed the magus.

"And Ornon's assistant is home with a black eye," Eddis finished. "A success all around, unless you are the former assistant to our Ambassador to Attolia."

The room was a small one, the paintings on the walls all around it and the delicately carved screen that formed the low ceiling making it seem even smaller. There was no place to sit but the floor and no place to rest the lamp, so Sejanus had been standing for some time when his father arrived.

"I shouldn't be here," he said. "We should not meet."

Erondites grunted. "I want a report."

"I am a success." Sejanus shrugged; the lamp in his hand moved, and the shadows flickered wildly around the room. The satyrs on the wall seemed to dance and leer. "There is not one attendant who has not disgraced himself and the king. He is ready to purge them all."

"Not yet," said Erondites. "I don't want them dismissed yet. He must take the mistress first, so that she can tell him whom to choose as new attendants."

"You are less successful than I," said Sejanus.

The baron glowered. "She's beautiful, newly widowed, and the stupid ass persists in dancing with her sister."

"Why not use the sister, then, if she has caught the king's eye?"

"She reads plays. She embroiders. She is artless, unwed, and useless. Her sister is twice widowed and quite adequately prepared for the task of leading the king by his nose. It has to be her. I told their father to beat them both, and the younger one especially. She won't dance with the king again. What about you?"

"What about me?"

"I don't want you dismissed as well. You're the one attendant who must stay."

"Depend on it," said Sejanus. "He won't let me go."

"I have heard otherwise."

"He relies on me. The other attendants don't realize it, but the king and I are becoming allies and better friends every day. He won't dismiss me when he throws out the rest."

"Be sure of it," the baron warned.

"Oh, I am," said Sejanus.

After they left, Eugenides shifted a little on the rafters above the carefully carved and pierced wooden ceiling, more screen than a ceiling, in fact. He sat cross-legged in the dark and considered the room below, conveniently out of the way, but not far from the royal apartments. With no furniture in it, too small to be useful for any legitimate purpose, it was guaranteed to be empty. The architect who designed it, and directed the carving of the wooden screen for the false ceiling, had been Eugenides's many-times-great-grandfather. He'd called it "the conspiracy room."

Silent as an owl, Eugenides made his way back to his room and his bed. Lying there in the dark, he whispered to himself, "So Sejanus is my dear friend. How strange that I did not know. And poor Heiro is suffering for dancing with me. Sejanus, dear, dear Sejanus, what are you playing at, I wonder?"

The next night, he danced again with the Lady Themis's little sister, Heiro. "That was beautifully done," he told her.

"Excuse me, Your Majesty?"

"I mean the way you tried to avoid dancing with me, in a way calculated to make me insist on doing just that. Just this." He gestured to the dance as they separated.

When they met again, he said, "Do you know, I heard someone describe you as artless?"

"I don't know what you are talking about, Your Majesty."

"Neither did he," said the king.

"Your Majesty—"

"Was the beating very bad, my dear?"

She stumbled slightly. He took her arm.

"You're tired. Let me take you to a seat." The dancers around them parted, and he led her through.

"I can finish the dance with your sister."

Her grip on his arm tightened.

"Just a single dance, dear," said the king. "Then I promise I'll move on. I can't allow you to be beaten for casting yourself between me and the rather rapacious clutches of your sister. I do wonder why you think I am worth saving."

"Maybe because I have eyes in my head, Your Majesty," said Heiro.

Eugenides was briefly taken aback. "Well, I will have

to watch my step then, won't I? And you will have to point out to your father the advantages of having one of his daughters admired by the king, even if it is the wrong one. If it saves you from a beating, you may always call on me." He bowed over her hand.

He could feel her shaking, and looked over his shoulder to see her father approaching. "He will wonder what you see to admire," said Heiro.

"That's easy," said the King of Attolia. "Tell him I like your earrings."

"Your Majesty might like to dance with my friend, Lady Eunice. She's a pretty girl," Heiro said quickly.

"I like pretty girls. Who else?"

She mentioned a few more names, but fell silent as her father arrived looking thunderous.

"She claims she's unwell," said the king with petulance. "She suggests I finish the dance with her sister."

Her father's brow cleared. He led her away. Lady Themis and the king returned to the dance.

Two weeks later, Costis was sitting on the steps outside the mess hall, enjoying the sun that slid between the tall, closely packed buildings. It wouldn't last. The sun moved with infinite patience across the sky, and the shade crept inch by inch across the stairs. It would reach him soon, and he must move with the sun or be content with the chill of the shade. With luck, Aristogiton would arrive before he had to make a decision. Aris would be coming off duty very soon. He and Costis were scheduled for a three-day leave and intended to spend it hunting in the hills a day's ride from the city.

Costis had his gear packed and had been waiting most of the day. Aris was very busy with his new duties while Costis's life was suddenly filled with leisure.

Teleus had explained that his position was indeterminate while his future was under consideration. Probably he would be transferred to a border fort in the north, perhaps even at his old rank of squad leader. That bright hope made Costis's days drag, filled with anxious anticipation. In the meantime, he continued as lieutenant-at-large with light duties filling in watches and supervising the parade marches of boys in the training barracks.

The shade was creeping closer. Costis looked up at the sound of running footsteps, a barracks boy with an urgent message, he supposed, but it was no barracks boy who hurried around a corner and into the narrow court. It was someone from the dog runs, a kennel apprentice by his uniform. He stopped, gasping, in front of Costis.

"My master sent me to ask for help. The hunting dogs have been released into the court. There are bitches in heat, and the dogs are fighting. We can't get them back to their runs without help. Can you bring guards to help, sir? My master is afraid the king will have the dogs slaughtered and him, too."

Costis sent him on to the officer of the day in his office, then he fetched the layabouts out of the nearest dining hall and led them off toward the kennels.

"Why hurry?" grumbled the men. "Why spoil a good joke?"

"Because it's no joke for the Master of Hounds," Costis said.

"No joke for us, either," said someone else when they reached the court. They had come through the palace and were on the porch outside the palace doors that led out to the hunting court. From there, steps led down to a barking, snarling chaos of dog. The noise assaulted the ears and overwhelmed the shouts of the men working below. The kennel keepers with sticks and ropes were trying to drive one dog at a time out of the pack and lead it back through the open gate to the dog runs. Already there were palace guards assisting where they could. Some stood on the steps below the portico, catching at the stray dog pushed up the stairs by the melee. A hunting dog stood lower than a man's waist but higher than his knee, and weighed half what a grown man did. It was no laughing matter to seize one and keep hold of it without being bitten.

A dog raced up the stairs toward Costis, heading for the open palace doors behind him. Costis and his men shouted and waved the dog back. It shied down the steps again.

"SHUT THAT DOOR!" Costis roared above the

din, but had to point to make his meaning clear. Two guards went to work swinging the twelve-foot-high doors to seal off the palace from the hunting court.

Next Costis checked the other exits. There were only four: two large gateways and two small arched doorways. One of the large gates was open, and led back into the kennels and the stables. In normal circumstances, the animals would have been brought through that gate to gather in the court before leaving with the royal hunt. The other gate led through the outer wall of the palace to the hunting road into the royal preserves. It was safely shut, but stairs on either side of it led up to the palace walls. Costis was glad to see guards already blocking the top as well as the bottom of the stairs. With more waving and pointing, Costis sent men to block the entrances into the palace gardens. Shouting at the top of his lungs, he sent men to the stables to fetch pitchforks, rakes, and brooms. There was little hope of dragging the dogs one by one back to their runs before the king arrived. They would have to drive the entire wild, barking mess through to the stable yards and deal with the problem there.

There was no way to know how much time they had, but Costis assumed the king must be scheduled to pass through soon, or the dogs wouldn't have been released.

Two dogs snapping and snarling at each other threw

themselves against his knees, and he almost went down. The Master of Hounds caught him by the elbow and steadied him. Costis explained his plan, and the two men separated to gather the kennel keepers and soldiers into a circle around the dogs. With brooms and rakes they stood shoulder to shoulder and began to force the dogs through the gates and into the yard beyond. More guards had come from the palace to join them. Looking to his left, Costis was surprised to see Aristogiton, sword in hand, prodding the dogs.

"What are you doing here?" he shouted.

"What?"

Slowly the tenor of the barking changed as the dogs moved together. Costis tried again. "I thought you were on duty?"

"I am," answered Aris.

"Where's the king?"

"In the garden. He was supposed to meet the Secretary of the Navy, but he canceled. We left him in the garden to come help here," Aris shouted, and nodded over his shoulder toward the small arched doorways behind them.

The noise had lessened, and they could hear each other without shouting, though they still had to raise their voices.

"The king canceled?"

"No, the secretary."

If the king hadn't been scheduled to pass through the

hunting court, then why had the dogs been released? Someone had to have known in advance that the secretary was going to cancel his appointment. Costis's knees understood before his head did. They felt suddenly weak, and his stomach roiled. Costis looked up at the palace wall, where the guards still stood blocking the route to any stray hound, looking down into the court-yard and not into the garden. His hands were shaking.

"Oh my god," he prayed to Miras. "Oh my god, oh my god."

"What?" Aris still didn't understand.

Costis dropped his rake and grabbed him by the shoulders. "Where did you leave the king?"

"In an alley, just beyond the naiad fountain and the reflecting pool. What is the matter? I left Legarus at the entrance."

"And at the other end?"

"There's a gate. It's locked. Costis, for god's sake, it's locked and it's not fifteen feet from the guards on the palace wall."

Costis reached for hope. "Do they know the king is in the garden? Did you send a message up to the wall?"

No, Aris hadn't.

"Get your men. Give me your sword." Costis grabbed at the buckle and stripped belt, sheath, and sword from Aris and began to look wildly through the crowded court for Teleus. He had to have come with the guards.

Teleus looked up at his shout. His eyes met Costis's for a moment, then turned to look at the guards on the wall above him, taking in the situation at a glance. Costis was already running, naked blade in hand and sheath in the other, for the nearest entrance to the garden.

This was not the relatively small queen's garden. This was the much more expansive palace ground. It had never seemed so large and so full of pointless obstacles—shrubs, fountains, paths that curved in serpentine courses between waist-high banks of flowers that made it impossible to move as fast as he desperately needed to go.

If he choked on a bone and died, I wouldn't care. It wasn't true.

Costis prayed as he ran. To Miras, his own god, and to Philia, goddess of mercy, that she would preserve the king from harm. "Oh, Goddess, please let the little bastard be all right," he prayed. "Oh, please let there be nothing wrong. Let this be a mistake. Let me look like a fool, but keep him safe, ten gold cups on your altar if he is safe."

The gods above knew that the king could be laid out by a toddler with a toasting fork. What hope had he against an assassin, trained as a sword is sharpened, honed to one purpose, to murder? Costis could only pray that he would not be too late.

Blood on the flowers, blood on the green grass, blood blossoming like a rose in the still waters of a fountain. In his mind Costis saw it all. What would the king think when the assassins came? He would call his Guard to protect him, and there was no one there but Legarus.

Costis's feet pounded on the path. When it dropped down a set of stairs to run beside a long rectangular reflecting pool, Costis leapt from the top of the steps to the bottom and at the far end of the pool went up more steps in a stride. Behind him he heard someone stumble. There was a grunt, and a splash.

At last he rounded a hedge and came face-to-face with Legarus, who had heard running feet and had been drawn away from the entranceway in the hedge. He had his sword out, and Costis was lucky not to run right onto it.

"GET OUT OF THE WAY!" he roared, and Legarus fell back in confusion.

"Attolia! Attolia!" Costis shouted in warning as he ran beside the hedge. Out of breath, he reached the opening and hurtled through it.

The king sat on a stone bench in an open space at the far end of the alley between tall hedges and flower beds. There was a fountain, with a shallow pool underneath. His legs were stretched out, crossed at the ankle and resting on the tiled lip of the pool. No doubt he had been contemplating reflections of the clouds in the water or watching the fish. Costis could see the amused smile he had prayed for, the lift of one eyebrow. It was for nothing, all the panic, and the running. There was no one there but the king, quietly sitting by a fountain, and Costis, standing in the gap between the hedges with a naked weapon in hand, looking like an idiot frightened by shadows.

The king was safe and, as usual, laughing at Costis. Costis didn't care. He hunched forward in relief, gasping for breath. His sword still in his hand and his hands on his knees, he smiled back at the king as the assassins stepped into view.

They must have been concealed by the bushes, but to Costis they appeared as if by magic. One minute they were not there, the next they towered over the slight figure on the bench. Costis screamed an inarticulate warning and stumbled forward, but he might just as well have stayed in the hunting court. It was hopeless before he had taken his first step and over before he'd crossed half the length of the long, narrow alley between the high hedges. There was nothing for him to do.

His steps slowed of their own volition as he got close to the fountain. Numb, he stared at the body there and the spreading cloud of blood. It was what he had imagined and yet nothing he could ever have imagined. He looked at the blood on the graveled path and at the body there. There was more blood on the grass. It wasn't the king's blood. It wasn't the king's body. Costis heard footsteps behind him and turned to see Teleus, wet from falling into the reflecting pool.

Teleus looked as stunned as he felt. Side by side they stared at the blood pooling at their feet, and side by side they turned to the king, who stood with his hand on his hip and his back toward them.

"Your Majesty?" Costis's voice came out in a whisper.

The king turned his head. His usually dark skin was so pale the scar on his cheek showed against the lighter skin around it. He was almost green with pallor, as Sejanus had once described him. It wasn't fear. It was rage.

Softly he said, "I thought that being king meant I didn't have to kill people myself. I see now that was another misconception."

Teleus and Costis stood like garden statuary.

"Where are my guards, Teleus?" He was still speaking softly. Three men dead and he wasn't even breathing hard, Costis noted.

"WHERE ARE MY GUARDS?" the king shouted.

The birds twittered nervously from the bushes around them in the silence that followed.

"Here, Your Majesty." It was Aristogiton, his men crowded behind him, at the entrance to the alley.

"And where have they been?" In almost a whisper, the king addressed only Teleus.

"They were drawn off by the noise of hounds released in the hunting court, Your Majesty. They went to help get the dogs contained before you returned to the palace." Teleus was very calm.

"I see," said Eugenides. He looked at the corpse at his feet. "Have them clean up this mess. That one"—he nodded toward the man farthest away—"may still be alive. You and Costis can take him where someone can ask him who sent them. I am going back to the palace . . . now that the dogs are safely out of the way . . . to make my groveling apologies to the queen."

He stepped toward the path.

"Your Majesty shouldn't be alone," said Teleus.

Eugenides turned back. "Your solicitous attention to my health is appreciated, Teleus, but it's too late for that," he said.

"Please," said the captain humbly. "Take Costis and the squad leader."

Eugenides considered. "Very well," he agreed with cold reluctance.

Aristogiton and his men hurried toward Teleus, responding to his summoning wave. Costis waited while the captain gave the squad leader his orders, then Costis and Aris caught up with the king, who had already started back to the palace. He was walking slowly, his hand still on his hip. Costis had never seen him so dignified. His stately dignity faded a little when they got close enough to hear the curses he muttered under his breath. He was less inventive than usual, and by the time they reached the reflecting pool he was repeating the same phrase again and again like a chant.

Walking so slowly, Costis had ample time to consider his commitment to the goddess Philia. Ten gold cups.

With all the money he had, added to all he could conceivably borrow from the moneylenders in the city, he could afford one gold cup. His father might have enough for another. The priests wouldn't expect them all at once. Only if Costis waited too long, or died before delivering on his promise, would he risk the goddess's displeasure. That displeasure would spread to his family, in which case his uncle might be willing to give the gold for two more, possibly three. If harvests were poor, or other signs of the goddess's ill will appeared, he might empty the family treasury and buy four cups. That still left four unpaid for, and anyway, Costis hated the idea of asking his uncle for money.

He was thinking of full-size drinking cups, made by a goldsmith and decorated with figures. If he offered the goddess ceremonial cups instead, smaller models of drinking cups, very plain ones, his money would go farther. It might stretch to three small (tiny) cups, and his father's to three more. And if he saved every coin, wore the clothes the army provided, ate the food the army provided, which was nourishing enough, if occasionally infested, and if he never spent a copper in a wineshop with his friends, he might pay for the remaining four small (very small) cups, in ten or fifteen years. He could just forget his oath, he supposed, and hope the goddess didn't notice.

The king reached the top of the stairs that led down to the reflecting pool and stopped. He turned a little to face Costis, his hand still pinching his side.

Guilt-stricken, Costis gasped in horror, "No! No! I'll get the ten cups, I swear it!"

The king's coat was light gold, the color of the hills in the autumn heat, embroidered in matching satin threads. His tunic underneath was a contrasting dark mulberry color. The blood didn't show against the fabric, but it welled between the king's fingers, and its bright stain spread in a messy spiderweb across the back of his hand.

"Costis," the king said in the patient voice of someone dealing with the insane, "I just need a little help on the stairs."

Of course. The stairs. With a wound in his side, the stairs would be difficult. Costis pulled himself together and looked over to Aris, standing there as pale as the king. "Go for the physician," he said.

"No!" the king contradicted sharply. Both Costis and Aristogiton turned to him in surprise.

"Oh, gods all damn it," the king said softly. He lifted his hand to rub his face, saw the blood all over it, and put it back on his hip. He turned carefully to look at the walls of the palace itself. The heads and shoulders of spectators were visible on the guard walks at the top.

The king looked back at the walls that circled the grounds. More people.

"So, so, so," he said, defeated. "Get the physician. Have him meet me in my rooms."

Aris went.

Eugenides stood with his head bent and his shoulders bowed. "How many cups, Costis?" he asked without lifting his head.

Costis flushed. "Ten."

"Silver?"

"Gold."

"Ten gold cups for my sake?" He looked up, surprised. "I thought you hated me."

"I do."

Eugenides started to laugh and gasped instead. Costis put a hand on either shoulder to steady him.

"I have a superstitious fear of falling," Eugenides admitted. "Let me put an arm over your shoulder while we get down the stairs."

Costis ducked his head and presented his shoulder.

The king didn't move. "Wrong arm, dear," he said, dryly. He had to use his left hand to cover the wound, because he had no right one.

Embarrassed, Costis stepped around behind the king to the other side. The king's arm dropped heavily across his shoulder. When Costis straightened, the hook hung just in front of his eyes. For the first time, he could see its knife-edge. There was a smear of blood on it, and one corner of the cuff of the king's coat was soaked.

Costis flinched and looked away from this compensation to the king's handicap, only to find himself staring directly into the king's face instead. Eugenides matched Costis look for look, his expression grave, his eyes like pools of darkness deeper than Costis could penetrate. For a moment Costis could see, not so much what was hidden but that there were things hidden that the king did not choose to reveal. Things that were not for Costis to see. There was no understanding him, but Costis knew he would march into hell for this fathomless king, as he would for his queen. So long, he worried, as they didn't order him in opposite directions at the same time. What he would do when that happened, Costis couldn't guess.

The king's arm tightened across his shoulder, and Costis broke free of his thoughts and started down the steps.

The king's left foot landed awkwardly on the stair. He hissed.

Costis reached across to support him with his right hand, and his concern must have shown on his face.

"Hoping to get out of paying for those cups?" the king asked.

Costis snapped the hand back to his side, and the king laughed.

"Miniatures?"

"Full size," said Costis obstinately.

"Was it to keep me from getting hurt? Because this"—he stopped for a breath—"this hurts."

"I'm not sure. I think I prayed that you would be safe, Your Majesty."

"That's more ambiguous." Eugenides considered. "I'll have to die for you to be free of that promise."

"I'll get the cups, Your Majesty."

The king shook his head. "You would spend your life paying for them."

Costis would never pay off the debt. He'd prefer to march into hell, but that option wasn't available. Odd that you could be so angry at someone and devoted to him at the same time. "I'll get them," Costis said simply.

"Costis, I am speechless."

"Not noticeably, Your Majesty." His entire life, which he had been hoping for the past two weeks might be restored, was gone again. He wished the king wouldn't laugh at him.

They walked beside the reflecting pool. There was a great black hole in the water lilies where Teleus had fallen in. The water that had come with him when he'd climbed out of the fountain had splashed onto the edge work and was drying in the sun. One smashed lily trailed across the edge and into the water. Eugenides began again, hesitantly. "As it was undertaken on my behalf, we might ask the royal treasury to address the debt."

Ten gold cups would hardly be noticed by the royal treasurer. Costis swallowed.

"Have I offended you? I didn't mean to."

Costis shook his head. "No, Your Majesty. Thank you, Your Majesty."

"Which goddess should we dedicate them to?"

"Philia."

She was an Attolian goddess. Not one of Eugenides's gods. "I see. I suppose it's good to curry favor where you can. You never know who might rescue you when you overreach."

Costis believed in his gods, prayed to his gods, and sacrificed to his gods, but Eugenides was rumored not only to believe in his gods but also to speak to them and to hear them answer. The idea made Costis uncomfortable. The gods may have walked the earth in the time of the legends, but he preferred to think of them safely on their altars.

"Of course, that's assuming I live," said the king. "I might not." He sighed. "I probably won't live to see my bedchamber." If these were death agonies, they were fake ones, Costis thought, and was sure of it when they reached the shallow stair at the far end of the reflecting pool. No one on the verge of death has the strength to pile one foul word on top of another like a man compiling a layered pastry of obscene language, from the bottom step all the way to the top.

He was more concerned when the king's steps slowed

as they approached the hunting court, and the halt was accompanied by no curses or complaints. Then he heard voices coming toward them and realized it wasn't the pain, it was the anticipation of company that had stopped the king in his tracks.

The crowd came trampling across the flower beds, guards, nobles, and servants.

Eugenides made a noise. Costis bent his head to hear.

"Arf, arrf, bark, bark, bark, yap yap," muttered the king.

They were quickly surrounded. Voices hammered at them from all directions, and there were faces pressing close on every side. Hands, whose owners Costis couldn't see, tried to pull the king away. Costis pulled back, and the king yelled in outrage. Costis wondered if somewhere in the crowd was a man who would finish the work the assassins had begun.

"Hey," he said loudly to a well-dressed middle-aged man who stood in front of him, but was turned toward the king. "Hey!" Costis said again, and the man turned. Costis put his hand out flat on the man's chest and shoved. All of the muscles in his arm and in his back pushing like a ram, he drove the man backward until he bumped into the man behind him and both fell with arms windmilling. To avoid being dragged down, those who could stepped back, crowding the people behind them and leaving an open space in front of Costis.

On the edges of the crowd he could see guards. They were on the outskirts, like the palace servants, only spectators on the scene. It was not their place to approach the king without being directed to do so. Costis recognized most of them by sight, if not by name. He trusted them more than the yammering nobles around him.

"To the king!" he shouted, and the guards, after a startled look, to be sure it was they who were being addressed, came. They shoved their way through the crowd.

Costis said, "Don't let anyone get close."

Costis was half-carrying the king, whose steps had faltered. Costis could feel him tremble. There didn't seem to be any point in following the curving path if the flowers were already trampled, so Costis made directly for the gateway into the hunting court.

Frantically, he bent his head to the king who appeared to be choking. Costis made a grumpy noise. The king was laughing.

"That was the Baron Anacritus you just dumped on his backside. Did you know?"

"No. I don't care either. Where are your attendants?" Costis asked bitterly.

"I dismissed them while I went for my quiet walk. No doubt someone is telling them right now what fun they are missing. They will be here soon."

"Not soon enough," said Costis.

"Anxious to get rid of me?"

"Why can't you act like a proper king?" Costis hissed in his ear.

They reached the hunting court at last.

"Oh gods, stairs," Eugenides muttered in despair.

Costis sighed. The king had a long way and many stairs ahead of him. The royal apartments were on the far side of the palace. It would be best, probably, to find the nearest staircase and climb to the walks at the roofline. That would take him across to the inner palace, and from there he could go down and then up again to his rooms.

Thinking that surely someone else would escort the king that far, Costis was eyeing the first set of steps ahead of him. They led up from the hunting court to the portico entrance to the palace. Eugenides was looking at his feet. He didn't see the queen arrive.

She came through the palace doorway ahead of her attendants, who joined her one by one, all showing signs of haste. The people on the stairs moved silently out of the queen's way, and she looked down at the king, who still hadn't looked up. Walking stiffly, she came silently down the stairs. The guards broke their cordon to admit her.

She reached for Eugenides, touched him on the face. He leapt backward like a startled deer, so explosively that Costis almost fell over trying to hold him. The queen snatched her hand back as if she had been burned.

There was a collective gasp from all around and then silence. Nothing stirred in the courtyard, not even the air, while the queen looked down at the king and the king looked down at his feet. Costis's heart sank—for king and for queen, and for himself, who was uncomfortably loyal to two people at the same time.

The queen had begun another slow step backward up the stair behind her when the king caught her by the wrist and pulled her forward. He pulled Costis as well. Costis was sufficiently taller than the king that bringing his shoulder down to provide support put him off-balance. He had to shift his footing with care, and shift it again as the king let go of Attolia's wrist in order to catch the robe at the elbow and pull her closer.

The king lifted a hand to her cheek and kissed her. It was not a kiss between strangers, not even a kiss between a bride and a groom. It was a kiss between a man and his wife, and when it was over, the king closed his eyes and rested his forehead against the hollow of the queen's shoulder, like a man seeking respite, like a man reaching home at the end of the day. "I didn't have the gardens searched," he said. "I'm sorry."

Costis realized his mouth was open, and shut it. He couldn't step away without pulling the king's arm off his shoulder, but he could look in some other direction, so he did that. He looked at the court, filled with people who were slower than he to realize that their mouths were hanging open. So many stunned faces all in rows. Costis could have laughed, but was still too shaken himself.

"I'm sorry if I startled you," said Attolia softly.

"You didn't startle me," said Eugenides. "You scared the hell out of me."

Attolia's lips pressed together. "You needn't admit it out loud," she reproved him.

"Hard to deny it," Eugenides answered. Costis could hear him smile.

"Are you badly hurt?"

"Hideously," said the king, without sounding injured at all. "I am disemboweled. My insides may in an instant become my outsides as I stand here before you, and no one will even notice." He reached up again to touch her face, trying to wipe away the bloody fingerprints he had left, but only making them worse. "My beautiful queen. Your entire court is staring at you, and I can't blame them."

They were, too. The queen turned to look. Her glance swept through the crowd like a reaping sickle through grain. Mouths slammed shut on every side. There was a scuffling sound as the people in the back shifted, trying to screen themselves from view. The queen looked back at the king, who was broadly grinning.

"Where are your attendants?" she said. She looked at

Costis for the first time, and at the other soldiers with sudden scrutiny. "Where are your guards?"

"With Teleus," Eugenides answered quickly. "Costis and these others were conveniently near to hand. I left the others to clean up."

"I see. Still, you should not be standing here." She signaled to a guard. "Lift him."

"I think I will walk," said the king.

"Maybe a stretcher?" the queen suggested innocently. "You can lie down."

"Like Oneis carried off the field? I think not," said Eugenides. His arm pressed against the back of Costis's neck, and they started up the stairs.

· CHAPTER EIGHT ·

THEY laid the king down on his bed. The crowd
had thinned as they crossed the inner palace, and
as they reached the final set of stairs, he'd let his guards
carry him. He'd accused them of laziness for not offering sooner. When Costis looked at him in reproach,
he'd said, "Stop giving me the evil eye, Costis, I am
mortally wounded. I deserve some consideration."

The room was filled with people talking. Those
who knew the details of the assassination attempt
were sharing their information. The guards were
sorting themselves out under the direction of the
lieutenant who had been in the guardroom. The
queen was near the door speaking to her attendant,
who was wiping the king's bloody fingerprints from
the queen's cheek. The last few hangers-on, those
who had talked their way past guards at various doorways along the route, were in the guardroom, hoping
to be admitted by the guards posted there. One by

one, the silence by the bed drew their attention.

Even the king was quiet. Exhausted, relieved, he lay boneless and silent. The skin was dragged thin across his cheekbones. His sweaty hair stuck to his face, and his eyes were closed. His hand, clutching the fabric of his tunic, had relaxed and slipped down to his side, revealing what the careful bunching of the cloth had concealed.

The tunic had been split by a knife stroke from one side to the other. As the edges of the fabric separated, those by the bed realized how much blood had been soaking, unseen, into the waist of the king's trousers. The wound wasn't a simple nick in the king's side. It began near the navel and slid all the way across his belly. If the wall of the gut had been opened, the king would be dead of infection within days.

He should have said something, why hadn't he? Costis wondered. In fact, the king had. He had complained at every step all the way across the palace, and they'd ignored it. If he'd been stoic and denied the pain, the entire palace would have been in a panic already, and Eddisian soldiers on the move. He'd meant to deceive them, and he'd succeeded. It made Costis wonder for the first time just how much the stoic man really wants to hide when he unsuccessfully pretends not to be in pain.

The king must have noticed the silence. He opened his eyes. Everyone else was looking at his abdomen;

Costis watched his face. Seeing him look anxiously around the room until his eyes fixed on someone by the door, Costis knew that he hadn't been trying to deceive the palace, or calm the Eddisians. He hardly cared if the palace was in a panic. There was only one person he'd been hiding the extent of the injury from, the queen.

Costis saw him pull himself together as she approached the bed. Of all impossible things, he tried to look smug. "See," he said, still playing his role, "I told you I was at death's door," but he wasn't fooling them anymore, not Costis and not the queen. The queen's eyes were slits, and her hands were clenched in fists. She wasn't frightened; she was angry. He could hardly, at this point, reassure her by telling her the wound wasn't serious. Costis almost saw him wince. The king opened his mouth to speak.

"It isn't very deep," the Eddisian Ambassador said from the other side of the bed. He was leaning over the wound, looking critical and mildly disappointed. Eugenides didn't miss a beat.

His head whipped around. "It is . . . too . . . deep!" he insisted, outraged.

The attendants looked shocked and then amused.

"Your Majesty," Ornon said in supercilious tones, "I've seen you get deeper scratches with a cloak pin."

"Damned clumsy with a cloak pin," one of the attendants muttered.

"I wasn't using it on myself," the king snapped. He turned back to the ambassador. "I was enjoying that little moment of horrified attention, Ornon."

"Forgive me, Your Majesty," Ornon replied. "But I think you've been closer to death than this."

The king looked up at the queen, who, relieved by Ornon's opinion as she would not have been by the king's, still looked down at him in displeasure. "I doubt it," she said. "I could disembowel you myself."

"I did say I was so—" The king broke off to shriek in rage and pain, and everyone but the queen jumped. "What in the name of all gods is that?" the king shouted.

The physician, nervously clutching a bloody swab, said, "It's a mixture of aqua vitae and v-vital herbs."

"It hurts, you bloodsucking leech. I didn't leave that torturing bastard Galen in the mountains so that you could take his place."

"I'm so sorry, but it w-will prevent infection, Your Majesty."

"It had better if it hurts that much, and you had better warn me before you put any more on."

"I will, Your Majesty," the doctor said, carefully wiping the wound with another clean cloth.

"When you've finished admiring it, you can put a bandage on it," the king said impatiently.

The palace doctor, who was a thin, nervous man, stared, concentrating. "I'd like to put stitches in where the cut is deepest. And stitch the muscle first." He looked up at the queen for approval.

"It doesn't need stitches," the king said warily.

"Because it's not very deep," someone in the crowd muttered. The king looked around with a black look, but didn't see the speaker.

"Petrus has been my personal physician for a number of years," said the queen. "With the crown's money, he operates a charitable hospital in the city where he has studied a number of new medical techniques. If he believes stitches are suitable, I suggest you let him put them in."

"Just here," said the doctor, "at the side where the wound is deeper. Had it been this deep for the entire length, your assassin would certainly have ruptured the peritoneum."

"The what?"

"The gut."

"Ahh," said the king, and then "Aagh!" a moment later. "What is that, an awl?"

"Oh, no, Your Majesty, no, as you can see, it is a very fine needle."

"It doesn't feel like a needle—it feels like you've spent too much time working on people who don't pay you and you should—ow! Ow! Ow!"

Costis closed his eyes, appalled. The king couldn't lie on a deathbed with a sense of dignity. The attendants were all on the verge of breaking into laughter, and the king, far from minding, was enjoying every minute of it.

The queen's lips thinned.

"I am very sorry," the physician said helplessly.

"Stop apologizing and hurry."

"Your Majesty, I . . ." Petrus looked as if he was about to cry.

Ornon spoke firmly from behind the doctor. "Your Majesty is upsetting his physician." The ambassador stepped closer to the bed. He and the king locked gazes.

Eugenides looked away. "Oh, very well," he said, sulkily. "Tell him to get on with it." He took a breath and let it go in a brief huff of audible petulance.

Ornon encouraged the doctor with a pat on his shoulder and stepped back. The doctor bent over the wound again. The king made a face, but was silent. The doctor looked up momentarily in astonishment but returned to his work, eager to finish before this reprieve passed.

The king lay still and made no sound. As Petrus pulled his first stitches tight, the king took a deeper breath and didn't let it go. After a long count of ten, he softly released the breath and took another.

There were three people between Costis and the queen. Costis knocked all three of them aside like pegs in a counting game and dropped to his knees in time to catch the queen as she collapsed into his outspread arms.

He'd seen her, white as wax, from the corner of his eye and, seeing her waver, had known she was fainting, but too late to do anything but catch her.

"The queen!" someone shouted in alarm, and the king erupted like a wild animal caught in a snare.

He tried to sit up, and the men around him held him down. He struggled. Someone sensible used both hands to pin the hook, with its knife-edge, to the bed. Someone less sensible tried to consolidate his grip on the king's other arm and staggered back, holding his face.

"My stitches, my stitches!" the physician yelled.

"Your Majesty, Your Majesty!"

"Damn your stitches!" he snarled. "Let me up."

With one hand free the king was forcing himself to a sitting position, but more people were pushing him back down, all of them shouting. Someone fell back from the end of the bed, kicked solidly. The doctor cried out again, all his work going to waste.

Costis saw no good to be had by involving himself in the melee. He watched as Ornon stepped forward, seized a man efficiently by the hair, and pulled him sharply backward. The man sat down hard, and Ornon stepped into the space he had left by the king's bed. He splayed his hand across the king's face and slammed his head back hard against the pillow. Keeping his hand planted on the king's face, he leaned over and roared into his ear, "The queen is fine!"

Eugenides was still. The men around the bed froze as well.

"Irene?" the king called.

"She fainted. That's all," Ornon said more quietly. "There is a great deal of blood. She is a woman and she was upset. It is not a surprising reaction."

Costis looked down at the woman in his arms. She had a name. She was Irene. He'd never thought of her having any name except Attolia, but of course she was a person as well as a queen. Lying in his arms, she felt surprisingly human, and female. Costis, suddenly uncomfortable with his burden, was relieved when Hilarion lifted her out of his arms and carried her away to the guardroom. Her attendants followed after, clucking like hens.

Costis got to his feet.

On the bed, Eugenides stirred restlessly. "Upset at the sight of blood?" he said. "Not my wife, Ornon."

"Your blood," the ambassador pointed out.

Eugenides glanced at the hook on his arm and conceded the point. "Yes," he said. He seemed lost in a memory. The room was quiet. As Costis struggled toward a new understanding of the king and the queen, he knew everyone else in the room was doing the same. Except perhaps the physician, who was holding needle and thread in his raised hand, waiting anxiously for instruction.

"Get on with it," said the king. He hardly seemed to

notice when the stitching began. He looked toward the doorway, toward the queen, but spoke to the Eddisian Ambassador. "I think, in future, Ornon, I will stick to upsetting my physician."

· CHAPTER NINE ·

"Y OUR Majesty," Costis whispered.
Eugenides opened his eyes and turned his
head on the pillow. Costis was on his knees by the
bed. The room was dark. The only light came in the
open door of the bedchamber past the guards standing there at attention. They'd let Costis go through
unchallenged, as though they hadn't seen him. They
knew why he was here.

The king blinked.

"Your Majesty, I am sorry to wake you, but I think
only you can help."

"What time is it?" the king asked, hoarsely.

"It's the dog watch, an hour until dawn."

"Early, then," the king murmured, "not late."

"Your Majesty, she's going to have them all executed."

"All who?" His eyes were bright with fever.

"The captain, my friend Aris, and his entire squad.
She had them arrested yesterday afternoon after she left

here and said they will be executed in the morning."

"In an hour?"

"Your Majesty, she has promoted the senior lieutenant to the captain's position, but the men are saying they won't serve under him." He rushed on, "If you can stop her, Your Majesty, please, can you? Aris didn't know the danger, I swear to you. He thought the garden was safe."

"Why didn't you come sooner?"

"You were asleep. They gave you lethium."

With effort, the king dragged his hand free of the sheets. "I remember," he said. "I didn't want it. It always makes me feel like I've been dead." He rubbed his face. "Has she sent for them?"

"Not yet," said Costis.

"Ah."

"Your Majesty, please."

"Costis, I can't publicly reverse her orders."

"But she would listen to you," Costis pleaded.

"Privately, she might. If there were time. But she's angry, Costis. I knew she would be."

Costis dropped his head. He had seen so many impossible things in a day, he had hoped for one more.

"Wait," said the king. "Just wait." He twisted his head. "Is there water? Lethium leaves you dry as a bone."

Costis poured him a cupful, and then refilled it twice when the king emptied it. Eugenides had hauled himself, wincing, to a more upright position to drink. He sighed heavily and stared into the invisible distances. He asked at last, "Do you know any archaic?"

Costis almost flew down the stairs and through the turning passages of the palace. He relied on the early hour to keep his way clear. He cut through the kitchens, escorted on his way by the grumbling and complaints of the kitchen folk already awake and at their work, to reach the stairs that led down to the queen's prison, only to be brought up short by the deliberate shuffling of the prison keeper. Costis forced himself to match the man's strides. There was no point getting ahead of him. The prison keeper had the keys, and like all the prison keepers, he was jealous of his power here in Her Majesty's dungeon. He would make no haste for a queen's guardsman.

Costis waited while the keeper jingled through the keys and slowly unlocked the cell. Then, his patience exhausted, he wrenched open the iron-barred door. He saw Aris first, sitting on the floor, his knees drawn up and his arms locked around them. Excess chain lay in tangled loops around his feet. He raised his head to look at Costis, then dropped it again and reached out a hand to touch the man lying beside him gently on the shoulder. "It's time, Legarus," he said softly.

Legarus was crying. The rest were dry-eyed, but Legarus was crying. No wonder, Costis thought. It was

Legarus who had been the ostensible cause of their sudden promotion, an arrangement by some lover in the palace, everyone had assumed. But the promotion hadn't been arranged for Legarus's benefit. Nepotism had only been a disguise. Someone had wanted on duty that day a squad of neophytes, who, in their inexperience, could more easily be distracted from their duty. His lover had used Legarus and left him to die.

Costis turned to Teleus, who was getting to his feet. "There is no hope, Costis," Teleus said flatly, seeing the look in his eye.

"There is," Costis insisted.

"No," Teleus stubbornly refused. "I should never have agreed to promote Aristogiton's squad. I would not have done it for the queen's bodyguard, and I shouldn't have done it for the king's."

"The squad you promoted? They also die?"

"They also failed."

Costis wanted to seize him by the shoulders and shake him. "And the Guard? She has promoted Enkilis, you know. The men won't follow him."

"They have pledged their swords to the queen."

"They aren't just swords. They are men. They follow you. Without you, their discipline will fail, maybe their loyalty. They are the keystone of the army. You are the keystone of the Guard. The queen cannot afford to lose you."

"Do you think I don't know that?" Teleus asked.

"You have to stop her."

"She knows it, too, Costis," Teleus said sadly. "Even if I could stop her, who am I to do so? It is her decision."

"What if she is making a mistake?"

"Who am I to question the queen's judgment?"

"She is human like us all, Captain." Costis remembered how she had felt in his arms the afternoon before. "She must make mistakes sometimes."

"Oh, yes," said Teleus bitterly. "Rarely, but we are all living with the fruits of her greatest error. Still, we cannot remake her decisions. She is the queen."

"Then ask her to reconsider. Just that. Ask her to take the time to be sure it is the right decision."

"How?" asked Teleus.

The throne room was bright with lights in every sconce. The chandeliers were great wheels of light suspended in the air. The crowd was thick, though the day had not yet begun. No one would miss a chance to see the Captain of the Guard sent to his execution. It was relatively easy for Costis to slip in and stand anonymously near the door. The king had warned him to deliver his message to Teleus and then go directly to his rooms to wait there for the storm to pass, but Costis couldn't go yet. He wasn't sure what Teleus had decided to do. Too soon, the prison keeper had swung the door open and the rest of the jailers had assembled to escort the prisoners to the queen. There had been no more time to convince Teleus. Quickly, Costis had repeated the phrase in archaic and translated it into the demotic. He had no idea if Teleus knew any archaic or if he would be able to remember an unfamiliar sequence of sounds at a moment like this. Costis had no idea why this phrase, the invocation of Hephestia used in the spring festival in Eddis, might remind the queen of past mistakes. He only knew that the king had promised that it would. All Costis could do was follow the prisoners and their keepers and then step away as the prisoners were led into the throne room. He would wait until he knew if his friend was going to die. If Aris was sentenced to die, Costis wouldn't leave him.

On her throne, Attolia held every eye. The empty throne beside her, which she had occupied only a few short months before, might have been invisible, might never have existed, for all of its significance to the people in her presence.

She looked down at the men before her. Only Teleus could speak for them. He looked from left to right like a man hesitating before he chooses his way. Then he raised his face to the queen. "*Oxe Harbrea Sacrus Vax Dragga Onus Savonus Sophos At Ere.*"

The room darkened as a sudden morning draft swept through the open windows near the ceiling and blew through the chandeliers, guttering their flames. In the flickering light, the queen seemed to swell with rage, seemed to burn with it like a flame, simultaneously motionless and ceaselessly moving. The fabric of her robe wrinkled across her knees very slightly as the hands holding it clenched into fists. Costis drew a breath, sucking at air that seemed too solid to inhale.

"What?" said the queen, daring him to repeat it.

"We invoke the Great Goddess in our hour of need for her wisdom and her mercy," Teleus said in the demotic.

"*Ere* translates as love, a rather ruthless love, not mercy, Teleus. The Great Goddess of Eddis is not known for her mercy."

"My Queen," Teleus began.

"Your Majesty," snarled Attolia. Everyone in the room recoiled, excepting only Teleus.

"No," he said. "Relius was right and I was wrong. You are My Queen. Even though you cut my head from my shoulders, with my last breath as a noose tightens, to the last beat of my heart if I hang from the walls of the palace, you are My Queen. That I have failed you does not change my love for you or my loyalty."

"Yet you prefer his mercy to my justice." She meant the king. She knew where the message had come from.

"No—" Teleus shook his head dumbly, held his hands out in supplication. "I only—" but she cut him off.

"Have it then. Free him." She snapped out the order

to the prison keepers. "Free them all." Then she rose from the throne and stormed for the door, leaving behind her attendants, her guard, all of them struck motionless by her anger.

The guards at the door hesitated, unsure if the queen meant to leave the room without her entourage.

"Open the door!" she shouted, and they leapt to obey. She swept through the doorway and disappeared down the hall beyond. Her attendants and her guard came to life, and streamed behind. The rattle of chains and the crash as they dropped to the floor was the only sound as the crowd, like water released from a smashed jug, dispersed in every direction, through every door except the one the queen had used, everyone seeking urgent business elsewhere.

Costis, packed in with the crowd, turned and hurried off himself. Not in the battle for Thegmis, or even in the garden with the assassins, had he been so frightened. The queen had passed him, so close he'd felt the stir of air, and he had guessed that if she had turned her head, only a little, and met his eyes, he might have died right there, so potent was her anger.

Without stopping and without speaking to anyone, he went like a badger to its hole. He hurried down the stone hallway of the barracks and slipped through the narrow doorway into his quarters. He threw himself down on the cot, leaning his back against the wall and pulling his feet up like a child afraid of nightmares under the bed. He wrapped his arms around his legs and sat. After a time he yawned. The building around him was quiet. There was an occasional sound of footsteps in the stairwell and in the courtyard outside, but nothing out of the ordinary. No shouting, nor the tramp of feet mustering out to arrest one small, unimportant guardsman. He yawned again. He had been awake all night. He rested his head against the wall and fell asleep sitting up.

Hunger and a stiff neck woke him hours later. He stretched painfully and decided that sooner or later he would have to leave his room or starve. He also had better check the duty schedule. Officially, he was still enjoying his three-day leave to go hunting with Aristogiton, but emergencies might have changed the schedule, and if he hadn't been arrested already, maybe he wouldn't be. Maybe his part in the play enacted in the throne room would be overlooked in the moment and forgotten in the future. He could only hope so. He went to the mess hall.

It was almost empty. Tight little groups of men huddled together, talking in voices that carried only as a murmur. Costis sliced himself some bread and cheese and helped himself to a cup full of olives and ladled the day's stew into a bowl. He piled the bread on the stew, the cheese on the bread, balanced the cup of olives on top of the cheese, and still had a hand free to collect a cup of watered wine. He sat by himself. Almost before he had unstacked his meal, he was surrounded.

"Any news?" the men settling on the benches around him asked.

"I've been in my room since dawn," Costis said.

"So we have news for you," someone said.

"Maybe," said Costis. "Teleus and the others were freed. I know that much."

"Were you there?"

"You weren't on duty?"

"I was in the crowd."

"Aeeie, that was a stupid place to be."

"So," Costis agreed. "I won't do that again."

"You went back to your quarters? You haven't heard anything else?"

"Like what?" Costis asked warily.

"Like the fight between the king and the queen."

Costis put his cup down. In whispers they told him the news.

The queen had gone directly from the throne room to the king's apartments. "I would see My Lord Attolis," she demanded angrily. Never had she addressed him before by his name as king.

"I am here," he had answered, stepping into the doorway wearing a nightshirt and robe, rumpled and pale, but resolute. He had been waiting for her. He'd leaned against the doorway for support, while the roomful of perplexed attendants scattered like chaff trapped in a small space with a high wind.

As the queen raged at him, he responded, first calmly, then with his own heat. "Is there no one that you will see punished?" the queen shouted. "Are you so fond of Teleus now that you preserve his life at all costs?"

"I only asked you to reconsider."

"There is nothing to reconsider!"

"You know why I need him."

"Not anymore," the queen declared with finality.

The king ignored the finality. "Now more than ever," he insisted.

"He has failed—"

"That is not entirely his fault!"

"Then you will unmake my decisions?" Attolia dared him to try.

"You said I could," Eugenides flatly replied.

Pushed too far, the queen lashed out. The king made no effort to avoid the blow. His head snapped around, and his forehead struck the doorjamb. He staggered and caught himself. By the time he opened his eyes, she was at the door and then she was gone.

Before his attendants were released from their dumb-struck paralysis, he had stepped through the door and swung it closed. It slammed with a report like gunshot, and they heard the tumblers of the lock fall into place.

Sejanus attempted a cutting comment, but it missed

its mark in the uneasy confusion, and its edge blunted on a sullen unanticipated sympathy for the king.

"Yesterday, I thought he loved her," Philologos said plaintively.

"I think he did," said one of the others.

"And she—"

"And I think," said Hilarion, cutting short further discussion, "that we are not all needed here, and as all of us have been up through the night, some of us, at least, should go to bed." He put a hand on Philologos's shoulder and pushed him toward the door that led through the king's wardrobes to the cell-like, semi-private rooms where the attendants slept. "Who knows but that you will get up to find that the world has inverted itself yet again?" He looked around the room at the other attendants as if in warning, but spoke to Philologos. "Remember, the love of kings and queens is beyond the compass of us lesser mortals."

If anyone noticed, no one commented that he had called the Thief of Eddis a king.

"She didn't love him," the guard to Costis's right said. He sounded relieved. "It was a sham."

Before Costis could disagree, the man on his left said, "Of course, it was a sham. Would our queen be cow-eyed for the goatfoot that stole her throne? Are you mad?"

Costis opened his mouth again.

"And would you still be loyal to her if she were?" The man across the table spoke.

Costis closed his mouth.

The men around him shrugged their shoulders in contempt. The question was moot to them. Their queen would never be other than beautiful and passionless in their eyes, and their low opinion of the king was in no way changed by what they would have seen in any other man as insane courage in facing Attolia in a rage.

"I would," said Costis stolidly.

His comrades eyed him in confusion. The question put forward had been so preposterous, it had already been forgotten.

"She is my queen." Costis frowned at Lepkus, the man across from him, daring him to disagree. "Nothing else matters," he said. "I will be loyal until the day I die."

Someone sucked in a breath. The question was no longer rhetoric and doubtful conversational exaggeration. Their loyalty was being questioned, and there was only one response possible.

"Of course," said the men around them. Some of them taking offense at the question, they all reaffirmed the unswerving loyalty of the Guard. "Of course."

"Not everyone will," said someone down the table. Costis couldn't see who. He leaned forward to look. It was Exis, squad leader in Costis's old century. He was a patron, educated, and known for being clever.

"The Eddisian will find people to support him," said Exis. "He is the king, remember, and he can make it worth their while to bolster his power. The queen will need us."

"Who will win if the king and the queen are at odds?" No one could doubt that they would be. No woman could slap her husband across the face and still pretend affection. No man could be slapped and still pretend to be a man.

"Who will win?" Exis suggested with a shrug, "Baron Erondites."

If the king and the queen fought each other, the Baron Erondites would wait until they were both too weak to oppose him and then attack. Inevitably. The men around the table nodded in unhappy agreement.

"Where are you going, Costis?" they asked when he pushed himself to his feet.

"To check the duty schedule, and if I am not on it, to my room. I can await my fate there."

"Don't look now, but I think your fate is on its way. Our new captain just came in, and he is headed your way."

"New captain?"

"You hadn't heard? Enkelis already had the captain's gear packed and moved out of his quarters. He says the queen freed Teleus, she didn't reinstate him. He tried to run Aristogiton off, but Aristogiton told him to his face that he hadn't been relieved of his oath of service and he wouldn't leave until the queen told him to go. We've all been waiting for the queen to come out and settle Enkelis, but the day is almost over, and she hasn't left her rooms. Aristogiton and his squad are confined to quarters. Nobody even knows where Teleus is."

The new captain arrived at their table, and the men respectfully stood. Enkelis nodded at Costis. "You are wanted. Clean yourself up and come with me."

Costis stepped between the guards and into the king's guardroom. Sejanus smiled. "Our dear whipping boy is among us again. What brings you, Costis? Hope for revenge?"

"I'm on duty. I am to remain on duty until relieved or until the king dismisses me."

"And whose orders are those?"

"My captain's, Lord Sejanus. From whom else would I take my orders?"

Philologos got up from his bed to find that the world had not reinverted itself and was in fact exactly as he'd left it, much to his distress and the distress of many others. The queen did not leave her apartments. The king, when they eventually knocked on his door, got himself out of bed to open it, and told them to go away. He did admit the Eddisian Ambassador, but their conversation did not go sweetly, and Ornon stalked out in a rage.

The queen's attendants refused to admit anyone to

the queen, and refused to carry in messages, though some did leave on unrevealed errands. Ministers were left to their own devices. Counselors counseled themselves. There was no break in the ordered routine of government, but the palace seethed with disquiet.

Costis ate his meals in the king's guardroom and slept at night for a few hours on the narrow bench that ran around the walls. The attendants took it in turn to sleep on the wider benches at either side of the doorway to the bedchamber. They were on hand, in case the king called in the night, but he did not.

The next day there were more visitors. Costis, torn by conflicting loyalties, made a mental note of those who came. These were men who might start a new government with the king. They waited in the guardroom while the attendants stepped in to ask if the king would like to see them. Mostly he said no, though he did allow Dite to come sit by his bed for a while. Lady Themis was turned away. An hour later her younger sister was admitted by the guards at the hallway door. She looked pale as she asked an attendant if she could see the king.

"His Majesty is not—"

"Let her in," said the king from the bedchamber.

Lifting his eyebrows in surprise, the attendant waved Heiro toward the door. She went to the bedside and sat.

They talked in low voices for a while. The king, holding her hand in his, said, "I hope your father appreciates what a good friend you are to me."

"Thank you, Your Majesty," she said softly, and left.

The king slept then for the rest of the afternoon.

· CHAPTER TEN ·

Costis woke with a start that rolled him off the narrow bench and onto one knee beside it. Groggy, he struggled to wake fully. He'd been asleep for only an hour or so, and had slept only a few hours altogether since the king was attacked. There was screaming. The screaming had woken him. Rubbing his eyes, he staggered across the guardroom and pushed between the men standing there, shoving aside attendants as needed and wondering why they stood like posts in his way. Only when he reached the door and struggled himself with the latch did he understand. The door was locked. The king was screaming on the far side, and they could not get in. He pounded at the door, but it was as solid as the ages. He shouted into the face of the attendant standing helpless beside him, "The key! Where's the key?"

"We have no key," Cleon shouted back.

Costis threw up his hands. Spinning, he looked around the room and snatched the gun out of the hand of the first guard he saw. Leaning it into the crook of his elbow, he pulled open the leather cartridge box on his belt. Even fuddled with sleep, he could load the gun. The gestures were automatic. He tore the paper cartridge open with his teeth and poured a bit into the priming pan, closed the pan and tipped the rest into the barrel, dropped the bullet, still wrapped in paper, into the barrel and rammed it home, then replaced the rammer in its groove beside the barrel and lifted the gun.

"Get back!" he shouted at the men watching him in confusion. "Get back!" he shouted louder when they didn't move. Not until he put the muzzle against the lock of the door did they understand and dive for cover. There was a burst of light and a shattering blast from the gun. Costis blinked the afterimage from the muzzle flash out of his eyes and looked through the smoke. The door had a chunk as wide as his hand chewed out of it, but the lock still held. Costis reloaded. Everyone in the room was shouting, but no one stopped him. He raised the gun again. This time he turned his face away before he fired. When he looked back, the lock was twisted metal and the door was slightly ajar. He blew out his breath in relief. He'd felt the wind of the second bullet as it ricocheted off the door and past his ear. He didn't want to have to fire a third time.

The king was sitting up in bed, the bedclothes twisted under him. He was propping himself on the stump of his right arm and staring down into his blood-covered hand. His nightshirt was spotted red. The room appeared to be otherwise empty, but Costis checked every corner and the latches on the windows to be sure there was no intruder before he turned back to the king, his knees beginning to weaken in the aftermath of the excitement, his hands to shake. By that time the king was surrounded by his attendants, all of them calling suggestions.

"A drink of water, Your Majesty."

"Some burnt wine?"

"Go away," he said, his voice rough with sleep.

They had never seemed more like yapping dogs to Costis, although he couldn't really blame them. With the possible exception of Sejanus they all seemed rattled.

"Just have a sip, Your Majesty," said one, offering a glass.

"Just a nightmare."

"A clean shirt—"

"*Go away!*" Eugenides shouted. "*Go away!*"

The attendants backed off for a moment, but then closed in again. They opened their mouths to speak, but the queen's voice interrupted from the doorway. "I think His Majesty's wishes are plain."

Every attendant turned to her, aghast.

The queen looked back at them. "Go," she said, "away."

They bolted for the door.

Costis, beginning from the far side of the bed, and

trying to leave with a little dignity, was the last to reach the door. He looked back. The queen was settling on the edge of the bed, ungainly with hesitation and at the same time exquisite in her grace, like a heron landing in a treetop. Without meaning to, he stopped to watch.

She reached out and touched the king's face, cupping his cheek in her hand.

"Just a nightmare," he said, his voice still rough.

The queen's voice was cool. "How embarrassing," she said, looking at his maimed arm.

The king looked up then, and followed her gaze. If it was embarrassing to wake like a child screaming from a nightmare, how much more embarrassing to be the reason your husband woke screaming. A quick smile visited the king's face. "Ouch," he said, referring to more than the pain in his side. "Ouch," he said again as the queen gathered him into her arms.

Costis turned in confusion to the attendants standing around him. They looked as surprised as he, and Costis felt it wasn't any of their business, anyway, how the king and queen resolved their quarrel. It wasn't any business of theirs at all. He reached back for the door. Hooking his hand into the hole where the lock should have been, he seized it by the splintered wood and swung it closed.

The attendants looked at him in outrage, but no one said a word that might draw the attention of the queen.

Costis looked over the shoulders of the attendants and met the eyes of his guard.

"Clear the room," he ordered.

At that, the attendants did protest in low but vehement tones. Sejanus's voice cut through. "By what authority do you act with such confidence, Squad Leader?"

Costis didn't answer. Sejanus knew his rank and the rank hardly mattered. Even as a lieutenant he had no authority over a king's attendant.

"How do you propose to enforce your order?" Sejanus added in his infuriating and condescending drawl, and in doing so, gave Costis the answer.

"At gunpoint, if necessary," Costis said.

Sejanus's hand went to the knife at his waist. Without a moment's hesitation, half the guards in the room put their hands on their own swords and the other half grounded the butts of their guns and started loading them.

Costis didn't take his eyes off Sejanus. The rest of the attendants were sheep. Where Sejanus went, the others would follow, and when Sejanus lifted one shoulder and exhaled his contempt, Costis knew he had won.

"I'm sure none of us wish to disturb Their Majesties," said Sejanus.

In the hallway outside the guardroom, Costis posted his guards. He stood at the door himself after he had checked the rest of the king's apartment to be sure it was empty. The hallway was crowded with the king's attendants and also with the queen's women. Someone had fetched the benches from down the passage and moved chairs out of the receiving rooms. Costis stifled a yawn and put a hand to his ear, which had begun to throb. It was swollen and stiff with drying blood, and when he looked, he saw blood on his shoulder as well. Evidently the ricochet of the second bullet hadn't entirely missed him. The queen's senior attendant approached, and he stiffened. Phresine was an older woman with graying hair neatly twisted away from her face. She smiled at him and stepped close enough to wipe his ear with a white cloth. It was wet and smelled of lavender.

"Well done, Lieutenant," she murmured as she worked gently to sponge away the blood. When she was done, she smiled again at him and settled on a bench not far away.

Her support was reassuring in the face of the baleful glares from the king's attendants, and Costis was sorry when she left only a little later. Another of the queen's attendants, Luria, came down the hallway to speak to her, and when they had exchanged their whispered words, the older woman stood. She nodded to the other attendants, and all the queen's women glided away, leaving the guards and the king's attendants alone with each other in the hall.

✦ ✦ ✦

It was a long night.

The king's attendants played dice or cards, or lay on the benches and slept. Costis and his guards stood at their posts. Costis wished the king's attendants could go away, as the queen's attendants had gone, but he supposed they should be available should the king call for them, as unlikely as that might be. Finally most of the attendants slept.

The guard changed for the dog watch of the night. Costis sent his men back to their quarters but stayed at his post. Only his authority could keep the attendants out of the guardroom. There was no sign of the new captain, Enkelis, although he must have heard about the confrontation between the guard and the attendants. There was no sign of any of the other lieutenants, though they must also have heard. No doubt, they thought it was safest to leave the matter in Costis's hands and avoid any responsibility for the outcome, Costis thought dryly.

There was a gray light visible in the atrium at the end of the hallway when Phresine returned. Standing in front of Costis, with her back to the others in the hallway, Phresine held out a gold seal ring, set with a carved ruby.

"Come with me, please, Lieutenant," she said.

Costis shook his head, surprised. He couldn't leave the king's door.

She looked up at him gravely and lifted the ring a little higher. It was the seal ring of the Queen of Attolia. Holding it, Phresine spoke with the voice of the queen. To disobey her was to disobey a direct order from the queen.

Costis looked over his shoulder at the closed door behind him. Then back at the queen's attendant. She offered him no further explanation. He knew, even if he had told no one, that his orders to guard the king, day and night, had come through Enkelis, from the queen herself. He looked again at the crowd in the passage, trying and failing to imagine what might justify leaving the king and queen unguarded.

"My men?" he asked the attendant.

"Leave them here, if you wish. They are not needed."

"Very well." The king would be adequately guarded without him. He instructed the squad leader on duty to admit no one to the king's apartments until the king or the queen summoned them. Then he followed the queen's attendant.

In the queen's opulent guardroom, he left his sword and the gun he had appropriated from another guard. No one proceeded further into the royal apartments armed. He followed his guide through a passage and various interconnected rooms to a small chamber, an anteroom by its furnishings, with a couch and a desk and a closed door. Knocking gently, Phresine pressed the latch and opened the door. She was a small woman, and Costis could easily see over her shoulder into the room. On a gilded chair, waiting for him, was the queen.

Costis blinked.

He walked forward automatically, but his mind was rooms away. Three steps into the queen's bedroom, he could take in the whole room, paneled in wood, carpeted in gold, with chests and a desk and various chairs and a bed, raised on a dais, with a cloth-of-gold spread. It had no bedposts, no canopy, and no curtains to hide the sleeping occupant.

Costis knew, even before he saw the dark hair on the pillow, who it was. If he hadn't been so tired, he wouldn't have been surprised. Eugenides had long since proven that he could move through the palace of Attolia as he pleased. Clearly, both he and the queen could travel to the queen's room in private if they chose.

"He took a few drops of lethium several hours ago, so I don't think there is a particular need to be quiet," said the queen. Costis turned toward her and hastily pulled himself to attention. Nothing could stop the flush of red creeping to his hairline.

She was amused.

"I want you to stay here until he wakes."

"Yes, Your Majesty."

"You may sit."

"Thank you, Your Majesty."

Costis didn't move.

"Tell an attendant when he wakes."

"Yes, Your Majesty."

When she was gone, and the door had closed behind her, Costis drew a shaking breath and glanced around the room. Moving cautiously, he approached the bed. The king's face was turned away. Costis bent to look at it closely, aware that he was taking a liberty very few must have. Eugenides looked very different in his sleep, younger and—Costis searched for a word—gentler. Costis had never thought the king's expression strained until he saw that strain, by the action of a few drops of poppy juice, relieved.

Thoughtful, he stepped back from the raised bed. There was a low upholstered chair nearby. Costis settled hesitantly onto it. The buckles of his breastplate dug into his side, reassuring him that this was not all a dream.

The morning light was dim. The skies were still gray. Costis yawned. As if in answer to a prayer, Phresine arrived at the doorway with a tray in her hands. He snapped his mouth shut and stood, feeling guilty for sitting down.

She smiled to put him at his ease. "I thought you might like breakfast," she said.

"Thank you, ma'am," Costis whispered. "I'm not sure I should."

"Of course you should," she said. Her voice was low,

but she didn't whisper. "You aren't here on guard duty. He has men in the guardroom to keep him safe. You're here in case he is . . . unwell when he wakes." She put the tray down on a small table beside Costis's chair, and crossed to the bed to lay her hand on the king's forehead. He didn't stir. She slid her hand around his face to cup his cheek and bent to kiss him on the brow, like a mother kissing her child.

Costis stared.

Phresine smiled. "The liberties an old woman can take," she said. "Even with a king." She slipped through the door, leaving Costis alone again.

The queen's bedchamber was as golden as a honeycomb and as peaceful as a tomb. Though Costis was occasionally aware of the quiet bustle of coming and going in the rest of the apartment, the silence in the bedchamber was soporific. He stood and paced across the carpet to keep himself awake, and looked with interest, but not too close an interest, at the queen's writing desk with its tidy rows of inkwells and pens, and at the row of carved beads on a shelf and the assortment of tiny amphoras on a tabletop. Then he sat back down to watch the king sleep.

Once Eugenides's head turned on the pillow and he opened his eyes. He looked around the room, puzzled but unconcerned. His gaze settled on Costis. Costis leaned forward in his chair and said, "Go back to sleep."

Eugenides obediently closed his eyes.

Costis smiled. Behind him someone chuckled and he started. It was Ileia, one of the younger of the queen's attendants, with her dark hair escaping from its silver net and curling against her neck. She was leaning against the door frame with her arms crossed. "I didn't think he ever did as he was told," she said, smiling.

"I only told him what he was going to do anyway," said Costis.

"That would be the trick," Ileia agreed.

Later, when Eugenides stirred again, Costis was relieved to think the king might finally be waking. Costis was stupid with fatigue. The day had passed with creeping slowness, and his eyes were desperate to close. Even when he held them open, they seemed unwilling to focus, and it took time to realize that the king wasn't waking, he was having another nightmare.

Costis dropped forward onto his knees beside the bed. "Your Majesty?"

The king flinched as if flame-bitten, but he didn't wake.

Suddenly he was completely rigid. His eyes were open, but he wasn't seeing anything in front of him. He struggled for a deep breath, and Costis, to forestall the scream he knew was coming, grabbed the king hard by the arm and shook him.

A heartbeat later the king was on the far side of the

bed, eyes wide and a six-inch knife like a sudden miracle in his left hand. Costis kept his hands out in front of him, easily seen, and held very still and spoke very calmly.

"You were having a nightmare, Your Majesty."

"Costis," said the king, as if he was struggling to recognize him.

"Yes, Your Majesty."

"Squad leader."

"You made me a lieutenant, Your Majesty," he said carefully.

The king focused. "Yes, I did."

He lowered the point of the knife. It was shaking, but the color was coming back into his face.

"Irene," he said softly.

Costis turned to see the queen in the doorway. When he looked back at the king, the returning color had drained away again.

The queen stepped around the end of the bed and came up beside the king to put her arms around him.

The king leaned against her and said apologetically, "I am going to be sick."

"Put that down, then," said the queen, lifting the knife from his unresisting fingers and tossing it onto the bedcovers. With one arm around him still, she reached with the other for a basin set on a table beside the bed. She held it for him and stroked the king's forehead as he threw up.

"My god, how humiliating is that," said the king as he lay back on the pillow.

"Survivably so," said the queen.

"Easy for you to say," said the king. "You weren't throwing up."

"Tell me what I should say, then," the queen asked.

The king sighed. Forgetting Costis standing nearby, forgetting possibly that anyone or anything else in the world existed, the king said shakily, "Tell me you won't cut out my lying tongue, tell me you won't blind me, you won't drive red-hot wires into my ears."

After one moment of gripped immobility, the queen bent to kiss the king lightly on one closed eyelid, then on the other. She said, "I love your eyes." She kissed him on either cheek, near the small lobe of his ear. "I love your ears, and I love"—she paused as she kissed him gently on the lips—"every single one of your ridiculous lies."

The king opened his eyes and smiled at the queen in a companionship that was as unassailable as it was, to Costis, unfathomable. Deeply embarrassed to be witness to this private moment, he glanced at the door, thinking of escape, but the way was blocked by two of the queen's attendants, present but as immobile as doorposts, both looking carefully at the ground. He wished the floor could open and swallow him, the floorboards split apart and he and the upholstered chair and the small three-legged table all be sucked down out of sight. Assuming, of course, that it could happen without a sound, and without drawing the attention of the king or queen.

"Costis is here, and Iolanthe and Ileia," the queen reminded the king.

"Costis," said the king vaguely. "Younger version of Teleus? No sense of humor?"

"The same," said the queen, a trace of amusement in her voice.

The king lay still, but his color was slowly coming back to his face, and his breathing eased. He opened his eyes and looked up at the queen still bending over him.

"I'm sorry," he said.

"You were right," she said.

"I was?" The king sounded bewildered.

"The apologies do get boring."

Eugenides chuckled. He closed his eyes again and turned his head from side to side on the pillow, relaxing overworked nerves. Looking more like himself, he said, "You are treasure beyond any price."

He sounded more like himself, too, and Costis realized that what he had taken for the roughness of sleep was the king's accent. While half asleep, he had spoken with an Eddisian accent, which was only to be expected, but Costis had never heard it before, nor had anyone he knew. Awake, the king sounded like an Attolian. It made Costis wonder what else the king could hide so well that no one even thought to look for it.

"If you are feeling more yourself, there is a problem best addressed immediately," said the queen.

"In my nightshirt?" The king wriggled, as ever, out of straightforward obedience.

"Your attendants. I have spoken to them. You will speak to them as well."

"Ah. They have seen me in my nightshirt." He looked down at his sleeve, embroidered with white flowers. "Not in your nightshirt, though."

He was fully awake and himself again.

He said, "Don't you think we should know first what message Iolanthe is holding on the tip of her tongue?"

Iolanthe, who had been waiting patiently with her message, said when the queen turned to her, "Your Majesty's physician is here."

"Someone else who has seen me in a nightshirt," muttered the king.

Petrus, when he came to the door, was followed by two guardsmen, and looked as if he might have been propelled by them rather than his own motive force. He reinforced this impression by dropping to his knees as the guardsmen stepped back. The queen waved a dismissal, and they continued backward through the door before she turned to the doctor.

"Your Majesty, p-please—" he stuttered before she cut him off.

"Clearly you found something in the lethium. What was it?"

"Q-Quinalums," he said. "The king's lethium has been tainted with powdered quinalums." He twisted his long fingers together nervously. "I am sure Your Majesty knows that they are used in the temples t-to open the minds of the oracles to receive the gods' messages. Misused, they can cause death. Even the smallest amounts in the untrained result in—"

"Screaming nightmares?" suggested the king.

"Yes, Your Majesty."

The queen looked at the physician appraisingly. If the king could make a throne seem like a stool fit for a printer's apprentice, the queen could make a rumpled bedspread into a throne.

With an effort that Costis recognized as heroic, coming from such a timid man, Petrus pulled himself together. "Your M-Majesty," the physician said more calmly, "I cannot prove my innocence. The only defense I can offer is that I am not a brave man and not a stupid one. It was not I who altered the king's medication. Please believe that there is nothing on this earth that would have induced me to do so."

"I am not sure that is a risk I am prepared to take," said Attolia.

The man was sweating. "The hospital," he said, "the

experiments and—and your patients depend on me. Please, Your Majesty . . ."

The queen lifted her chin abruptly. "Very well," she said.

The physician breathed a sigh of relief. He tried to recover a little of his lost dignity. "The taste of the quinalums was obscured by the lethium. Another physician might not have realized that quinalum was present."

"Though the screaming nightmares might have given him a hint?" the king asked dryly.

"Yes, Your Majesty. Perhaps I should examine Your Majesty?"

A dark look from the king and a nod from the queen dismissed him.

When he was gone, the queen pulled at the covers, straightening them around the king.

"You trust him?" she asked.

Costis wondered what signal he had missed between the two of them.

"I know something you don't," the king told her.

"Who put the quinalums in the lethium?"

"That, too."

"You will see your attendants. They have run unchecked long enough."

"I'm very tired," he said pathetically.

"Now." She rose and left.

✦   ✦   ✦

Filing through the door, the king's attendants stood in a group between the bed and the windows. Costis didn't envy them the conversation they had evidently had with the queen. He was still standing by the chair near the head of the queen's bed and would have chosen to be almost anywhere else in the world, but neither the king nor the queen had dismissed him. Excepting the queen's hint to the king, and his comment about Costis's deficient sense of humor, neither of them had seemed to take note of him at all.

"I can't doubt that the queen has made her displeasure at your performance very clear," the king began.

"Yes, Your Majesty."

"And she has left your punishment to me?"

"Yes, Your Majesty."

"Well, pick up your heads and stop looking like criminals. If Her Majesty has excoriated you, then I think you have been punished enough already."

Costis suppressed a wince. He might have pitied the attendants after their talk with the queen, but he hadn't forgiven them, and he didn't think the king should either. Eugenides might know how to deal with their queen, perhaps better than anyone could have guessed, but the king mishandled his attendants. One and all they lifted their heads and looked up with varying degrees of relief. Sejanus's smirk was already back.

Only Philologos was unwilling to be let off so easily.

"Your Majesty," he said sternly. "We have behaved shamefully. You should not overlook it."

"I shouldn't?" The king was amused.

"No." Philologos was not.

"You tell me," said the king. "What should I do?"

Philologos didn't smile back. "We should be dismissed, if not banished outright."

His fellow attendants looked at him as if he was out of his mind.

"That's a little fierce, isn't it?" said the king. "To deprive your father of his heir and his only son because of schoolboy tricks?"

Maybe Philologos hadn't thought this through, but he didn't waver. Exiled, he might still inherit his father's land and property, but would hardly be able to administer them from outside the country. His father, in the interests of his property and dependents, would likely be forced to disinherit the young man and choose another heir, a cousin, probably, if the man had only one son, or a daughter if she could be safely married to a man who would hold and defend the family's land.

"For schoolboy tricks?" the king repeated.

Philologos licked his lips. "The snake was not just—"

"Philologos," Hilarion interrupted. "Before you betray a man's misdeeds, you might check to see if he has the same sense of nobility as yourself. However, as you have done so"—he turned to the king—"perhaps you can exile those of us responsible for the most grievous offenses against you, Your Majesty, and send Philologos back to his father."

The king appeared taken aback. "I am surprised, Hilarion, to see your nobility can rise to the occasion, but I hadn't intended to exile any of you. Not even for the snake. I think it is all in the past now. We can leave it there."

"Your Majesty, at the very least we should all be dismissed from your service," Philologos insisted. "Whatever he implies, I—"

"Put the snake in my bed," the king finished for him. "Yes, I know. He was trying to save you from yourself, but he didn't need to. I knew who delivered the snake, and who put the sand in my food. Who sent poor naive Aristogiton with the note to release the dogs, and which of you poured ink all over my favorite coat." As he looked in turn at each attendant as he spoke, it was undeniable that he did, in fact, know. If they had looked chagrined before, they looked at him now with something very like horror. Except Sejanus, who still managed to look both smug and amused. The king turned to him last. "And I know who put the quinalums in the lethium, Sejanus."

Sejanus only smiled down his nose. "You can have no proof, Your Majesty."

"I don't need proof, Sejanus."

"You do if you don't want every baron to rise in revolt. Your absolute power really only extends as far as the barons will allow before they rise against you. Not to mention that any member of the barons' council can question the king's treatment of one of his men. A majority of the barons can vote to overturn your judgment, and if you have no proof, they will."

"Of course, if the subject in question is already executed, it is merely a matter of paying compensation."

Sejanus stared him down. "I don't think you would go so far, Your Majesty. It is no easy thing for the barons to accept an outsider as king. If outraged much further, they will revolt, Eddisian garrisons or no Eddisian garrisons."

"Oh, I might safely go as far as I like without outraging anyone. You can't tell me you really think your father would lift a finger to help Dite."

"Dite?" Sejanus seemed surprised.

"Who else are we discussing? I admitted him to my room yesterday. I admitted him to my confidence, and he attempted to poison me. Who else could it have been? The Lady Themis? Or perhaps her sister? Heiro's a little young to engage in political murder, don't you think?

"I don't need any more proof than I already have, Sejanus. I can have him arrested today, and I will. I can have him dismembered piecemeal this evening. We will see how many clever songs he sings and plays with no hands and without his tongue."

Sejanus was still shaking his head slowly back and forth.

"Your father won't care. He will thank me for relieving him of an embarrassment of an heir and for making the way clear for you to inherit." He smiled. "You won't mind either, will you? We know how much you hate your brother. While you, Sejanus, are my very dear friend, whom I will keep by my side even if I were to turn out every other attendant."

Sejanus paled. His disdainful smile faded. "I poisoned the lethium," he said suddenly, forcefully.

"What?" The king raised an eyebrow, as if he'd heard incorrectly.

"I put the quinalums in the lethium. I have a friend who is a priest. He got the powder, and I added it to the lethium yesterday."

The king asked, "Now, why would you do that?"

"I hate you," Sejanus answered, as if he were reciting the lines in a play. "You have no right to the throne of Attolia."

The king blinked in astonishment.

"I am very sorry it didn't kill you," said Sejanus venomously. "I thought I put in enough to kill a horse."

"In that case, I suppose I will have you arrested."

"Very well, Your Majesty." Sejanus was all disdain again.

"*And* your brother."

"No!"

"You have confessed. I feel sure you are willing, under persuasion, to reveal his complicity."

"My brother had nothing to do with it. I acted alone. I acted entirely alone."

The king, looking down at the bedcover, ran his hand across the embroidered cloth and said nothing. The silence went on.

Sejanus swallowed. When he swallowed again, it was his pride. As the other attendants looked on, more puzzled than anything else, he said, "Your Majesty, I will confess to any crime you name, but my brother is innocent."

"You've already confessed to attempted regicide," said the king. "What else could you confess?" He looked up from where he had been carefully smoothing the embroidered cover, and seeing his face, Costis felt the shock like a physical blow. If Attolia could look like a queen, Eugenides was like a god revealed, transformed into something wholly unfamiliar, surrounded by the cloth-of-gold bedcover like a deity on an altar, passionless and calculating. "Do you think I intend to leave your father an heir?"

Gods in their heaven, Costis thought, did Erondites have only the two children?

He had seen a temple fall once, in an earthquake. Small gaps had appeared between the stones, and these had grown until each separate stone tottered in opposition to the ones below. First the columns supporting the porches and then the walls had tumbled down. So, piece by piece, did the king hammer out the enormity of the disaster Sejanus had precipitated on his house.

"Your father disinherited your sister and all children of hers when she married against his wishes. He did it formally. That's why he couldn't disinherit Dite. A wise man doesn't leave himself with only one heir. He had to keep Dite, because there are so many things to kill a man off between one day and the next—disease, war . . . poison, for instance. Also, there was a chance that Dite might succeed with the queen and marry her. What a coup that would have been for the house of Erondites. But Dite didn't succeed; I married the queen. Poor useless Dite.

"Now your father loses both of you together. He could get rid of your mother, remarry, and get himself another heir, but he doesn't need a baby, he needs a full-grown heir who can fend for himself and support his father."

"You have no evidence against Dite. I won't give you any."

"And my barons might not like evidence dragged out of your screaming mouth?" the king asked.

"I will retract my confession. I can deny that I ever made it."

"You have a point. But I have one, too. I have many of them, sons and nephews of barons, all standing here on the verge of being banished for what even your most sensitive barons would agree is egregious misbehavior. How ironic that they have been forced into this compromising position . . . by you." He waved at the attendants. "Do you think they will lie for you, Sejanus? They may not like me, but they hate you by now. And their families hate your father. He has bribed, bartered, and black-mailed his way to power, but mostly blackmailed. No single baron can risk offending him, but if there is a way to bring him down, with no risk to themselves, every baronial house will jump at it."

"I still won't give you any evidence against Dite. Not that you could execute him for."

"I don't need to execute him, Sejanus. All I have to do is banish him for being an embarrassment to the throne. I have all the evidence I need for that."

That stupid song, thought Costis.

Sejanus thought it through, and like a puppet with its strings cut, or like the temple collapsing on itself, he landed on his knees before the king with a force that must have rattled his teeth in his head.

"He cannot support himself," Sejanus said.

The king agreed. "He has no money. Your father hasn't provided him any for years. He has lived on the queen's charity and spent every coin she has given him. Within a month he will be begging on a street corner somewhere on the Peninsula, and within two months groveling in the mud for a crust of bread, and within the year, he will be dead. On the other hand, if you try to retract your confession, I will have one dragged out of him, and then I will have him drawn and quartered.

You can decide which is preferable. After all, he might make a living for himself, selling his songs from a gutter on the Peninsula."

Sejanus put a hand to his head.

"Your father won't support him." The king hammered on. "What would be the point of an heir who cannot manage the family from exile? Your father will instantly disinherit him and pick another heir. Only . . . if a man chooses someone, not his own offspring, as heir, he must obtain the approval of the throne. Me. My approval. "

Sejanus buried his face in his hands.

"Your cousins, your uncles, your every illegitimate sibling will be scrambling before the day is out. All of them straining to be the next Baron Erondites, all of them stabbing each other in the back. They must be chosen by your father, so they will seek his favor. They must be approved by me, and so they will seek mine. If we cannot agree, and your father dies without an heir, the entire estate reverts to the throne. I will choose an heir for him."

The king looked from the diased bed down at Sejanus. "The house of Erondites," he promised, "will not survive."

They could hear Sejanus's breathing, baffled by his carefully manicured hands.

"Your Majesty." He dropped his hands, but didn't look up as he spoke. He concentrated his gaze on the floor, as if he had this one last thing to say and meant to say it well. "My brother has served the queen loyally. He would serve you as well. He has never been anything but loyal. Please. Please let your revenge fall on me, who deserves it. Not on my house. Not on my brother. Let me confess to any crime you like and be punished in any way you choose." He licked his lips. "I beg you."

"It isn't revenge, Sejanus," said this new incarnation of the king. "I wouldn't destroy an entire house to destroy one man. But I would destroy a man to destroy a house. Your brother will be exiled, your house will fall, not because I happen to hate you, but because Erondites controls more land, and more men, than any four other barons stacked together and has proved to be dangerous over and over. Its very existence is a threat to the throne. It will not survive," he said again.

He gave Sejanus time then to think it all through, to find some escape, but there was none. The baron's son cast a brief glance at the other attendants, but he'd lost his hold over them. Even if he retracted the confession, he had made it in front of too many witnesses. They were the younger sons and nephews of the most influential barons in the state and they would repeat everything they had heard to their uncles and fathers. The council of the barons wouldn't support someone who'd confessed to the attempted murder of the king. His father had too many enemies who would be delighted at the fall of the house. There was no hope, and only Dite's fate lay in his hands.

"I will not retract the confession," said Sejanus. "I will give you any evidence you need, except against Dite, if you will exile him instead of killing him."

"Thank you," said the king.

Sejanus looked up at last. Then, with a little effort, he shrugged, like a man who has lost a bet on a footrace or a roll of dice. Accepting a shattering defeat with some dignity intact, he was more likable than he ever had been in the past. Costis almost felt sorry for him.

Sejanus saluted the king. "Basileus," he said, using the archaic term for the fabled princes of the ancient world.

He looked over his shoulder as if to summon the guards in the doorway who were stepping forward to lift him to his feet, and he left the room without another word.

The attendants exchanged glances in the silence after his departure, but they didn't speak. The queen entered and sank into a chair. The king inched himself backward with a grimace and settled back against the headboard.

Two of the queen's attendants had come in behind her: Chloe and Iolanthe. All of the king's attendants but Sejanus remained, as well as Costis, still standing uncomfortably by the small upholstered chair. The room was full of people.

"Ninety-eight days," said the queen, folding her hands in her lap. "You said it would take six months."

Eugenides picked at a nub in the coverlet. "I like to give myself a margin. When I can."

"I didn't believe you," the queen admitted with a delicate smile.

"Now you know better." The king smiled back. They might as well have been alone.

The queen turned her head to listen. There was shouting in the guardroom. Costis tensed. His hand went to his belt, looking for his sword.

"That will be Dite," said the king. "He must have been in the outer rooms. I may as well see him."

The queen rose and stepped behind the embroidered screen in front of the fireplace. Her attendants withdrew. The king's attendants remained, digesting the fact that their helpless, inept king had promised his wife to destroy the house of Erondites in six months and had done it in ninety-eight days.

Dite, when he came to the door, braced by two guards, was as white as his brother had been by the time he left. He, too, dropped to his knees by the king's bed, but he didn't look at the floor. He stared up at the king's face, seeking answers.

"I warned you," said the king, in a level voice.

"Yes, Your Majesty."

"And I told you to warn your brother."

"I know, Your Majesty. I did warn him. Even though I didn't believe what you told me, but why would my brother try to poison you?"

"He didn't," said the king, and when Dite stared at him at a loss, he explained, "He confessed to protect you. He thought you put the quinalums in the lethium."

"I didn't!" Dite protested.

"No," said the king. "I did."

"Why?" Dite asked, helplessly. "Why?"

"I didn't drink any of the filthy stuff," the king snapped. "Dite, I don't need quinalums to give me nightmares; they come on their own. The gods send them to keep me humble."

There was no stroke of humility about him, and if Costis had ever wished to see him look more like a king, his wish was answered. He found the prospect was unsettling.

"Then my brother is guilty of no crime?"

"Oh, he's guilty of a crime, Dite. Just not guilty of the one he confessed to. He's guilty of leading, cajoling, and bullying every single one of my attendants into criminal misbehavior." He swept his eye over the attendants. "And conspiring with your father to have them all dismissed, excepting himself, so that I could choose new attendants more to the liking of the Baron Erondites. With Sejanus's help, of course, and the help of the mistress the baron had picked out for me—only I kept dancing with her sister—who, by the way, has lovely earrings."

"I see," said Dite, hesitantly.

"No, you don't. Neither did I. Because Sejanus, in the process of corrupting my attendants, was supposed to be making himself indispensable to me, which he dramatically and inarguably failed to do. Your father wanted me neatly snared. Your brother wanted me dead. He was on a balcony overlooking the garden directing the assassins to where they would find me."

"But you had no proof?"

"None that I wanted to bring into the light of day."

"So you put quinalums in the lethium and got him to confess to that."

"I did. Would you prefer, now that I have had him arrested, that I extract a confession for the crime he did commit?"

Dite lifted his hands hopelessly. "You will execute him?"

The king shook his head. "No."

"Thank you," Dite gasped. "Oh, thank you."

"Don't," said the king, holding up his hand. "Don't thank me. Your father will be somewhat more tractable so long as he thinks there is some hope of Sejanus's release. That is the only reason Sejanus lives. Unfortunately, it eliminates any chance that your father will support you in your exile, Dite, and is no favor to you."

Dite dropped his eyes, but didn't complain. Painfully, the king leaned to his right, reaching with his left hand to flick open the drawer in the table beside the bed. Catching it by its strings, he pulled out a purse, then reached back for a folded document. Sitting back up, he tossed the purse to the edge of the bed and handed the document to Dite.

"You can use some of the money in the purse to address . . . family matters. The rest should get you to the Peninsula. The paper is a letter of introduction to the Duke of Ferria. He is holding the position of court music master open for you."

Dite turned the packet over in his hands. "Ferria," he said in wonder.

"I'm sorry, Dite."

Dite shrugged away the apology. "You have spared my brother when you could have killed him and you have offered me an escape from the cesspit of my family and this court. You know what it means to me, to make music in the court of Ferria. You've put a purse and an impossible dream in my hand. I don't know why you should apologize."

"Because I am exiling you, Dite. I intend to raze your patrimony and salt its earth. You emphatically do not need to thank me."

Dite got to his feet to take his leave of the king. Still looking at the paper and the purse in his hand, he said, "You never said why Sejanus would want you dead."

The king looked sad then, and answered gently, "For your sake, Dite."

Dite's head came up.

"Brotherly love." The king shrugged.

"And you let us live, and give me this." He held up the paper and the purse.

"I think we have cleared the difficulties between you and me, Dite."

Dite nodded. "Fortunately so, for me. I did warn him, as you asked me to."

"It isn't your fault he didn't believe you," said the king. "Nor that he is as fond of you as you are of him. It may save him someday, when I no longer need him alive."

Dite looked at him. "I hope so. I beg so, Your Majesty. He is very dear to me."

"You need to be on ship by nightfall."

"I will be," Dite assured him. He glanced at the embroidered screen before the fireplace and then back at the king. Then he said, with a bow and a smile, "Be blessed in your endeavors."

The king chuckled. "Good-bye, Dite."

When Dite had left, the queen stepped from behind the screen, speaking as she came. She said, "If he considers my court a cesspit, I wonder why he has remained here so long."

"He was in love," the king explained.

"With whom?" Attolia asked.

The king laughed. "You."

She said nothing, but her cheeks grew pink as she sat in a chair near the bed. "That is a joke?" she asked at last.

The entire court knew that Erondites's older son was in love with the queen. The entire country knew it. Costis suspected it was common knowledge as far as Sounis.

"That is ridiculous," she said.

The king agreed. "Like falling in love with a landslide. Only you could fail to notice."

She shook her head in disbelief and started to speak. But before she did, she looked from face to face at the other people in the room and observed the truth reflected there. Her cheeks grew pinker. She turned back to the king.

He said, "Sejanus and his brother pretended to dislike each other. It kept Sejanus in his father's good graces, and Dite above suspicion and therefore able to be close to you, at least until I stepped in to claim you. Sejanus was jealous of me on his brother's behalf. He hoped that if I were dead, you might come to accept Dite's love for you."

"The difficulty with Dite that you two have settled," she said thoughtfully, disbelieving the conclusion she had reached. "You were jealous . . . of Dite?"

The king, the master of the fates of men, before their eyes was reduced to a man, very young himself, and in love. Picking again at the coverlet, he answered, with his eyes cast down, "*Wildly.*"

The queen's lips thinned, and her eyes narrowed, but even her control was not equal to the task, and she had to lift her hand to cover her smile and then duck her head. Her shoulders shook slightly as she laughed.

"I shall throw something at you," the king warned loftily. "You are embarrassing me in front of my attendants."

The queen lifted her head, but kept her hand in place a moment more. When she lowered it, she was almost serene. "As if you cared," said the queen. With an observing eye, she added, "You're tired."

"Yes," he admitted, and this was clearly the truth.

There was more color in his face than could be accounted for with a blush. She lifted a hand to lay on his forehead, but he leaned out of reach.

"Go away," he said.

"As your wishes are clear, I will," she murmured, and rose. "You will send them away and sleep now?"

"Yes."

She bent to kiss him and was gone.

As if you cared.

If the attendants had felt chagrined, horrified, or foolish before, they were now feeling very, very small.

"One of you go get me some clothes," said the king.

"A nightshirt and your robe, Your Majesty, right away."

"I said clothes." The king sighed and rubbed his face. He did look tired. "The new blue silk from the tailor's. Pick something to go with it." There was a subtle warning in the words.

"Yes, Your Majesty." One attendant bobbed his head and started for the door.

The king turned to Costis. "Go get a squad ready to escort me."

Philologos protested naively, "You said you were going to rest."

The king only flicked a glance in his direction. "I lied."

After Costis had informed the squad on duty in the queen's guardroom, he waited, watching the attendant hurry past with the king's clothes. Another headed out carrying a message. A short time later the king himself appeared, trailing worried attendants.

Hilarion stepped faster, passing the king. Once ahead of him, and between the king and the door, he stopped and turned around to ask bluntly, "Where are we going, Your Majesty?"

The king tilted his head and looked up at him through narrowed eyes. Hilarion swallowed, but the king chose to give him an answer. "So far today I have pardoned people I would have preferred to exile, exiled the only member of this court that I like, and imprisoned for life a man I would have preferred to execute. I am going to the palace prison to indulge myself. I think I deserve it. You may stay here."

"No!" A little too loud. "I mean, please, no, Your Majesty. We should be with you." Or the queen would have their heads, thought Costis.

"I will have my guards with me. They are sufficient."

"Your Majesty." It was Philologos. "We are your attendants, aren't we?" His expression was equal amounts pleading and resignation.

The king rolled his eyes, but gave in. "Three of you may come."

He left it to them to choose. Hilarion and Sotis, now that Sejanus was gone, were the two obvious choices. Costis was a little surprised when Philologos also stepped forward and even more surprised when the other attendants backed down. The three followed the king out the door.

Costis hesitated, then followed them. He'd been told by the queen to stay with the king until dismissed and he hadn't been dismissed.

They reached the grand staircase that led down four levels to the ground. The king glared at the steps in front of him.

"If we may assist you, Your Majesty?" Hilarion offered.

"You may not."

Putting his hand on the marble railing, he went

down. He moved slowly, without any obvious sign of difficulty, but Costis noted that the king was sweating by the time he reached the ground floor.

They crossed the palace and circumnavigated the kitchens to reach a stairwell that led down to the palace prison. The prison was entirely underground and lay beneath the courts between the palace and the stables and hound pens. The hound pens probably smelled better, Costis thought. He hated it down here.

At the bottom of the stairwell the guard sat on a three-legged stool. He didn't rise until he saw the king, and then did so with barely concealed reluctance. With insulting leisure, he led the way into the prison. The chief of the prison guards, in their guardroom, bowed to the king, looked at the hook at the end of the king's arm, and hid his smile. It seems he knew which prisoner the king was seeking.

"This way, Your . . . Majesty."

By stepping forward as the prison keeper opened the cell door, Costis blocked the king until two of his own guards had gone in, and he had stepped in himself, but the prisoner was no danger. He was chained to the stone bench on which he lay, and the chains, like the guards, were a superfluous security. The cell stank of cess and vomit, and the prisoner hadn't moved when the door opened, not even to turn his head. The growth of his beard covered his chin, and the bruises obscured the rest of his face. His arms lay across his chest, one hand swollen and black. The fingers were like grotesque sausages, and Costis looked away. There was a cloak bundled behind him. Perhaps it had been used as a blanket at one time, but the prisoner lay now without it. Recognizing the fabric, Costis was stunned.

He looked more carefully at the man lying on the bench. Even knowing who he was, Costis saw no sign of the assured Secretary of the Archives in the battered and bruised face, but bunched behind him was undeniably what remained of Relius's elegant cloak.

Costis stepped aside to let the king enter and took his place by the doorway.

"A chair," said the king. He considered the prisoner and then turned to Philologos. "And some water. Get it from the kitchen."

Philologos hurried out the door.

The chair was brought, and the prison guard set it beside the king with a flourish.

"If there is anything else you desire, Your—"

"I desire"—the king interrupted in a level voice—"never again to see your living face."

The smug condescension of the prison keeper wavered as he backed out the door. The attendants exchanged knowing glances. Eugenides sat in the chair that had been brought and leaned back carefully. "So, Relius," he said finally, "are you ready to discuss the resources of your queen?"

It was a curious question, like an echo without a source. As if Relius had once asked the king the same question and the king was casting it back to him. Costis felt a chill travel down his spine.

A sound came from the figure lying so still in his chains. "I thought you would come somewhat sooner for your revenge," Relius whispered.

"I've been indisposed."

"I heard. One does hear things, even down here."

"I remember." The king looked around the cell as if reacquainting himself. "It was a room very much like this. I don't remember a bunk, but maybe I just didn't see it. Does she know that you came back to question me after she left?"

Costis swallowed, feeling more uneasy with each passing moment. Relius had questioned the king. When he had been a prisoner of Attolia, Relius had pressed him for information about the Queen of Eddis.

I am going to the palace prison to indulge myself. I think I deserve it.

Costis exchanged a glance with the rest of the guards in the cell. They were veterans. They'd seen this sort of thing before. They didn't want to be here either.

Relius shook his head almost imperceptibly. "She didn't want to know then."

"And you weren't foolish enough to tell her later?"

"No. Though she will have guessed."

"Did I tell you anything?" the king asked conversationally.

Costis shuddered from head to toe.

"No," Relius said. "You begged in demotic. You babbled in archaic. I would have pressed you harder, but I was afraid you would die. She didn't want you dead." The Secretary of the Archives finally turned his head to look at the king. "I wish I'd killed you."

"Brave words, Relius."

"No one here is brave. Just stupid. Did you come to hear me beg? I will. I have. You know the words." The tears rose in his eyes, and his voice weakened. "Please don't hurt me anymore. Please. Please, no more."

The king turned his face away.

"I don't know," Relius whispered, "if I was ever brave. But if I'd known that you would come back, I would have killed you then."

"If you had only known that I would end up here and you there? What a surprise it must be after all your years of service to the queen."

"No surprise that I am here. Only that you are here as well. Do you think I didn't know, from the very beginning, that this was where I must end?"

"Would you have served her if you did?" the king asked.

"Gladly," snarled the secretary, and had to pant for breath, having disturbed the equilibrium of his body's pain and his tolerance of it.

The king leaned forward then, and Relius cried out, but the king only slid his hand under Relius's head to lift it while he used the hook to pull the cloak forward. He laid Relius's head back down on the makeshift pillow.

Philologos came back with a skin jug in his hand.

Sotis took it from him, and, following the king's indications, he bent to tip it into Relius's mouth. The secretary swallowed once. Before he could swallow again, the king said confidently, "You must hate her now."

Relius's eyes rolled. He looked at the king and deliberately spat out the precious water. He struggled to lift his head, so that he could look the king in the eye. "If I were here for fifty years," he said, gasping, "and she released me, I would crawl, if that was all I could do, to her feet to serve her."

The king shook his head in amusement and disbelief. "That is impossible. After what she has done to you?"

"It is what I taught her to do."

"So you would serve her still?"

"Yes."

His amusement and his disbelief wiped away, the king leaned closer.

"So would I." He spoke so quietly that Costis had to strain to hear the words. It was too much for Relius to take in. He only stared.

"What do you want from me?" he whispered. The

tears rolled from the corners of his eyes. "You are here for your revenge. I cannot stop you. So take it. Whatever you want you can take. No one can stop you."

"I want you to believe me."

"No." His breathing was ragged as he fought to suppress sobs that would rack his already aching body. His face twisted in pain.

The king was at the edge of the seat, leaning close to Relius's ear. Costis couldn't hear what he said next, but he heard Relius cry out. "What difference does it make what I believe when I will be dead soon, like Teleus?"

The king sat back, making a face at the pain in his side. "Then there is something you haven't heard. She pardoned Teleus."

"Liar," Relius cried. "*Liar.*"

"Well, yes, I am," the king agreed, turning his head to listen to the sound of footsteps approaching in the passage. "However, this is one truth I can prove. Unless I miss my guess, and I doubt that I could, the angry footsteps currently stamping toward us belong to the captain himself."

The king was correct. It was the captain and a squad of guards. He came through the door and stopped just behind the king's chair.

He didn't speak. He reached around the king's shoulder to offer him a folded paper.

"Let me guess," said the king. "My queen has

transferred Enkelis and reinstated you, and your first task is to get me back to bed?"

He opened the paper with one hand, spreading it across his knee, and read the message it contained.

He smiled down at it.

"I will spare you, Teleus, the difficulty of attempting to conduct me bodily back to bed. You can finish what I have begun here, instead."

Teleus flinched in horror and disgust. He looked across the cell to Relius, and the shock on his face faded into grief. Relius looked back without hope. Teleus was alive because the king had interceded on his behalf, and he knew where his duty lay. "I am at your service, Your Majesty," Teleus said, sickened.

Eugenides got out of his chair in order to turn around fully, so that he could see Teleus's face. "You misunderstand me, Captain. I am pardoning him."

Teleus, who had faced his failures and his death and the death of his friend and accepted his own salvation at the hand of a man he despised, ran out of the strength to accept any more. He contradicted the king. "Her Majesty has condemned him."

Eugenides, wounded and tired and surrounded by the walls and the stench of the prison where he had lost his hand, responded, not mocking but snarling, "Am I king?"

The way a crack in the face of a dam widens with accelerating speed, letting more and more water surge through, Teleus's voice rose with every word until he was shouting loud enough to be heard across a parade ground, the deep profundo painful in the small cell. "Do you think that matters?" he bellowed. "Do you really imagine it is your orders taken here?"

What else he shouted was lost, its meaning obliterated as the king shouted back, equally impassioned and incomprehensible, their words ricocheting against the walls and clashing into meaningless noise that made Costis long to cover his ears. If Teleus swelled with rage, the king burned with it. No matter that Teleus was nearly a head taller than the king, if Teleus meant to overwhelm him with his physical presence, he failed. Like a feral cat against a barnyard dog, the king stood his ground, and the two shouted until Teleus caught sight of the Secretary of the Archives. Relius had turned his head away, trying hopelessly to shut out the sound. Abruptly Teleus fell silent, letting the king's last words ring uncontested.

"I CAN DO ANYTHING I WANT!"

The prison keeper chose an inopportune moment to look around the doorway into the cell. He and the king locked gazes, and the king's eyes narrowed while the prison keeper's widened. Then the angry flush in the king's cheeks faded away. He let the queen's message drop from his hand, his face as white as the paper it was written on. He reached for the chair, and his hook banged awkwardly over the top of it. He was swaying as he turned to catch his balance with his remaining hand. Philologos was nearest and raised his hands to help, but backed away. They waited. The king held the chair, stared into invisible space, and slowly his color came back. He started to speak twice, and stopped. He experimented with a small breath, then took a deeper one, and finally spoke without turning his head.

"I don't care whose orders you think you are following, Captain, but you will see that Relius is moved to the palace infirmary and some physician, other than the butcher down here, treats him. Get Petrus. I will take your squad with me. You may keep mine. Send Costis to his bed before he falls over."

He waited to see if Teleus was going to argue.

It was Relius who spoke from where he lay, his voice thready but defiant.

"You cannot buy my loyalty."

The king made a noise too harsh to be a laugh. He stepped around the chair, and holding his side with his left arm, he leaned close to the secretary. "You said no one down here was brave." He lifted his hook near Relius's face. Relius closed his eyes tightly, and the king ruefully withdrew it. Painfully he crouched down until his knees were on the filthy floor and one elbow was supporting him on the bench. He lifted his hand away from his side, lifted it to Relius's face, brushed the sticking hair off his forehead, and said, speaking very gently, so that a man exhausted and in pain could understand, "You are pardoned, Relius, because I want you to be. Not because I want your loyalty." He waited while the words sank in. "You can retire to a farm in the Gede Valley and keep goats, and be loyal to whomever you want. I don't care.

"You are pardoned. Do you understand?"

Relius's head nodded a fraction. Eugenides brushed his hand across the secretary's forehead one more time. His words were still gentle, but he smiled as he said, "Don't let Petrus put in too many stitches. They hurt like hell."

He got to his feet slowly, but he didn't make a sound. His attendants twitched, but didn't offer to assist. The king stepped across the cell toward the door, his left leg moving slower than the right, making his steps uneven, his left arm pressed against his side. As he passed Teleus, he didn't look at him.

"Her Majesty charged me with your safe return to bed," Teleus said stiffly.

"I am going directly there. When you have seen Relius to a comfortable bed, you may tell Her Majesty so."

When the king was gone, the prison keeper returned, creeping back. Teleus sent for something to carry Relius on. "Carry him where?" the keeper asked. He'd heard every word from where he'd stood in the hallway. He didn't need to ask.

"Never mind," said Teleus curtly. He crossed to Relius's side. "Are your ribs broken?" he asked.

"Nothing but the hand, I think," Relius whispered.

Teleus leaned over to lift the secretary's head. His strong fingers cradled his friend gently while he pulled the cloak away. He used the cloak as a wrapping. "Get that damned chain off," he said, and the keeper hurried to the task. When it was done, Teleus lifted his friend himself. Holding him in his arms, he carried him out of the cell. The guard trailed behind him.

"You can't carry him all the way to the infirmary," the prison keeper called.

"He can hand him to me," said a guard as he was leaving.

"And me," said another as he went through the door, leaving the keeper alone in the cell.

"Your Majesty," Hilarion wailed, sounding more like Philologos.

"I lied." The king interrupted without lifting his head and without pausing as he continued painfully up the stairs.

With no choice, the attendants followed. They had been left behind at the landing when they had stepped off the stairs, mistakenly heading in the direction of the royal apartments.

The top of the staircase let out onto the walks

around the roof of the palace, near the Comemnus tower. All of the towers around the palace were named. The Comemnus was taller than the rest of the roof by only a single story. It had been added to the palace by the current queen's grandfather in a day of flamboyant architecture and was made of two colors of stone, speckled like a lattice and faced with decorative brickwork. The king paused as if admiring it, then went up the decorative brickwork as if it were a staircase and disappeared over the edge of the roof.

Consternated, the attendants stared at one another. After silent prodding Philologos called, "Your Majesty?" but there was no answer.

Hilarion put his hands to the brickwork and cautiously began to climb, not sure how he would continue when his path took him over the edge of the wall and out above empty space. He didn't find out. He'd gone no more than a few careful steps when the king's voice came over the edge of the tower roof.

"I will have you granched," he said quietly.

Not wanting to end his life hanging impaled on stakes, Hilarion stepped hastily back down.

It was more than an hour before the king came down, and Relius had long been in his bed in the infirmary before his attendants and guard returned the king to the royal apartments.

✦ ✦ ✦

Weaving with fatigue, dismissed by Teleus when they were halfway to the infirmary, Costis returned to his room, freed himself of belt and breastplate, and fell, otherwise fully dressed, onto the bed.

CHAPTER ELEVEN

THE long summer's day was ending. The sky was still bright, but the sun was gone. The last of the swallows were flicking across the open spaces between the buildings and the first bats could be seen flicking with them when Dite left the walled city of Attolia and made his way through the open streets to the docks where a ship was awaiting him. If he'd imagined going off alone, with just his bag on his shoulder and some of the king's money in his pocket, there were obvious complications to this plan. He needed to take his music and his instruments and had had to hire one of the palace boys to carry them. When the boy saw the number of cases, he doubled his price and went out to fetch a handcart. Dite's friends had helped him pack all afternoon, insuring that it took much longer than necessary and that he had to put in a number of useless but appreciated last-minute gifts. His friends walked with him as he followed the handcart.

They were very merry, all of them. The house of Erondites might be tumbling to destruction, but they saw cause for celebration. Dite was going to the court of Ferria to be music master. Ferria—where they were translating the great works from the ancient world and reading them aloud in the plazas, where the artists were changing the world of painting overnight, where the wealthy patrons of the city demonstrated their status by keeping able-bodied men to do nothing all day and most of the night but make music.

They followed him onto the ship and helped him stow his possessions in his tiny cabin. Then they stood about on the deck admiring the sky, the ship, the crew, the bay. Dite pulled at one young man's sleeve and drew him aside. He handed him two letters and a heavy purse.

"Will you deliver these for me, Kos? I couldn't do it myself. The purse and the letter with it are for my mother."

"God of wealth, Dite, where did you get this much? It isn't the king's silver, is it?"

Dite admitted that it was. "I kept some of it," he said, "but I wanted my mother to have the rest. She might need it."

"If your father decides he needs a younger wife. I understand. What's the other letter?"

"That's for Sejanus. If the king allows it, will you

deliver it? I tried to visit him, and they wouldn't let me. No one is to speak to him."

Kos agreed. The captain of the ship finally came to put off anyone who didn't intend to sail for the Peninsula. The ship set out toward Thegmis, and the dark came down.

Inside the walled city, in the walled palace—under it, where it stank and there was no air except what came in, as if by mistake, through tiny openings into the rare light well—the dark hardly mattered. The only light all day had come from burning lamps outside the cell. Sejanus sat with his back against the rough stones of the wall. He was fortunate. He was privileged. He had a mattress on his stone bed; he had a window, no bigger than his face and barred, that connected to an air shaft, like a chimney, that went to the surface. He wasn't chained. From time to time he walked over and pulled himself up on the bars so that he could put his face close and suck a breath of air not soggy with the smells of the prison.

When the prison keeper brought him food, he asked, he begged, for news of his brother, but the man wouldn't speak. He left the food and went away.

The Baron Erondites, in his villa surrounded by quiet fields and the occasional sound of the animals in the stable and barn, ate his dinner with absentminded pleasure, unaware of the messenger riding toward him on a fast horse. The night grew older, the dark cooled and blanketed the noises of the farm and the city alike. The Baron Erondites went to his bed, satisfied with his day. In the city, the palace grew quiet. Sejanus slept at last, as did Dite, rocked by the waves of the wine-dark sea.

In the palace infirmary, the moon shone through the arched windows. The lamp beside the only occupied bed burned with a tiny flame, and the dark gathered in the corners of the room and the recesses of the high ceilings. Relius was awake. He had heard the door on the far side of the infirmary open and close again, and he watched as the king crossed the large room toward him. His steps made no more sound than the moonlight falling through the windows, nor did the stool scrape against the floor as he settled onto it and hooked his ankle around one of its three legs. He might have been a dream, and Relius was not sure he was not.

Relius cleared his throat and whispered, "I had heard that you moved through the palace at night unattended."

"In the past, perhaps," the king admitted. "But not tonight." Lifting his head, with effort, from the pillow, Relius could make out figures in the gloom on the far side of the room.

"My punishment," said the king, "for walking in the gardens when I knew they hadn't been searched. I have promised to keep them with me."

Relius said nothing.

"I'll keep the promise until I know I can get away with breaking it," said the king. "It may be some time. She was"—he searched for a word, looked as if he might be dismissing *enraged, livid, furious,* and said— "not pleased."

Relius still said nothing. He was waiting.

The king knew. "It occurred to you some time ago that this would be a fine revenge." He lifted an arm to wave at the empty room around them. "One night here on clean sheets in the warmth of the brazier with a lamp beside you to chase the horrors away and then, in the morning, back to the cold and dark of one of those little rooms under the palace."

It was as if the king pulled the thoughts out of Relius's head on a string.

Relius had to try twice to get words out. "Is that what this is?" he whispered. He shifted his head on the pillow, searching for an answer in the king's expression.

"No."

Relius still stared without blinking. "Oh, gods," he said, and closed his eyes. He seemed to shrink beneath the bedcover.

The king agreed with what Relius left unsaid. "It is exactly what I would tell you, whether it was true or not. There is nothing I can say to keep you from lying here all night anticipating the worst. Even if you are not hauled away in the morning, you will only worry that the prison guard will be here in the afternoon, or the late watches of the next night or the next, and maybe, after enough nights have passed, you might begin to think you were safe all along. But there are hours and days and weeks of suffering between now and that point, aren't there?" His voice was quiet.

"Should I beg again for your mercy?" Relius asked, looking away.

"You should believe me," said the king more forcefully. "But you won't. Would you believe the queen? Shall I bring her here to tell you it isn't all a cruel trick?"

Relius twisted to face the king in astonishment and in horror.

"No!" The protest was surprisingly robust.

"Why not?"

"I failed her."

"You won't even ask?"

"I will never—" speaking so forcibly he was reminded of his pain and his vulnerability. He broke off.

"I thought so," said the king. "I left her to sleep and brought you this instead. She wrote it out earlier."

Eugenides lifted a roll of paper in his hand. He offered it to Relius. "You hold the bottom," he said. He laid the roll across Relius's chest. One of Relius's hands was wrapped in bandages, but he used the other to pinch the edge of the scrolled paper as the king lifted. Once it was open, the king squeezed the scroll at the top, keeping it open while he folded it and laid it on the edge of the bed. He pushed the cuff on his other arm along the fold to make a gentle crease.

He held it up again, so that Relius could see the words as he read them aloud. "I, Attolia Irene, here pardon my Secretary of the Archives, Relius, for his crimes and his failures, because of his many services to me and for the love I bear him."

Relius swallowed. Eugenides released the paper and straightened out the fold. It rolled back up.

"For the love she bears you, Relius."

"It's paper," said Relius, blinking back tears. "Put it over the bedside lamp and it will be ash."

Eugenides shook his head, but Relius's eyes were closed again, and he didn't see. "Relius," Eugenides commanded, and the Secretary of the Archives opened his eyes. "It's her word. If I drop it into a brazier, the paper will burn, but her word is not so easily consumed. She wouldn't lie to you."

Relius shook his head. "You are the king," he said.

It was his last possible denial. The king countered, "If she thought that I, as king, intended to overrule the pardon, she would never have written this. It would be a lie, and she wouldn't lie to you," he repeated.

"No," Relius said shakily, "she . . . wouldn't." His breath of relief ended with a gasp.

"I am sorry I couldn't come sooner, Relius. I did not mean to leave you alone here so long."

The king sat beside the secretary, neither of them

speaking, until Relius was asleep. When the king got up, he stood a moment, hunched over, before he straightened with an almost inaudible sigh.

In the morning, Costis skipped sword training, had a leisurely bath in the bathhouse, and went directly to breakfast in the mess hall. He picked a place by himself, but he was not alone for long. A group of other guards instantly rose and settled around him like a flock of birds. Their haste made Costis uncomfortable, but there was no way to leave without giving offense.

They wanted news and Costis was their most likely source.

"We heard that the king has had Lieutenant Sejanus arrested on some trumped-up charges." To them, he was still the loyal lieutenant.

"They weren't trumped up," Costis said, before he recalled that the charges were exactly that.

"He confessed," Costis said, but the guards had seen him waver. They looked at him so skeptically that Costis added firmly, "Sejanus attempted to kill the king."

"Don't we wish he'd succeeded," said Domisidon, a leader in the Third Century.

Costis winced. He would have agreed wholeheartedly just a few days before. Or perhaps not. He had raced to the king in the gardens before he knew that Eugenides was more than he appeared and before he knew that the queen loved him. What had shifted his opinion of the king? It might have been Costis's suspicions of Sejanus, but he thought it was more likely the king's tears, and the realization that the king, no matter how obnoxious, suffered just like any other man, from teasing without mercy, from isolation, from homesickness.

Exis was down the table, watching Costis with lifted eyebrows. Costis shrugged. "I think it is worth remembering that Sejanus is a true son of Baron Erondites."

The guards understood that. Whatever their thoughts about the king, they knew the danger that Erondites posed for their queen. "At least now we know why the queen has been pretending her affection for the king. She's made him her puppet," Exis said dryly.

"He's no one's puppet," Costis warned, but they laughed.

"You sound like his attendants," said Domisidon. "No one believes them either."

"Tell us about the attack in the garden," Exis asked. "Only you and Teleus witnessed it, and the captain won't talk."

Costis delayed. He wasn't sure why he didn't want to talk about the events in the garden. "I slept most of the afternoon yesterday. Tell me your news first."

He learned that the king hadn't gone directly to bed as he'd promised.

"What was he doing on top of Comemnus tower?" Costis asked.

"Admiring the view," someone said.

Costis recognized one of Teleus's squad from the prison cell the day before. "Did you see him?" Costis asked, too quickly. "Which way was he looking?"

The guard eyed him strangely. "I couldn't see. What difference does it make?"

"Never mind," said Costis hastily. "I'm glad you eventually got him back to his room."

"Her Majesty's rooms. It seems he is staying there."

Another guard leaned into the conversation. "I heard that he wanted to leave again, but the queen's attendants put lethium in his wine."

"I heard they put it in his food. He refused the wine and fell asleep anyway."

The guards laughed unkindly.

"So he lied," said Costis with a forced laugh. "It's what he does best."

"Well, you would know, wouldn't you?" said the man on his left.

"Tell us about the fight," someone else said, and others around the table echoed. "Tell us about the fight with the assassins."

Glancing up, Costis saw that Aristogiton had come to join them as well, a wine cup in his hand and his mouth full of bread. Costis smiled in delight. "I thought you were confined to quarters?"

Aris smiled back, his cheeks bumpy. "The queen reinstated me yesterday morning, as a squad leader still in the upper cohort, no less, at the same time that she reinstated Teleus as captain and threw out Enkelis."

"She threw out Enkelis?"

But this was old news to the guard. They wanted to hear about the assassination attempt, and they wouldn't be put off.

"Aristogiton says he arrived too late to see anything but the bodies on the ground. Tell us what really happened, Costis."

Costis reluctantly told them what he had seen of the assassination attempt, that there were three men, that the king had taken the long knife away from one of them and used it to cut the throat of another. He'd then thrown the same knife at the last assassin as he tried to escape.

"He wasn't armed himself?"

"How did he get the knife away, then?"

Costis shrugged. It hadn't been a training demonstration. There hadn't been time to observe carefully while he was running flat out toward the king. "It happened too fast."

"I see," said the man on his left.

He clearly saw something Costis didn't, by the tone of his voice, but there was no time for more conversation. A barracks boy was at his elbow with a message. Costis was commanded to appear in the queen's guardroom immediately. He got to his feet. "I have to go." He excused himself, not wanting to give offense.

"Of course you do," said someone down the table into his wine cup.

Costis hesitated. Whatever they were thinking, the men at the table clearly shared the same thoughts. Costis couldn't stay to press the matter. He would ask Aris about it later.

He had to go back to his quarters for his breastplate and his sword. Then he hurried to the queen's guardroom, where he took the sword off and racked it. An attendant who had clearly been waiting for him led him into the maze of interconnected rooms to the anteroom to the queen's bedchamber.

The queen and Ornon were there.

"What he tolerates, he does so for your sake, Your Majesty."

"What you are saying, Ambassador, is that he can be led, not driven." The queen's voice was chilly.

"Your Majesty, what I am saying is that I have never seen him driven, and rarely led either. However, if you were to twist him around your finger and could conceivably grind him under your heel in the process, you have to know that I would be eternally grateful. I would die a happy man."

The queen chuckled at this admission, and Ornon smiled, but grew quickly grave. "His health was broken, Your Majesty. His constitution is not what it was before . . ."

"Before I cut his hand off."

"Before you cut his hand off." Neither of them would mince matters. "The wound is not serious, but he will be in real danger if there is infection, and we cannot afford to have him die. Your Majesty may choose to use other measures and keep this one in reserve. It is your decision, of course." Costis doubted that this was true. Eddis held a sword at Attolia's throat, and Costis had heard that there were agreements written into the treaty that gave the ambassador certain authorities superior to the queen's.

The queen still considered.

Ornon said, "I have seen him jump across atriums four stories above the ground, a distance that would make your blood freeze, and I heard him once confess that he sometimes thinks the distance is beyond him. He always jumps, Your Majesty. The Thieves are not trained in self-preservation. I beg you would take my advice."

"You could summon them on your own authority."

"I would never presume."

He was presuming, and he wasn't going to give up until she agreed.

He smiled again. "He has accepted certain restraints;

that doesn't mean that they no longer chafe. If they come from another source, he might find them easier to bear."

"Why?"

"Mostly because he can complain about them."

The queen nodded, conceding the point.

"Then we are in agreement?"

"Very well."

Costis and the attendant stepped hastily to the side, and Costis ducked his head as the queen passed. When she was gone, he started for the doorway, and stopped when Ornon reached for his sleeve.

"Your whole goal in life is to make sure the king stays in bed. Has that been made clear, Lieutenant?"

"Yes, sir," Costis answered, wondering how the task had fallen to him, but too well trained to ask.

Ornon, smiling very slightly, answered the unasked question. "Obviously, His Majesty the king isn't going to take direction from his attendants and would probably eviscerate them for giving it. He won't take it from me either, but he might, just might, be more suggestible to your advice. If he does take offense and eviscerates you, well, then not much is lost. Politically speaking," Ornon added, "of course."

"Of course, sir," Costis said politely.

"I suggest you try anything that works to keep him in bed, including bludgeoning him. Her Majesty's attendants used lethium in his soup, but it was a short-term solution. He was up again in the middle of the night, while Her Majesty and her attendants slept. Do your best, Lieutenant, and don't worry too much if he threatens to have you executed, because if you fail, it only means that it is your queen who will have your head." Ornon patted him on the shoulder and stepped aside to allow Costis to pass.

It was apparent, even from across the room, that the king was worse off than he had been the day before. He lay in the bed with his head turned to one side. His face was pale, his normally dark skin yellowed. His eyes, when he opened them to look at Costis, were overly bright.

"What are you doing here?" he asked without lifting his head.

Costis bowed stiffly. "I am here to make sure that you stay in bed, Your Majesty, because if this offends you and you order me summarily executed, it is no loss. Politically speaking."

The king smiled. "You've been talking to Ornon."

"Yes, Your Majesty," said Costis, still stiff.

"If I get up, I suppose you will be punished?"

"So I have been told, Your Majesty."

"You needn't worry. I don't feel like dancing just at the moment. You will have a sinecure, a pathetically easy job." He yawned.

He fell asleep soon thereafter, leaving Costis somewhat relieved and simultaneously depressed as he faced another very boring watch.

The king slept most of the morning. He woke just before noon with a violent start, but if he had had a nightmare, no visions from it lingered. He ate a little soup, after poking at it suspiciously and being reassured by Phresine that it had no lethium in it, and soon went back to sleep. When he woke in the afternoon, he looked better, but Costis's relief was short-lived. The king was fretful and bored, casting dark looks at Costis out of the corner of his eye. Costis saw summary execution approaching. He could not, as Ornon had suggested, bludgeon the king over the head, and he suspected that nothing short of that would keep the king in bed much longer.

He was rescued by Phresine. She came in to sit with the king, first asking Costis to move the small upholstered chair closer to the bed. She leaned to rest a hand on the king's forehead. He sighed petulantly.

"If I asked you nicely to go away, would you?"

"No, dear. I have become very fond of the lieutenant and hate to see him saddled with an impossible task. I'll just stay a moment to be sure you aren't tiring yourself."

"By putting lethium in my food. You won't get away with that twice."

"I know," said Phresine. "It's a pity."

The king eyed her thoughtfully. "This is ridiculous, you know."

Phresine folded her hands in her lap and looked pleasant and unhelpful.

He conceded defeat. "Tell me a story, then," said the king. "Keep me occupied."

"A story?" Phresine was surprised. "What makes you think I can tell stories?"

"Insight," said the king. "Go on."

Phresine protested.

"A story, or I am getting up," threatened the king, and twitched the bedcovers aside.

Phresine, in her turn, conceded defeat. "Very well," and she smoothed the bedcovers back in place. "I have just the one in mind."

"As long as it isn't instructive."

"How do you mean, my lord?" Phresine was prim again.

"I mean I'm not appearing in this drama. I don't want to hear the story about the wayward, self-indulgent boy who learns the error of his ways and grows up to be a model of decorum and never cuts anybody's head off for spite."

Phresine smiled. "You wouldn't do such a thing, my lord."

"I might. I remember suggesting it to Eddis any number of times."

"You wouldn't do such a thing, my lord," Phresine repeated calmly.

"No, I wouldn't. I hate killing people. There's a secret

you need to keep to yourself because I will have to kill people whether I want to or not. Yet another reason no sane man would choose to be king."

Phresine looked very pained at the king's bitter humor, but only commented with a word. "Awkward."

"There you have it. Don't give me an instructive story."

"Not I," said Phresine. "Do you know the story of Klimun and Gerosthenes?"

"No."

"That's not surprising. It's a story from Kathodicia in the north, where I was raised. It's a very remote place."

"I was there."

"Really? Not many can say so."

"I was six. My grandfather took me. I don't remember anything but towers of rock."

"Well, Klimun was a king of all Kathodicia in the time before the archaic. He was a great king, a powerful ruler respected by all."

"Now I know this isn't about me."

"Hush," said Phresine, and began her story.

Klimun didn't begin as a great king. He was a prince only of his people, a Basileus, in a small valley surrounded by rolling hills. In the Kathodicia, young men as well as young women visit the temple of the moon when they have reached their majority. They leave offerings on the altar there, and depending on the young man, they ask a favor of the goddess or make a demand.

Phresine smiled and gave an example: "O Goddess, I have brought you a silver plate, so you must make all of my ewes bear twins this season."

Klimun was not an Annux, not a king over other princes yet, and as I said, his city was not a powerful one. On the contrary, it was on an evening when there was starvation and sickness and death among his people that Klimun made his way up the sacred path by moonlight to the temple.

His city had been fighting with the surrounding cities for many years. Outside its walls, the fields had been stripped bare by passing armies and the olive groves were nothing but stumps. Fields can be reseeded every year, but there is little point in planting trees that will be cut down before they grow old enough to bear fruit. So, where there is no peace, there are no trees. Inside, the city was filled with slaves taken after Kathodicia's victories, but so many times had Kathodicia suffered defeats, and so many of her citizens were serving out their lives as slaves in other cities, that Kathodicians were scarce inside their own walls.

All the cities nearby were the same. Their fields produced little, and their orchards nothing. When they ran out of food, they looked for others to steal from. The people in the weakest cities starved. So all the cities sacrificed to their patron gods and goddesses, begging for their favors to make them victorious over their enemies. Everyone expected that when Klimun went to the temple, he would do the same and promise the goddess that every city they defeated they would sack for treasures to fill her temple. He didn't.

Suppliants usually brought silver to the temple of the moon, or pure white cloth. Sometimes they brought expensive perfumes, but by and large they brought things in silver or white to please the taste of the goddess. Klimun brought a tree. He brought the sapling of an olive and placed it in the open center of the temple where the moon shone down on it.

The goddess, to whom no one had ever given a tree, came down with the moonlight for a closer look. The moon was young that night, and she appeared as a girl nearly Klimun's age. She had shone on him in the past, and seen what her light had revealed in him.

"Most people bring me more precious gifts, Basileus," she said.

"O Goddess," said Klimun, "I have brought you the most precious silver in my city. The silver leaves of the olive. Like all suppliants at your altar, I come begging a favor. Please, Goddess, make me a good leader for my people. Let me bring them peace, and I swear I will cover the hills around the city with silver, in your honor. Everywhere the moon shines around the city it will strike the silver leaves of the olive, I promise."

She considered the empty hills around the city and the rows of broken stumps. "It would be pretty," she said aloud, "covered in trees." She told Klimun, "Very well, cover the hills with olive groves, and I will bring the peace they need *to live. But you will have to free the first captive that you see when you leave the temple, and never let the moonlight find you telling a lie. Failing that, your olives will be razed and your city, too."*

Klimun agreed. He waited out the night at her altar, and, in the morning, walked back down the sacred path. The sun was not yet over the horizon, and the road was still dark between the trees. He heard a shout and rushed into the bushes, where he saw a slave—

"I knew I would be in this story somewhere," Eugenides interjected.

"Oh, no," said Phresine, "this was a humble slave."

"Ouch."

"Though very courageous."

"Not me," whispered Eugenides to his pillow.

"Shhh."

The slave was struggling with some animal. Klimun drew his sword before he realized that one of his own hunting dogs had somehow gotten itself entangled in a snare. It was frightened and enraged, snarling at the slave as the slave worked to free it. While Klimun watched, the cord around the dog's neck snapped. Klimun was fond of the dog and wished he had seen it first, not the slave. The dog was certainly more valuable, but he remembered his word to the goddess. He struck with his sword and killed the dog as it went for the slave's throat.

Klimun freed the slave, who was named Gerosthenes, and told him he could go home. But Gerosthenes's family was long

dead, and there was no home for him to go to. He was grate-
ful to Klimun for his life as well as for his freedom, and he
said he would stay and serve the prince for the rest of his life.

"And that is different from being a slave in what way?" Eugenides asked.

"I think the difference lies in the choice," Phresine said gently.

The king looked away.

"One more interruption, and you won't hear the rest of the story," she warned him.

"Yes, Phresine."

"Good."

As she took a breath to speak, he said, "Have I mentioned that I am king?"

She exhaled in exasperation. "And I am an old woman, and boys with fevers who want to hear a story shouldn't interrupt, king or not."

"I'm not a boy," said Eugenides, sounding like one.

"A boy," said Phresine, "and your wife just a babe herself to an old woman like me."

Eugenides grunted in disagreement, but was then, at last, quiet, and Phresine went on.

Perhaps even Klimun didn't know why Gerosthenes
would choose to stay with him, but he was glad of it. He
liked Gerosthenes, and the two quickly became friend and
friend, not master and servant. Klimun was a very good
leader, and he was true to his promise to the goddess. He
immediately began the replanting of the olive groves and he

invited the princes of neighboring cities to discuss a peace. If he wasn't wholly truthful, he was truthful by and large, because one cannot tell a lie during the day and be sure that it won't come home to roost in the evening. The other princes found that he was honest and that he could be relied upon.

As he proved himself to his allies, his reputation for honesty and true dealing grew, and the peace among the cities grew as well. Not all of the cities, of course, but peace held well enough that the olive trees grew higher and higher and the year came nearer when they would begin bearing fruit.

The goddess's stricture lay very lightly on Klimun. He was honest by nature and, after many years, honest by habit as well. I don't suppose he had to remind himself very often about his promise to the goddess, and after a time, he began to forget it. I am not saying he started to choose lies over truth; on the contrary, he was honest in his dealing with princes and with paupers. He was kind and he was generous. I am just saying that as the days and years slipped by, he forgot his initial reason for hewing so close to an honest course. Ever since the gods created the world, mortals have been forgetting from where their blessings come.

But the gods make their bargains for a reason, and they do not forget. Not in ten years, not in twenty, not in a lifetime. Every night the moon shone her light on the earth, it bathed Klimun especially bright. She watched him, waiting for him to break his word.

The king, lying on the bed, listening to Phresine, looked uncomfortable, but he didn't speak.

Now, in the year when the olive trees were near to bearing fruit, there was a new prince in one of the nearby cities, the city of Atos. The Basileus of Atos had died, and it was his only son who had come to power. The old prince had made a few treaties with neighboring cities, but he had never brought his son to the bargaining table, and no one knew if this young man would stir up old troubles the way some young men do.

Klimun decided that he would have a look at this young prince and see for himself if he was a danger. He decided to go to Atos and wander among its people. If they talked about war and vengeance, then Klimun would know what sort of man led them. If they talked of peace and their harvest, Klimun would know they followed the lead of their prince and that he would be a good man. If he saw the prince himself, he would know how the young man treated his citizens. That was the way to learn the most, he thought.

The harvest festival was coming soon. It would be a good time for a stranger to wander through a city without drawing attention. So Klimun, taking only Gerosthenes with him, set out. He arrived in good time for the festival. Once he was there, he told everyone he was a farmer and that his farm was just beyond the border of the land that the city controlled. He was no citizen of the town, he explained, and he was unsure of his welcome, but the townspeople were good to strangers, and they welcomed him to the festival. He drank wine with new friends and asked them what they thought of their prince. "See him for yourself," he was told at the wine bar. "He will judge the wrestling contest."

Klimun was no longer a very young man, but he was still young enough to enjoy a wrestling contest, and he decided to enter this one. He won all of his early matches. In the afternoon, he won again, until there was only one match left before he reached the laurels. The new prince judged the final match, and Klimun was able to get a good look at him. He seemed proud, but he judged fairly when he could have cheated and allowed his own citizen to win. Some people might have been angry to see a stranger win the city's prize, but the prince didn't seem offended when he awarded the match to Klimun, and the laurels as well. The prince went back to his pavilion, and Klimun, for his labors, received an amphora of wine and an invitation to join the prince for the evening meal.

Now, it dawned on Klimun that it would be hard to sit down with the prince for a meal, and expect the prince not to know him when they eventually met again. The prince might well be angry at being deceived. So Klimun made hasty excuses, found Gerosthenes in the crowd, and the two slipped out of the city as quickly as they could. They had hurried some ways beyond the fields of the city when they came across an old woman on the road. She told them that a horse and rider had recently passed, and in her hurry to get off the road, she'd dropped all the coins she had earned that day selling cakes at the festival. They were there somewhere in the dirt of the road, but the light was failing, and so were her eyes. She begged Klimun and Gerosthenes for their help.

Klimun judged they were well away from the city of Atos, and they stopped to help her look for her money.

They were still looking for the coins on the road when they heard horsemen. They stood at the verge and waited for the horsemen to pass, but the riders swept up and pulled their mounts to a stop. The horses' hooves stamped in the dust, and the horseman in the lead spoke.

"Our prince wishes to know why a man would decline an invitation to eat with him. So we have come looking for the farmer who won the amphora at the city today to ask him why he left so hastily. Are you that farmer?" He was looking pointedly at the amphora in Gerosthenes's hand.

This was a difficulty indeed. Standing in the deep twilight by the road, Klimun racked his brains for a story to tell. Perhaps there was a shrewish wife who wanted him home. Perhaps she didn't know he'd left and he must make it back to his farm before she was undeceived. At all cost, he must think of a reason not to go back to the prince. He didn't notice that since they had paused to look for the old woman's coins, the evening had grown not darker, but brighter. The moon had come up, it had cleared the horizon behind him, but Klimun didn't see it, and he never thought of the bargain he had made with the goddess of the moon.

"Phresine," said Eugenides, looking uncomfortable. "I should have stipulated a story with a happy ending. I don't like this one. Tell me a different one."

Phresine ignored him. The king set his jaw, but he listened.

Now, Gerosthenes, standing with the amphora in his arms, was facing the horizon where the moon had crept into the sky. He remembered Klimun's promise, but what could he do? Klimun had gathered himself to speak. His mouth was open, and the words were on their way from heart to tongue. Gerosthenes could hardly shout, "My prince, don't lie." Horrified, he knew there was nothing he could say.

"Phresine . . ." The king looked genuinely unhappy. Costis didn't believe for a moment there had ever been a real Klimun, or a real Gerosthenes. He looked at Phresine for some understanding of the king's distress, but Phresine was looking into space and seemed unaware of the king's unhappiness.

"So," she said, "Gerosthenes hit Klimun over the head with the amphora."

"Ha," the king snorted in relief. Phresine affected not to notice this any more than his earlier distress. She continued.

Well, this was a surprise to more people than Klimun. It was the Prince Atos himself who nudged his horse forward from the back of the group of horsemen and asked why Klimun's friend had wasted an amphora of their best wine on Klimun's head.

Klimun was wondering that himself. He looked at Gerosthenes, who looked at the moon. Klimun followed his gaze and turned to see the moon over his shoulder.

"I see that you are enlightened," said the young prince. "Do please enlighten us as well."

Seeing no other choice before him, Klimun did so. "My friend has most earnestly recommended that I remember a vow I have taken never to lie by moonlight, and to tell you truthfully that I am Klimun, Basileus of Kathodicia, that I came here in secret to see the new prince of this city and judge him by his behavior among his people."

"And what was your judgment?" the young prince asked.

"You are proud, but fair, and I do not think you are a warmonger."

"I'm flattered," said the prince.

"You may be flattered, but I am no flatterer," said Klimun, "at least not by moonlight."

"Then I think you are what my father said I should value above all others, a man I can trust, and we should be allies," said the prince.

"Then I would be both flattered and honored," said Klimun, "but I am not sure that I am worthy of your trust." Humbly he turned to the old woman, still standing nearby, and said, "Goddess, I have broken my promise to you. If not for the action of my friend, I would have lied. I believe your olives and my city are forfeit," he said sadly.

"You told no lie," said the goddess, for goddess she was, as both Gerosthenes and Klimun had realized.

"But I would have lied."

"Your friend prevented you."

"Yes." Klimun agreed, but saw only that he had been tried and found wanting.

"If you were not the man you promised to be, all these

years, he would not have been your friend, here in your moment of need. I do not think the moonlight has uncovered anything it should not have seen," she said gravely, and then she was gone, leaving Klimun very relieved and a group of horsemen awaiting an explanation.

"Thank you, Phresine," said the king, humbly.

"Thank me by eating some more soup and sleeping for a while."

"Will there be poppy juice in it?"

Phresine shook her head.

"Good. My wife and I agreed that only my wine was to be poisoned."

Phresine went to fetch him more soup.

By the time the king had eaten a little, he admitted he was tired and slept again. Costis was grateful. In the late afternoon, the queen came to sit with the king and sent Costis to the guardroom. Teleus arrived with the change of the guard and told Costis he could go.

The air was heavy as Costis crossed the large open courtyard behind the public rooms of the palace. Costis stifled a yawn, surprised at how tired he could feel after doing nothing all day. From the courtyard, he cut through the breezeway that connected the front part of the palace to the complicated collection of buildings that made up the residential portion of the palace for the court. There was a passage at the east end that bypassed the public rooms and led to a terrace. From the terrace, one could go by steep staircases down to the barracks and the training grounds of the Royal Guard.

Sleepy and hot, he stepped around the broken pieces of several roof tiles that must have fallen from somewhere high above the terrace. There was a crash like a crockery jar exploding behind him, and he jumped forward out of the way of the next batch of tiles that slid down. He looked back at the mess on the terrace, thought longingly of an afternoon nap, and went instead to report the fall to the palace secretary in charge of roofs.

Thoroughly awake after that, and hungry, he headed for the mess hall. The guard who had sat at his left earlier in the day was sitting at a table alone, and he waved for Costis to join him. Costis, after pouring himself a glass of wine, did so.

Domisidon, sitting nearby, looked up, saw Costis, and said, "The king's lapdog arrives."

The guard beside Costis laughed, then stopped. "I'm sorry, Costis, it isn't your fault. What happens to you now, do you know?"

Costis thought. "I have no idea. I was pretty much done being a fake lieutenant. I thought they might farm me out to a border fort—maybe when Prokep came down from the north. I guess that might still happen."

"But you've saved the king's life?"

"Not really," said Costis. "He mostly did that himself."

"Of course. I forgot."

They thumped him on the shoulder and elbowed him good-naturedly. But there was something behind the good nature, not condescension, commiseration perhaps. He didn't want to ask outright what they meant by their pity. He was afraid he knew the answer, and he didn't like it. Costis excused himself and went to look for Aristogiton.

In the night, Relius woke, gripped by sudden terror. The infirmary around him was dark, the high ceilings lost beyond the glimmer of the night candle by his bed, the heavy air around him silent. Under the light pressure of the sheet and thin blanket, he was rigid with fear, and he had to close his eyes to fight the impulse to thrash his way free of the covers, of the bed, and of the infirmary. There was no escape, no hope of escape. It was an emotion beyond rational thought, and not until the king spoke did Relius realize he was not alone.

"It's the dog watch of the night," the king said softly.

Relius gasped and opened his eyes to see the king sitting in the low chair near the foot of the bed. As he watched, the king stood, and hooked the chair with his foot to slide it closer to Relius's head and sat again.

His statement seemed at first irrelevant, but it wasn't.

The dog watch of the night was a bad time for those haunted by nightmares. The king had to know that for himself.

Relius lifted his head briefly. The king turned to follow his gaze to the silent group of attendants near the door. He turned back to look down at Relius with a bitter smile that was gone almost as soon as it appeared and was replaced by an expression of surprising calm. He sat quietly by the bed as Relius, through sheer will-power, steadied his breathing and relaxed his body. The darkness around them became slowly less threatening.

"Why save me, Your Majesty?" Relius asked softly.

"You think it was a mistake?"

Relius opened his mouth and shut it again.

"You want to say yes and no at the same time," the king guessed.

"I am having trouble separating my own self-interest from that of my queen," Relius admitted, sounding a little pedantic and apologetic about it.

"You sound like Sounis's magus. He had a similar problem once."

"The risk that you take is too great," Relius said, "and you gain nothing by pardoning me."

"The greatest risk was to the queen, and the risk lay in your death, not your pardon."

Relius puzzled over this, and the king gave in to exasperation.

"You don't know what I mean. She is so strong, and

you assume that strength has no end, no breaking point. You and Teleus are among the few she still trusts enough to love, and you say yes, she should have you tortured and killed. What were you thinking?"

"If she pardons people because she loves them, someday someone that she loves will betray her and all of Attolia with her. A queen must make sacrifices for the common good," Relius said.

"And if what she sacrifices is her heart? Giving it up a piece at a time until there is nothing left? What do you have then, Relius, but a heartless ruler? And what becomes of the common good then?"

"The queen could never be heartless."

"No," said the king. "She would die herself, Relius, or lose her mind first and then her heart. Could you not see it happening? Or is your faith in her strength really so blind? Everyone has a breaking point. Yet you never stop demanding more of her."

Relius was quiet while he thought. "And yours? I thought we found your breaking point."

Eugenides winced, but he responded with a self-deprecating noise. "Ornon says, Ornon-who-always-has-something-to-say says, the Thieves of Eddis don't have breaking points. We have flash points instead, like gunpowder. That's what makes us dangerous."

"You don't like Ornon," said Relius.

"I wouldn't say that."

"Because you don't like to speak the truth?"

Eugenides made a wry face. "Ornon and I have a great deal of hard-won respect for each other," said the king.

"Won how?"

"Well, he almost managed to avert a war. I've heard he did a splendid job of working the queen up to killing me on the spot when she caught me. If it hadn't been for the Mede Ambassador's timely and provoking interruption, I would have been safely dead, and there wouldn't have been a great deal of blood shed."

"You've heard?" Relius asked.

"I wasn't there for Ornon's part."

He'd been puking on the wet floor of a cell of the queen's prison. Not far from where Relius himself had been.

"Ornon's respect for you?" Relius asked, taking the conversation back to a less perilous topic.

The king only smiled. "Even ex-Thieves don't spill their secrets, Relius."

He left a little later. Relius lay alone with his thoughts. What kind of man, he wondered, referred to himself as "safely dead"?

The king, passing through the guardroom and back to the queen's bedroom, asked, "Where's Costis?"

"He was released at the end of the afternoon watch."

"By whom? I didn't give him leave to go."

"The queen sent him to the guardroom, Your Majesty."

"Then why isn't he here?"

"The captain dismissed him at the end of the after-noon watch."

"I want him."

"The captain?"

"No, you idiot—" He broke off as the queen appeared in a doorway opposite. "You're awake," he said.

"Phresine is not," pointed out the queen.

"Oh?"

"You gave her lethium."

"She gave it to me first."

The queen looked at him, eyes narrowed, and said nothing. He waved at his attendants. "I dragged them like a ball and chain all the way across the palace and back."

"If sterner measures are called for, we can find a larger ball and chain." The queen turned and disappeared into the apartment.

"Oh, dear," Eugenides muttered as he followed, without sending for Costis after all. The queen's sterner measures, dispensed by the Eddisian Ambassador, arrived before dawn.

Costis wasn't in uniform, he wasn't even particularly clean, when he learned the next morning that he had been sent for. He had checked the duty schedule the evening before when he was hunting for Aristogiton and couldn't find him. Aris had been on duty. Costis was assigned no duties for the foreseeable future, and he had enjoyed a quiet morning pottering around in his own room, giving his sword and breastplate and the assorted shiny bits of his uniform a thorough cleaning. He had polishing grease on his nose and his fingers were black when someone slid back the leather curtain across his doorway without knocking on the door frame first.

When Costis lifted his head from the sword he was cleaning, prepared to be angry at the intrusion, he found no lowly barracks boy in the doorway. It was Ion, one of the king's elegant and carefully turned-out attendants.

Ion, looking far from elegant, stared at him in horror. "Get dressed. Get clean. You are supposed to be in the queen's guardroom."

"When?" asked Costis, getting to his feet.

"Now," said the attendant, "hours ago. You were supposed to be there when the king asked for you just now. He said he wanted you last night, but we didn't think he meant it."

"And now he's angry?"

"Now the queen is angry."

Moving fast, Costis tipped water from a pitcher into a bowl and began to scrub his face.

The queen was waiting in the antechamber to the bedroom. As before, she had Ornon with her. They were both waiting. She stood as Costis entered. No, Costis thought, she didn't stand. She rose—like a thundercloud towering in the summer sky. He could try to explain that he hadn't known he was supposed to remain on duty, and that he'd been dismissed by the captain himself. He could also rush back to the guardroom, snatch his sword out of the rack, and throw himself down on it. Likely with the same results.

"You will not leave the apartment without royal permission," commanded the queen. "You will eat and sleep here. You will remain in the king's presence until he dismisses you, and you will endeavor in every way to ingratiate yourself sufficiently that he does not dismiss you."

"Yes, Your Majesty."

"Ornon"—her eyes flicked to the Eddisian Ambassador briefly—"believes the experience will be instructive. Try to learn something."

"Yes, Your Majesty." The queen watched him for a moment. She offered this opening, if there was anything else Costis wanted to say. But Costis was silent. Seeing himself in her eyes, he remembered what he hadn't thought of in days, not since the assassination— that he was a lieutenant in name only, and what had brought him to this place at this time in the royal apartment was his failure, failure to keep his temper, failure to keep his oath. Failure to do his duty. He had nothing to say.

The queen left, followed by Ornon. Shaking, Costis went to the door of the bedchamber to find the king.

Two men in Eddisian uniform sat in chairs by the window. They had pulled a small table over and were casting dice on the inlaid wooden top. Costis eyed them suspiciously as the king repeated what the queen had just told Costis in the anteroom. The king sat in bed, surrounded by papers and vellum sheets spread in haphazard patterns. There was an open leather mail pouch incongruously rough on the soft embroidered cloth of the spread.

"I have more company than I need," said the king. "You can go to the guardroom."

Costis cleared his throat uncomfortably. "The queen said I should stay."

"And no doubt, you are therefore afraid to go. I would be, too. Stay, then, and I shall introduce you to Aulus and Boagus, my dear relatives, who have joined me to while away my convalescence."

Costis couldn't help wondering if these were the cousins that had held him down in the rainwater cache. "Watch out for Aulus," the king warned acidly. "Like the bull he resembles, he has been known to crush people with a single misstep."

Aulus eyed the king for a moment without comment, then rose from his chair. Aulus, Costis realized, was *huge*. He hadn't appeared so large when he was sitting, but standing up, he seemed to almost fill the room. He loomed over the king as he bent to collect the papers and reports on the bed.

The king pinned a paper to the spread with his hook. "I am reading that!" he insisted. Aulus took no notice. He merely pulled the paper until it tore free. He put the shredded piece onto the stack he had built and shoveled the entire stack into the messenger pouch. Then he looked at the king and lifted a single admonishing finger as thick as the haft on a hand ax.

"I told you. One more nasty comment and it would be time for a nap." His accent was thick enough to cut with a knife, and it seemed to add a syllable to every word.

"You cannot keep me in bed!"

"Of course I can," said Aulus calmly. "A damn sight easier than I can get you to do anything else. I'll lie down on top of the covers on this side. Boagus can lie on the other. You'll be trapped like a kitten in a sack, and before you can work out a suitable revenge, Boagus and I will be safely posted to a distant and very invisible location, far beyond the reach of his royal petulance the King of Attolia." He nodded significantly. "Ornon promised."

The king stared dumbfounded, then attempted to reason. "I have important—"

"Gen," Aulus interrupted. "You've been reading since the sun came up. You're ragged, and you need a rest."

Eugenides glanced at Costis. Costis straightened,

prepared to defend his king to the death against this huge Eddisian nanny.

Aulus sighed wearily. "Gen. Go to sleep."

The king grudgingly slipped down under the covers. To Costis's awed delight, the enormous Eddisian actually straightened the covers and tucked them in.

Aulus went back to the window, but didn't begin the dice game again. He whistled a quiet tune Costis didn't recognize, filled with long, soothing notes. Before the second repetition of the tune, the king was asleep.

Boagus got up to check on him, hanging over him for a long time and watching him carefully. Finally he nodded at Aulus and stepped back to his chair. He and Aulus made themselves comfortable, both putting their boots up on the small wooden table, negotiating wordlessly how four feet might be simultaneously squeezed onto it. Then they closed their eyes like professional soldiers who know better than to miss a chance for rest, and appeared to fall asleep themselves.

When Costis moved, just shifting his weight from one foot to the other, not only one but both of the Eddisians opened an eye to look him over. Costis didn't move again. The king slept until the watch trumpets blew their noon fanfare. When he'd eaten, Aulus let him have his reports back.

In the afternoon, apropos of nothing, Aulus said, "I heard you were scared white by your jailer yesterday."

Gen did not look up from what he was reading. "That would be Ornon talking again," he said.

"Yes," said Aulus, smiling.

"No," said the king, looking up at last. "I was not scared white by one of my jailers."

He looked down—pretended to go back to what he was reading, but didn't. Instead he fiddled with the nubs of the embroidery on the bedcover. Boagus opened his mouth, but at a signal from Aulus, he shut it again. They waited. Aulus appeared to be willing to wait forever.

"I nearly had them killed, every single one of them, garroted, gutted, and dead."

Costis remembered the sick look on the king's face and the sudden long silence in the cell.

"Your captain, too?" Aulus asked.

"Oh, certainly. He would have been first in line." He pushed his hand through his hair. "I told him I can do anything I want," he admitted.

"Ahh," said Aulus, "I suppose he thought that was the King of Attolia talking?"

"I suppose he did."

Boagus shook his head. "You really can do anything you want, now." Eugenides's glare made him throw up his hands in the air and add hastily, "Not that you couldn't always."

Aulus chuckled. "If I had a gold coin for every time I heard you say that you could do anything you wanted, I'd be rich," he said, "as rich as—" He searched for an appropriate comparison.

"As Ornon before he lost all his sheep," Boagus finished for him. The two soldiers laughed, and even the king smiled. Reinforcing Costis's suspicion that Eugenides had been responsible for Ornon's lost sheep, Boagus asked, "Do you still baa like a lamb when he walks into the room?"

Eugenides shook his head. "Ornon took me aside first thing after the coronation ceremony and explained that it would be beneath my dignity."

Aulus and Boagus stared. Eugenides's expression was bland.

"He said that?" Aulus asked.

"He did," the king confirmed.

"What did you say?" Boagus asked suspiciously.

"I promised to bark like a sheepdog instead."

The Eddisians chuckled again.

"You don't, though?" Aulus had to ask.

The king eyed him with disgust. "Give me some credit," he said, and when Aulus was visibly relieved, added, "Not when anybody else can hear me."

The Eddisians roared.

The king laughed more quietly, holding his hand against his side. Even Costis smiled. He quickly straightened the smile. It wasn't his place to laugh with the king, but he was pleased all the same.

A figure appeared suddenly in the doorway. Costis's

hand went to his empty sword belt. Aulus and Boagus crouched forward in their seats and then relaxed. The figure was Ornon. Squelched laughter leaked out like the flames of a poorly snuffed candle.

"Ambassador Ornon," said Eugenides in a slightly choked voice. "How good of you to drop by."

"I believe you have been having a joke at my expense, Your Majesty," Ornon said, crossing the room to sit in a chair by the fire screen.

"We wouldn't dream of it, Ambassador."

"I am so relieved. I might have to suggest a celebration to mark your return to health. A day of special audiences, perhaps." As the king's expression changed he added, "A royal parade?"

"You wouldn't."

"Well, I do think it would be a fine way to reassure the populace, but not if Your Majesty disliked it."

"Thank you. I dislike it very much. My apologies if we have offended you."

"Not at all." Ornon's dry smile registered points scored on either side, then faded. "If you are done laughing, send your keepers away. I am afraid I have news."

"Bad news?"

Ornon shrugged. "Good for our hopes of peace and a unified triumvirate to stand against the Mede. Bad news," he said gently, "for the heir of Sounis."

Laughter gone, the king said, "They have his body, then?"

"No. Not yet. But we have reports that Sounis is retaking the countryside. If the rebels had him alive as a hostage, they would have said so by now."

"I see."

Ornon signaled the Eddisians. "Perhaps you would excuse us?"

The king waved Costis out of the room as well.

Costis followed the looming bulk of Aulus out of the bedchamber and through the anteroom and from there to a waiting room filled with the paraphernalia of women—embroidery stands, sewing tables, a harp, and, looking uncomfortably out of place, the king's attendants. The queen's attendants were nowhere to be seen, displaced by the men who had little to do to serve their king and instead sat kicking their heels. They looked at the Eddisians and at Costis with hostile eyes.

"There is a guardroom," said one of the attendants pointedly as Aulus settled into a chair.

"There is a guardroom, Your Highness, I am sure you meant to say," said Aulus as he leaned back and hooked a table closer with one booted foot and then rested the foot on top of it. Both chair and table creaked alarmingly. "I'm sure it's a very nice guard-room."

He smiled. The attendants took his meaning. They looked as if they thought Aulus might be pulling wool over their eyes, but none of them had the nerve to call what might not be a bluff.

Costis didn't think it was a bluff. Aulus looked very little like a prince, but that meant nothing—Eugenides didn't look like a king. Ornon needed someone to sit with the king and restrain him, someone who would be safe from Eugenides's retaliation. A prince of the house of Eddis would be a natural choice if there was one on hand. No prince of Attolia would serve as a common soldier, but that also might be different in Eddis. Costis didn't think Eddis had any brothers, but this might be a close cousin of Eddis's and a prince of the house.

Costis realized that the entire room was now looking rather pointedly at him. He wasn't a baron, or the heir of a baron, or a prince. What was he doing in the waiting room? The king's attendants clearly thought he should go. Trying to look as if he really didn't care what they thought, he looked toward Aulus for his opinion.

"Huh," said Aulus. "That's a good question." He turned to Boagus. "Go ask what Gen wants done with his pet guard."

Boagus went and came back. "He said he wants Costis in the guardroom round the clock. He says you can go to hell."

"Are you Costis?" Aulus asked.

Costis nodded.

"Off you go, then," said Aulus. Costis went. As he started for the door, Aulus bellowed, "Go to hell yourself, you silly bastard." The knickknacks on the table almost seemed to rattle. The attendants looked pained.

As Costis stepped through the door, he caught a glimpse of one of the queen's attendants looking through the doorway from another room. She was equally pained.

Costis spent the rest of the afternoon in the guard-room, feeling no more welcome than in the attendants' waiting room. He'd expected to be greeted when he arrived. He nodded to the lieutenant on duty. The lieutenant looked right through him. Puzzled, Costis had looked around the room at the men standing on guard at the door and at the others in more relaxed poses around the room. No one met his eyes. Men who'd seemed comfortable working with him a few days earlier looked away. Shrugging, Costis picked a spot on a padded bench and sat. He was off duty, even if he couldn't leave.

Teleus came through the guardroom later and stopped to speak to him. No one else had all afternoon. Teleus only asked what the king's orders were, and then he left. Dinner was brought up for the attendants. When they were finished, Costis ate what he suspected were leftovers alone in a makeshift dining room. They were nice leftovers, at least, better than he would have eaten in the mess hall. Phresine showed him where he could sleep, in an interior room with no windows, a narrow bed, and a washstand. There were chests stacked along one wall, and Costis guessed the dismal spot was probably a closet cleaned out to make room for him. Hard to believe the royal apartments, so lavish elsewhere, would otherwise have such a plain corner. Expecting better of royal closets, Costis went to bed disappointed.

In the morning, stiff from a poor night's sleep, he shaved and washed as well as he could in the fresh water brought to the washstand, then presented himself to the king. He arrived in the middle of an argument.

"I am not interested in one of your moon promises," Aulus was saying.

"It doesn't really matter if you believe me," said the king. "I am throwing you out. The promise was just a sop to keep your feelings from being hurt."

"And if we refuse to go?"

Boagus was cleaning his fingernails with a knife.

"I have a whole guardroom full of brawny veterans who'd enjoy a chance to drag two Eddisians out of here, particularly if you kicked a lot and they could kick you back."

Aulus shook his head sadly. "I'm disappointed."

"Well, I am fed up. Get out."

Aulus considered, then leaned back in the chair. It squealed in agonized protest. "Noontime. When the watch trumpets blow. We'll leave then."

"Oh? I shall magically be healed then, and you won't need to hang over me like an anxious cow? What of any significance is going to be different at noon?"

Aulus crossed his arms across his chest and said, "Ornon will owe me three gold queens."

The king's brow cleared. "I see. Very well. You leave at noon."

"And . . . ," said Aulus.

"If you aren't leaving until noon, there isn't going to be any 'and.'"

"And," Aulus insisted, "you keep your pet Costis with you. If you break your promise to rest easy, he will send a message to the queen, who will pass it to Ornon, who will send for us."

He looked at Costis to see if he accepted the responsibility. Costis, in turn, looked at the king. The king said, "I thought you and Boagus were heading for some unnamed post in the hinterlands."

"Soon," Aulus assured him.

The Eddisians left at noon. Costis stayed. The king smiled at him occasionally, but otherwise ignored him. He read papers and wrote things out on a lap desk. He called in people to speak to him, and when he did, he sent Costis into the anteroom and asked him to close the door. He called Costis his watchdog when the queen visited. The queen actually smiled at Costis, which warmed Costis right down to his toes.

After another solitary meal, Costis went back to his closet and to bed. He woke in the dark to knocking on the door. The king was leaving and, in keeping with his promise, had sent for Costis.

Relius was relieved. The king was apologetic.

"I couldn't be here last night," the king said as he settled onto the stool.

"Teleus told me this afternoon that you had Eddisian visitors." One night apart had elided their community, and the exchange of small talk was awkward.

"One particularly large one sitting in my room all night. How is your hand?"

"Fine," Relius answered automatically, then flinched. His hand hurt, the swelling gross, though the bones were now set. At least it was still on the end of his arm. The king's hand was gone.

"Relius," the king spoke softly. "I should have been here last night. I am sorry."

"There is little reason for you to take such care, Your Majesty."

The king put his hand on Relius's shoulder, his only hand, Relius couldn't help thinking. "You're being stupid. She was within her rights. So were you."

"How can you think that?" *Safely dead.*

"Well, it's something like a tenet of my profession. When you fail, and failure is inevitable, you pay the penalty."

"But me you pardoned."

"You aren't a member of my profession." It was too glib. He sighed. "Maybe I should have said that if you fail, you must be willing to pay the penalty. You were willing, Relius. That's what I went to that cell to find out. As to the actual payment of penalties, you have no idea how many times my cousin, who is Eddis, rescued me from well-deserved agonies. What else did you and Teleus talk about?"

Relius let him change the subject. "He's angry about Costis."

"I'm not happy myself." The king checked to see if their voices carried to the far side of the room. "So, I have something to ask you."

In the morning, Costis was cautiously optimistic. Even with the midnight excursion, the king seemed better. The circles under his eyes had faded, and his color was improved. In the afternoon, he was sitting in the sun at the window warmly wrapped in an embroidered robe when the queen arrived. Costis stiffened to a more precise form of attention, but the king didn't appear to notice the opening and closing door. Attolia brushed her hand along his shoulders, and he turned to smile at her, but then turned back to the view.

"Homesick?" she asked.

"Thinking of Sophos."

"I see."

"Is there news?"

Attolia shook her head, dropping gently into a chair beside him.

"Ornon said there would be if he were alive."

"Most likely," said Attolia. "You were fond of him?"

The king shrugged. "He was very likable—Eddis would have married him."

"Do you know whom she will marry now?"

"Sounis, I suppose."

"But she hates Sounis," said the queen.

"She is the Queen of Eddis. Queens make sacrifices."

Attolia was quiet, then. "She would have been happy with Sophos?" she asked softly.

"I think so. They had exchanged a number of letters."

"I never understood why she didn't marry you."

The king settled further into the seat with a snort. "Maybe the prospect of being driven out of her mind put her off," he said.

The queen smiled. "What did she see in Sophos, then?"

It took the king some time to find an answer. "He was kind," he said at last.

"And you're not?" Attolia responded sharply.

Finally the king turned to look at her, his eyebrows raised in amusement. He shook his head.

"No," she observed thoughtfully. "You aren't, are you?" Then she dropped her eyes in a mocking imitation of demurral and said, "You've always been kind to me."

The king laughed out loud. He held out his arm, and she leaned against him.

"What a lie *that* was," he said.

Of course, the king was kind. Costis would be dead if he weren't. And the queen wouldn't love him, if he was unkind to her. Costis was puzzling through the convolutions of human relationships, which were so unlike the neatly arranged patterns in a fireside story, when a light touch at his sleeve made him turn. Phresine was trying to close the door. He looked from Phresine to the king and queen and, flushing, stepped back into the anteroom. Phresine pulled the door closed, leaving the king and the queen alone.

Costis didn't see the king again until the next morning. He arrived at the bedchamber door just as he had the day before, and found two of the king's attendants, Ion and Sotis, waiting there. Ion opened the door, and smiled unpleasantly as Costis passed through. Sotis cleared his throat to announce Costis's arrival, and the king looked up from the papers he was reading. He was fully dressed and sitting on top of the bedcovers.

"What are you doing here?" he asked.

It was like a kick in the gut, leaving Costis dumb, and he hesitated in confusion.

"I don't need you. I am officially recovered," the king said. "You can go back to your regular duties." After a moment he looked pointedly at the door behind Costis, and numbly, Costis withdrew. Ion closed the door behind him, and in the anteroom, Sotis assiduously studied the braid on his cuff as Costis passed by.

Between the anteroom and the queen's guardroom, Costis considered what his "regular duties" were and decided he didn't have any. Certainly he didn't have any that involved remaining at loose ends in the queen's guardroom under the hostile gaze of its veterans. He went through the guardroom and all the way through the palace, back to his own room without stopping. He flung off his armor, kicking the breastplate under the bed and then cursing the pain in his toes. Breathing heavily, he forced himself to drag the breastplate back out and hang it carefully in its accustomed place, and tidied away the rest of his duty armor. Then, in less formal dress, he went to the mess hall. Perhaps his mates would be less hostile than the veterans.

If anything, they were worse than hostile. Their unexplained pity had grown thicker and more difficult to ignore. Feeling more angry instead of less, Costis went to find Aristogiton and cornered him in an alley between two of the barracks buildings as he was coming off duty.

Without preamble he began, "What the hell is going on?" He asked even though he thought he knew.

"What do you mean?" Aris replied with innocence

that rang completely false, even to Aris. He winced as he spoke.

"Are you going to tell me or am I going to beat it out of you?"

"Costis, why don't we go—"

"Now," said Costis. "Here."

"If you insist—"

"I do."

"They think the assassination was a fake. Maybe the assassins were real, or maybe even they were faked. What they really think is that you and Teleus killed the men who attacked the king and he's taking the credit."

"They think he lied?"

"After all, he is a l—"

"THEY THINK I LIED?"

Costis turned away then, and Aris jumped to catch his arm. Costis shook him off, already starting back down the alley the way he had come, toward the mess hall, but Aris knew his friend too well. He grabbed him again and this time held him harder.

"What are you doing?" Costis said, trying to pull free.

"What are *you* doing?" Aris asked, refusing to release him.

"I am going to tell people I am not a liar, and I am going to beat the life out of anyone who says I am."

"No, you aren't," Aris said. "Really, you aren't. You won't convince anyone that way."

"Then how do I convince them?" He stared at Aris, his gaze sharpening, and Aris backed away. "What about you?" Costis said. "You were there. Why didn't you tell them?"

"I wasn't there," said Aris. "Not when the assassins died. By the time I got there with my squad, it was all over."

"But you believe me."

"Of course I do," said Aristogiton.

Costis raised his hands to Aris's chest and pushed him away hard. He rebounded off the wall nearby. "No. You don't," Costis said bitterly.

"I hadn't talked to you since the attack," said Aris, as angry as Costis. "How was I to know? Costis, you owe him. You knocked him flat on his back, and he let you off. How was I to know," he said again, "that he didn't call in his debt and that you didn't let him get away with it because of your confounded asinine patron sense of honor?"

"You should have known!" Costis was shouting and made himself stop. He didn't know up from down anymore. He didn't know right from wrong and couldn't make sense of the simplest events. He'd been nothing but blindsided by every tortuous twist in his life since the Thief of Eddis became king. Why should he expect Aris to know more? "I apologize. I am very sorry." He stepped away.

"Costis, wait." Aris clutched at his sleeve. Costis shook him off, and this time Aris didn't try to hold him.

In the morning, Costis was summoned to the office of the captain. Tersely, Teleus informed him that he was a squad leader again. He would have a squad, although not the same one as he had had before, nor in the same century. His belongings would be moved from his quarters near the other lieutenants to the rooms above the dining hall in one of the barracks. Just as tersely, Costis accepted his assignment, was dismissed, and headed for the door.

"Costis," Teleus called him back. "If you show them that you are angry, it will only make every wild rumor that much more believable."

"Thank you, Captain," said Costis. "I will try to remember."

Costis didn't announce his outrage to the Guard in a speech at dinner, but he met every sympathetic look with a challenging glare, daring anyone to suggest to his face that he was a liar. The squad Teleus had scripted for him had older unassigned men and a few trainees just out of the recruitment barracks. The older soldiers brought the trainees up to date, and they watched Costis with round eyes for the first few days. Costis might have been in a foul mood, but he was also fair, and they gave him no trouble.

On his off-duty nights Costis found he didn't care for the company of the other guards and took himself down to the wineshops in the city of Attolia. Three times he ended up in fights. He must have acquired some particular curse, because what should have been a business of a few punches thrown turned to knives and broken furniture. The third time, he was picked up by the watch and taken before Teleus, who eyed him as if he were a stranger, and reminded him that he could be broken back to line soldier or dismissed from the Guard if he was a disgrace to his rank.

Costis tried to take the warning to heart, but was somehow fighting again the next day. He was outside a wine bar when two drunks accosted him, pretending to be veterans and demanding that he honor their service by buying them another bottle of wine. It was a common pitch, and Costis brushed by after refusing. The drunks took offense, and Costis would have come to a sticky end if a passing stranger hadn't intervened. One of the drunken men grabbed Costis by the arm, while the other pulled a wicked beltknife from his tunic. Fortunately, the stranger was there to drop a stool from the wine bar onto the head of the knife-wielding assailant. When the drunks saw their advantage was gone, they quickly lost interest in the fight and stumbled off. Costis thanked the stranger, who looked at the crowd that was gathering and suggested that he and Costis should both slip away as well, before they found themselves explaining the event to the city's watchmen. Costis thought it was a wise suggestion and managed to blend in with the crowd and head back to the barracks without another reason to be called before the Captain of the Guard.

Sitting on his bed, unlacing his sandals, Costis admitted to himself that he had been spoiling for a fight. Every day he'd told himself that the king didn't need him anymore and so had dismissed him—there was no insult in that. He had been valuable to his king, and he should be happy knowing that much. Kings are kings and incomprehensible. Eugenides had revealed that in the palace garden. Costis misunderstood. That was all. He reminded himself that he was better off than the king's attendants, who were laughingstocks for their persisting wariness and deference to Eugenides. No one believed the warnings they'd sounded after the fall of Erondites. If the members of the court were more cautious in dealing with the king, it was because they believed that he was now the instrument of the queen. To the court, Costis had heard, the king seemed as harmless as ever and the attendants looked ridiculous. Costis should be happy he was spared that. He went to bed wishing he believed everything he told himself.

Aris meanwhile paced in his own tiny quarters not far away. He was still serving in the palace, while Costis was not. Their working paths never crossed, and Costis always seemed to have disappeared into the city when Aris was looking for him. Aristogiton wanted to know who had first started the rumor that the assassination had been faked. He was afraid that he already knew, and that it was Laecdomon.

· CHAPTER TWELVE ·

THE Queen of Eddis sat at a desk scattered with papers. There was ink on her fingers and a smudge on one cheek. She looked up from her work and smiled when the Magus of Sounis was introduced to the room. "How is my honored prisoner?" she asked.

The magus wrapped his robes tighter and sat in the chair by the desk. "I am enduring my captivity very well," he said. "But I cannot find a morning chill refreshing, and I would like to return to my nice warm country."

"You know that you may go when you like," said Eddis.

"Unfortunately, my nice warm country is consuming itself in a civil war, and there are too many people who would slit my throat if they could. One of whom being the king, who may still hold it against me that I was abstracted from his service by your nefarious, under-handed, incorrigible former Thief. My 'confinement' will have to continue until Sounis sends for me."

"You heard this morning in the court about the progress Sounis has made. It won't be long until things are settled and he negotiates your release. I will miss you when you go."

He smiled at her fondly. "No less than I will miss you, Helen. Did you send for me for a reason?"

"I thought you might like to see Ornon's latest report."

"I would," said the magus. "Did it come by the diplomatic pouch, or has he sent home another assistant ambassador?"

"It came by the regular route. He is growing anxious."

"Gen is still acting the buffoon?"

"Yes, but Ornon has begun to worry more about getting what he wished for. You've heard about the fall of Erondites?"

"I did, but what has Ornon been wishing for?"

"Well, he didn't approve of the tactics of his assistant, but he has been trying every way that he thinks might work to get Eugenides to take the reins of power. Mostly, I think he's put his faith in rational argument, and he lectures Gen every opportunity he gets. It has only just dawned on him that if he succeeds, Eugenides will be King of Attolia."

"And this is not happy news?"

"King," Eddis emphasized, "of Attolia."

"I see," said the magus, and he did. "We will have a

very powerful king, and a powerful queen as well, as our neighbors. But also, a committed ally," the magus pointed out. "You did not release him from his oaths of loyalty to you."

Eddis shook her head. "Eugenides never took any oaths of loyalty to me. The Thieves never swear loyalty to any ruler of Eddis, only to Eddis itself."

She met the magus's stunned look with a smile. "The Thieves of Eddis have always been uncomfortable allies to the throne, Magus. There is the niggling fear that if you fall out with a Thief, he might see it as his right and his responsibility to remove you. There are some checks, of course. There is only ever one Thief. They are prohibited from owning any property. Their training inevitably generates the isolation that makes them independent, but also keeps them from forming alliances that might become threats to the throne. It is not the folly you might think."

"Why didn't I know this?" the magus asked, his sense of his own scholarship deeply offended.

Eddis laughed. "Because no one ever talks about the Thief. Haven't you noticed?"

The magus nodded. He had registered the superstitious reluctance to discuss the Thief or anything to do with the past Thieves of Eddis. It almost amounted to a taboo. He'd been trying to compile a more complete history of Eddis while he had access to the queen's library and had been puzzled to find no mention of the Thieves there.

"I did hear a rumor about Eugenides and a comment he made to the Captain of his Guard," he said.

"Now how did you pick that up?" Eddis asked, amused.

"I got one of your guards drunk," the magus admitted. "But I am right? The Thief of Eddis has a certain freedom to do whatever he wants?"

"And an accompanying responsibility," the queen pointed out.

"Even without an oath," the magus said, "you cannot believe that Eugenides would ever betray you or your interests?"

Eddis looked away. "If Sophos is gone—" she said.

"We don't know that he is," the magus interrupted. Like Eddis and Eugenides, he refused to give up hope for the missing heir of Sounis. More than either of them, he felt conscience-stricken to have been safe in Eddis when Sophos disappeared, even though his presence in Sounis would have meant little to the king's nephew. The King of Sounis had forbidden the magus to continue educating his heir. He had feared the magus's influence and had sent Sophos away from the capital city to be tutored by someone else.

"But if he is gone, if he is dead, and not a hostage somewhere," the Queen of Eddis asked, "would you see me marry Sounis, then?"

She turned back to the magus, but he, in turn, had looked away. He answered very reluctantly, "Yes."

No more needed to be said. They both understood that if Eugenides was King of Attolia, he would face difficult and painful decisions that he would make in the best interests of nations, not individuals, no matter how much he might love them.

Relius had been moved from the infirmary, but not into his own apartment. In his own rooms he would have been in the center of all his webs of intrigue, surrounded by the papers and codes and histories of his work. Those rooms, no doubt, had been locked up. Once emptied of his personal effects, they would be turned over in their entirety to the new Secretary of the Archives. The thought gave him no pain. It was surprising how remote his past life now seemed. His thoughts only pained him when he struggled to bring his previous work to mind, and he did not do that much. If he considered anything at length, it was some memory of his childhood or the flight of a bird past his window. Mostly he lay in his bed as blank and free from thought as a newborn baby. His days were immeasurably restful.

Darker thoughts crowded in during the deepest hours of the night when he woke listening to the secret mystifying sounds of the sleeping palace. Many nights, the king was there. Pleasant, irreverent, and distracting, he eased Relius past nightmares and self-recrimination. Some nights he said nothing at all, just comforted with his presence. Other nights he related the events of his day, spewing out his insights and analyses of the Attolian court in a devastatingly funny critique that Relius suspected was as much a relief to the king as a distraction to Relius. Occasionally they talked about plays or poetry. Relius was surprised by the breadth of the king's interest. He knew a great deal of history. Several nights they argued the interpretation of great events until Relius was exhausted.

The king's arguments were spiced with "the magus says this" or "the magus thinks that." Relius and the magus had crossed paths many times, never on academic matters, and Relius was fascinated by this revelatory view of an old opponent. He thought that when he had healed sufficiently, and withdrawn from the capital, he might write the magus a letter and open a correspondence on Euclid, or Thales, or the new idea from the north, that the sun and not the Earth might be in the center of the universe. As he healed and memories of the world he had moved in grew more distant, he imagined, very tentatively, a new life opening in front of him.

The lamp beside his bed was lit. If the king came this night, he would arrive soon. When the door opened after a light knock, he turned his head, but the greeting on his lips died, as his forgotten world crashed upon him like a breaking wave. The king stood in the doorway, but not alone. His arm was linked through the queen's and he guided her into the room. She stood by the bedside while Eugenides fetched a chair, and then she sat. Relius lay on the bed watching, unable to look away from her as she seemed unable to break from his gaze.

Eugenides looked from one silent face to another. "You must speak sometime." He brushed his wife's cheek with his hand and bent to kiss her softly on the cheek. Some of Relius's longing must have showed on his face because the king turned to him with a smile.

"Jealous, Relius?" With no sign of embarrassment, or of jest, he brushed the former secretary's hair back and kissed him as well.

It was laughable, surely, but as the king left, Relius blinked the water from his eyes. The kiss had been gentle, and the king's eyes as he delivered it had not smiled.

The flame in the lamp guttered, the sound unnaturally loud. The queen spoke at last, saying softly, "I failed you, Relius."

"No," Relius protested. He lifted himself on his elbows, disregarding the dull aches such movement reawakened. It was imperative that the queen not mistake his culpability. "I failed. I failed you." He added awkwardly, "Your Majesty."

Sadly, she asked, "Am I no longer your queen, then?"

Shocked, he whispered, "Always," breathing his soul into the word.

"I should have known that," she said. "I should have had more hope for the future instead of re-creating the past."

"You had no choice," Relius reminded her.

"So I thought, that it was another *necessary* sacrifice, like so many we have made together. I was wrong. I did trust you, Relius, all these years; I shouldn't have stopped." She leaned forward and straightened the covers, smoothing the wrinkles from the white sheeting. "We cannot forgive ourselves," she said. Relius knew that he would never forgive himself, that he didn't deserve forgiveness, but he remembered what Eugenides had said about the queen's needs. He had considered it during the lonely night hours in the infirmary. "Perhaps we could forgive each other?" the queen suggested.

Relius pressed his lips together, but nodded. He would accept a pardon he knew was undeserved if by doing so he could relieve his queen of any part of her burden.

The queen asked, "What do you think of my king now. Is he impetuous? Inexperienced? . . . Naive?" She repeated his words back to him. Her voice, reassuringly calm, achingly familiar, eased a little of his distress and shame.

"He is young," Relius said hoarsely.

It was Attolia's turn to look surprised, the slightest lifting of one eyebrow.

Relius shook his head. Tongue-tied, he had mis-spoken. "I meant that for ten years, or twenty . . ." He hesitated to put his thoughts into words, as if speaking them aloud might work against his hopes.

Attolia understood. "A golden age?"

Relius nodded. "He doesn't see it. He doesn't want to be king."

"Did he say so?"

Relius shook his head. He hadn't needed to be told. "We talked about poetry," he said, still speaking hesitantly, "and about a new comedy by Aristophanes about farmers. He said you had chosen a small farm for me, and suggested I write a play about it." Relius was a man whose entire life had depended on insight. "He didn't marry you to become king. He became king because he wanted to marry you."

"He says he will not diminish my power or rule over my country. He intends to be a figurehead."

"Don't let him," Relius said, and then pulled himself back, in case he had overreached. Gently his queen waved away his concern.

"Am I not sovereign enough, Relius?" she said. There was no smile on her face, but it was there in her voice, and Relius, who knew her every intonation, heard it and breathed more easily.

The queen said, "No matter how securely I hold the reins of power, so long as I had no husband, my barons had to fight, afraid that someone else might seize that power. Only if they could be certain that that goal was out of their reach, and out of their neighbors' reach as well, would there be peace, Relius. Oh, there are stupid men among them, and a few warmongers, but mostly, you and I know that they fight me because they are afraid of each other. If there were a king, secure in his power, the barons would unite.

"I have bought all the time I can against the coming of the Mede," she said. "If Attolia is not united when they strike again, then we are all, king, queen, patronoi, and okloi, lost. But it is not up to me alone, Relius, whether or not Eugenides will be king or just appear as one."

"He refuses?"

"He refuses to either defend or assert his position. He just . . . looks the other way and pretends he doesn't hear. He cannot be led, or driven. The Eddisian Ambassador has tried everything, I think, including extortion, and failed. I think he is afraid."

"Ornon or the king?"

"Both. Ornon looks more and more like a man at the edge of a precipice every day. But I think Eugenides is afraid."

"Of what?"

"Of failing," said Attolia, as if that fear, at least, Relius should have recognized. "Of stealing my power from me."

"You would only be stronger."

"I know," Attolia soothed him. "I did not say that I am afraid. He is, though, I think. Afraid of his own desire for power. He is not unused to wielding power, but it has always been in secret. I could, of course, command him to be king. He will give me anything I ask."

"That would only confirm your sovereignty, not his," Relius objected.

"So," agreed the queen.

Relius considered her, sitting beside him. She didn't seem unduly concerned. "I am confident, My Queen, that if you have met your match, so has he."

"He is stubborn," Attolia reminded him, "and very strong."

"Surely he revealed himself in the fall of Erondites?" Relius asked.

"The barons have come trooping through my bed-chamber, to have a new look at him."

"And?" prompted Relius.

"He simpers. He preens."

Relius snorted. "I suppose that the barons reported that the plan must have been yours all along, that the king was your witless tool."

"So." The queen nodded. She looked down at her hands, lying quiet in her lap, while Relius imagined the scene the king must have enacted, no different from the scenes he himself had witnessed when the king was playing the fool.

"You must force him into the open," Relius warned her.

She raised her head, and he was aghast to see her eyes bright with tears. "I am tired of driving people and forcing them to my will. I am like a war chariot with bladed wheels, scything down those closest to me, enemies and my dearest friends alike."

"I failed you, My Queen," Relius reminded her.

"You served me. I rewarded you with torture and, if not for his intervention, with death. He loves me, and I reward his love by forcing on him something he hates. In the evening, after we dance, he rarely returns to the throne; he dances with others or he moves from place to place through the room. The court thinks he is trying to be gracious, sharing his attention. Only I see that he moves always toward the empty spot and the court moves always after him. He is like a dog trying to escape its own tail. He indulged himself in one brief moment of privacy and almost died of it. Relius, he hates being king."

Relius thought of his companion of the past nights and their wide-ranging conversations and the king's laughter.

Still diffident, he disagreed with his queen. "The Thieves of Eddis have always been set apart, Your Majesty. He has had very little company in his life, and he isn't used to it. But there are other words for *privacy* and *independence*. They are *isolation* and *loneliness*. Drive him out. Whether he wants to or not, he belongs in the open. The world needs to see what a king he is."

"Whatever the cost to him?"

"No man can choose to serve only himself when he has something to offer to his state. No one can put his own wishes above the needs of so many."

"Take care," the queen said softly. "Take care, my dear friend."

Relius lay very still.

"I am an exceedingly effective scythe," the queen said.

Relius smiled wanly back. "And I offer you justification out of my own mouth. There is no house waiting for me in some obscure village in the Gede Valley, is there?"

"Not in the Gede Valley, no. There is one in the Modrea, two floors and an open court, as well as an atrium, a study downstairs. There's a little land at the back, for goats."

Relius waited.

"Or you could stay with me. I need you still. Attolia needs you still."

The tears rose in Relius's silent eyes. He closed them and thought in the darkness about a house in the Gede Valley or the Modrea with a study downstairs and a small fountain, no doubt, and the sound of goats, and peace.

"I am what you have made of me," the queen said softly.

Relius smiled through his own tears. "And you may mow me down a hundred times, My Queen, with my best wishes. But I am a failure and a wreck. I cannot see how I could be of any use to you."

"You are not a failure, and for my sake, I hope you are not a wreck. As to what use you may be, shall we wait and see?" she asked.

When Relius agreed, sadly relinquishing in his thoughts the quiet farm in the Modrea Valley, Attolia asked if he had changed his opinion on whether the king should be driven to a task he hated, now that he himself had been manipulated by the queen.

"I only hope you can be as effective with the king," Relius said.

Attolia admitted the challenge. "The whole Mede Empire was easier to redirect," she said. "Ornon was right to say that he could not be driven. I don't know why he continues to try."

"I think he is providing a foil for you, My Queen, and waiting for you to make your move."

"I made it already," said Attolia. "On my wedding night. You have heard no doubt the events of our wedding night?"

Relius looked away. "He said that you . . . cried," he said softly.

"But not that he cried as well," said the queen, amused at the memory. "We were very lachrymose."

"Is that what he told Dite in the garden?" Relius asked, fitting puzzle piece to puzzle piece.

"I think so. I haven't asked either of them outright.

Would you like to hear more romance of the evening? He told me that the Guard should be reduced by half, and I threw an ink jar at his head."

"Is that when he cried?"

"He ducked," said Attolia dryly.

Grown more confident of the queen's humor, Relius said, "I had not pictured you for a fishwife."

"Lo, the transforming power of love."

"The Guard," Relius said thoughtfully.

"Your own pet worry," said Attolia.

"Will you reduce it?"

"You know why I have not. Because I cannot, not with the Mede raising its armies and my barons still divisive. The Guard is the loyal heart of my forces."

"And your barons will go on being divisive so long as Eugenides is a figurehead."

Attolia waited.

"And Eugenides is resisting being king. And?" prompted Relius.

Attolia raised her hands in a mockery of helplessness. "I agreed to reduce the Guard."

Relius waited.

"With the condition that he needs to ask Teleus and have Teleus agree."

Relius laughed outright. He was sufficiently healed that no pain forced him to stop.

The queen said, with a ladylike chuckle, "I believe

you handled me just the same once. When you told me I could install an okloi general just as soon as I had the approval of the council of barons."

"And I was right," said Relius. "Once you had shown you could sway that council, you could install anyone you wished."

"Am I not right?"

"Entirely right. Teleus won't bow to superior force. He won't bow to reason either, and damn his pigheadedness, he won't bow for his own salvation, but he'll bow to a king. If Teleus thinks Eugenides is a king, it will only be because he is one. It is a brilliant strategy, My Queen."

"It is good to hear you say so," said Attolia quietly, looking at her hands, resting still in her lap. "I have missed your advice."

The queen gathered her skirts, preparing to rise. Hesitantly, Relius lifted his hand to stop her. "My Queen," he said, "when you said that you had trusted me all these years . . . ?"

The smile she so often hid in her voice came to her face then. It was a smile Relius had been privileged to see before. He knew he shared that privilege with few others. It pleased him deeply to know that one of those others was the king. "Yes, Relius," said the queen, smiling. "I have trusted you, and no, that does not mean that I have not had you watched and that I do not have spies that watch my spies, and spies even that watch those."

"Good," said Relius, relieved.

The queen shook her head and warned him, "That is over now, my friend. You have been elevated to a new rank, where you are trusted unconditionally. Don't look so uncomfortable. I have learned that there is a flaw in your philosophy. If we truly trust no one, we cannot survive." She bent to kiss his cheek, then gathered her skirts and was gone. Relius was left behind in the quiet room, considering a new philosophy.

The events of the state rolled on. The queen showed every sign of affection for her king, and it was accepted as a necessary artifice. The courtiers walked warily of Eugenides; though he was no more than a tool for the queen, he was obviously a dangerous one. The Guard clung to a sense of offense on behalf of their captain. The great states of the Continent politely disbelieved any rumors of war from the Mede Empire, and the King of Sounis slowly recaptured control of his country, though there was still no word of Sophos, the missing heir. Sejanus was tried for conspiring to commit regicide, giving evidence that the assassins had been sent by Sounis. The queen, supposedly at the direction of the king, ordered that he be spared the ultimate penalty for his crimes, and he was sent to be incarcerated in the hinterland. The last of the assassins died in the queen's prison after revealing that his services had been provided to the King of

Sounis by Nahuseresh, the former Ambassador to Attolia from the Mede Empire.

The attendants stood listening to the muffled sounds of destruction. That they could hear anything at all was indicative of the violence of the proceedings on the far side of the heavy wooden door. At each crash they winced. Glad to be in the king's guardroom, not in his bedchamber with him, Ion met Sotis's glance and rolled his eyes.

The king had moved back to his rooms a week earlier. Where he slept was anyone's guess. The attendants knew that they put him to bed in his bedchamber, and that when they knocked at the door in the morning, he was there to unlock it. Now they knew that this was the entirety of what they knew.

In an interview that morning with the new Secretary of the Archives, the Baron Hippias, Eugenides had learned that the assassins from Sounis had been sent by Nahuseresh. Afterward, the king had excused himself graciously from the queen and returned to his rooms for what was supposed to be a change of clothes before lunch with a foreign ambassador.

But he hadn't changed his clothes. Instead he had silently waved his attendants out of the bedchamber and closed the door behind them with a benevolent smile, and then, as far as they could tell from the noise, he'd broken every breakable thing in the room.

The noises stopped some time before they heard the door unlock. The king depressed the latch and let it swing open behind him as he turned back toward the center of the room. The attendants paced hesitantly into the destruction. There were broken bits of the side chairs scattered across the carpet. The hangings above the king's bed were ribboned tatters.

"The person who describes this to the queen will be flayed." The king spoke quietly. The attendants moved from nervous to fearful.

"Your Majesty," said Ion. The king didn't seem to be listening. Ion licked his lips and tried again. "Your Majesty," he whispered. The king turned and looked at him impassively. "I-I am sure . . . I assure you . . . no one here will speak of it."

The king passed his hand across his face. "That will have to do," he said. "I will change in the wardrobe. Cleon and Ion can attend me. The rest of you—" He looked around at the wreckage. "Clean up what you can."

"Sacred altars," Lamion whispered when he was gone. "Does he think there will be anyone in the palace who doesn't hear about this?"

Philologos passed the velvet ribbons of the bed hangings through his hand. The bedpost nearby was marked as if hammered over and over with a pickax. The wood was splintered and gouged. The holes were surprisingly deep.

"They won't know details. They won't hear any from us."

"They won't need to," said Hilarion.

Philologos poked his fingers into the holes.

The attendants began collecting the remains of the chairs. They looked helplessly at the wall, splattered with overlapping explosions of different colored ink. The unbreakable inkwells lay on the carpet. Fine ceramic pieces of the more fragile inkwells crunched underfoot. One inkwell, lying on its side, was carved diorite. It had left a dent in the plastered wall. Below the king's scriptorium was an array of writing utensils swept from its surface. Pens and nibs, papers and the weights he used to hold them while he wrote, were all scattered in mute testimony to frustration and rage.

Silently the attendants contrasted the evidence before their eyes to the calm behavior of the king as he had returned from the audience with Hippias.

"Our little king doesn't like people trying to assassinate him."

"He isn't angry because someone tried to kill him," Philologos said sharply.

"How do you know that, Philo, dear?"

But Philologos had had enough of being condescended to. "Because, Lamion, I am not as dumb as you think I am, even if you are."

By the time Lamion had parsed this to be sure there

was in fact an insult at the end of it, Hilarion had laid a restraining hand on his arm.

"So, tell us, Philologos, your insight."

"He isn't angry because Nahuseresh tried to have him killed," Philologos told them. "He is angry because he can't go kill Nahuseresh in return."

"Because he is king," agreed Hilarion.

"Not because he's king," Philologos said, disgusted by their dull wits. "*Because he has only one hand,*" he said, voicing the king's bitterness as his own.

The attendants looked around them at the mess, at the fabric sliced again and again until it hung in threads, and the bedpost marked by gouges. They looked back at Philologos with new respect.

"*That's* what he doesn't want the queen to know about."

No one disagreed. They turned their attention to cleaning what they could and arranging for the wall to be repaired, and discussed, very carefully, how they might suggest to the rest of the court that the king's tantrum was caused by his dislike of Nahuseresh, and nothing else.

Costis panted as he hurried up the stone steps past the last flickering lamp and onto the dark walk that ran around the roof of the palace. Aris was waiting for him at the top. Behind them rose the dark bulk of the inner palace. In front of them was the city with a few lights burning on its dark streets and farther out the harbor, with the dim lights on ships glowing against the deeper black of the sea. Costis shivered. The night air was cool, and he'd raised a sweat hurrying across the palace after the messenger Aristogiton had sent to knock on his door frame and wake him in the early hours of the dog watch of the night.

"What is it?" he asked, not happy to have been dragged out without an explanation. "Your messenger wouldn't—"

"Shh," said Aris, and pointed out toward the outer wall. His eyes not yet accustomed to the dark after coming up from the lighted courtyard below, Costis saw only a dim silhouette against the sky.

"That's not—" Costis whispered.

"The king. Yes, it is," said Aris.

"He's on top of the crenellations." Costis had patrolled this wall many times and knew those crenellations. They rose from the parapet, about two feet high and each about three feet long, narrowing to a ridge along the top. As he watched, the king moved to the end of one crenellation and then hopped across the intervening space to the next.

Costis opened his mouth to say, "Why doesn't someone tell him to get down?" when he realized why Aris had summoned him from his warm bed. "No," he said firmly, "not me."

"Costis, please."

"Where are his cursed attendants?" Costis hissed.

"Behind you," said Ion.

Costis whirled to see a handful of them standing in the dark. They had been no friend of Costis's when he was with the king. They'd made it clear that their waiting room was no place for common soldiers, and now they wanted him to tell the king to get down off the wall before he fell and broke every bone in his body.

"Go to hell," said Costis. He turned back to the stairs.

"Costis, please," begged Aris.

"It isn't my business," said Costis. "Besides, he probably does this sort of thing all the time at home."

"Maybe he does, but not with a wineskin in his hand," said Ion, flatly. Staring, Costis could see the wineskin swinging as the king jumped to the next crenellation.

"It's not my business," Costis insisted, as flatly.

"It's my business," said Aris, catching him by the arm. "I'm on watch. If he falls, Costis, I'll hang for it. Please."

Costis said nothing.

"We'll all hang for it," said Hilarion. "I know why you don't want to get involved. You certainly owe us no favors, but I swear on my honor, Costis, name your price and we'll pay it, if you can get him off that wall."

✦   ✦   ✦

Costis approached slowly, careful to scuff a little as he stepped. He didn't want to startle the king.

"Costis," said Eugenides, without turning around, "I should have realized they would drag you out of bed. I apologize."

He swung around then with a little stagger that made Costis's heart leap into his throat.

Head down, swinging the wineskin by the leather thong at its neck, the king walked along the crenellation. Costis paced beside him.

"Your Majesty, please get down," Costis said hurriedly. The king was almost at the end of the crenellation, and he dreaded what would happen when he got there.

"Why? Costis, I'm not going to fall."

"You're drunk."

"Not that drunk," said the king. "Watch." He tossed the wineskin to Costis, who caught it and clutched it in horror as the king turned himself upside down and balanced, one hand on the narrow ridge of the stone.

"Oh, my god," said Costis.

"O *my* god," said the king, cheerfully. "You want to call on the god appropriate to the occasion. After all, your god would probably be Miras, light and arrows and all that sort of thing, whereas my god is a god of balance and, of course, preservation of Thieves, which I suppose, technically, I am not." He straightened up. "Maybe I shouldn't push my luck," he said.

"I wish you wouldn't," Costis said faintly. "Your god might be offended."

"Costis, my god is not a ten-devotee-to-the-average-dozen, got-a-priest-on-every-corner kind of god who is always being badgered by his worshipers. He keeps a very close eye on me, and what may look completely stupid to you is merely a demonstration of my faith. Give me back my wine."

Remembering the way the king's cousin had dealt with him, Costis held out the wineskin. The king reached for it, but he guessed Costis's intent and pulled his hand back before Costis could catch him to yank him to safety. The king laughed like a little boy and windmilled his arms for balance.

"Costis," he said with mocking disappointment, "that's cheating."

"I don't know what you mean, sir."

"I am not sure I trust you."

"You can trust me with your life, My King."

"But not with my wine, obviously. Give it back."

"Get down and make me."

The king laughed again. "Aulus would be so proud of you, and Ornon, too. You are a quick learner."

But Costis didn't have Aulus's size, or his history with the king, and Aulus had been dealing with a very sick, bedridden Eugenides. Costis had none of his advantages.

The king chuckled in the dark, a warm sound that

Costis couldn't help responding to, though he was immediately exasperated with himself as well as the king.

"I've been thinking. Don't you want to know what I have been thinking about?"

"Only if you are thinking about getting down," said Costis, his exasperation showing.

"Is this a sense of humor, Costis?"

"I do have one, Your Majesty."

"Good for you," said the king. He started to walk back the way he had come. Costis followed, still clutching the wineskin.

"Your Majesty, please get down. My friend Aris is really a very good man, and if you fall off that wall, he's going to hang for it, and so will his squad, most of whom are also nice men, and though I can't say I really care if your attendants hang, there are probably many people that do care, and would you please, please, get down?"

The king looked at him, eyes narrowed. "I don't think I've ever heard you say that many words in a row. You sounded almost articulate. I was thinking of Nahuseresh," said the king, getting back to his subject. He looked over his shoulder at Costis. "Do you know, you can't strangle a man with one hand?" he said very seriously. "It's probably why I have only one. It narrows one's options. I may make a poor king with one hand, but the gods know I'd be no king at all if I had two."

"Your Majesty . . ."

The king rubbed his hand over his face. "And I was just thinking of you, and here you are, you poor silly bastard, trying to tell me to get down off this wall."

He swung around again, walked the length of the crenellation, and before Costis had time to draw breath to protest, he hopped neatly to the next.

"You present me with a difficulty, Costis, as I owe you something better than what you are in line for now—death by falling roof tile."

Diverted, Costis said, "That was an accident," and reconsidered even as he spoke. The old broken tiles could easily have been scattered on the ground beforehand. Broken roof tiles were easy to come by in every trash pile around the palace.

The king turned his whole body to look at Costis, swaying for a moment before he balanced.

"How did you know about the roof tiles?" Costis asked.

"I am omniscient, I know everything. Or at least I did before I had to tow four attendants, a squad of guards, a guard leader, and a stray lieutenant around behind me wherever I go. To be honest," the king admitted, "I didn't know. You just told me. All I had was an educated guess because it's a fairly common form of assassination. There's the true course of political savvy for you, good guesses. Tell me, in the course of your blundering innocence, have you noticed any other attempts on your life?"

Costis thought a moment. "Yes," he said, hesitantly, "maybe." He convinced himself—surprised at how little effort it took. "Yes."

"Yes," agreed the king. "It's a dangerous thing to be seen as the confidant of a king. Knife fights in wineshops, aggressive drunks, and a stray arrow at the butts. Any others?"

"Are those guesses, too?" Costis stared in disbelief.

"No."

"You are omniscient."

The king shook his head. "I asked Relius for the names of two competent men to keep an eye on you. I couldn't keep you in the guardroom for the rest of your natural life. And you, you stupid bastard, had already wandered away once and gotten under a load of roof tiles."

"What men?"

"You met one after the knife fight in front of the wineshop."

Costis remembered the stranger.

"Their powers are limited, however. They can watch, but sometimes there's not a damn thing they can do. It was just luck the arrow missed you. So, so, so," said the king. "I had hoped that your very obvious outrage at being dropped like a used glove would have protected you, but obviously it hasn't.

"I could hide you in the hinterlands, but frankly, I

don't know enough people that I trust in Attolia. I could call on my cousin who is Eddis and ask her to hide you, but even more frankly, I will admit that having to do so would be embarrassing." He looked over at Costis and said, "I hate being embarrassed." He rubbed his side, and Costis knew he was thinking of Sejanus. "I saw him on that balcony, and I sat there like an idiot wondering what he was doing." He shook his head in self-disgust and moved along the wall. Costis followed after him.

"I hope you know that I could once jump from the palace to those roofs over there." He eyed the empty space below him and said sadly, "If I tried now, I'd probably eviscerate myself when I landed. But it does give me an idea for what to do with you. In the morning I will tell Teleus that I am detaching you from the Guard. You won't like it," he informed Costis unsympathetically, "but then, you shouldn't have hit me in the face . . . all those many lifetimes ago."

It did feel as if lifetimes had passed since Costis had knocked the king down in the training yard. That was some other soldier, a simpleminded one with no idea how complicated life could become.

"Really," said the king, "I've gotten a lot of thinking done tonight. In spite of my entourage."

"Is that what the wine is for? To help you think?"

"Oh, the wine. The wine, Costis, is to help hide the truth. It doesn't work. It never has, but I try it every once in a while just in case something in the nature of wine might have changed."

"The truth, Your Majesty?"

The king cocked his head at him. "I'm not going to tell you, Costis, you idiot. I'm trying to bury it, remember? Hide it from myself, hide it from the gods. Because not wanting the prize the gods have arranged for you— that just might offend the hell right out of them. If you are going to reject the gods' rewards, Costis, you have to go very carefully." He shook his finger in admonishment. "You can't let *them* know that you hate being surrounded every minute of every day by people who think you should be acting like a king, and that you cannot possibly stand one more day listening to prating idiots tell you how lucky you are while a man you hate is laughing his guts out on the far side of the Black Straits, and there's not a damn thing you can do about that because you are trapped in the only disaster you've ever gotten yourself into that you absolutely cannot get out of." He turned and walked back along the parapet. He didn't falter, but landed on the next crenellation in a stiff-legged jolt.

He said over his shoulder, "Do you know, it's the first time I've ever been caught in something I can't get out of?" His laughter was bitter. "Because I don't want out of it, Costis. I'm terrified that if they know how much I hate it, they might take it away." He stopped then, as if realizing what he'd just said, all that he'd admitted out loud. "Oh, my god," he said, "the wine isn't working, is it?"

He swung his body around and turned again toward Costis, but his momentum continued to carry him away. He took several teetering steps backward. Then his eyes widened, and Costis could see their whites in the dim light. Instead of recovering, he recoiled farther. One foot stepped out over the abyss. The king reached with his hand and caught at nothing and, though it was impossible, still hung there, suspended, over the open air.

"My god," the king whispered, not in prayer.

And Costis heard, as clearly as he'd heard the king speaking, another voice. It said, "Go to bed."

Then the king was falling toward Costis, and Costis was tossing the wineskin aside in order to catch him. As his feet hit the walkway, the king's knees buckled, and Costis held him, his own knees weak. He couldn't tell which of them was shaking more. The king sucked at the air, drawing each breath and holding it. Costis remembered the doctor putting in his stitches, but these were more the hissing breaths of a man who has just cut himself or foolishly reached for a hot iron handle and burned his fingers. When the king finally straightened, Costis didn't let him go and the king didn't pull away. He stood, head down, with his hand on Costis's shoulder, until the shaking finally subsided. He laughed a little then and shook his head.

He pushed Costis away and stumbled off in the direction of his waiting attendants.

Trying to believe that he hadn't seen what he'd seen or heard what he'd heard, Costis followed, telling himself that it wasn't true that he and the king and even the stone under their feet were nothing but tissue, transparently thin, and that for a moment, the only real thing in the universe had been there on the parapet with the king.

"I am beginning to sense a certain amount of fraud in the reports of poets, Costis," said the king, over his shoulder. His voice was almost steady. "Maybe someone lied to the poets. Maybe it's just me. Do you know what the gods said to Ibykon on the night before his battle at Menara?" the king asked. "At least, what they said according to Archilochus?"

"Something about courage," Costis said automatically, busy with his own thoughts, busy trying not to think them. Gods belonged in temples and distant mountaintops, or floating on clouds. His every feeling revolted at the idea of hearing one speak.

The king quoted:

> Rise and slay. Throw your chest against your enemy.
> Stand like an arrow when the enemy's spear thuds at your feet.

"And for Roma . . . ," the king quoted again.

> To you alone, Eldest,
> the Fates have given unassailable rule.

> *Time alters all things,*
> *except this one thing.*
> *For you alone,*
> *the wind that bellows the sails of rule*
> *makes no shift.*

"That was Melinno."

"I know that," said Costis. "My tutor once made me memorize the entire lyric."

"No 'Glory shall be your reward' for me. Oh, no, for me, it is, 'Stop whining' and 'Go to bed.'" He snorted. "I should know better. Never call on them, Costis, if you don't really want them to appear."

They had reached the knot of attendants and Aristogiton anxiously waiting for them.

"I believe I will go to bed now," the king very stiffly informed his attendants, as if daring them to comment, which they didn't. He started down the stairs, his hand still on Costis's shoulder, pushing him along slightly and leaning on him for balance. He seemed suddenly very tired, but he moved without hesitation from the wider main hall through this wing of the palace into the narrower passages on the way back to the royal apartments. His attendants and his guard trailed behind.

They reached a staircase around a light well. The king turned up the stairs. One attendant raised a hand in a moment's silent protest, but dropped it again. They followed up the stairs to a passage that looked somehow familiar to Costis, though he didn't fully recognize it until they reached a tiny office and passed through it to a balcony looking out on a larger atrium. They had been here before.

"Dammit," the king said, looking out over the atrium.

The attendants shuffled their feet. They weren't gloating. They didn't even want to remember that they had ever gloated in the past.

"Well, this time I am not walking around," the king said in disgust. "You can go the long way." He assumed an expression of long suffering. "Obedient to my god, I am going directly to bed." He sat down on the railing and swung both legs over at once, dropping down onto the rafter below before the attendants could stop him. To Costis, who'd reached for him too late, he said, "Worried?"

"Your Majesty, you just—" Costis stopped.

"Just what?" the king prompted wickedly.

Nothing would induce Costis to say out loud that the king had almost fallen from the palace wall and that Costis had seen him manifestly saved by the God of Thieves.

The king smiled. "Cat got your tongue?"

"Your Majesty, you are drunk," Costis pleaded.

"I am. What's your excuse?" For hearing gods and seeing impossibilities.

The king relented. "Safety is an illusion, Costis. A Thief might fall at any time, and eventually the day must come when the god will let him. Whether I am on a rafter three stories up or on a staircase three steps up, I am in my god's hands. He will keep me safe, or he will not, here or on the stairs."

The attendants did fruitlessly throw themselves at the railing, but he was out of their reach. Ignoring them, he continued on along the rafter, leaning gracefully to step around the trusses where they dropped from the roof in diagonals to join the rafter.

"He's a lunatic," someone muttered. "A raving lunatic."

Costis wasn't sure. He knew what he'd heard on the rooftop, even if he didn't believe it. Even if he woke the next day believing it had all been a dream. The next day, he thought, when he would no longer be a member of the Guard.

"Your Majesty," Costis said again, more loudly than the attendants. The king turned, swaying just a little. He put his hand to the truss slanting down beside him.

"Yes?"

"You said you owed me something better than death by falling roof tile."

"Yes?"

"Can I ask for something?"

The king appeared to think. "You can ask," he said.

"I'm king, Costis, not a genie. I don't grant wishes."

"Come to sword training with the Guard in the morning."

The king peered at him as if he were having difficulty seeing. "Costis? Do you have any idea what my head is going to feel like in the morning?"

"You said that you would speak to Teleus tomorrow. Will you come?"

"Why?" asked the king, suspicious.

"Your side has healed. You need the exercise." When the king continued to look dubious, he added, "Because I am asking."

"All right," the king said at last. "All right, I will be there. Yech," he muttered as he moved away.

Costis and the attendants watched, hearts in their mouths, as he crossed the atrium. No one moved or spoke until he reached the far side and pulled himself up onto the balcony there. Costis swung then, to face the attendants.

"That is my price," he said. "You get him to sword training in the morning."

"Do you know what he's going to be like in the morning?" one asked.

"Costis . . . we can't just . . ."

"You can," he insisted. "I've seen you badger him. Every one of you."

"That was before."

"Then you'll just have to pretend nothing has

changed. Get him to sword practice in the morning."

They wavered.

"When I said, name your price, I was thinking of silver," Hilarion admitted.

"I wasn't."

"All right," he capitulated, "if that is your price, but you are obviously a lunatic, too."

They turned back through the doorway and made their way to the staircase. Costis stopped on a landing one flight down and watched the attendants and the squad of guards continue. He went back to his room, getting slightly lost on the way.

In the morning, he was up and dressed early. He went down to the mess hall, which was empty, and fetched himself a piece of a loaf from the day's baking. He was one of the first men on the training ground. The other guards stretched and chatted with one another. They ignored him. He paced, and tried not to look anxious. If the king didn't come, he would have to face the awkwardness of training alone. He'd already discovered that no one would spar with him. Having shown up this morning, he knew his pride wouldn't let him leave without some semblance of practice. He prayed the king would come.

He had slept badly, waking off and on through the night haunted by the voice he'd heard on the parapet. In the morning light, the whole episode seemed part of one muddled nightmare. Costis preferred it that way.

At last the king came. He came late, with his face still creased from sleep, when the training ground was filling and guards had settled into pairs and begun sparring throughout the courtyard, except in the empty space where Costis waited by himself. The first thing the king did was walk to one of the fountains along the wall and stick his face into it. He shook his hair off his face, flicking drops of water sparking into the air. Then he crossed the open square to Costis, leaving his attendants behind.

"Shall we start with the first exercises?" He was looking down at the button on his cuff. It was undone, and he was awkwardly holding his sword and trying to button the cuff at the same time.

"I don't think so," said Costis, and when the king looked up, Costis swung at his head.

Costis wasn't close, and the king jumped back. The sword passed harmlessly in front of his nose.

"Costis, what do you think you are doing?"

"Sparring, Your Majesty."

"Most people cross swords before they spar and they say something introductory like 'Begin!' before they swing."

"We can cross swords if you will put yours up, Your Majesty."

"But I don't want to spar."

"I didn't think you would," Costis said, and swung again.

The king jumped back again. He still hadn't gotten his button through its buttonhole.

"Dammit, Costis, have you lost your mind?"

"No, Your Majesty."

"I am not going to spar with you."

"Then I am a dead man, Your Majesty."

"Oh?"

"Your attendants will have me arrested if this doesn't start to look like a sparring match soon. They are headed this way."

The king glanced briefly around. The guards on either side had stopped sparring and were standing to watch.

"I'll hang, Your Majesty," said Costis, cheerfully. "Assuming I'm not tortured."

"And you are thinking I wouldn't want that to happen?"

"I know you don't."

"Only because I have another job for you to do."

Costis smiled.

The king scowled. "This is extortion."

Costis lifted his sword up. The king didn't want him to die, and not because of an errand that needed doing. The king had dismissed him in order to protect him from the reprisals of the powerful. The king wasn't going to let him hang. Last night's bizarre episode was forgotten. Only the memory that he hadn't been betrayed by the king mattered. Costis felt wonderful.

A moment later the sword he'd been holding clattered to the ground. Costis looked from the sword to his stinging fingers and back to the sword.

"There," the king said nastily. "We're done. I'm going back to bed." The attendants had paused. More people were staring.

"I don't think so, Your Majesty." Costis picked up the sword and raised it again.

There were a few exchanges this time before the king's sword slid over the top of Costis's guard and the flat side of it smacked him on the cheek.

"You drop your point in third," said Eugenides.

Costis flushed, remembering the king's comment at their first practice together. He had sparred for weeks with the best swordsman he'd ever encountered in his life and was no better for it because he'd dismissed the king's advice.

"Done now?" the king asked.

"No, Your Majesty."

The king sighed. He backed a few steps. Watching Costis warily, he popped his sword between his teeth, and giving up on the buttonhole, he rolled up his sleeve before he spat the sword back into his hand.

"Ready," he said.

They began.

"Has it occurred to you, Costis," the king said conversationally between thrusts, "that the only reason I am alive now is that those three assassins took me for a prancing lightweight?"

It hadn't occurred to Costis. "You will have the Guard to defend you now," he said.

"I was supposed to have the Guard to defend me then. I am not reassured."

"You will," Costis insisted.

"Oh?" said the king. "You think they will see I do know how to use a sword and lo, they will come to heel? I don't think so, Costis."

It wasn't as simple as that, Costis knew. There had been suitors before for the queen's hand, suitors who were capable with a sword, and the Guard wouldn't have followed them across the street into a wineshop. Nonetheless, Costis was certain that the Guard, if they knew him, would follow the king. He just didn't have the words to explain why, and was too hard-pressed to stop and think of them.

The king attacked; Costis defended. The king hit him hard on the thigh. Hopping backward, Costis disengaged, but the king kept coming and hit him twice more, once on the same thigh and once on the elbow. Costis retreated faster. The king watched, his eyes narrowed.

"Frankly, Costis, if they all fight like you, I am still not reassured."

This time, Costis's sword rose into the air in an arc before hitting the ground with a rattle. He went to pick it up.

"Too late to stop now, Costis," the king said, and attacked again.

Costis snatched up his sword and retreated. The men sparring around him moved to make room and then circled around, all pretense of minding their own business gone.

"So, Costis," said the king, as Costis watched him warily, "you asked for this. Why?"

"You compromised my honor."

"I compromised *your* honor? Which one of us hit the other in the face?"

"They think I lied on your instructions. That Teleus and I killed the assassins in the garden and let you take the credit."

"Oh, that," said the king with a shrug. "That isn't your honor, Costis. That's the public perception of your honor. It has nothing to do with anything important, except perhaps for manipulating fools who mistake honor for its bright, shiny trappings. You can always change the perceptions of fools."

The wooden swords thwacked against each other, and Costis was driven back again. The circle of onlookers broke and re-formed again around them. Even after the weeks of practice, it was disconcerting to fight against someone left-handed. The king's sword came from the wrong direction, and it came too fast for Costis to be sure he could parry it, so he retreated. The circle of men widened to give him room, but the men were starting to jeer.

"Come on, Costis," someone shouted. "You're going the wrong direction."

That was easy for him to say, Costis thought. His arm and his thigh didn't ache, and his face didn't burn as if a hot iron had been laid on it.

Other watchers remembered that Costis, even in disgrace, was their man. There were a few cheers on his side, and his heart rose. Costis took a breath and tried to steady himself. When the king moved toward him, Costis held his ground. The king attacked in first, exactly as they had practiced for so many tedious hours. Costis parried, his arm moving automatically. The king attacked again, still in first. Costis parried. Costis remembered their first lesson when he had thought he would have to take his beating and make the king look good in the process. Instead, the king was making him look good. Eugenides continued to attack in first, harder and faster, and each time Costis parried. His arm knew its business better than his head did. He didn't need to think, only to react—in mounting terror as the king's blows came faster and faster. Should he change to another attack, Costis was not going to be able to defend himself. The king's wooden sword was going to break his arm, or his ribs, or his head, but just as Costis thought he would surely break down, the king slowed and backed off. The guard watched in silent appreciation.

"Ready?" asked the king. Costis nodded. This was the part where he wouldn't look good. It was a farce. Costis didn't stand a chance of defending himself, though he tried. The king moved too fast; he attacked in ways that were entirely a surprise to Costis, who had a soldier's command of a sword, not a duelist's.

The guards around him shouted advice, but it was hopeless.

The king slipped through Costis's guard; he slipped under it, catching him on the thigh or the knee, or over it, knocking him on the head, hard enough to sting, but not hard enough to finish him. And with every hit, the king shouted directions in a harsh voice Costis had never heard. "Don't lower your guard!" Whack. "Don't swing so wide!" Whack. "Don't leave yourself open!" Whack. "Don't . . . lower . . . the . . . point . . . in . . . third!" With each stroke, Costis was more rattled. His defense fell apart. The king disarmed him, and then disarmed him again. Costis stood amazed.

"H-How did you do that?"

"No!" shouted the king. "You don't stand there like a buffoon. Get your sword!" he roared, and raced at Costis. In a panic, Costis dove for his sword and missed. The king's sword fell on his exposed and undefended posterior. Yelping, Costis scrambled for the sword and managed to twist and block the next blow as it fell and the next as he crawled away from the king. The guards roared with laughter. Costis got to his feet and raised his sword, but he was laughing as well, and the sword shook in his hands. He backed as the king advanced. Giving up even a show of self-defense, he waggled the sword in front of him, until he bumped into a wall and realized he'd been backed into a corner of the courtyard.

The king stood in front of him, arms crossed, sword hanging from his hand. "Are we done?"

Costis looked at the men standing behind the king, smiling and relaxed.

"Yes, Your Majesty," said Costis.

"Good," said the king. "I want my breakfast. I want a bath." In a weak voice he added, "I drank too much last night, and I have a headache."

He tucked his wooden sword under his right arm and extended his hand to Costis, pulling him out of the corner.

Costis moved carefully, moaning. With the excitement of the sparring over, he was realizing that some of the blows hadn't been light.

"Serves you right," said the king. "You haven't even apologized."

"I'm very s-sorry, Your Majesty," Costis said immediately.

"For what exactly?" the king prompted.

"Anything," said Costis. "Everything. Being born."

The king chuckled.

"Will you serve me and my god?"

"I will, Your Majesty."

"Then come out," said the king, helping him, "knowing that you'll never die of a fall unless the god himself drops you."

· CHAPTER THIRTEEN ·

"Y OUR Majesty," said a humorless voice, and the
king turned away from Costis. The cheerful
atmosphere faded. The guards shuffled their feet.

"Teleus," said the king. His smile gone, he looked at
the captain with a waiting expression.

"If a man can expiate his debts in bruises, Your
Majesty, there are others who would clear their
accounts."

"I think not, Teleus," said the king, and started to
step around him. Teleus moved to block him.

"You won't get out from under your debt so easily,
Teleus," said the king, "and you have little to gain by
trying."

"And little to offer Your Majesty," Teleus agreed.
"Except a challenge."

He flicked a glance at Costis, and the implication
was obvious.

The king shook his head, still not rising to the bait.

"If I were to beat you, Teleus, your Guard would only think that you had let me. There's little point in that."

"What, then, if I beat you, Your Majesty?"

"The day hasn't come, Teleus, that I would let you beat me."

"I think you wouldn't have to, my lord."

The king warned him, "Teleus, I can have your head off."

"Of course you can, Your Majesty." He ducked his head in submission, and the king had started away when Teleus added under his breath, "With a word."

The king stopped and his head went up. "I can do it with a sword, too, Teleus."

Teleus stepped back and into a guard position.

"Very well," said the king, and he raised his own sword. "But I won't have you accused of not trying your hardest. I know that it is worth my while. How shall we make it worth yours? Shall we make a bet, Teleus? I beat you, and the queen reduces the Guard by half. You win, and she doesn't."

The guards standing around them looked at each other in horror.

Teleus thrust his chin forward. "I know that you have badgered her to weaken the Guard," said Teleus. "I will die before I let you do it."

"You don't have to die, Teleus. Just beat me."

✦ ✦ ✦

Feeling that all his good work had been undone, Costis could do nothing but leave them to it. He turned and was walking toward a bench along the wall where he could sit and nurse his bruises when he heard the wooden swords clack and the king yell. He whirled in time to see the king still in the air, both feet off the ground, the sky suddenly blue, the morning mist gone, the sunshine glowing in the sky and on the stones and on the king, and everything frozen for a moment like the carved frieze in a temple, as the flat side of the king's extended sword smashed against Teleus's undefended neck.

Teleus went down like bricks falling. He dropped his sword on the way and clutched at his neck with both hands, digging his face into the ground, struggling to hold the pain and trying to breathe. Half-controlled impulses made his legs twitch, and he shuddered.

The king looked him over and said impassively to the nearest barracks boy, "Ice."

The boy ran, and the soldiers parted to let him through. The king went to Teleus, first squatting down, and then sitting beside him.

"You didn't know I could do that, did you?" he asked, conversationally.

"I did not, Your Majesty," Teleus gasped.

"My grandfather killed a man that way once, using the edge of the wooden sword."

"I hadn't realized the Thieves of Eddis were so warlike."

"They aren't, mostly. But like all men, Teleus, I have two grandfathers." Teleus rolled his eyes to look up at him, and the king said, "One of mine was Eddis."

"Ah," said Teleus.

"Ah, indeed," said the king. "Here is the ice." He took a canvas bag from the barracks boy and felt the lumps of ice through it. Then he laid the bag on the hard ground and used the metal cuff at the end of his arm to crush the ice into smaller pieces and then lifted the bag onto Teleus's neck.

"Does that feel better?" he asked.

"Not really," said Teleus.

"Well, Costis will hold it for you. I see I have business with Aristogiton."

He got to his feet and walked away. Costis stayed with Teleus, holding the ice on his neck until he took it himself and got to his feet. Teleus looked around. Costis did as well. The king was in the center of the courtyard circling warily around one of the men in Aris's squad.

Costis asked, "Where's Aris?"

One of the guards turned to look at them in surprise. "He already whacked Aris on the head. Let him off lightly," he added, looking significantly at the captain holding the ice to his neck. "Now he's working on Meron."

Costis protested, "He can't fight all of them."

Aris arrived beside them, and Costis turned on him. "What were you thinking?"

Aris shrugged. Obviously hoping that the captain would take no notice, Aris said quietly, "Nobody minded seeing you knocked down. It was good fun. But they started to get angry again when he knocked down the captain. I thought if he did to me what he did to you, they'd relax again. But he didn't. He just knocked my sword out of my hand after about three exchanges and tapped me on the cheek."

If Aristogiton had hoped the captain wasn't listening, his hopes were dashed. Teleus turned around. "And then?" he said harshly.

"Then he waved Meron out. I swear I didn't mean for him to take on the whole squad, sir."

Costis said in a worried voice, "I think he hurt himself, fighting the captain. That jump must have taken everything he had."

"I think he did, too. He'll have to stop after Meron. What is it, Aris?"

"It's Laecdomon, sir. I haven't told you, sir, and I didn't know who else to tell, but it was Laecdomon who wanted us to go help pen the dogs. He suggested it. And when we were arrested, he wasn't with us in the cell, sir. He said he was kept in a different cell, but I never saw him until after the queen pardoned us."

"I see," said Teleus grimly. "Where is he now?"

"I don't know."

"Maybe he isn't here this morning," said Costis hopefully.

"No," said Aris, "I saw him earlier."

"And you think he'll come out to challenge the king?"

"I think he's Erondites's man, Captain. He's not landed, and his family is from the baron's demesne. Everyone knows how the baron feels."

"You can kill a man with a wooden sword," Costis said, echoing the king's words.

"If you don't care what happens to you afterward," said Teleus. "Would Laecdomon care?"

"I don't know," said Aris. "The baron would reward his family."

"The king can't beat a fresh opponent," Costis warned, "and he won't know that it isn't just sparring for Laecdomon."

"Don't worry," said Teleus. "As much as I would like to see it, I am not going to stand here and watch him get knocked down dead by a zealot with a wooden club. Find Laecdomon and get him out of here."

Aris and Costis moved away through the crowd. The king finished his opponent. Meron rubbed his chest where the point of the king's sword had struck and smiled. The king looked through the crowd for the next man in the squad. Searching the crowd himself, Teleus was too late to signal the man to hang back. Teleus, from behind the king's back, waved to get his attention and then mouthed silent instructions.

But the king caught the expression on the guard's

face and turned his head slowly to look over one shoulder at Teleus. He looked back at his opponent. "Did he tell you to give me an easy match?"

The confused guard shook his head.

The king shook his head. "Oh, no, no, that won't do. I'll have to make you the same offer I made the captain. Beat me, and the queen won't reduce the Guard; lose to me, and she'll cut the ranks in half."

The man looked in panic from Teleus to the king.

"He still wants you to go easy, doesn't he? That's what he's saying behind my back. What are your brothers saying? What does the Guard think?"

"Pound him!" someone safely anonymous shouted from the back of the crowd.

The king nodded. "Come on, Damon. I know what you can do. I may be tired, but nothing less than your best is going to be enough."

Damon attacked. Laughing, the king retreated. Damon attacked again, and they settled to the business of thrusting and parrying, and if Damon had meant to give the king an easy fight, his intentions were soon swept away as the king leaned in as they closed over the practice swords and whispered something in his ear. No one could hear what he said, but its effect was galvanic.

Damon was a better swordsman than either Costis or Aris. The king wasn't using his flashy technique. He parried and attacked carefully and precisely, wasting no energy. He hung back occasionally to catch his breath, and he began to favor his left leg just a little.

Damon pressed him, but the king always slid away. Then the king attacked with a sequence of moves that forced him back and back, barely parrying as the king swung and swung again and missed.

"Dammit," said the king, retreating. "I thought I had you."

Damon smiled. "I thought so, too."

Eugenides sighed dramatically. "Oh, press on, then," he said as he raised his sword. He was too tired to press an attack fast enough to touch Damon, but Damon wasn't good enough to get past the king's defense. The king began to twit him as the attacks failed. "That didn't work last time either. Are you going to try it again?" Frustrated, Damon was driven to overextend himself, and the king disarmed him. He stood ruefully as the king tapped him on the head and said, "Done."

Sticking his sword under his right arm and pinching it there, Gen used his hand to push the sweat-damp hair off his forehead. Then he walked with Damon toward the wall fountain, trailing the wooden sword so that its point dragged on the ground, bumping along behind him. They had taken no more than a few steps together when a voice called from behind them. The king turned.

"Laecdomon. Of course. How could I have forgotten you?"

"I don't know, Your Majesty. I hope that now that you have remembered me, you won't forget me again."

The guards fell silent. Teleus stepped forward, opened his mouth to speak, but the king shooed him away. Teleus had to content himself with a threatening look, which Laecdomon pretended not to see.

"Oh, I don't think I'll forget you, Laecdomon. I'll make you the same offer I made your colleagues. Beat me, and I will not reduce the Guard," said the king. He made a face and lifted the sword crosswise to his mouth and bit down on the blade, leaving both hands free, and swung his arms as if to relieve tired muscles. He spat the sword back into his hand.

"You'd have a wider smile, Your Majesty, if you did that with a real sword."

"It has not escaped my attention that everyone here objects to the way I handle a practice sword. Perhaps you'd like to tell me why?"

"The essence of the practice sword is to help you acquire the use of the real sword. If you don't treat it like a real sword, Your Majesty, you thwart its purpose. Here in Attolia," he said condescendingly, emphasizing Eugenides's foreignness, "we are taught to treat a practice sword with all the respect of a real weapon, so that no thoughtless mistakes are made."

"Oh," said the king, sounding amused, "in Eddis, we learn to keep track of the weapon we have in our hand."

He raised his sword. "Ready?"

"Ready," said Laecdomon.

"Begin."

"Captain?" Costis asked, worried.

Teleus shrugged. "I am not in charge here, Costis. If he chooses to walk into a trap with his eyes wide open, I have no authority to stop him."

Anxiously they watched the match.

The guards around the two men were silent and uncomfortable. There were no heckling comments and no shouts of support for Laecdomon. Everyone knew that there was more at stake than a sparring match, but something in Laecdomon's attitude discouraged any supporters. For the sake of the Guard, they didn't want the king to win, but they found it hard to root for Laecdomon either, so they stood silently and watched.

The king, favoring his left leg, spun on the right foot as Laecdomon circled.

"Captain," a nearby lieutenant said in an undertone, "Her Majesty is here."

The queen and her attendants had entered the training yard. She was not the only onlooker that had arrived. Most of the court seemed to have gathered. They lined the terrace above the training yard and were gathering on the walls that overlooked it. Costis looked at Teleus in growing apprehension.

Teleus crossed toward the queen. She was directing servants to place a dais and a chair. As they became aware of her, the men in the Guard opened their circle to give her an unobstructed view. As Teleus approached, she sat in the chair and calmly arranged the folds of her gown. Her attendants gathered behind her. The king's attendants drifted to flank them. Teleus bent down in order to speak to her quietly.

Her raised hand forestalled him. She waved Costis to approach.

"This was your idea?"

"No, Your Majesty. I mean, yes, I asked the king to spar. I had no idea this would happen." With an effort he avoided indicting Teleus with a glance.

"People do frequently seem to be surprised once my husband is involved."

"Your Majesty," said Teleus, "you must stop this."

"I? By what authority would I command the king?"

"He would stop if you asked," Teleus insisted.

The queen shook her head.

"Then I will stop it," said Teleus, and he turned.

"Captain." The queen's voice was soft, but Teleus turned back, subdued.

"He'll be killed," he warned.

"We must hope not."

"He's tired. He's injured. Laecdomon can kill him with one stroke. Let me arrest him before it is too late."

"Arrest the king?"

"Arrest Laecdomon," Teleus almost snapped, not appreciating the queen's humor.

"Arrest him for what? What proof do you have that this is anything but a sparring match?"

"Let me arrest him, and I will drag the proof out of him."

The queen shook her head.

"Why not?" Teleus asked helplessly.

"Because the king will not quit, Teleus," said Ornon as he joined them. "You must have noticed," he said. "He whines, he complains, he ducks out of the most obvious responsibility. He is vain, petty, and maddening, but he doesn't ever quit." Ornon shrugged. "Ever."

"He may not quit, but he will lose."

"Oh, I wouldn't place my money on it. I've seen him suffer setbacks." Ornon looked at the queen and away. "I have never seen him, in the end, lose. He just persists until he comes out ahead. No match is finished for him until he has won." Ornon shrugged expressively. "He won't quit, and he won't thank you for interfering."

There was a shout, and they turned back to the match. As Costis had done, the king was retreating. Laecdomon advanced, striking fast with his sword, driving the king back faster and faster. Finally the king responded. There was a furious interchange, and a sword spun in the air and hit the ground. For a moment there was no way to know whose sword had dropped. Then the two men separated, and everyone could see that Laecdomon was still armed.

Ruefully the king held up his hand.

Holding his breath, Costis hoped that it was just a sparring match after all. Laecdomon shook his head. Eugenides smiled.

"Your Majesty!" Teleus shouted, and indicated the crossbows aimed at Laecdomon. Costis hadn't seen them come, but they were the obvious solution. The king shook his head.

"You could default, Your Majesty," Laecdomon suggested with contempt.

"I think not," said the king, covered in sweat and breathing deep with exhaustion. "Though when you are finished, you may have to deal with my queen. You knew that when you started, didn't you?"

Laecdomon shrugged carelessly.

Eugenides shrugged as well. "According to the practice in Eddis, I cannot back up, so I will not here. Strike your best, Laecdomon."

With a sneer and perfect form, Laecdomon drew the sword back and swung for the king's head. Costis was not the only one to cry out, but the blow never landed. Without risk to his fingers from the edgeless weapon, the king grabbed for the blade of the sword, snatching it from the air and from Laecdomon's surprised grasp. He spun all the way around on his good leg, at the same time shifting his grip to just below the hilt. A heartbeat later the only sound in the stunned silence was the choking gasp as Laecdomon's breath was forced out of his lungs by the hilt of his own sword driven hard upward under his ribs.

Laecdomon collapsed like an empty wineskin. The king dropped the sword beside him. It rattled in front of his face.

"You forgot," said the king, into the silent air, "that it's a wooden sword."

Somewhere in the pack, a guard cheered, and the rest of the Guard joined him. The courtiers lining the walls began cheering as well. It was all quite deafening, thought Costis, looking up at the women waving their scarves, the open mouths of the aristocrats and soldiers alike.

Eugenides didn't respond. He limped slowly over to his own wooden sword and stooped awkwardly to pick it up. Trailing it on the ground behind him, he limped toward the queen, and the courtyard quieted as he approached and was silent again as he dropped to his knees before her and laid the sword across her lap.

"My Queen," he said.

"My King," she said back.

Only those closest saw him nod his rueful acceptance.

He lifted his hand to brush her cheek softly. As the entire court listened breathlessly, he said, "I want my breakfast."

The queen's lips thinned, and she shook her head as she said, "You are incorrigible."

"Yes," the king agreed, "and I have a headache and I want a bath."

Teleus stepped forward. "Perhaps His Majesty would like to visit the Guard's bath. It is closer, and he would be welcome."

The king had to consider. "Yes," he said. "That would be nice. Followed by breakfast."

Gravely, Teleus offered a hand to help the king to his feet. The queen smiled at them both. Costis could feel the grin he couldn't hide spreading across his face. He looked around at everyone smiling and knew why they did: because Eugenides was King of Attolia.

· CHAPTER FOURTEEN ·

COSTIS washed himself gently in the tepidarium
and limped to the steam room. He climbed to
the upper bench and relaxed with a flinch and a sigh
against the wooden slats behind him. The king had
not arrived. The guards were free to talk as they
chose. Costis listened with his eyes closed. His smile
faded when he recalled the king's response when
invited to join the guards in their bathhouse. He
must have known the offer was an honor since only
the guards were admitted here, but Costis had seen
the king hesitate.

The door to the steam room opened, and
Costis, seeing the king flanked by Teleus and his
lieutenants, understood why. It would be ridiculous to come into a steam room dressed in clothes,
or for that matter, wearing a metal cuff and hook
on the end of your arm. So Eugenides was as naked
as anyone else, but no one else used clothes as a

disguise, and none of them was as naked, therefore, as the king.

He chose Mede coats with the long bell sleeves because no fighting man who'd seen the muscles in the king's wrist would have underestimated him the way the Attolians had. His other wrist with no hand at the end of it appeared oddly narrow and delicate. Costis tried not to stare and found himself looking instead at the king's scars. The long line across his belly was an angry red, but there were other marks: ragged tears around his knees and elbows, and lighter shining bands around his ankles that could only be the mark of fetters, as well as the various lines left by edged blows on his chest and arms, and one long one on his thigh. There were also a number of bruises, some newly purple and black and some fading almost to nothing. Costis wondered where they could have come from.

Costis and the guards beside him shuffled aside to leave space for the king and Teleus on the upper bench, where the steam was hottest. When the king crossed to stand before the empty space, the guards could see that the muscles in his legs jumped with fatigue and his expression, when he looked at the steps up, was daunted. Teleus, already climbing, turned back to offer him a hand. Eugenides accepted the offer, and Teleus hauled him upward and dropped him onto the hot bench.

The king cursed and sighed as he leaned back. He turned his head toward Costis and explained the bruises easily. "Ornon never hesitates to hit me with a wooden stick," he said.

He hadn't kept in training by doing simple exercises. Moving through the palace as he chose, he must have practiced secretly with the Ambassador from Eddis.

"Don't be misled, Costis," said the king. "The beginning exercises are always important."

Flushing, Costis looked away. Across the room, someone bolder than Costis asked, "Did we give you all of those scars?"

The king opened his eyes and looked down at himself as if considering the scars for the first time. "I thought it was only the dogs that bit me, Phokis. Was it you, too?"

"No, Your Majesty," Phokis said hastily, and his mates laughed at him.

"Thank gods I don't have to hold that against you," said the king. "Nor the permanent decorations around my ankles and my wrist. Those came courtesy of Sounis." He held up his hand to look at the white patches that ringed it. "They were a nicely matched set, too, but that's ruined now." His evident lack of any distress about the result of his encounter with the queen left the guards gaping.

"This could have been one of you, though," said

Eugenides, running his finger along a short white ridge near the hollow of his shoulder. He looked at Teleus. "Was it?"

The captain shook his head.

"You transferred him? Are you worried about my taste in revenge?"

"Should I be?" Teleus asked bluntly.

"Not for that," said the king. "On the other hand, if you give me another morning like this one, I'll have you all packed up in chains and sold on the Peninsula as gladiators."

There was more laughter. "No more mornings like this one, Your Majesty," Teleus promised. "I admit that I find them painful myself."

"I'm glad to hear it. If I'd known that all I needed to do was hit you very hard with a stick, I would have done it months ago."

Teleus responded thoughtfully. "I would like to think there was more to this morning than getting hit in the neck with a practice sword." He looked gravely at the king. "It isn't an easy thing to give your loyalty to someone you don't know, especially when that person chooses to reveal nothing of himself."

He met Eugenides's eye, and this time it was the king who looked away.

He looked back to say, "For what was done, and not well done, I apologize, Teleus."

"No matter, Your Majesty. You are revealed at last."

The king looked down at his nakedness and back at the captain. "Was that a joke?" he asked.

"It does happen, on occasion. Do you know what you will do with Laecdomon?"

"Let him go," said the king.

"Some might think you are too merciful," Teleus said.

"But you don't."

Teleus shook his head. "He will go to Erondites and the baron will kill him."

The king agreed. "Erondites can't risk a connection between himself and a known traitor, and he will be afraid of whatever tales Laecdomon could tell. When Laecdomon is found dead in a ditch, everyone will see how Erondites rewards those who serve him."

"And if he doesn't suffer the ultimate penalty at Erondites's hand?" Teleus asked.

"Then I am still satisfied to let him go. If he disgraced himself, it was because I offered him the opportunity; if you tease a dog, it bites."

"Men are not dogs." Teleus leaned to give Costis a severe look. "A man should control himself."

"Easy for you to say, Captain."

"Not so easy, Your Majesty," Teleus assured him, "but I never hit you in the face."

"That's true enough," Eugenides agreed, without a glimmer of a smile. "But, then, I never meant you to."

He waited. When Teleus's eyes widened, Eugenides confirmed what the captain had guessed.

"I wasn't baiting you," said the king. "I was baiting Costis."

Costis sat back, dumbfounded. The loss of temper that had changed his life, the appointment to lieutenant. They hadn't been accident or caprice. "You made the notes on the Mede language," Costis accused the king, realizing that the small letters, though neatly formed, had shown the telltale shake of a man writing with his left hand.

"You sent them to me."

"I did," the king admitted.

"Why?"

"Your accent was terrible," said the king, in Mede, his accent perfect. "It's much better now."

"Why?" Costis asked again, demanding more. Teleus crossed his arms, silently seconding the request.

"Sometimes, if you want to change a man's mind, you change the mind of the man next to him first." Eugenides waved toward Costis, but he was talking to Teleus. "Archimedes said that if you gave him a lever long enough, he could move the world. I needed to move the Guard. I needed to move you."

"You changed Costis's opinion in order to change mine? And why does my opinion matter so much?" Teleus asked. "You could have replaced me."

The king shrugged. "I want the Queen to reduce the

Guard, and she said she will when I have asked *you* and you have agreed. So. May I reduce the Guard?"

"It is your decision. You are king."

"That is the question, Teleus. Am I king? Don't tell me that I have been anointed by priest and priestess or that this baron or that one has whispered meaningless sacred oaths at my ankles. Tell me, am I king?"

Teleus didn't pretend not to understand. "Yes, Your Majesty."

"Then I may reduce the Guard?"

"Yes, Your Majesty."

"Thank you." The king started to stand.

"Although you didn't win that match."

The king settled back down onto the bench. He eyed Teleus balefully.

"You never give up, do you? What is that supposed to mean?"

"It was your wager, Your Majesty," Teleus pointed out. "If Laecdomon won the match, you wouldn't reduce the Guard."

"In Eddis, a match runs until the first blow is struck."

"In Attolia, also."

"Well, I struck the first blow."

Teleus crossed his arms. "The object of the match is to practice swordplay, Your Majesty, not party tricks. A move that cannot be done with a sword is inadmissible."

"You are splitting hairs. You must have been talking to Relius, or was it Ornon?"

Teleus was obdurate. "You could not take a real sword out of a man's grip, not with your bare hand."

"Oh, Teleus," the king said, shaking his head sorrowfully. "So bullheaded and so wrong." Reaching across to Teleus, he held out his hand in a fist and opened it slowly like a flower. "I practice it with a wooden sword. I can do it with a real one, too."

Teleus lifted a blunt finger to gently trace the thin line of newly healed skin on the king's palm. "The assassin's sword. I don't know what to say, My King."

Eugenides shrugged. "Say I don't need to watch my own back anymore."

Teleus nodded. "I will be at your back, My King, until the last breath leaves my body."

"Very well, then," said Eugenides, and stood up as Teleus said thoughtfully, "I see, now, why Ornon was so confident of your success."

Eugenides climbed cautiously down from the upper bench. "Ornon was probably hoping I'd have my head bashed in, but I don't want your support under false pretenses, Teleus. Ornon wasn't thinking of circus tricks. He knew that if Laecdomon had ever become a real threat, I would have disemboweled him. Did you forget?" He raised his lamed arm, and looking at the truncated limb, they remembered the deadly nature of the replacement for his missing hand.

"You make people forget, with your long sleeves, pretending to be ashamed of it," said Teleus.

"Yes. But the truth is always right in front of you to see."

"So the Guard will be halved," Teleus said heavily.

The king sighed in resignation. Standing before Teleus, he said, "Teleus, the Guard made the queen. The Guard can unmake her. You can guarantee their loyalty now, but can you guarantee it twenty years from now? Forty years from now? You know you can't, yet you would entrust that Guard ten years, fifteen years, thirty years from now, with the power of kingmakers. Sooner or later the Guard's loyalty will be bought and sold like other men's, and the crown will go to the highest bidder. That is the course of history, Teleus. It is unchangeable. Keeping a private guard this large is like using a wolf to guard the farm. It may keep off the other wolves, but sooner or later it will eat you. I won't leave that legacy for my heirs."

"We keep Her Majesty safe," Teleus said, pain in his voice. "We have always kept her safe."

"Guard my back, Teleus, and I will keep her safe."

Moving more easily, but favoring his left leg, he went through the door, leaving the Guard and returning to his attendants, no doubt waiting outside.

"Will he keep her safe? Phokis could break him in half with one hand."

"If Phokis could lay a hand on him."

"Do you doubt him?"

The guards shook their heads.

"Basileus," someone hidden in the steam whispered. Others echoed the praise. "Basileus."

Only Teleus shook his head. Costis watched him, not surprised. "The Basileus was a prince of his people, what we call a king now," Teleus explained. "That one"—he nodded toward the closed door—"will rule more than just Attolia before he is done. He is an Annux, a king of kings."

As ever, the stories about Attolia, Sounis, and Eddis are fiction. There is no history here. This does not mean that representations of people and events from the real world have not crept in, but even those have been subject to fictionalization. There was a poet named Archilochus in the seventh century BC. We still have fragments of his poems, but the verse quoted in the book is not his. There was a playwright named Aristophanes who wrote comedies with titles like *The Birds* and *The Frogs*. I don't know that he ever wrote one entirely about farmers, but if he had, it would have been very funny indeed. The gods I describe aren't real, either. I made them up. The landscapes that surround the stories are based on the actual landscape of modern Greece and on what I imagine ancient Greece to have looked like.

But the setting isn't Greece, and it isn't meant to be ancient. With firearms and pocket watches, window glass and printed books, I hope it is more Byzantine than Archaic.

THE KING OF ATTOLIA

A young princess meets the god Eugenides — the original Thief of Eddis — and learns that she will become queen.

Eddis

The pony was fat and shaggy still from the winter. Its short legs flicked across the hard-packed road and Helen's own round, solid body bounced uncomfortably on its back. She had a bundle with her, but it was as small as she could make it, just blankets, a loaf of bread, and other bare necessities. She had her belt knife, and her own crossbow hung on the saddle with the cranking mechanism geared for her nine-year-old arms. With luck, anyone who noticed her riding up the road away from the palace would see nothing out of the ordinary and would forget her again quickly.

The Spring Festival was finally over and everyone was in bed recovering. Helen doubted that anyone but Xanthe, her nurse, would even wonder where she was. By bedtime, of course, Xanthe would be alarmed, but by bedtime she would have found the drawing chalked inside the door to Helen's sleeping room. Xanthe couldn't read, or Helen would have written a note. Instead, she had drawn a picture of her pony with its bundle of blankets and food, and a picture of herself waving good-bye.

It was only for one night, and Xanthe would eventually forgive her, but only if Helen made it away from the palace without drawing anyone's

1

attention. If her mother sent for her and Helen couldn't be found, people would assume she was playing with her cousins in some obscure part of the palace . . . so long as no busybody remembered that she had gone out on her pony. If that happened, his stall would be checked, and when it was found empty, the hue and cry would be frightful. Her aunts would start wailing that she and the horse had gone over a cliff or been eaten by a lion, and her father would send out the entire population of the capital city in a search. At the thought, Helen urged the pony on a little faster.

Finally, their path left the Sacred Way. It cut across the shoulder of the hill and then down to the valley road that led up into the hunting preserves. Out of sight of the palace, once among the trees, Helen relaxed. The pony slowed, and she patted his neck.

"Don't slow too much, Nestor," she told him. "We have a long way to go." The place she was heading for was more than half a day's ride away. She'd found it the previous fall when she wandered much farther than she'd intended. There had only been time for a quick look and a promise to return after the winter was over.

She had been out before on overnight hunting expeditions, and she'd sometimes spent whole days out on her own. This wouldn't be very different, and it was the only way she could explore her secret hideaway and still keep it secret.

The secrecy was essential, because without it the place wouldn't be hers alone. At the very least, she would have to share it with other children her age, but it was more likely that someone older, one of the new spears, would take it and chase the children away. Someone like her brother Pylaster, who had just left the boys' house and received his first spear, would declare it his personal kingdom, and only his closest friends would be allowed to join him there. He would lose interest eventually, when he wasn't a new spear anymore, but by then some other new spear would have claimed it. Helen would never have a chance.

By the time *she* reached the age when a boy received his spear, she would have left sword practice and horseplay behind and undergone the mysterious alteration that would make her a young woman with long skirts and jewels in her ears and no interest in anything sensible. She rolled her shoulders in distaste at the thought, but she had seen it happen to too many cousins to doubt its inevitability. Her mother must have her way. For the time being, however, there was freedom, exercised with discretion.

Helen arrived in the early afternoon. The day was gray and the spring wind was chilly. High up in the mountains there was still quite a bit of snow, and she shivered even in her sheepskin jacket. She wished the sun were shining. The narrow valley was dark and much less inviting than she'd anticipated. The temple itself, when she reached it, was

EXTRAS

desolate, the marble cold and gray and lifeless. She hesitated a moment before she swung down from Nestor's back. He was nervous and jerked at the reins as she tied them to a sapling.

He whickered, as if to say there was still time to make it back home before dark. "Don't be silly," she said aloud. She'd been looking forward to the trip all winter and she wouldn't quit, even though the high sides of the valley made her feel very small. She started for the temple with the stubborness that so often drove Xanthe to despair.

The temple must have been impressive once. Sitting sideways across the end of the narrow valley, its entrance porch at one end facing and nearly brushing the cliff face before it, it was as large as any temple Helen had ever seen. Its pillars and interior walls still stood, though most of its roof was gone. Rubble had fallen from the cliff face, burying the approach to the front entryway, but the temple's foundation was stepped on all sides, so it was easy for Helen to climb up to the terrace and slip between the pillars. Holes in the walls made it unnecessary to go through the front doors. Helen crawled across the tops of fallen stones nearly as high as her waist and slipped into the naos.

The floor was a dangerous wash of broken roof tiles mixed with the remains of the timbers that had supported them. The marble walls were bare. The statuary of the friezes had come down and smashed; lighter chunks of white marble were mixed with the roofing. Beside Helen was a piece from the head of a horse, and next to it was a broken-off hand with a bit of marble rein still running through it. The statue must have been beautiful when it was whole, and Helen was flooded by a sudden sadness. If Nestor had whickered again, she would have gone home.

He didn't, so she squared her small but sturdy shoulders and picked her way to a hole in the far wall. Halfway across, she paused to look toward the bare stone altar. The roof above was intact and the marble floor under it was mostly clear, but the pedestal that had once held a statue of some god or goddess was empty.

On the far side of the naos, there was a larger hole in the wall and an open path between the fallen stones. Once she was clear of the rubble and had a look at what lay before her, she stopped. She was so pleased that she hugged herself. The terrace on the far side of the temple was mostly free of broken masonry, and beyond it was an outdoor room, with the steep cliffs at the end of the valley for walls. The grass there was already green with the advance of spring. Under the gray skies, it seemed to glow with its own light. There were paths laid out, and the hedges of a garden, still visible, at one side. But mostly there was just the smooth carpet of the grass, and beyond it the opening of a cave in the cliffs.

The cave was a potential problem. Helen eyed

EXTRAS

it carefully for several minutes, then she went back for Nestor. It wasn't easy to coerce him up the stepped foundation and across the terrace behind the back of the temple, but once he reached the grassy carpet, he seemed happy enough, and she relaxed. The sun had started to break through the clouds, the sacred space behind the temple had begun to seem almost welcoming, and Nestor wouldn't have dedicated himself to the grass with such an appetite if he'd smelled a mountain lion's lair in the nearby cave.

She pulled off his bridle and left him to graze while she explored. The longer she stayed, the more at home she felt. Something very tight in her chest seemed to release itself, slowly unwinding, like thread off a spindle. On reflection, she decided the metaphor might not be apt. "I'd be in a mess the way Agape's yarn always is," she murmured to herself.

She looked into the cave first, which was high but shallow. There was a darker space at the back that led deeper into the mountain, but it was a crevice too narrow even for a child. A trickle of water came out of it and flowed in a channel to a basin cut in the rock. She had a drink and filled her waterskin before she whistled for Nestor to come have a drink as well. The water was cold and tasted of snow.

When the pigeons came home in the evening, she loaded her crossbow and shot quarrels at them until it was too dark to see where they fell. She did not hit a single bird. She had brought only the loaf of bread and a packet of sugared nuts for her dinner. Sighing, she went to gather wood for the fire. The dark was rising quickly and her skin prickled with cold. She collected a stack far larger than she would need.

She started her fire on the terrace looking out over her little territory, and rolled out her blankets beside it. Opening the bag holding her food, she looked into it dubiously. Glancing over one shoulder at a hole nearby leading into the naos of the temple, she considered how much the success of her return depended on luck. With much reluctance, she then tore the loaf in half and carried one half, and all the nuts, into the temple to lay them on the altar in front of the empty plinth. Better safe than sorry.

When she had eaten the remaining half of the loaf, she rolled herself in her blankets and lay down between the fire and her woodpile to sleep. Without waking fully, she could lift the sticks from the pile and add them to the fire. She listened to Nestor snuffling as he settled down for the night, then, without knowing exactly which moment it happened, she drifted off.

The cold woke her. The cold, and the feel of the empty marble under her hand as it searched for her woodpile. Thinking she must have used up all the wood closest to her, she extended her reach.

EXTRAS

Still no wood. Sighing with frustration, she opened her eyes to the dying firelight. Her woodpile wasn't there. She sat up, still half-asleep, and looked more carefully around the terrace. There was no wood. She looked back at the fire, which was a mistake. It made her night-blind, and once she had assured herself that the little campfire could not have burned through all her wood without leaving more ash, and that she hadn't mistakenly fed it all her fuel while asleep, she was left unable to see anything else.

She turned away from the fire and waited patiently for the blindness to clear, only to see at last that every stick of her wood was gone. She almost turned to check the fire again, but Helen didn't make the same mistakes twice. She looked elsewhere instead. Before she fully realized what she was searching for, she saw it: the glow of another fire burning nearby. Burning with her wood.

Her mouth firmed and her expression hardened. Brigands wouldn't have left her sleeping, and a decent person wouldn't have taken all of the wood, even if he'd had no time to gather his own. A decent person probably would just have joined Helen at her fire. Only a sneak would take all of her wood and leave her in the cold. The list of possible suspects was long enough. Any one of the new spears would have done it. They were so full of their own importance once they were out of the boys' house. One of her cousins, or perhaps Pylaster. The bread and nuts on the altar had been an unsuccessful sacrifice. Whoever had taken her firewood was going to announce her escapade to the palace, and there was going to be a tremendous din when she got home.

The cold shuddered through her, and she clenched her fists in frustration. She wanted to take their horses and leave the arrogant new spears to walk home, but she couldn't get Nestor across the terrace without waking anyone asleep inside the temple, and she wouldn't leave him behind. She would have liked to steal the wood back but doubted she could, and even if she were successful, the older boys would wake when they felt the cold, just as she had. There wouldn't be any secrecy the next time they took it. She might be very sturdy for a girl, but she was still only nine, and tiny compared to her brother's companions. However, she was determined not to creep up like a penitent to their fire. At least she could steal back enough wood so that she could sleep the rest of the night in the warmth generated by her own fuel.

She kicked off her blankets and got quietly to her feet. The firelight was definitely coming from inside the temple, which she felt was scandalous. One shouldn't camp inside a temple, even an abandoned one. Softly, she crept along the wall toward the light. She felt carefully for fallen blocks of stone but didn't encounter any. When she

EXTRAS

reached the hole in the temple wall, she found it more door shaped than she remembered, but the regular shape of the doorway was the least of the mysteries. She crouched in the darkness, just beyond the reach of the light from the fire burning before the altar, and stared. Whoever had stolen her wood, it wasn't a new spear.

She could see through the doorway and between the heavy interior pillars that held up the roof. The marble floor was clear of debris and scattered with carpets. Standing candelabras with fine wax candles augmented the light of the fire, which burned inside the repaired walls of the fire pit. Not only was the fire pit repaired, Helen realized, but the roof and the walls. The murals were restored, and so were the friezes above them. She laid a hand on the smooth-worked masonry of the doorway, then looked back to the interior.

Bathed in the light of the fire, a woman more beautiful even than Helen's mother lay on a couch with a little table beside her, and on it a bowl filled with pigeon eggs. As Helen watched, the woman selected an egg and cracked it on the edge of the table. The larger pieces of shell she tossed toward the fire, but the smaller pieces she carelessly let fall. When they landed on the pure white cloth of her gown, she brushed them to the floor.

Looking down at her from the altar was a young man. Helen thought at first that he might be the age of a new spear, but then he looked older and she wasn't certain. He was dressed all in gray, sitting cross-legged and eating nuts out of a silver bowl. Her nuts, Helen realized. She must have made a sound. The woman on the couch shifted a little and spoke to the figure on the altar. "Who is it?"

The young man looked over at Helen, and she pulled back into the darkness.

"It's Eddis," said the man, and Helen snapped her head around in surprise, looking up and down the terrace for her father.

"She's found her firewood missing," the man continued, inexplicably. Helen could see no one else on the terrace.

"You are eating her nuts," the woman on the couch said languidly. "It was unkind to take her fire as well."

"Nonsense," he responded. "If you think I am unkind, ask her to join us."

"I suppose we can make her forget again by morning." The woman beckoned Helen with one beautiful white hand. "Do come, dear," she said.

Against her better judgment, Helen stepped cautiously as far as the interior pillars.

"The last Eddis, is it?" the goddess asked, but she was speaking to the man. "Have I seen her before? She looks like her father."

"Have you seen her father?" the young man asked, amused.

"I'm not sure. Perhaps her grandfather. Certainly

EXTRAS

she is not a pretty girl, but I suppose that is neither here nor there with this one. What's your name, dear?"

"Helen," she whispered, too bewildered to be hurt by the casual condemnation of her looks. She might not have been hurt anyway; she knew she wasn't pretty and wasn't particularly bothered. She wondered if all this was a dream. A chill breeze from the open doorway behind her swept across the back of her neck and she shivered. It felt real.

"You're cold. Come closer to the fire."

Helen took another few hesitant steps. All of her wood was in the fire pit, and she could already feel its warmth. She saw that there was a third figure watching her from the base of the altar—another woman resting against a cushion. Beside her was a lap desk, as if she had just set it aside. She still held a white quill pen in her hand as she leaned forward to look at Helen.

Another shudder went through Helen, as if someone had walked over her future grave. She waited for it to pass, but it only grew worse until she dropped to a crouch, wrapping her arms around her knees and holding tight as she stared at the woman by the altar.

"Poor chick," the woman on the couch murmured, and Helen felt a breath of warm air caress the back of her neck. The shudder faded away and in its absence came a dreamlike feeling. The woman with the white quill pen was Moira, who recorded men's fates. She was the messenger of the gods. Sitting on the altar above her, so indecently comfortable in such a sacrilegious place, was Eugenides, the Thief. Helen didn't know who the third immortal was. The goddess of the temple, she assumed. A moment before, everything had been more frightening than she could bear. Now she accepted it with less excitement than she'd felt at the loss of her firewood.

"She isn't Eddis yet," Moira pointed out calmly.

"No, not yet," agreed the goddess on the couch. "But her Thief was just born, wasn't he? Yesterday? Last week?"

Moira laid down her pen, and unrolled the scroll on her lap desk. "Four years ago," she said dryly.

Her Thief? Helen wondered. There was a Thief at the Palace of Eddis, but he was old. He'd certainly been born more than four years before. He had a grandson, though, who was about that age. She remembered that the palace had been in an uproar after his birth, when he was named Eugenides after his grandfather and after the immortal who sat eating Helen's sugared nuts as if each one were a prize.

She looked up, and the Patron of Thieves smiled down at her. Such a wicked smile, Helen thought. Full of mischief and self-satisfaction and humor. He smiled like one of her grown-up cousins, Lycos, who had been exiled when Helen was six. She remembered him well; he could make you laugh one day and cry the next. When he left the court, she'd been heartbroken, and also relieved. She eyed Eugenides warily, but she had a generous nature. It tipped the balance in his favor, and she smiled shyly back at him. His own smile deepened in response, a nicer expression altogether, and Helen decided that she liked him very much, as if approval or disapproval of a god were an everyday affair.

"Have a seat here by me," said the goddess from across the fire, pointing to a cushion in front of her couch. Helen circled the fire and sat. From there, she could still see Moira, and also a heap of fabric that lay in a bundled pile beside the fire pit. Woven with different colors and kinds of thread, it was lumpy and soft in places and smooth and tight in others. Brightly colored and streaked through with dull browns and blacks, it still seemed to carry a coordinated pattern. Helen stared, trying to make it out, but too much cloth was hidden in rumples and folds.

Moira looked up from what she was writing on her lap desk. "Eugenides has stolen the fabric from the loom of the Fates. Little will happen in the world of men until they restring their loom."

"It was very bad, Gen," said the goddess over Helen's shoulder. "Everyone will be angry."

"You said you missed Moira."

"I did, didn't I? I suppose they will be angry at

14

me, too. Such a bore. Are the pigeons roasted, Moira dear?"

The recorder looked with narrowed eyes at a row of birds on skewers that leaned over the fire pit. "Not yet," she said.

"You aren't angry, are you, Moira?" the Thief asked in winning tones.

"No," said Moira. "You very nicely brought the weaving here, so I can catch up on my work while we visit."

"Moira is my daughter," said the goddess, behind Helen. "And we haven't seen each other for years. No, don't look it up, Moira; I don't need to know exactly how long. It is too long. You should tell those women to keep their own records."

Moira shook her head.

"Or the men. Tell the mortals to keep their own histories."

Moira smiled. "They do so much already. There is less and less work for me all the time."

"Good," said the goddess, her mother, who Helen realized must be the wind Periphys.

"I'm sure there will always be enough to keep you busy," said Eugenides. He had lain down on his stomach and had his chin propped in his hands. His knees were bent and his feet moved idly in the air.

"Busy enough," agreed Moira.

"I'd like some wine, I think," said the goddess. "Will you fetch me a cup, chickie?" When Helen looked over her shoulder, the goddess gestured to a table she hadn't seen before. She blinked, unsure if it had been there before the goddess gestured. It was in the dim light beyond the candelabras and she might have overlooked it. It was a low table with a silver inlaid top, covered with dishes of food and cups that matched the wine set. Helen got up and went to pour the wine into the mixing bowl. She carefully avoided looking at the food while she added water to the wine and swirled the two until they mixed, then turned to lift the bowl toward the altar.

She hesitated then, just for a moment; the wine sloshed in the bowl, but she steadied it without mishap. She had lifted the wine automatically for the blessing, but there was no impersonal statue of a god or goddess above the altar, just Eugenides looking sardonic. Helen considered turning to the goddess reclining on the couch, but she wasn't certain that this temple belonged to Periphys. It was unlikely that it belonged to Moira. Helen couldn't put it past Eugenides to make himself and his friends comfortable in someone else's temple. Amused, Eugenides resolved Helen's dilemma by waving one hand in benediction. The wine was officially blessed. Politely hiding her own amusement, she offered her reverence in his direction and turned back to the table to pour the mixed wine into a cup, careful not to spill a single drop. She then carried the wine to the couch and dropped to her knees, her eyes modestly lowered.

Instead of taking the wine, the goddess lifted a hand to brush Helen's cheek. She tucked a finger under Helen's chin and lifted it and looked into Helen's eyes. For a moment, Helen saw something beyond this slightly silly woman, something so vast that Helen felt as if she were staring up into the night sky and in danger of falling into it. "She will do," she heard the goddess say. "She will do very well."

"Of course she will," said Eugenides, dropping from the altar and stepping around the rumpled pile of the Fates' tapestry. "But what she wants just now is a pigeon, so take that wine cup or I will."

Periphys reached for the cup and directed Helen back to the cushion with a smile. "Are they done?" she asked.

"Well, I am tired of waiting, so I say they are," said Eugenides. He lifted two skewers away from the fire and carried them over. To Helen's surprise, he came to her first. He squatted down in front of her to look her in the eye a moment, as if he understood the growing distress that bubbled just beneath this odd sense of comfort that Periphys had provided. How could she be Eddis? Her father was Eddis. If Helen ever did inherit the throne, she would be Eddia, the feminine version of the state name, not Eddis. And that could only happen if her older brothers Pylaster and Lias died, and probably her younger brother Janus as well. A woman could

17

inherit the throne of Eddis, but only as a last resort. Helen might hold Pylaster in contempt most of the time, but she loved him, and Lias and Janus as well.

"Don't worry, little one, about what is to come," said Eugenides. "You will wake in the morning and all this will be a dream, gone before the dew leaves the grass. Now, eat your pigeon, which you don't deserve because you are a woeful shot. I will exchange with you for a pile of firewood and a handful of almonds." He handed her a skewer and waited until she took the first bite before he moved to Periphys. The goddess was offended at the wait, but the Thief returned her disaffected look with one of his own that left her flustered and defensive. She took the pigeon from him and turned a cold shoulder. He laughed and returned to the fire for two more pigeons, one of which he handed to Moira before he vaulted back onto the marble pedestal to eat his own.

It was quiet while they ate. Periphys sulked and picked at her food. But when she snuck a look over her shoulder at the Thief, he smiled. "You are dreadful," she told him.

Eugenides' smile only grew. Periphys sighed and rolled her eyes. Helen had a feeling that this had happened many times before. Sooner or later, the Thief was always forgiven. They talked then, Moira and Periphys and Eugenides, and like a child at any grown-up conversation, Helen understood less and less until she lost interest and concentrated on the pigeon.

She woke in the morning from her dream of gods and temples, lying on the terrace, wrapped in her blanket. The fire beside her was dead and she was stiff with cold. Shivering, she sat up. She looked first toward the empty space where her woodpile would have been and caught at the dream just as it was fading. There had been gods in the temple, she remembered, and the God of Thieves had eaten her almonds. Still shivering, she unwrapped her blanket and hurried between the fallen stones of the temple walls to the opening near the altar. The opening was a ragged hole nearly blocked by rubble, as it had been the day before. Inside the wall and the interior row of columns, the floor was again scattered with tiles and debris. The frescoes were gone and the fire pit was broken on one side. The dream seemed less real with each passing moment, but Helen clung to it as stubbornly as she had ever held on to anything in her life. On the far side of the fire pit, she dropped to her knees and swept her hands across the floor. In the cracks between the stones, there were eggshells. No large pieces, but small ones that might have fallen from the goddess's skirts.

Helen looked up at what remained of the roof over her head. In the rafters and in the niches of the metopes were a thousand pigeon nests. Of course there were eggshells between the stones.

She rose and stepped quickly away from the fire pit, past where the table laden with food had stood, and dropped to her knees again. On the dirty floor, among the debris, she found what she was seeking. A splatter of wax. Fresh and clean and white, it could only have fallen from the candelabras the night before. She used her belt knife to scrape up one perfectly round wax disc and pinched it between her finger and thumb. Her thumb fitting into the depression that had formed as it cooled, she rubbed the wax thoughtfully against her finger. Then she opened her heavy sheepskin jacket and slid the disc, just the size and shape of a button, wholly unremarkable in itself, into the small purse attached to her belt. She stood to look around the temple once again. There was no other sign that the events she remembered were anything but a dream.

She slipped a finger into the purse to nudge the small bit of wax. Determined not to forget what little she still remembered, she went to fetch her pony. Nestor was uncommonly uncooperative, jerking his head and sidling away from her at every opportunity. Finally, she lost her temper and stamped her foot on the green grass carpet outside the temple. "I am not going to forget!" she said. "And I don't care how distracting you are." Almost as if he were embarrassed, the pony lowered his head and meekly approached.

On her ride home, she was drenched by a

sudden shower, Nestor slid on a rocky part of the trail and almost went down, the wind blew particularly lovely white clouds across the sky, and a rainbow appeared as well. There were mysterious rustlings in the bushes and quite a few animals emerged to watch her curiously. Stubbornly, she ignored the distractions and instead went over and over what details she could remember from her dream: Lias and Pylaster and Janus dead, herself the last ruler of Eddis, the four-year-old boy who would be her Thief. From time to time, she slipped a finger into her belt purse to poke at the wax button and reaffirm her memories.

As she approached her home, worry curled up like smoke around her. If her mother had asked for her, if someone had noticed the missing pony, if Xanthe had panicked and revealed the message Helen had left . . . the possibilities infused every thought, until even the dream seemed less important than the coming moment of truth when she arrived at the entrance gate to the stableyard.

"Your Highness!" The stable master came himself to take Nestor's reins in hand. "Our royal Queen, your mother, was most concerned"— Helen's fists tightened on the reins in alarm—"that you would be back late from *this morning's* ride." Of course he had noticed the empty stall, and one of the stablers must have seen her bundle, but no one had given away her secret. Stony faced, the stable master said, "I assured her that I would send you to her when you returned."

"Th–thank you, cousin," she said, signaling her awareness of her debt to him with the familial address. She turned to go, but the stable master stopped her with a touch on her arm.

"If Your Highness had left a message to say where you were riding, I could have sent a messenger out. In the future, it would be a courtesy."

"Yes, of course," stammered Helen, happy to accept the bargain. He was willing to keep her secrets in the future, but only if he knew she was safe. She could go back. Automatically, she was searching in her belt purse as she hurried across the stableyard in response to her mother's summons. She could go back. The belt purse was empty.

She hesitated, looking at her empty hand. Go back? She considered again. It had been good to camp on her own in the mountain valley, but there were other places to explore, and it had been cold there, she remembered. The narrow valley held the winter chill. She would try someplace lower in the mountains next time. There was something else that she wanted to remember, but she couldn't think what. She hurried on across the stableyard, hoping it would come to her later.

She didn't remember. Not when she played with her cousin Eugenides, by far her favorite among all her many cousins, not even when the sickness came that took all three of her brothers in a matter of days. She never returned to the narrow valley high in the hunting preserves and never visited its abandoned temple again, though she continued her independent trips, skillfully maintaining a pretense of obedience to her mother's will with the complicity of Xanthe and the stable master and an ever-growing community of supporters.

She never thought of her dream again, until the morning she woke to find a wax button on the pillow by her head. Though it was as clean as if it had just dropped from an unregulated candle the night before, the wax hadn't soaked into the linen. It lay lightly on the cloth, and when she lifted it up, she could see the ridge she remembered, where her belt knife had scraped it free years before. When Xanthe came to the door, her cheeks wet with tears, Helen already knew that her father was dead.

"My Queen," said Xanthe, "you are Eddia."

Helen shook her head, still sorting through her newly returned memories. Knowing the consternation it would cause, and knowing she would overcome it, she said, "No, I am Eddis. The gods have told me so."

EXTRAS

Read on for an excerpt from

THE THIEF

· CHAPTER ONE ·

I didn't know how long I had been in the king's prison. The days were all the same, except that as each one passed, I was dirtier than before. Every morning the light in the cell changed from the wavering orange of the lamp in the sconce outside my door to the dim but even glow of the sun falling into the prison's central courtyard. In the evening, as the sunlight faded, I reassured myself that I was one day closer to getting out. To pass time, I concentrated on pleasant memories, laying them out in order and examining them carefully. I reviewed over and over the plans that had seemed so straightforward before I arrived in jail, and I swore to myself and every god I knew that if I got out alive, I would never never never take any risks that were so abysmally stupid again.

I was thinner than I had been when I was first arrested. The large iron ring around my waist had grown loose, but not loose enough to fit over the bones of my hips. Few prisoners wore chains in their cells, only those that the king particularly disliked: counts or dukes or the minister of the exchequer when he told the king there wasn't any more money to spend. I was certainly none of those things, but I suppose it's safe to say that the king disliked me. Even if he didn't remember my name or whether I was as common as dirt, he didn't want me slipping away. So I had chains on my ankles as well as the iron belt around my waist and an entirely useless set of chains locked around my wrists. At first I pulled the cuffs off my wrists, but since I sometimes had to force them back on quickly, my wrists started to be rubbed raw. After a while it was less painful just to leave the manacles on. To take my mind off my daydreams, I practiced moving around the cell without clanking.

I had enough chain to allow me to pace in an arc from a front corner of the cell out to the center of the room and back to the rear corner. My bed was there at the back, a bench made of stone with a thin bag of sawdust on top. Beside it was the chamber pot. There was nothing else in the cell except myself and the chain and, twice a day, food.

The cell door was a gate of bars. The guards looked in at me as they passed on their rounds, a tribute to my reputation. As part of my plans for greatness, I had bragged without shame about my skills in every wine store in the city. I had wanted everyone to know that I was the finest thief since mortal men were made, and I must have come close to accomplishing the goal. Huge crowds had gathered for my trial. Most of the guards in the prison had turned out to see me after my arrest, and I was endlessly chained to my bed when other prisoners were sometimes allowed the freedom and sunshine of the prison's courtyard.

There was one guard who always seemed to catch me with my head in my hands, and he always laughed.

"What?" he would say. "Haven't you escaped yet?"

Every time he laughed, I spat insults at him. It was not politic, but as always, I couldn't keep an insult in when it wanted to come out. Whatever I said, the guard laughed more.

I ached with cold. It had been early in the spring when I'd been arrested and dragged out of the Shade Oak Wineshop. Outside the prison walls the summer's heat must have dried out the city and driven everyone indoors for afternoon naps, but the prison cells got no direct sun, and they were as damp and cold as when I had first arrived. I spent hours dreaming of the sunshine, the way it soaked into the city walls and made the yellow stones hot to lean on hours after the day had ended, the way it dried out water spills and the rare libations to the gods still occasionally poured into the dust outside the wineshops.

Sometimes I moved as far as my chains would let me and looked through the bars of my cell door and across the deep gallery that shaded the prison cells at the sunlight falling into the courtyard. The prison was two stories of cells stacked one on top of the other; I was in the upper level. Each cell opened onto the gallery, and the gallery was separated from the courtyard by stone pillars. There were no windows in the outside walls, which were three or four feet thick, built of massive stones that ten men together couldn't have shifted. Legends said that the old gods had stacked them together in a day.

The prison was visible from almost anywhere in the city because the city was built on a hill and the prison was at the summit. The only other building there was the king's home, his megaron. There had also been a temple to the old gods once, but it had been destroyed, and the basilica to the new gods was built farther down the hill. Once the king's home had been a true megaron, one room, with a throne and a hearth, and the prison had been the agora, where citizens met and merchants hawked their jumble. The individual cells had been stalls of clothes or wine or candles or jewelry imported from the islands. Prominent citizens used to stand on the stone blocks in the courtyard to make speeches.

Then the invaders had come with their longboats and their own ideas of commerce; they did their trading in open markets next to their ships. They had taken over the king's megaron for their governor and used the solid stone building of the agora as a prison. Prominent citizens ended up chained to the blocks, instead of standing on them.

The old invaders were pushed out by new invaders, and in time Sounis revolted and had her own king again. Still, people did their trading down by the waterfront; it had become habit, and the new king continued to use the agora as a prison. It was useful to him, as he was no relation to any of the families that had ruled the city in the past. By the time I ended up there, most people in the city had forgotten the prison was ever anything but a holding pen for those who failed to pay their taxes and other criminals.

I was lying on my back in my cell, with my feet in the air, wrapped in the chain that led from my waist to a ring high in the wall. It was late at night, the sun had been gone for hours, and the prison was lit by burning lamps. I was weighing the merits of clean clothes versus better food and not paying attention to the tramp of feet outside my cell. There was an iron door that led from the prison into a guardroom at the narrow end of the building. The guards passed through it many times a day. If I heard the door banging, I no longer took any notice of it, so I was unprepared when lamplight, concentrated by a lens, flared into my cell. I wanted to look lithe and graceful and perhaps feral as I unwrapped my feet and sat up. Caught by surprise and nearly blind, I was clumsy and would have fallen off the stone bunk if the chain had not still been wrapped around one foot.

"This is the right one?"

No wonder the voice sounded surprised. I levered myself upright and blinked into the lamplight, unable to see much. The guard reassured someone that this indeed was the prisoner he wanted.

"All right. Take him out."

The guard said, "Yes, magus," as he unlocked the barred gate, so I knew who it was at my door late at night. One of the king's most powerful advisors. In the days before the invaders came, the king's magus was supposed to have been a sorcerer, but not even the most superstitious believed that anymore. A magus was a scholar. He read scrolls and books in every language and studied everything that had ever been written and things that had never been written as well. If the king needed to know how many shafts of grain grew on a particular acre of land, the magus could tell him. If the king wanted to know how many farmers would starve if he burned that acre of grain, the magus knew that, too. His knowledge, matched by his skills of persuasion, gave him the power to influence the king, and that made him a powerful figure at the court. He'd been at my trial. I had seen him sitting in a gallery behind the judges with one leg crossed over the other and his arms folded over his chest.

Once I had disentangled myself from the chains, the

guards unlocked the rings on my feet, using a key as big as my thumb. They left the manacles on my wrists but released the chain that attached them to the waist ring. Then they hauled me to my feet and out of the cell. The magus looked me up and down and wrinkled his nose, probably at the smell.

He wanted to know my name.

I said, "Gen." He wasn't interested in the rest.